big NATE

OUT LOUD

More

big NATE

adventures from

LINCOLN PEIRCE

Big Nate From the Top

Big Nate and Friends

Big Nate Makes the Grade

Big Nate All Work and No Play

Big Nate: Game On!

Big Nate: I Can't Take It!

Big Nate: Great Minds Think Alike

Big Nate: The Crowd Goes Wild!

Big Nate: Say Good-bye to Dork City

Big Nate's Greatest Hits

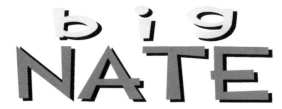

big NATE

OUT LOUD

by LINCOLN PEIRCE

Andrews McMeel
Publishing®

Kansas City • Sydney • London

Andrews McMeel Publishing, LLC
an Andrews McMeel Universal company
1130 Walnut Street, Kansas City, Missouri 64106

www.andrewsmcmeel.com

ISBN: 978-1-4494-7394-5

Library of Congress Control Number: 2011920757

These strips appeared in newspapers from April 2, 2007, through November 4, 2007.

Big Nate can be viewed on the Internet at www.gocomics.com/big_nate

ATTENTION: SCHOOLS AND BUSINESSES
Andrews McMeel books are available at quantity discounts with bulk purchase for educational, business, or sales promotional use. For information, please e-mail the Andrews McMeel Publishing Special Sales Department: specialsales@amuniversal.com.

For the Rhode Islanders

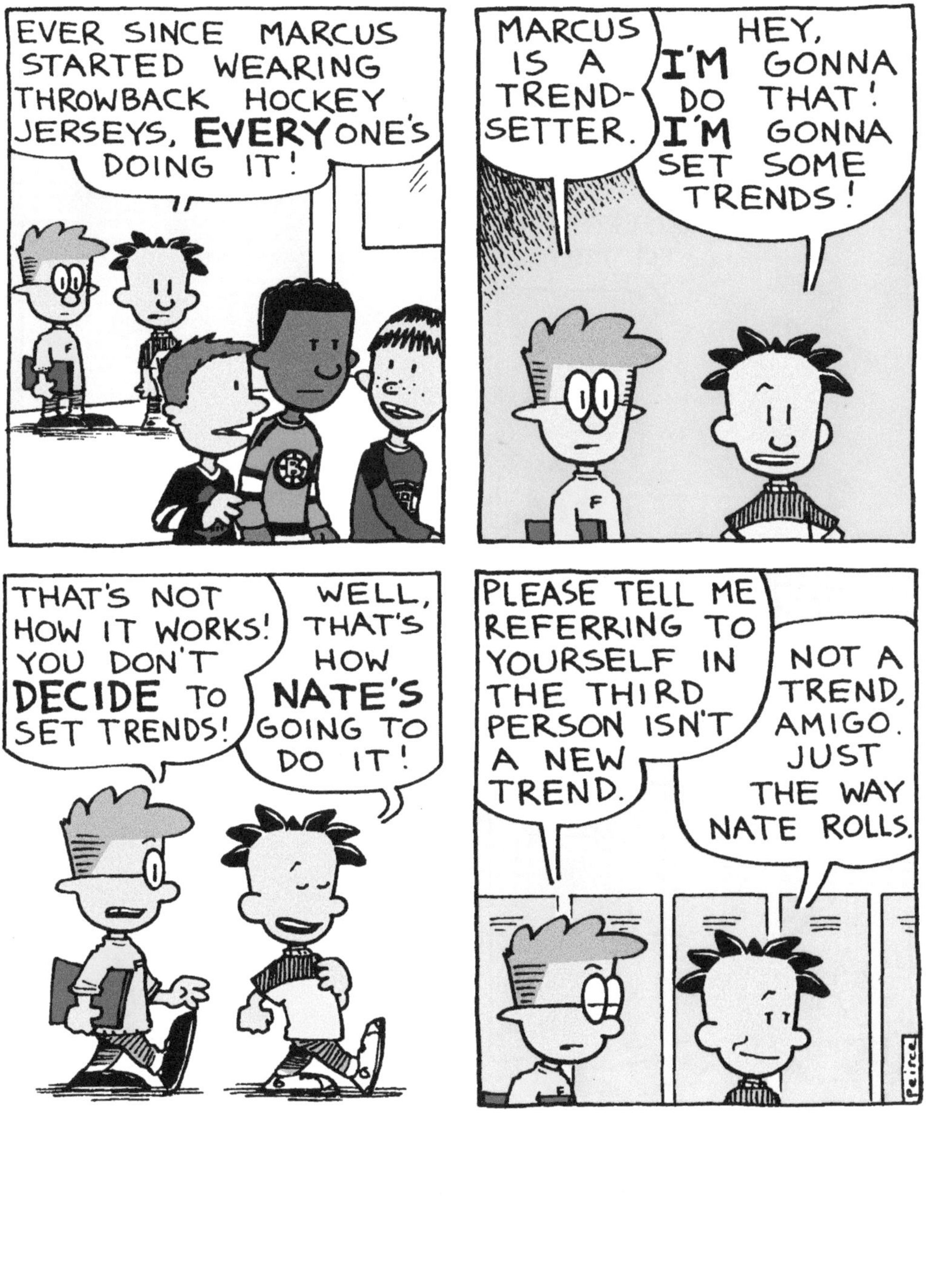
EVER SINCE MARCUS STARTED WEARING THROWBACK HOCKEY JERSEYS, **EVERY**ONE'S DOING IT!
MARCUS IS A TREND-SETTER.
HEY, **I'M** GONNA DO THAT! **I'M** GONNA SET SOME TRENDS!
THAT'S NOT HOW IT WORKS! YOU DON'T **DECIDE** TO SET TRENDS!
WELL, THAT'S HOW **NATE'S** GOING TO DO IT!
PLEASE TELL ME REFERRING TO YOURSELF IN THE THIRD PERSON ISN'T A NEW TREND.
NOT A TREND, AMIGO. JUST THE WAY NATE ROLLS.
Peirce

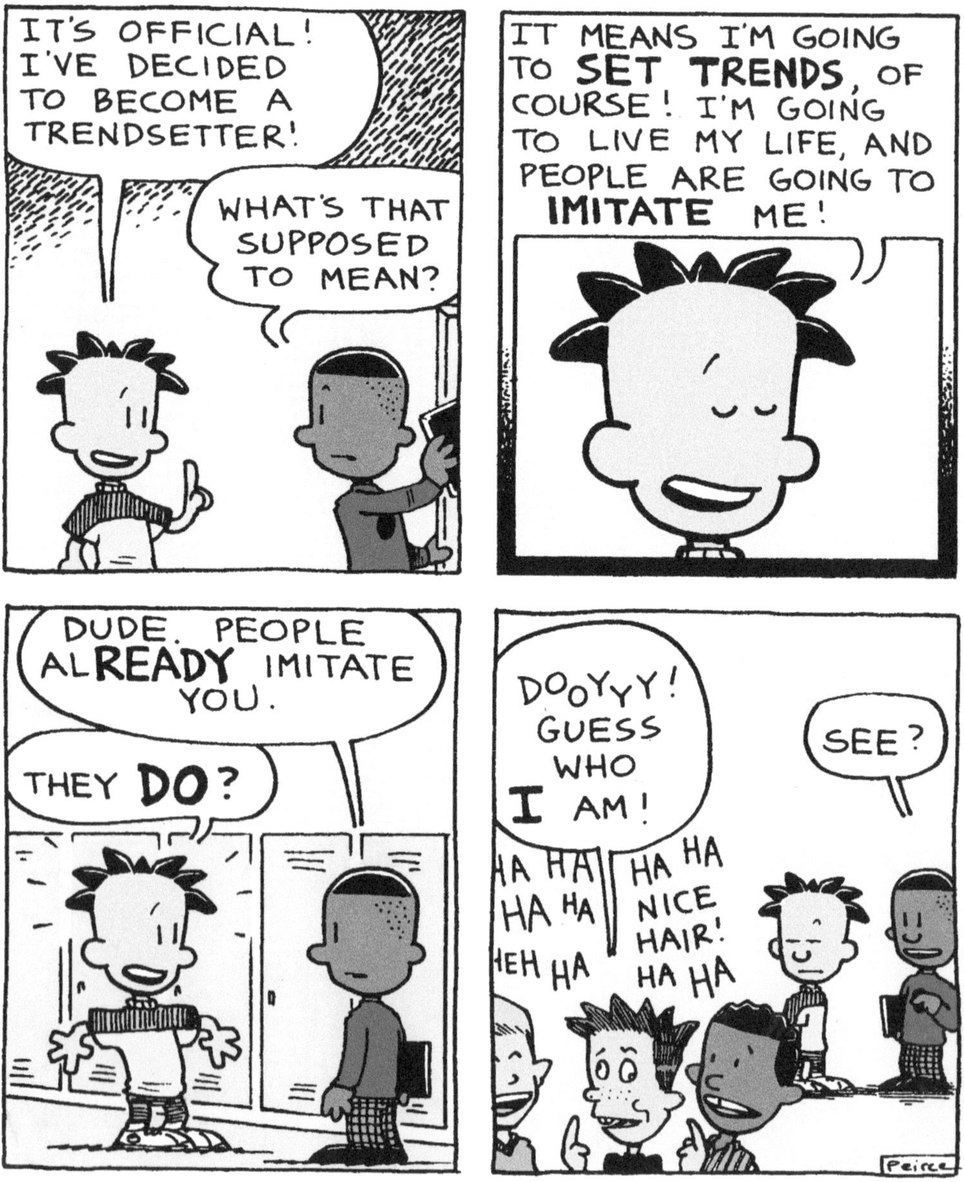
IT'S OFFICIAL! I'VE DECIDED TO BECOME A TRENDSETTER!
WHAT'S THAT SUPPOSED TO MEAN?
IT MEANS I'M GOING TO **SET TRENDS**, OF COURSE! I'M GOING TO LIVE MY LIFE, AND PEOPLE ARE GOING TO **IMITATE** ME!
DUDE. PEOPLE AL**READY** IMITATE YOU.
THEY **DO**?
DOOYYY! GUESS WHO **I** AM!
HA HA HA HA HEH HA
HA HA NICE HAIR! HA HA
SEE?
Peirce

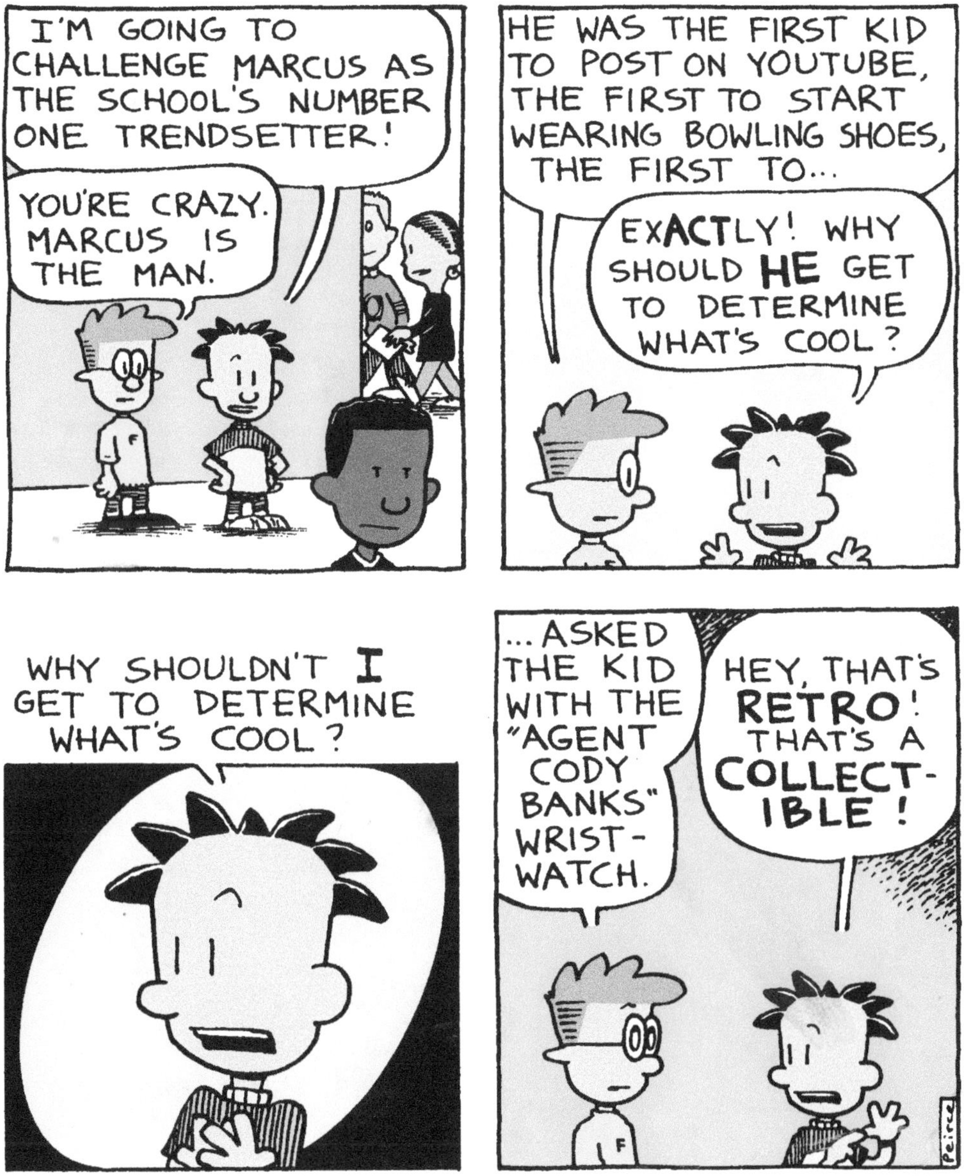
I'M GOING TO CHALLENGE MARCUS AS THE SCHOOL'S NUMBER ONE TRENDSETTER!
YOU'RE CRAZY. MARCUS IS THE MAN.
HE WAS THE FIRST KID TO POST ON YOUTUBE, THE FIRST TO START WEARING BOWLING SHOES, THE FIRST TO...
EXACTLY! WHY SHOULD HE GET TO DETERMINE WHAT'S COOL?
WHY SHOULDN'T I GET TO DETERMINE WHAT'S COOL?
...ASKED THE KID WITH THE "AGENT CODY BANKS" WRIST-WATCH.
HEY, THAT'S RETRO! THAT'S A COLLECT-IBLE!
Peirce

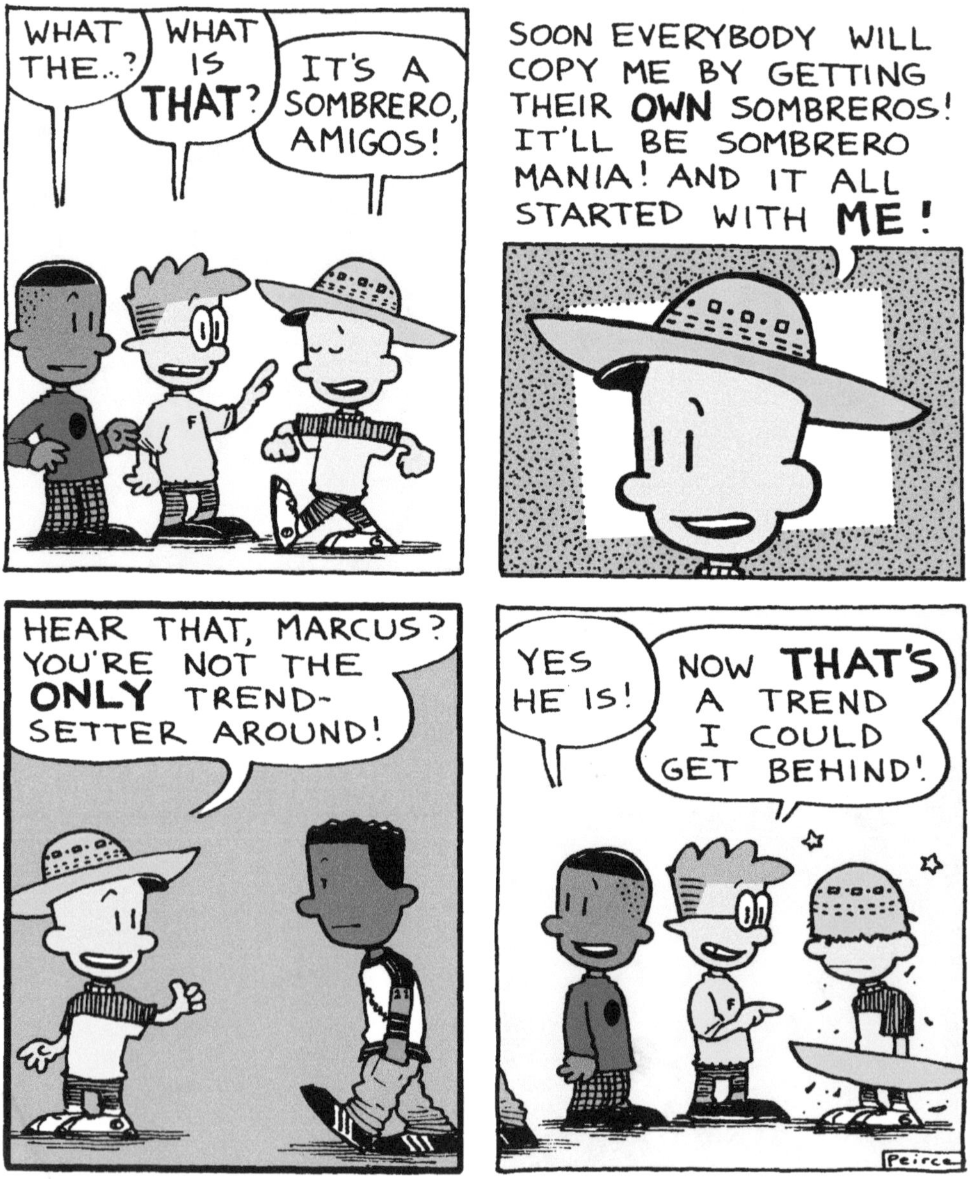
WHAT THE...?
WHAT IS THAT?
IT'S A SOMBRERO, AMIGOS!
SOON EVERYBODY WILL COPY ME BY GETTING THEIR OWN SOMBREROS! IT'LL BE SOMBRERO MANIA! AND IT ALL STARTED WITH ME!
HEAR THAT, MARCUS? YOU'RE NOT THE ONLY TREND-SETTER AROUND!
YES HE IS!
NOW THAT'S A TREND I COULD GET BEHIND!
Peirce

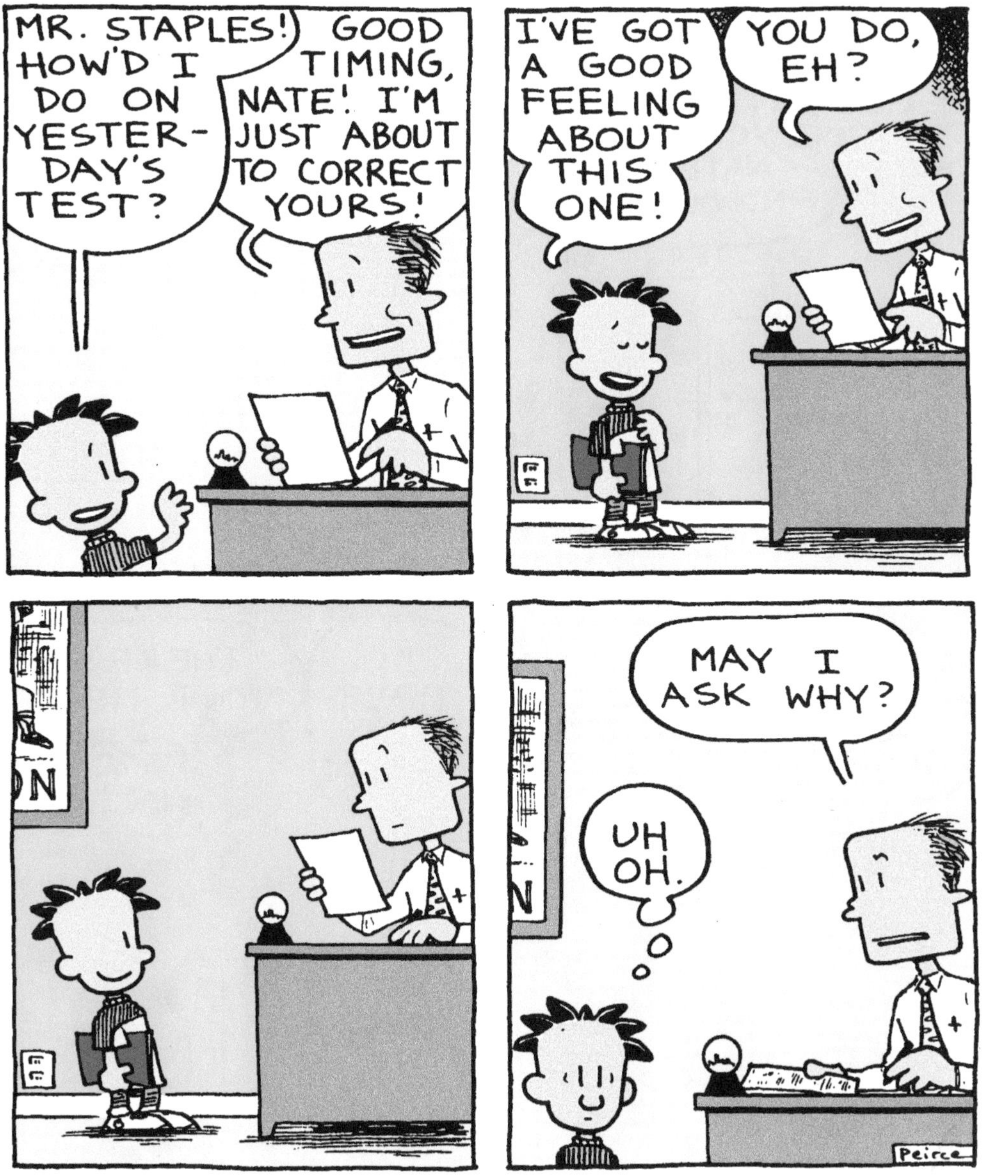
MR. STAPLES! HOW'D I DO ON YESTER-DAY'S TEST?
GOOD TIMING, NATE! I'M JUST ABOUT TO CORRECT YOURS!
I'VE GOT A GOOD FEELING ABOUT THIS ONE!
YOU DO, EH?
MAY I ASK WHY?
UH OH.
Peirce

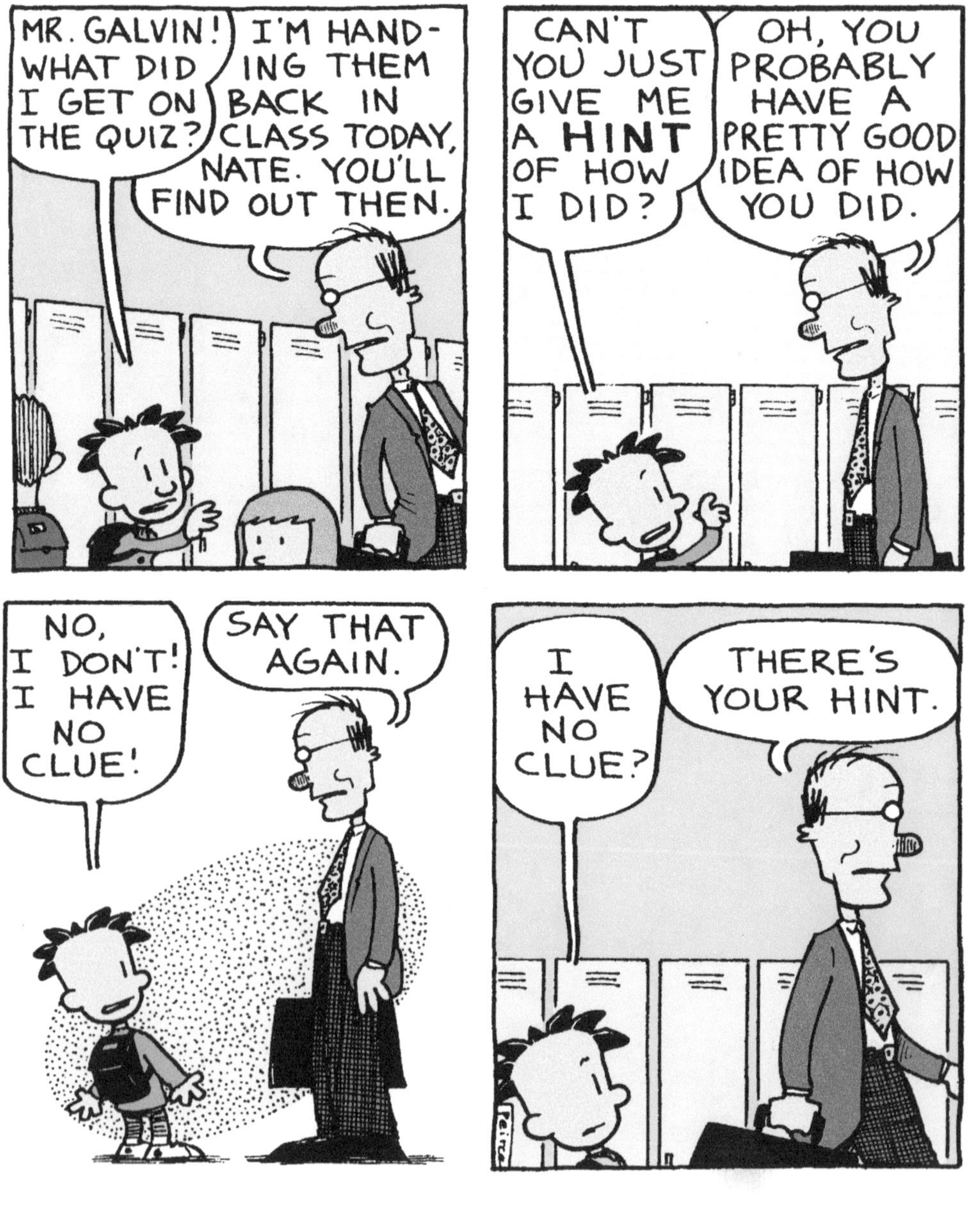
MR. GALVIN! WHAT DID I GET ON THE QUIZ?
I'M HANDING THEM BACK IN CLASS TODAY, NATE. YOU'LL FIND OUT THEN.
CAN'T YOU JUST GIVE ME A **HINT** OF HOW I DID?
OH, YOU PROBABLY HAVE A PRETTY GOOD IDEA OF HOW YOU DID.
NO, I DON'T! I HAVE NO CLUE!
SAY THAT AGAIN.
I HAVE NO CLUE?
THERE'S YOUR HINT.

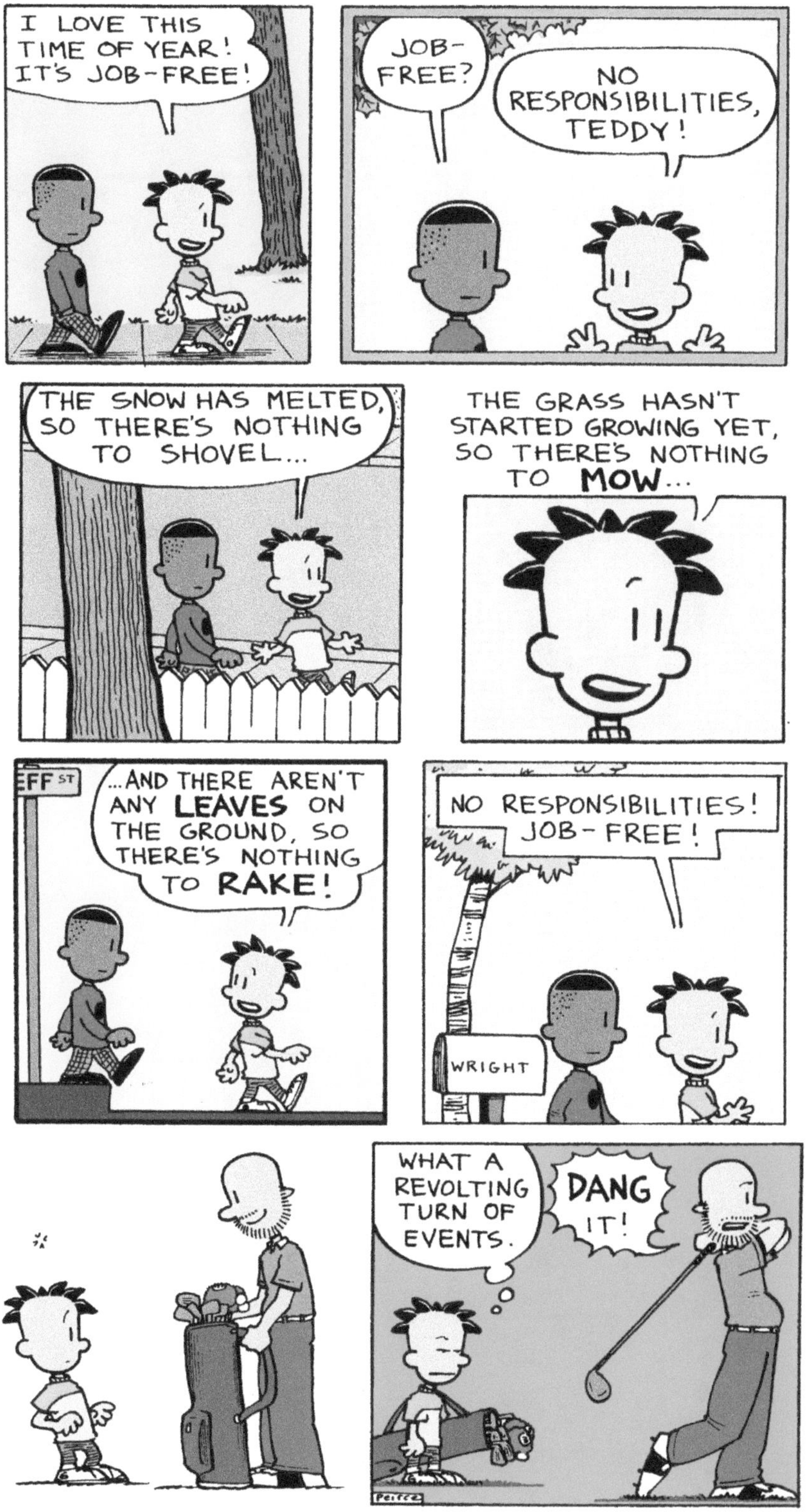
I LOVE THIS TIME OF YEAR! IT'S JOB-FREE!
JOB-FREE?
NO RESPONSIBILITIES, TEDDY!
THE SNOW HAS MELTED, SO THERE'S NOTHING TO SHOVEL...
THE GRASS HASN'T STARTED GROWING YET, SO THERE'S NOTHING TO MOW...
EFF ST
...AND THERE AREN'T ANY LEAVES ON THE GROUND, SO THERE'S NOTHING TO RAKE!
NO RESPONSIBILITIES! JOB-FREE!
WRIGHT
WHAT A REVOLTING TURN OF EVENTS.
DANG IT!
PEIRCE

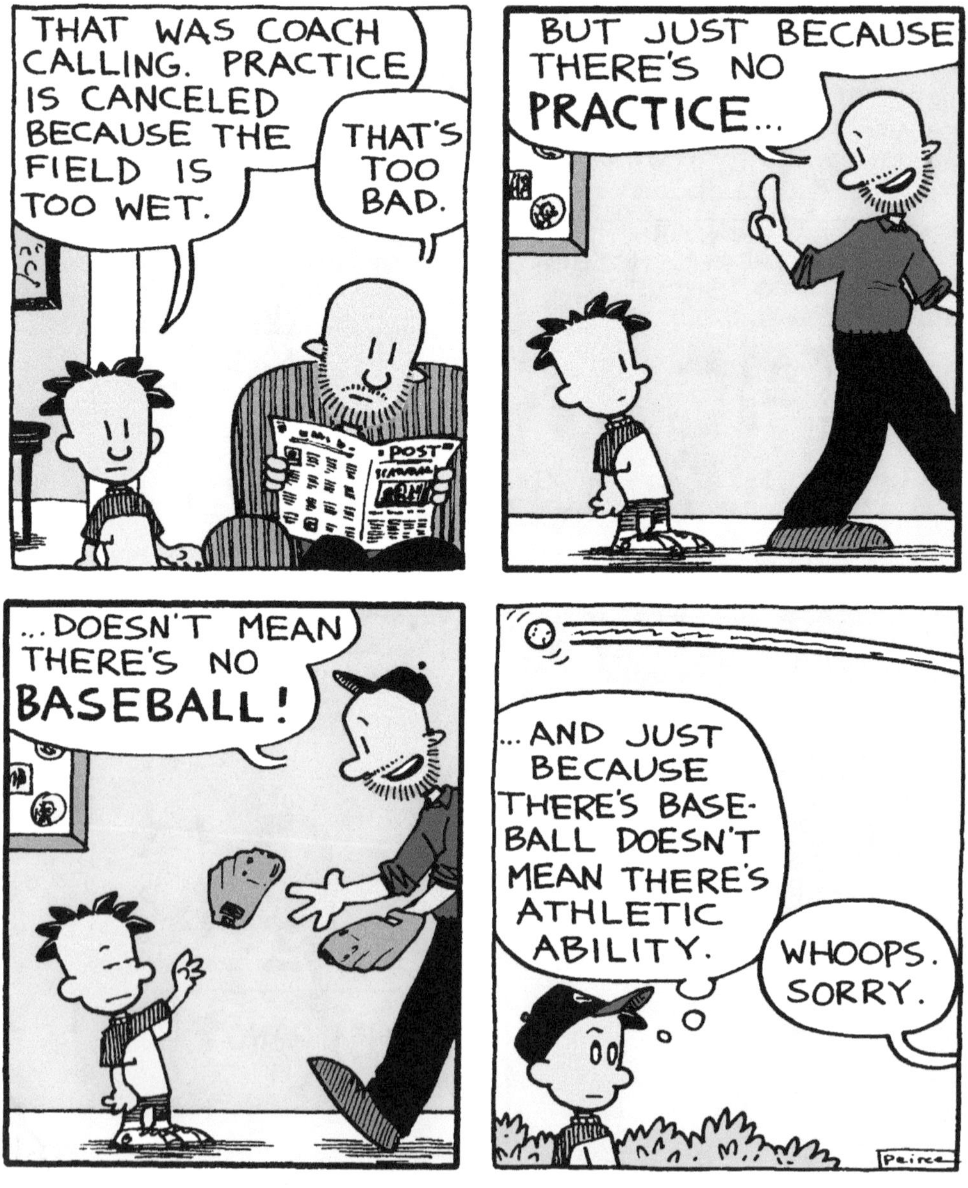
THAT WAS COACH CALLING. PRACTICE IS CANCELED BECAUSE THE FIELD IS TOO WET.
THAT'S TOO BAD.
POST
BUT JUST BECAUSE THERE'S NO PRACTICE...
...DOESN'T MEAN THERE'S NO BASEBALL!
...AND JUST BECAUSE THERE'S BASE-BALL DOESN'T MEAN THERE'S ATHLETIC ABILITY.
WHOOPS. SORRY.
Peirce

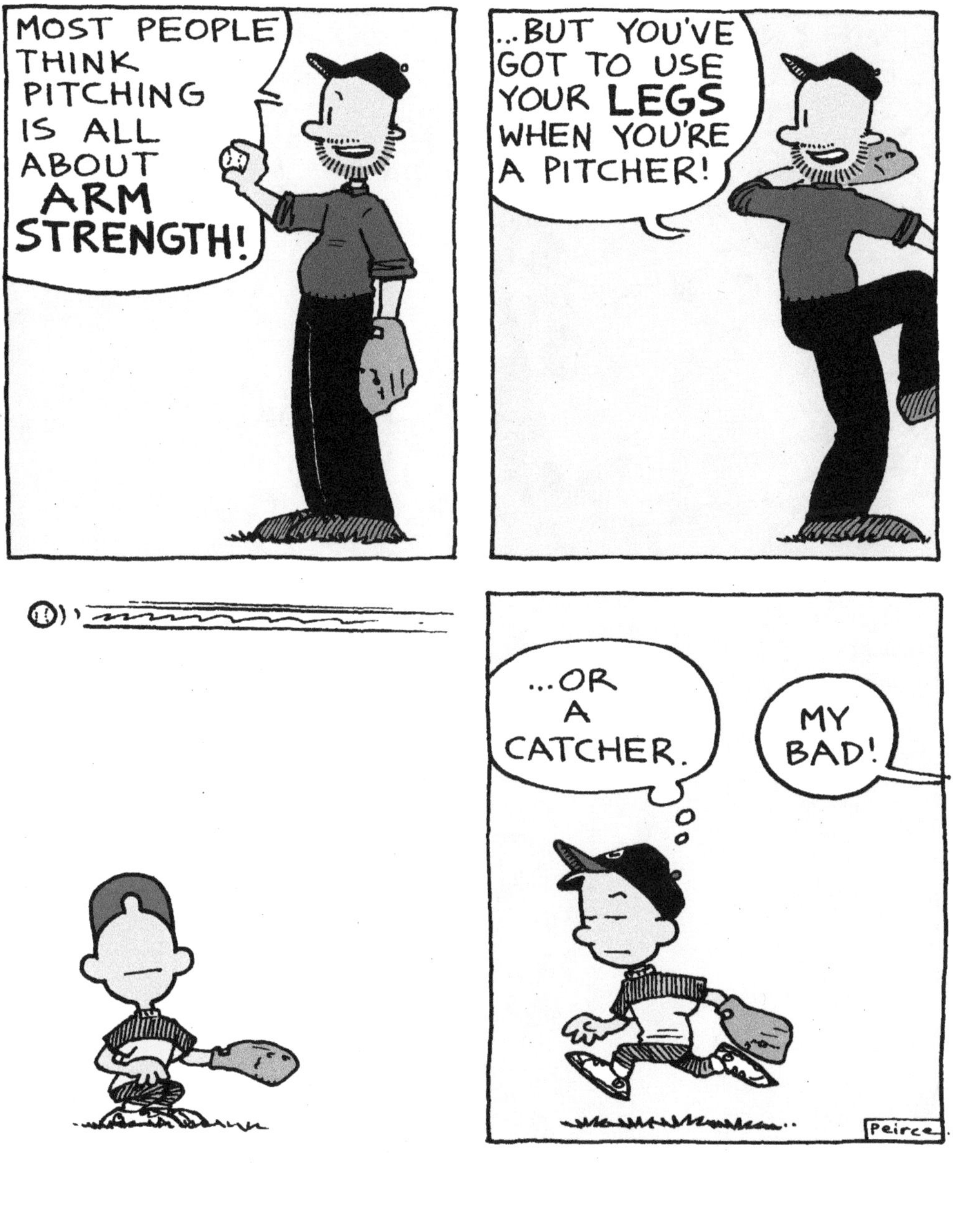
MOST PEOPLE THINK PITCHING IS ALL ABOUT ARM STRENGTH!
...BUT YOU'VE GOT TO USE YOUR LEGS WHEN YOU'RE A PITCHER!
...OR A CATCHER.
MY BAD!
Peirce

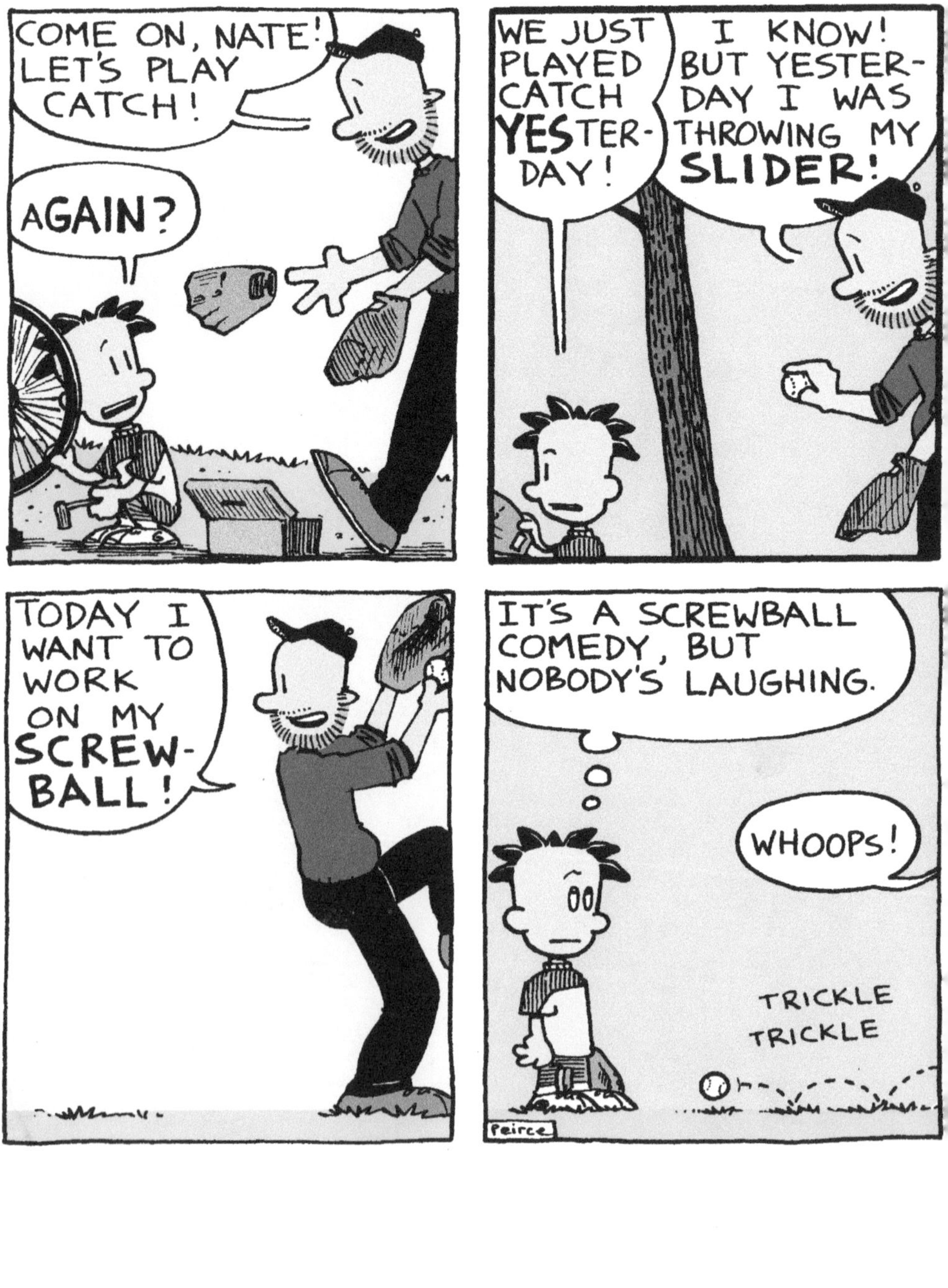
COME ON, NATE! LET'S PLAY CATCH!
AGAIN?
WE JUST PLAYED CATCH YESTERDAY!
I KNOW! BUT YESTERDAY I WAS THROWING MY SLIDER!
TODAY I WANT TO WORK ON MY SCREWBALL!
IT'S A SCREWBALL COMEDY, BUT NOBODY'S LAUGHING.
WHOOPS!
TRICKLE TRICKLE
Peirce

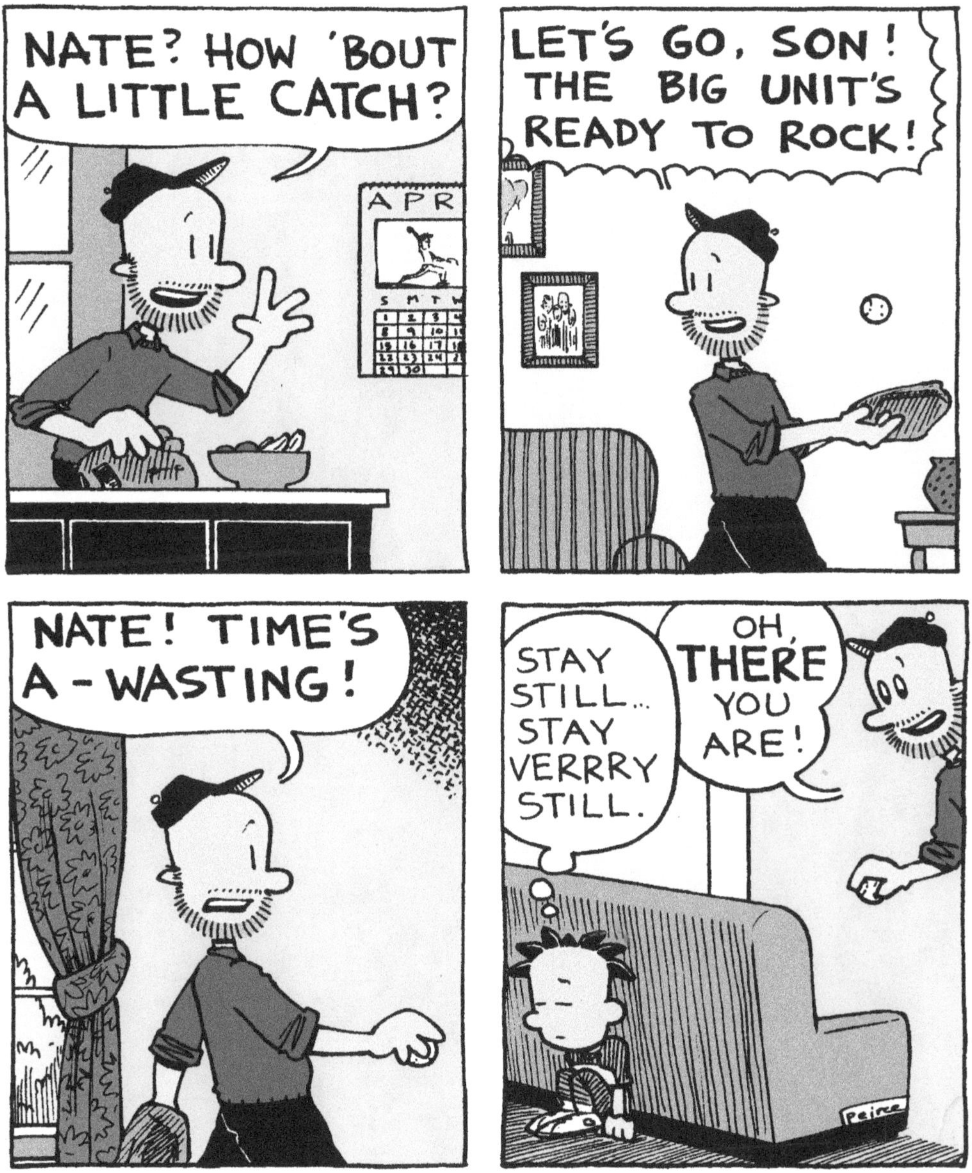
NATE? HOW 'BOUT A LITTLE CATCH?
APR
LET'S GO, SON! THE BIG UNIT'S READY TO ROCK!
NATE! TIME'S A-WASTING!
STAY STILL... STAY VERRRY STILL.
OH, THERE YOU ARE!
Peirce

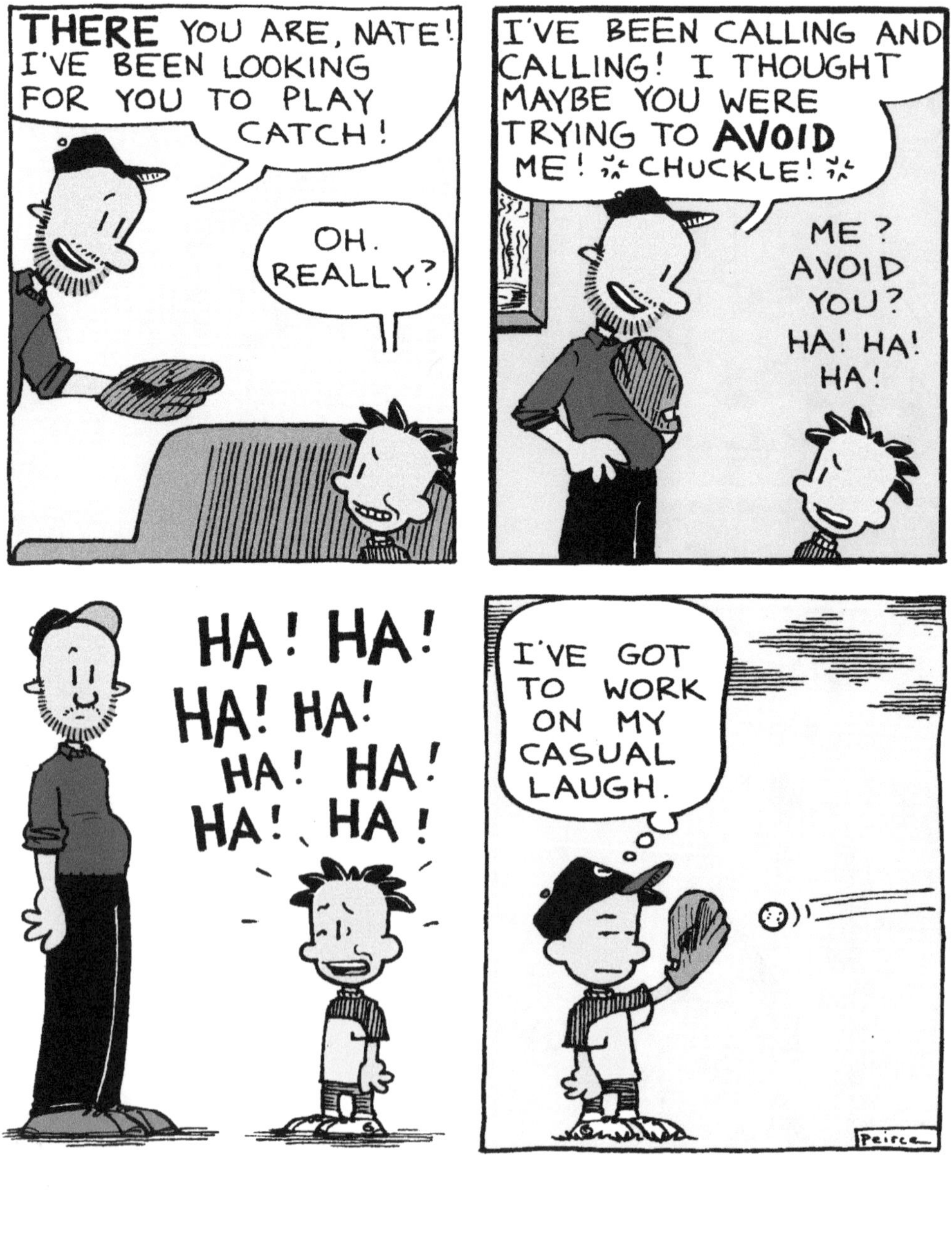
THERE YOU ARE, NATE! I'VE BEEN LOOKING FOR YOU TO PLAY CATCH!
OH. REALLY?
I'VE BEEN CALLING AND CALLING! I THOUGHT MAYBE YOU WERE TRYING TO AVOID ME! *CHUCKLE!*
ME? AVOID YOU? HA! HA! HA!
HA! HA! HA! HA! HA! HA! HA! HA!
I'VE GOT TO WORK ON MY CASUAL LAUGH.
Peirce

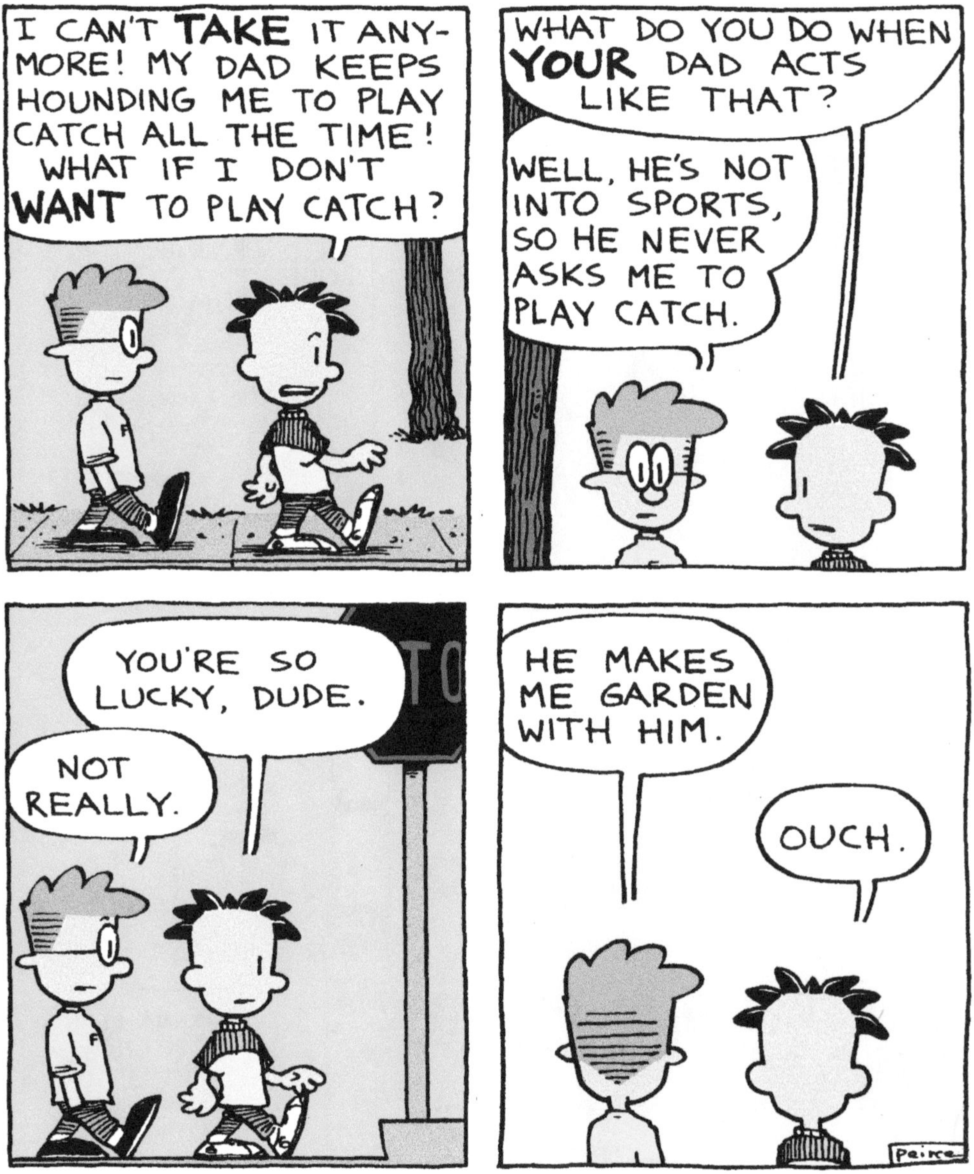
I CAN'T TAKE IT ANYMORE! MY DAD KEEPS HOUNDING ME TO PLAY CATCH ALL THE TIME! WHAT IF I DON'T WANT TO PLAY CATCH?
WHAT DO YOU DO WHEN YOUR DAD ACTS LIKE THAT?
WELL, HE'S NOT INTO SPORTS, SO HE NEVER ASKS ME TO PLAY CATCH.
YOU'RE SO LUCKY, DUDE.
NOT REALLY.
HE MAKES ME GARDEN WITH HIM.
OUCH.
Peirce

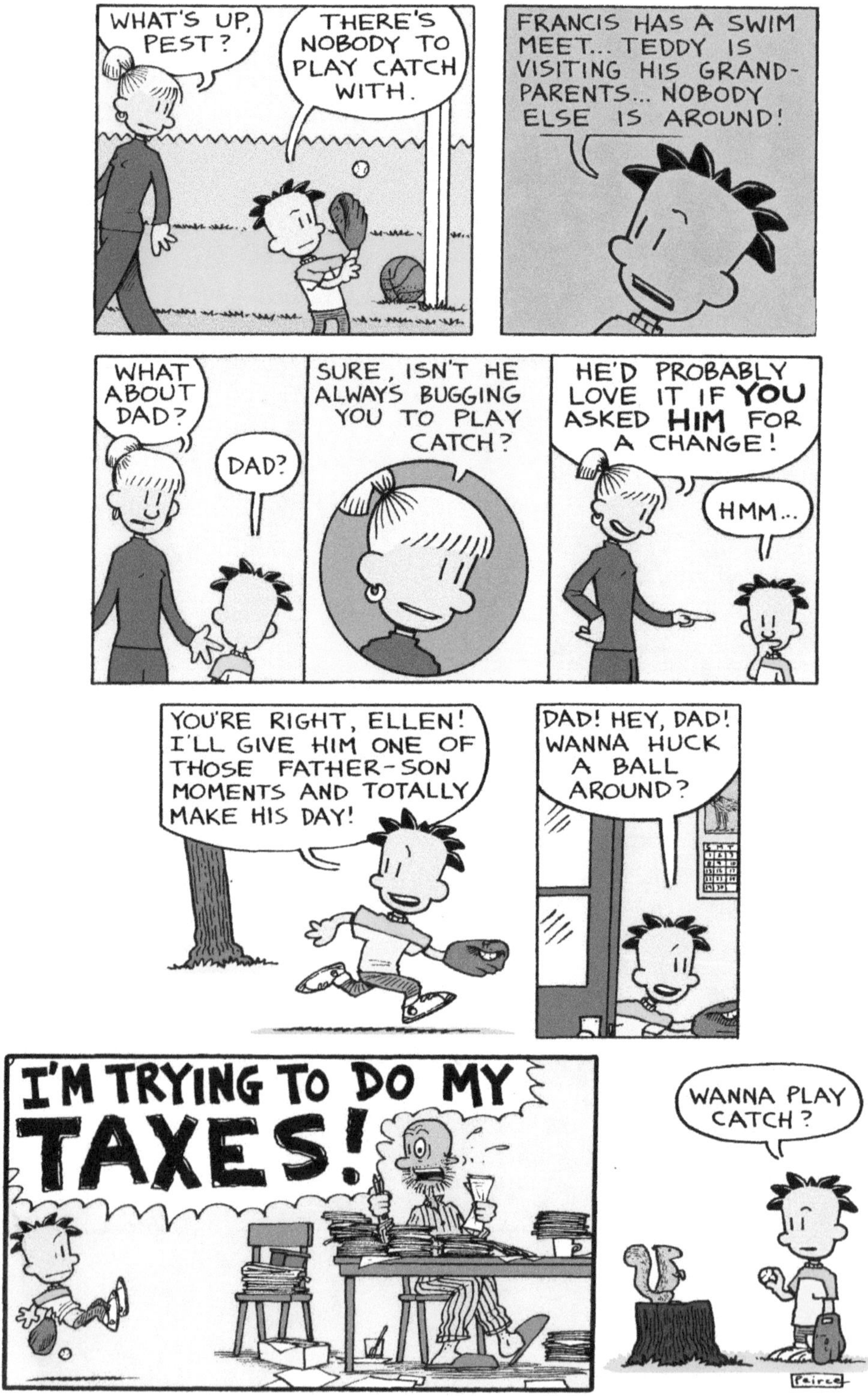
WHAT'S UP, PEST?
THERE'S NOBODY TO PLAY CATCH WITH.
FRANCIS HAS A SWIM MEET... TEDDY IS VISITING HIS GRAND-PARENTS... NOBODY ELSE IS AROUND!
WHAT ABOUT DAD?
DAD?
SURE, ISN'T HE ALWAYS BUGGING YOU TO PLAY CATCH?
HE'D PROBABLY LOVE IT IF **YOU** ASKED **HIM** FOR A CHANGE!
HMM...
YOU'RE RIGHT, ELLEN! I'LL GIVE HIM ONE OF THOSE FATHER-SON MOMENTS AND TOTALLY MAKE HIS DAY!
DAD! HEY, DAD! WANNA HUCK A BALL AROUND?
I'M TRYING TO DO MY TAXES!
WANNA PLAY CATCH?
Peirce

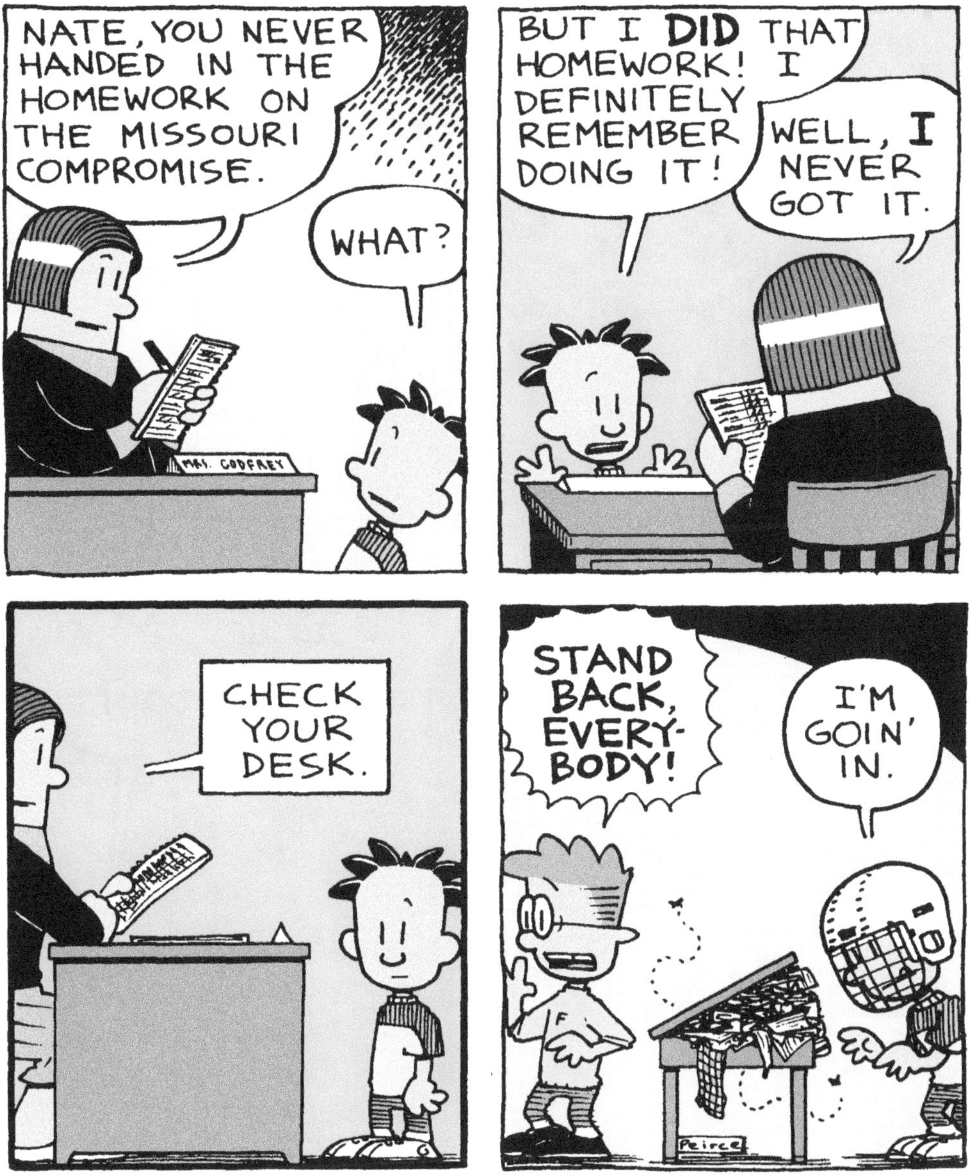
NATE, YOU NEVER HANDED IN THE HOMEWORK ON THE MISSOURI COMPROMISE.
WHAT?
MRS. GODFREY
BUT I **DID** THAT HOMEWORK! I DEFINITELY REMEMBER DOING IT!
WELL, **I** NEVER GOT IT.
CHECK YOUR DESK.
STAND BACK, EVERY-BODY!
I'M GOIN' IN.
Peirce

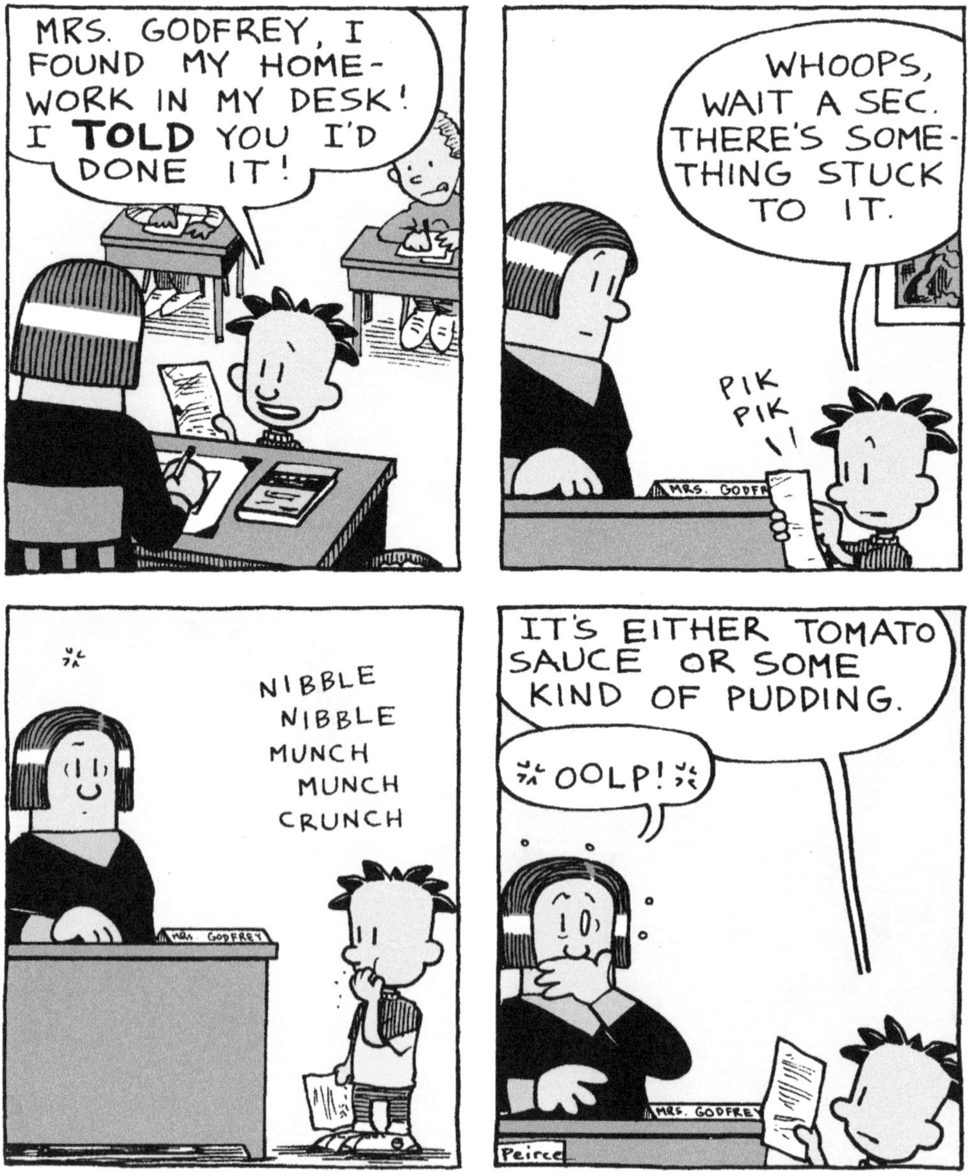
MRS. GODFREY, I FOUND MY HOME-WORK IN MY DESK! I **TOLD** YOU I'D DONE IT!
WHOOPS, WAIT A SEC. THERE'S SOME-THING STUCK TO IT.
PIK PIK
MRS. GODFR
NIBBLE NIBBLE MUNCH MUNCH CRUNCH
MRS. GODFREY
IT'S EITHER TOMATO SAUCE OR SOME KIND OF PUDDING.
OOLP!
MRS. GODFREY
Peirce

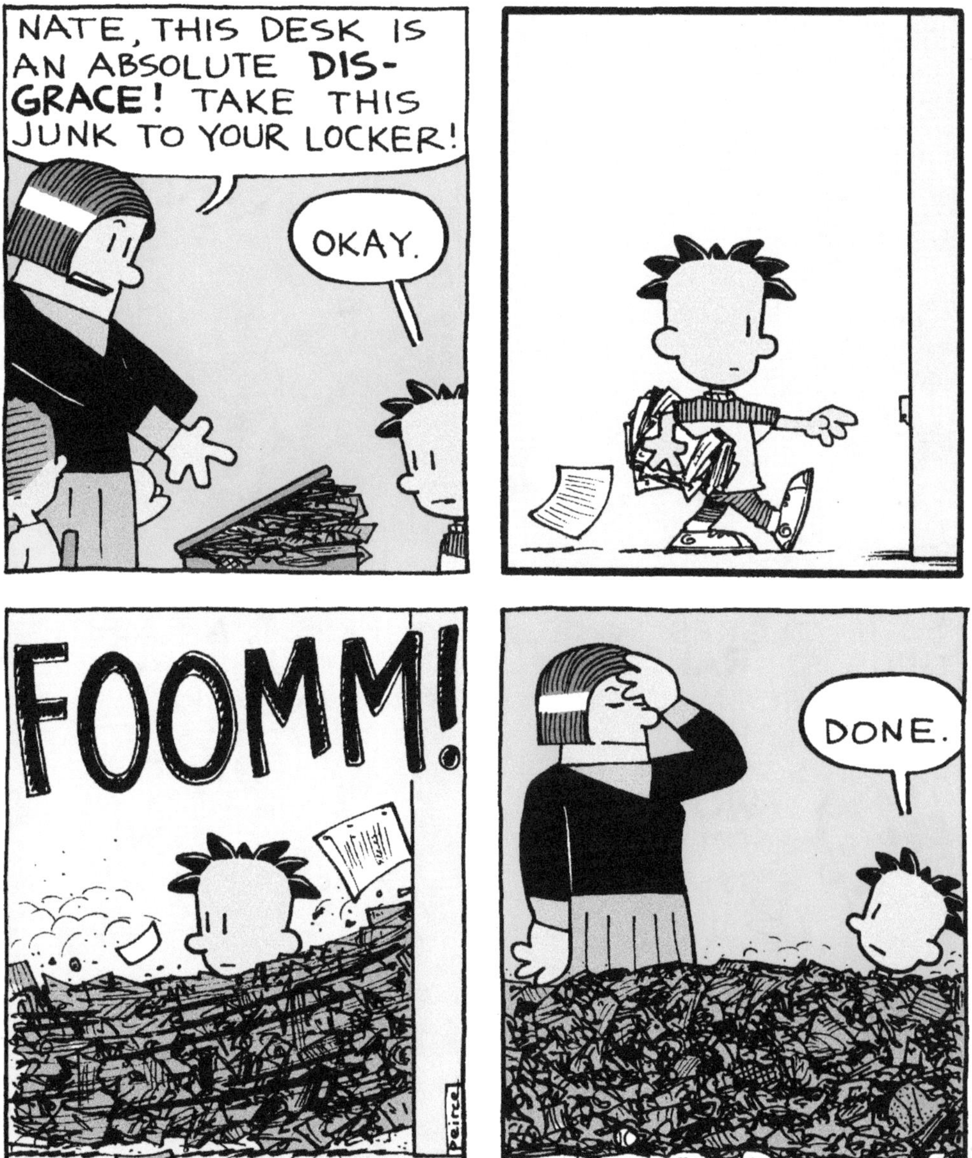
NATE, THIS DESK IS AN ABSOLUTE **DIS-GRACE!** TAKE THIS JUNK TO YOUR LOCKER!
OKAY.
FOOMM!
Peirce
DONE.

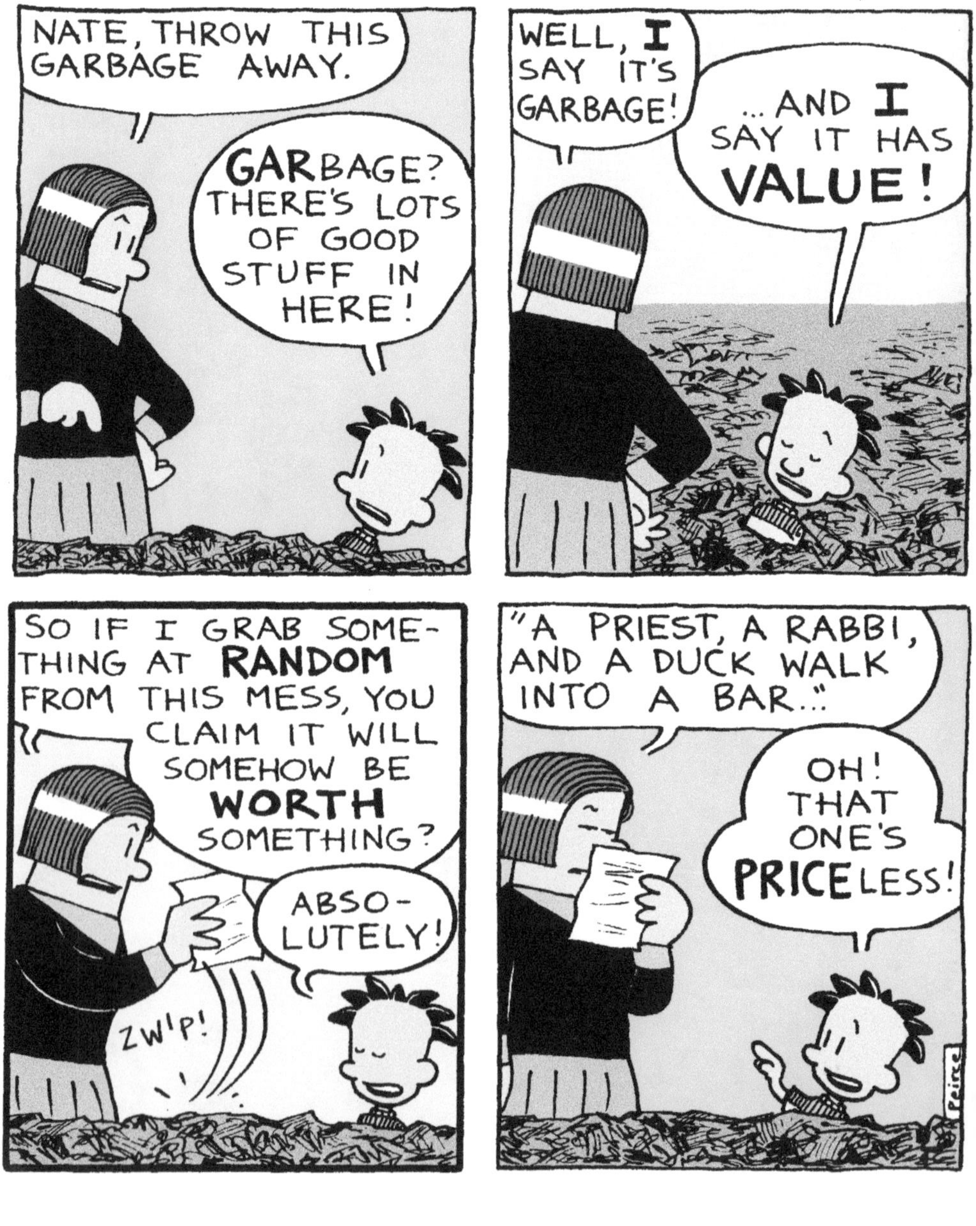

NATE, THROW THIS GARBAGE AWAY.
GARBAGE? THERE'S LOTS OF GOOD STUFF IN HERE!
WELL, I SAY IT'S GARBAGE!
...AND I SAY IT HAS VALUE!
SO IF I GRAB SOMETHING AT RANDOM FROM THIS MESS, YOU CLAIM IT WILL SOMEHOW BE WORTH SOMETHING?
ABSO-LUTELY!
ZWIP!
"A PRIEST, A RABBI, AND A DUCK WALK INTO A BAR..."
OH! THAT ONE'S PRICELESS!
Peirce

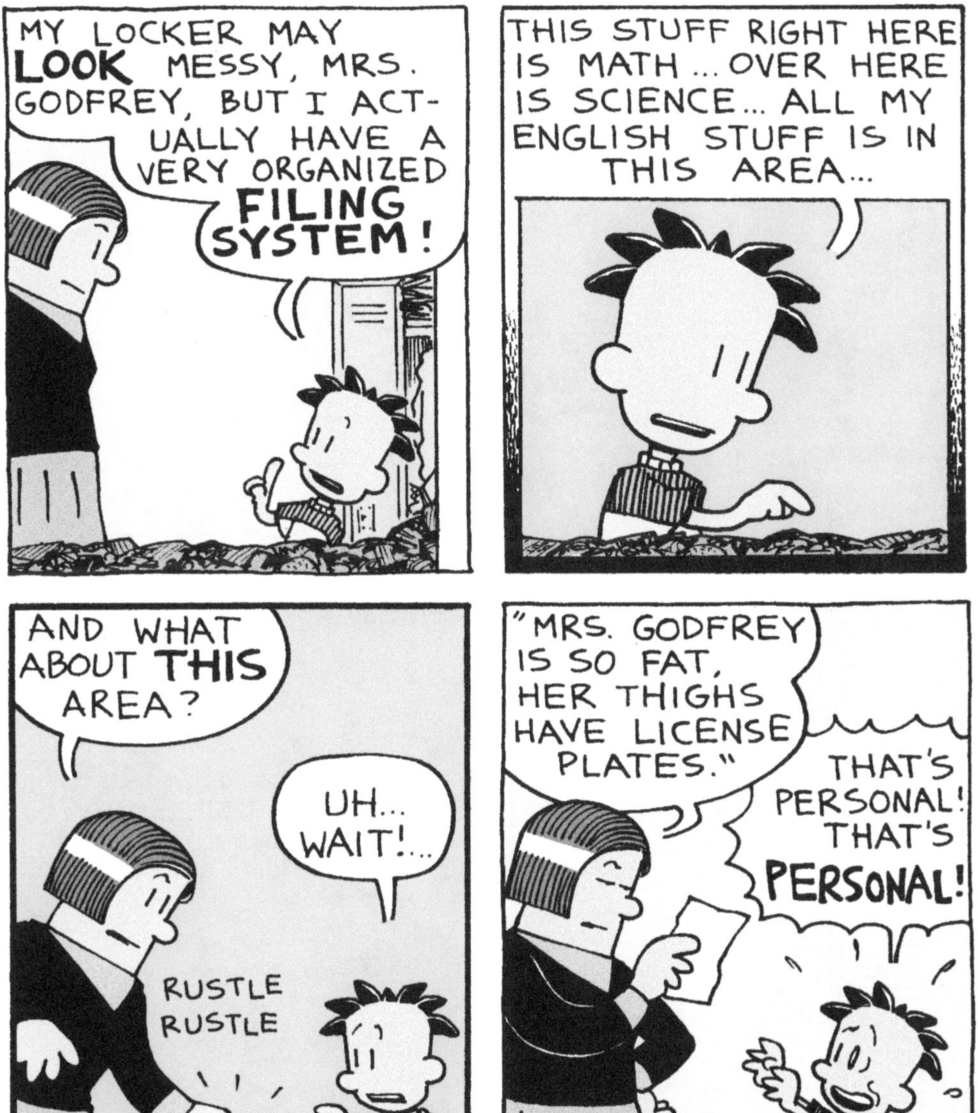
MY LOCKER MAY **LOOK** MESSY, MRS. GODFREY, BUT I ACT-UALLY HAVE A VERY ORGANIZED **FILING SYSTEM!**
THIS STUFF RIGHT HERE IS MATH ... OVER HERE IS SCIENCE... ALL MY ENGLISH STUFF IS IN THIS AREA...
AND WHAT ABOUT **THIS** AREA?
UH... WAIT!...
RUSTLE RUSTLE
"MRS. GODFREY IS SO FAT, HER THIGHS HAVE LICENSE PLATES."
THAT'S PERSONAL! THAT'S **PERSONAL!**
Peirce

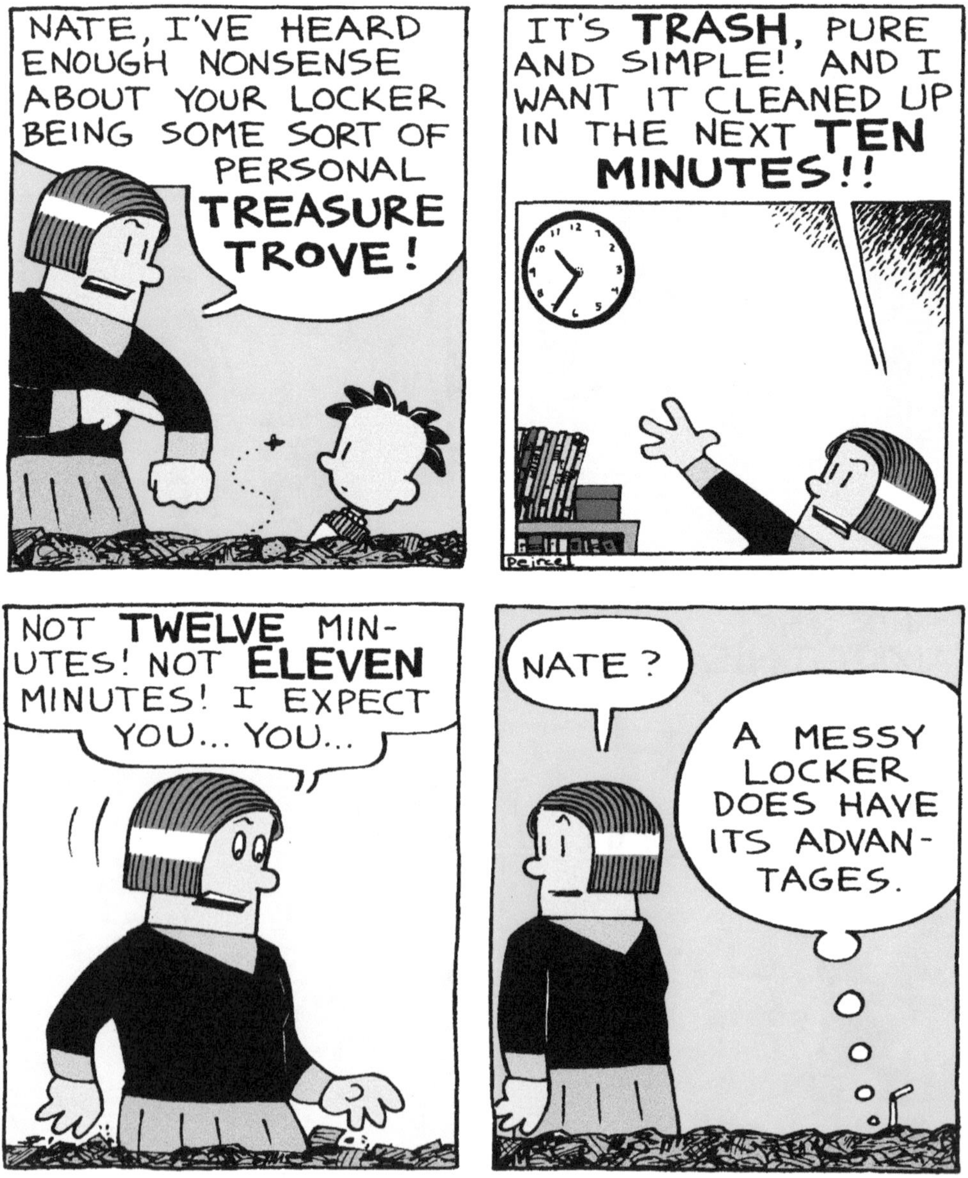
NATE, I'VE HEARD ENOUGH NONSENSE ABOUT YOUR LOCKER BEING SOME SORT OF PERSONAL **TREASURE TROVE**!
IT'S **TRASH**, PURE AND SIMPLE! AND I WANT IT CLEANED UP IN THE NEXT **TEN MINUTES**!!
Peirce
NOT **TWELVE** MINUTES! NOT **ELEVEN** MINUTES! I EXPECT YOU... YOU...
NATE?
A MESSY LOCKER DOES HAVE ITS ADVANTAGES.

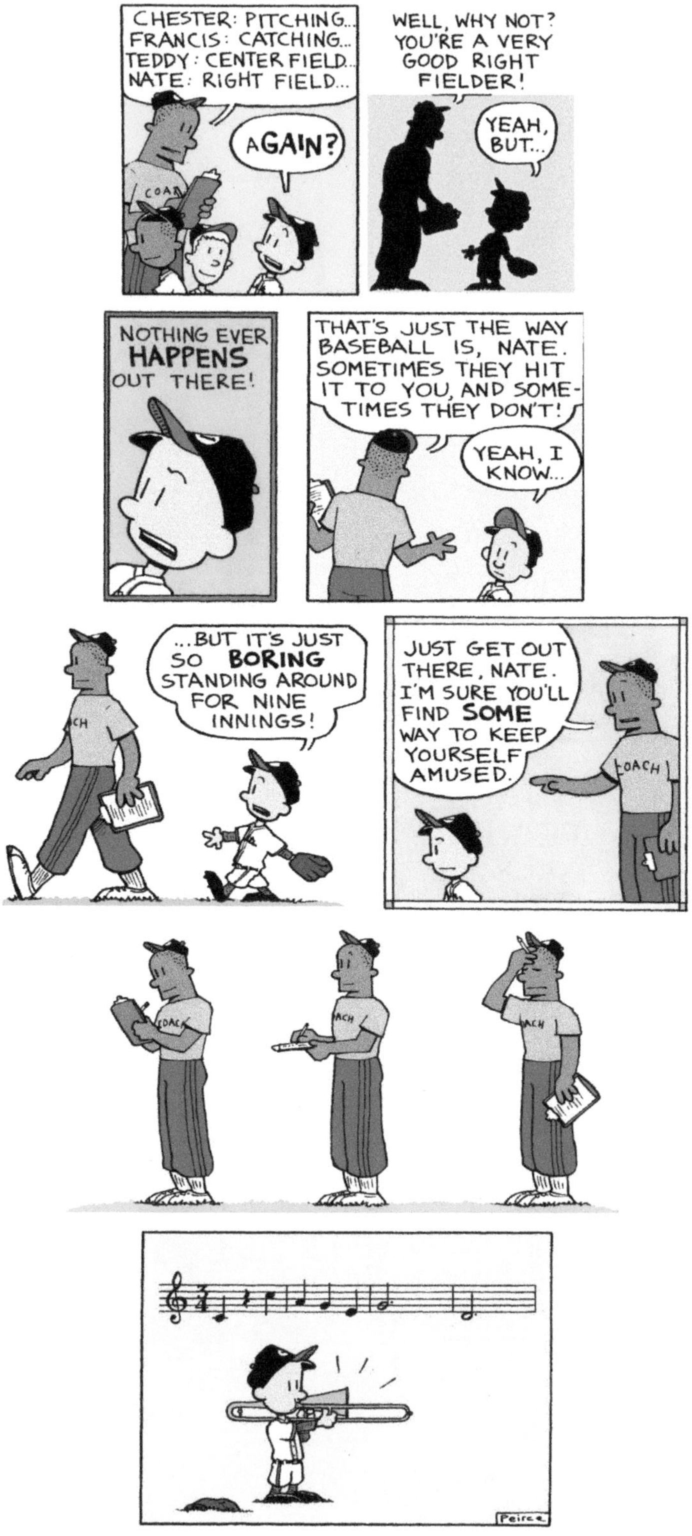
CHESTER: PITCHING... FRANCIS: CATCHING... TEDDY: CENTER FIELD... NATE: RIGHT FIELD...
AGAIN?
WELL, WHY NOT? YOU'RE A VERY GOOD RIGHT FIELDER!
YEAH, BUT...
NOTHING EVER HAPPENS OUT THERE!
THAT'S JUST THE WAY BASEBALL IS, NATE. SOMETIMES THEY HIT IT TO YOU, AND SOMETIMES THEY DON'T!
YEAH, I KNOW...
...BUT IT'S JUST SO BORING STANDING AROUND FOR NINE INNINGS!
JUST GET OUT THERE, NATE. I'M SURE YOU'LL FIND SOME WAY TO KEEP YOURSELF AMUSED.
Peirce

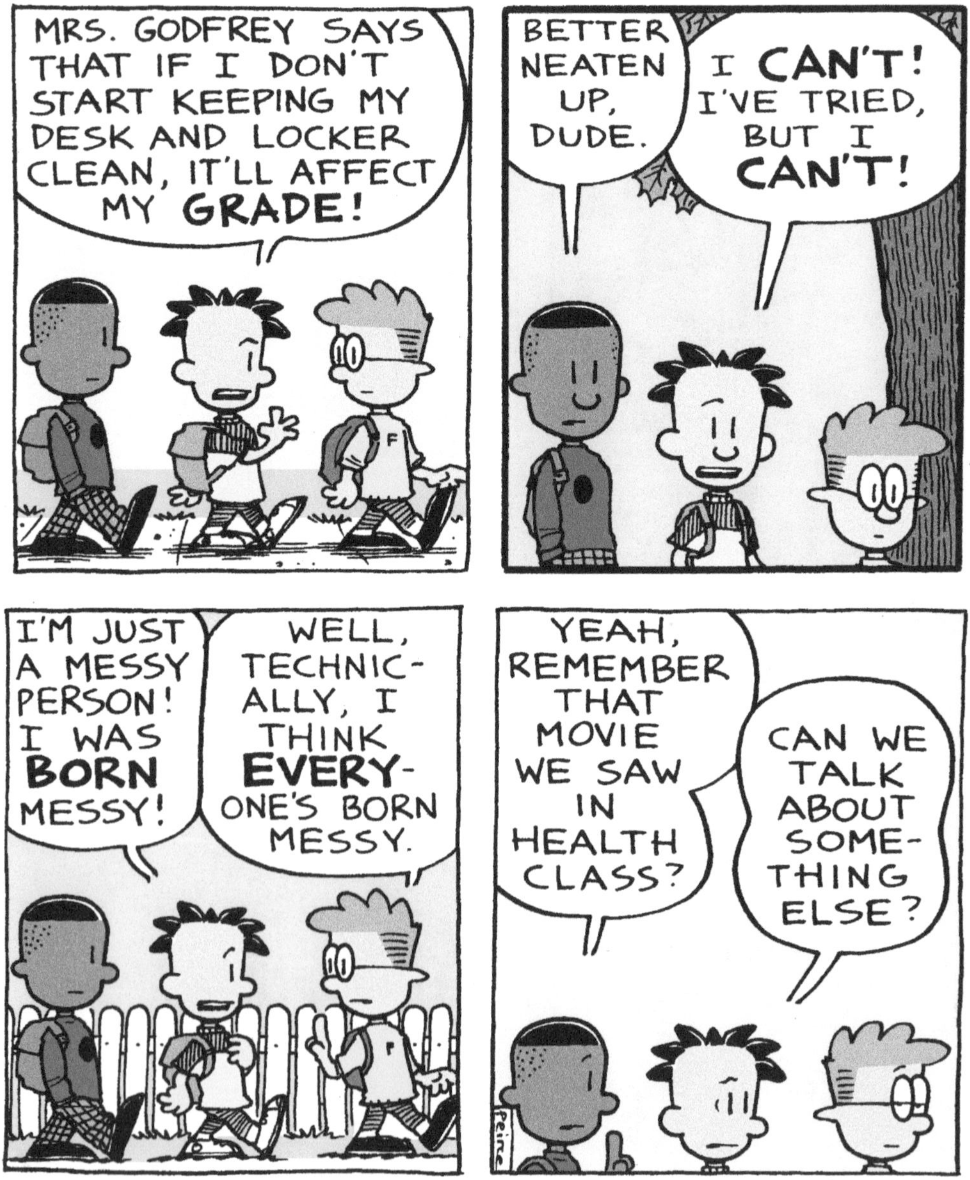
MRS. GODFREY SAYS THAT IF I DON'T START KEEPING MY DESK AND LOCKER CLEAN, IT'LL AFFECT MY GRADE!
BETTER NEATEN UP, DUDE.
I CAN'T! I'VE TRIED, BUT I CAN'T!
I'M JUST A MESSY PERSON! I WAS BORN MESSY!
WELL, TECHNIC-ALLY, I THINK EVERY-ONE'S BORN MESSY.
YEAH, REMEMBER THAT MOVIE WE SAW IN HEALTH CLASS?
CAN WE TALK ABOUT SOME-THING ELSE?
peirce

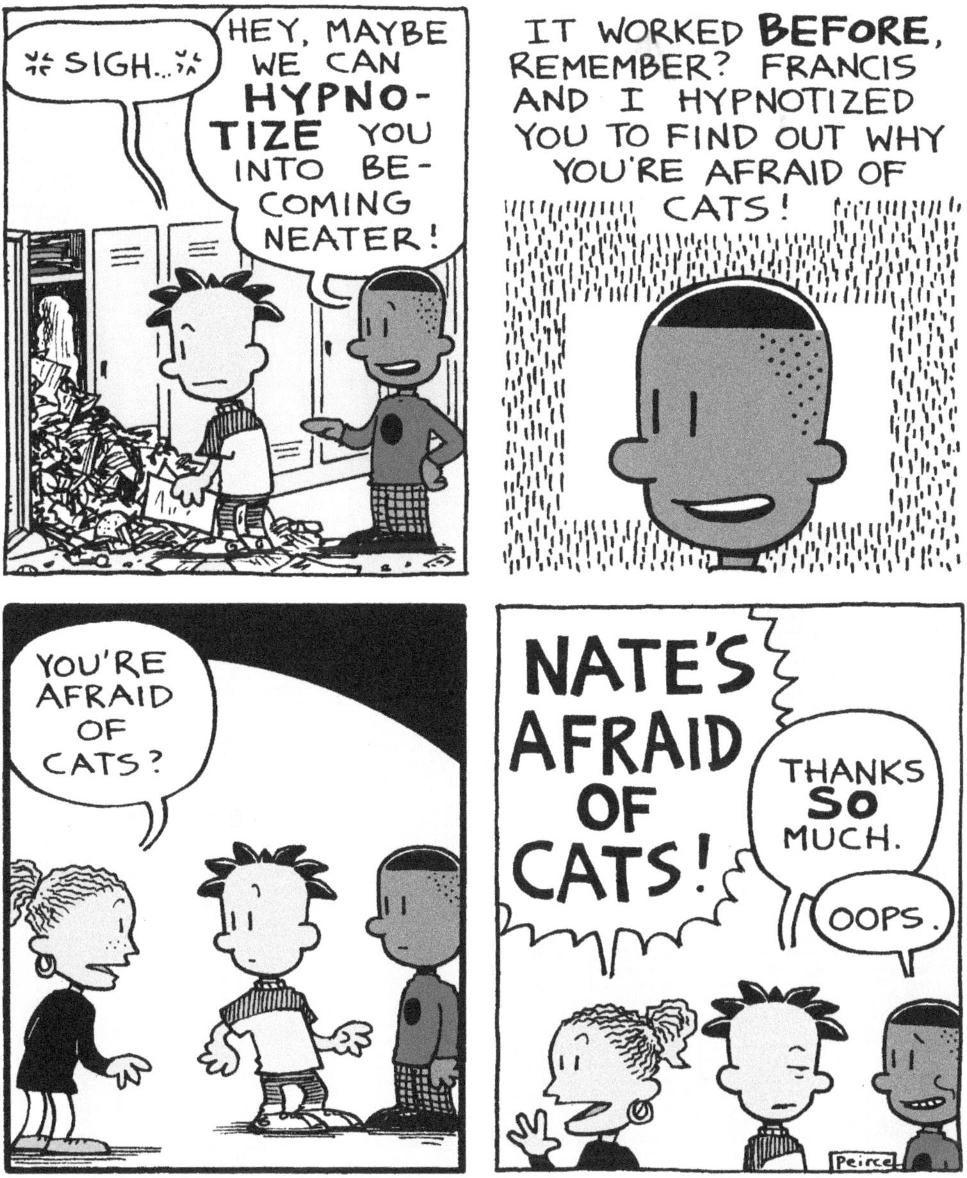
SIGH...
HEY, MAYBE WE CAN HYPNOTIZE YOU INTO BECOMING NEATER!
IT WORKED BEFORE, REMEMBER? FRANCIS AND I HYPNOTIZED YOU TO FIND OUT WHY YOU'RE AFRAID OF CATS!
YOU'RE AFRAID OF CATS?
NATE'S AFRAID OF CATS!
THANKS SO MUCH.
OOPS.
Peirce

READY TO GET HYPNO-TIZED?
I DON'T THINK THIS IS GOING TO WORK, FRANCIS.
YOU HAVE TO BE **SUGGESTIBLE** TO GET HYPNOTIZED! THAT'S NOT ME! MY WILL IS TOO STRONG! MY MIND IS TOO SHARP!
SNAP!
SHARP AS A SACK OF SAND.
ZZZZZZZZZZ
I DO THAT SAME TRICK WITH MY GERBIL!
Peirce

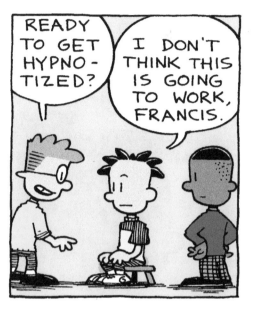

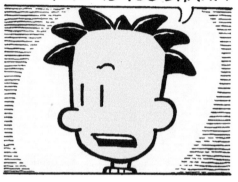

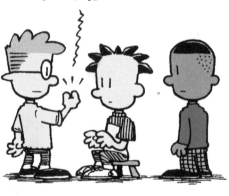

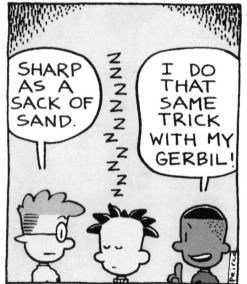

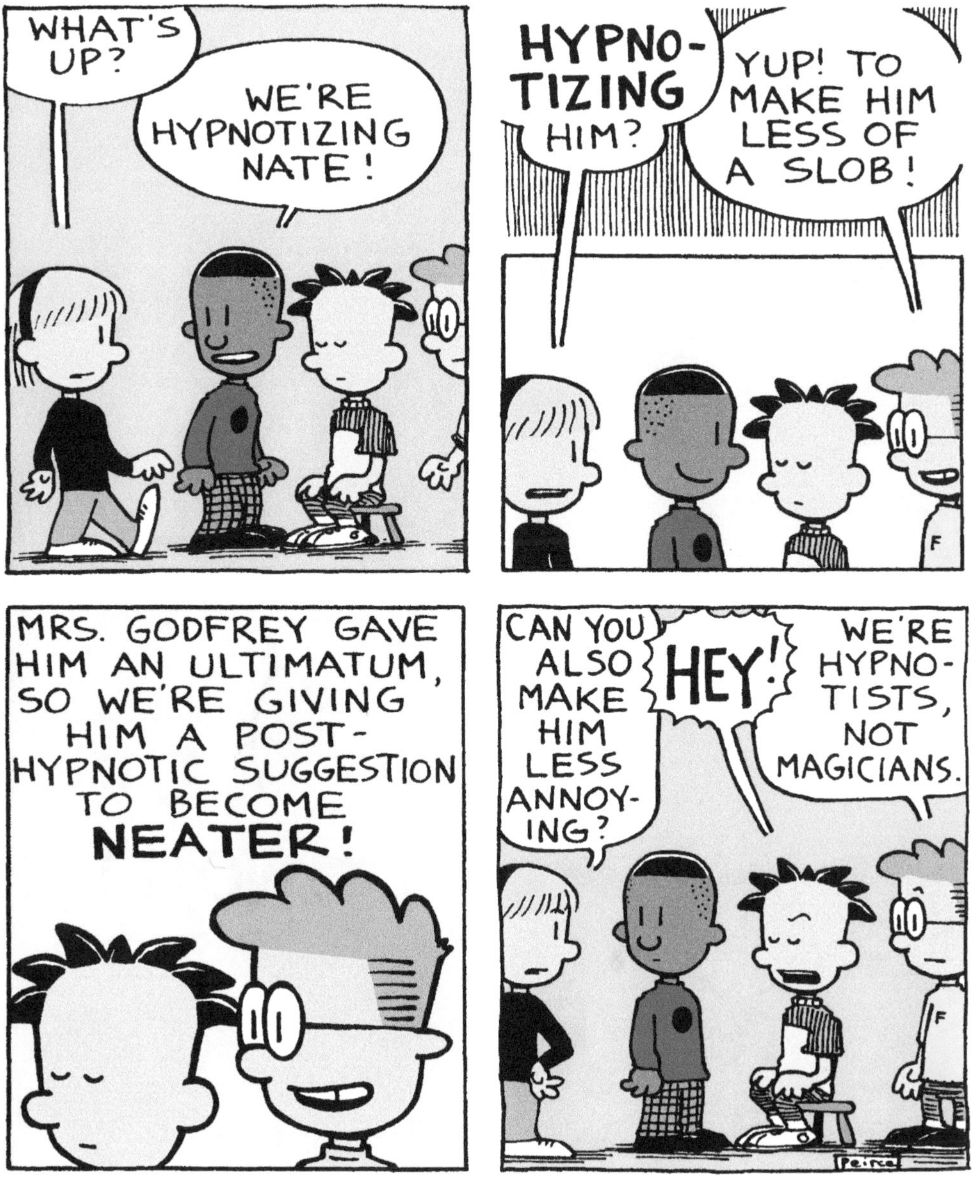
WHAT'S UP?
WE'RE HYPNOTIZING NATE!
HYPNO-TIZING HIM?
YUP! TO MAKE HIM LESS OF A SLOB!
MRS. GODFREY GAVE HIM AN ULTIMATUM, SO WE'RE GIVING HIM A POST-HYPNOTIC SUGGESTION TO BECOME NEATER!
CAN YOU ALSO MAKE HIM LESS ANNOY-ING?
HEY!
WE'RE HYPNO-TISTS, NOT MAGICIANS.
Peirce

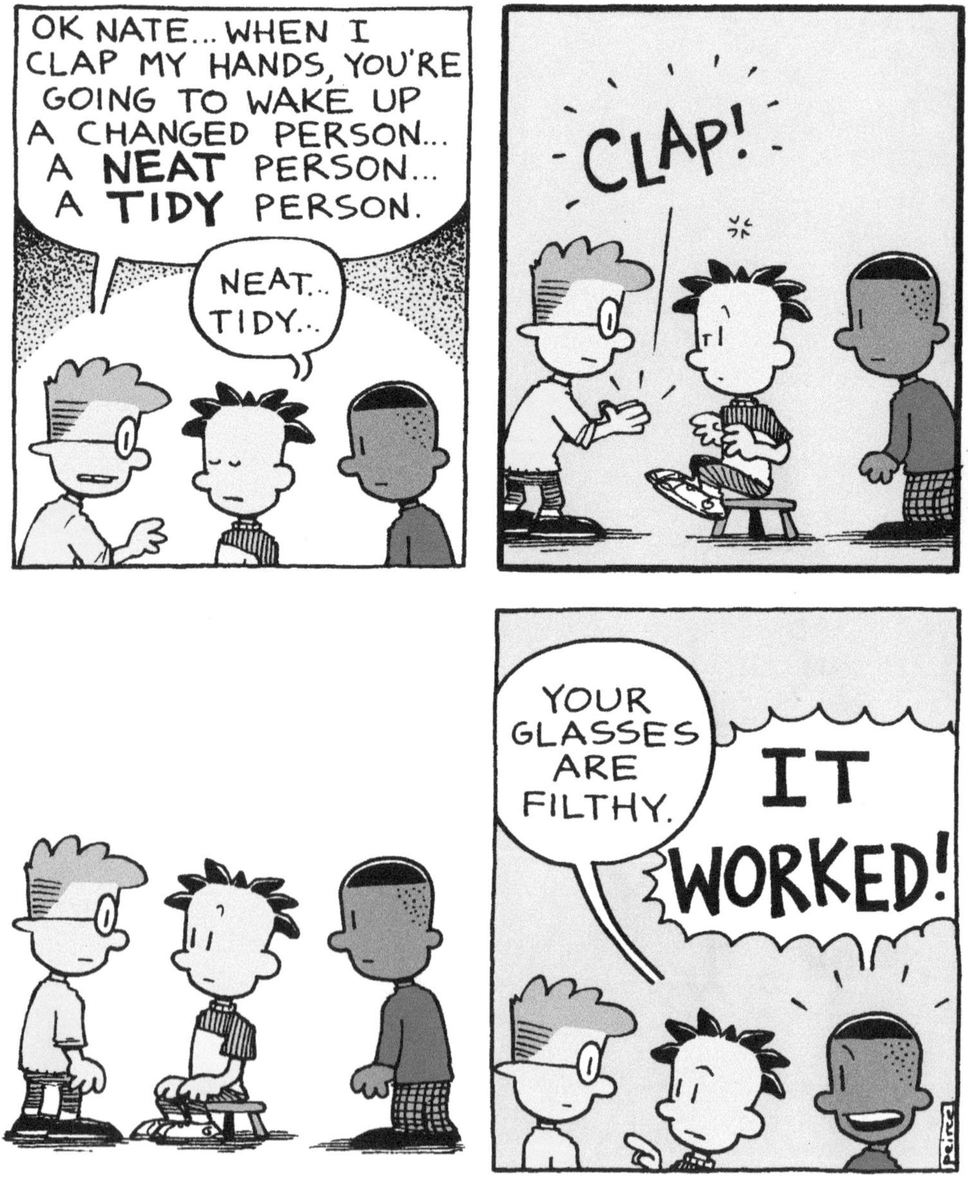
OK NATE... WHEN I CLAP MY HANDS, YOU'RE GOING TO WAKE UP A CHANGED PERSON... A **NEAT** PERSON... A **TIDY** PERSON.
NEAT... TIDY...
CLAP!
YOUR GLASSES ARE FILTHY.
IT WORKED!
Peirce

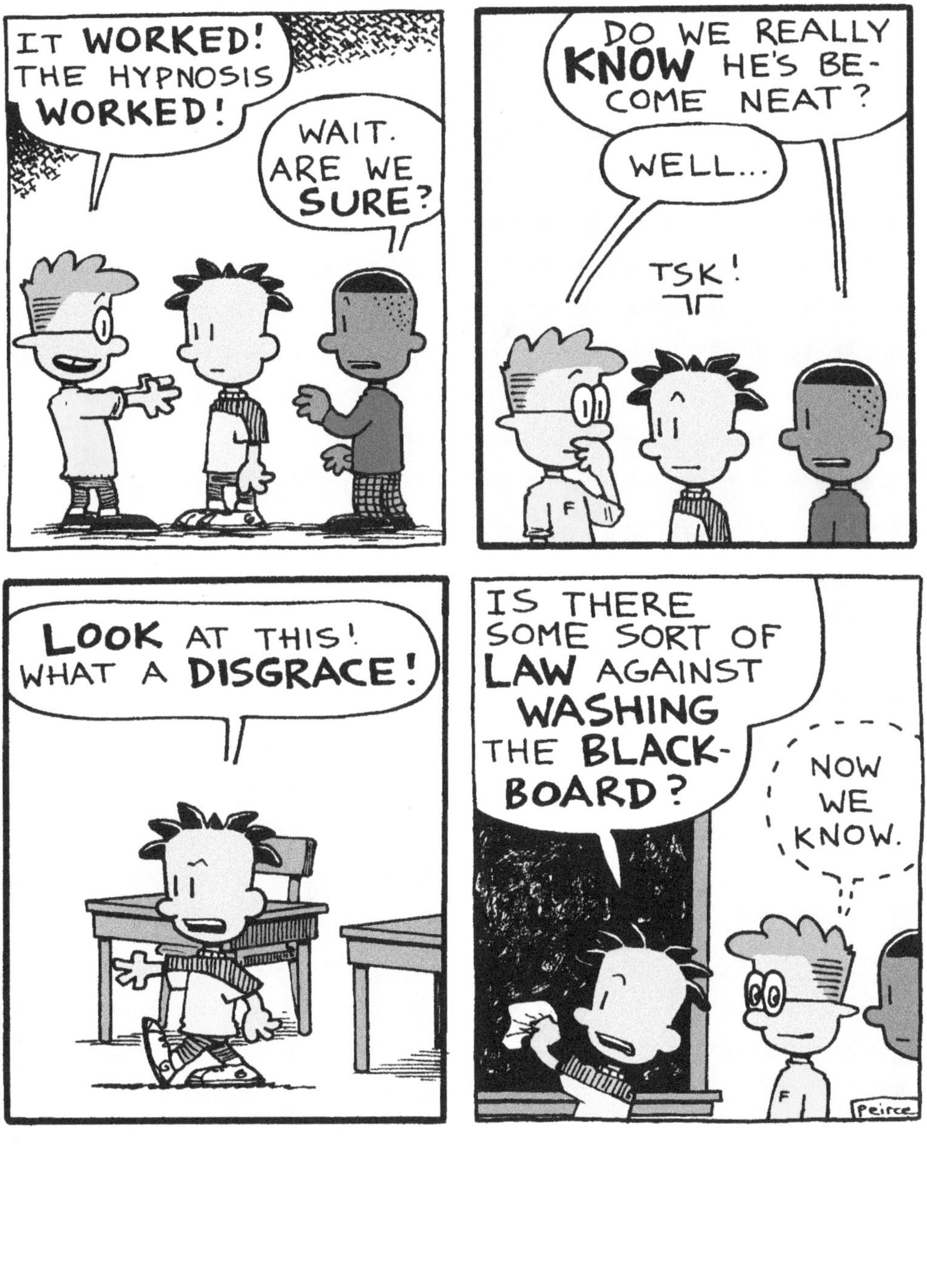
IT WORKED! THE HYPNOSIS WORKED!
WAIT. ARE WE SURE?
DO WE REALLY KNOW HE'S BE-COME NEAT?
WELL...
TSK!
LOOK AT THIS! WHAT A DISGRACE!
IS THERE SOME SORT OF LAW AGAINST WASHING THE BLACK-BOARD?
NOW WE KNOW.
Peirce

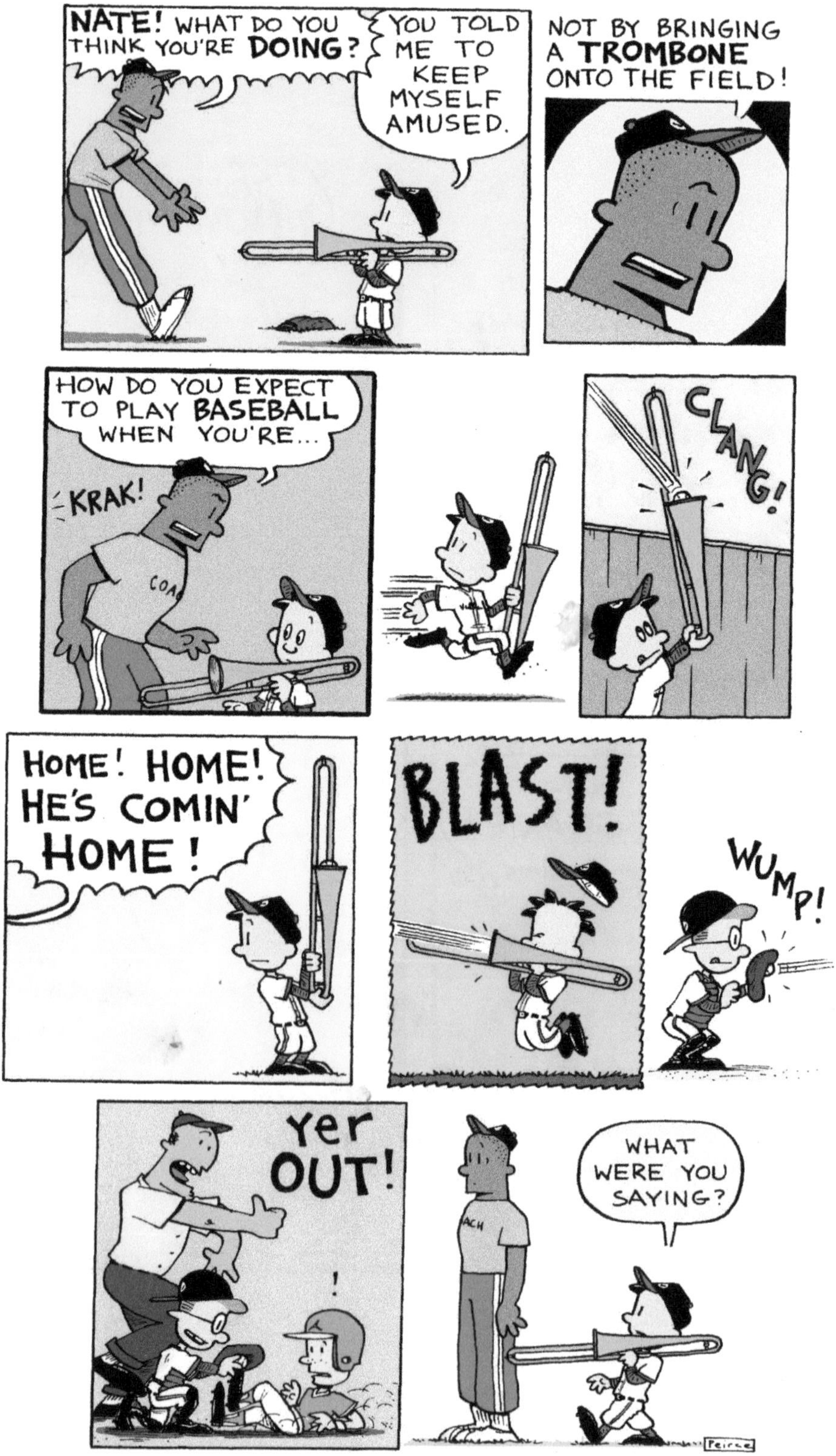
NATE! WHAT DO YOU THINK YOU'RE DOING?
YOU TOLD ME TO KEEP MYSELF AMUSED.
NOT BY BRINGING A TROMBONE ONTO THE FIELD!
HOW DO YOU EXPECT TO PLAY BASEBALL WHEN YOU'RE...
KRAK!
CLANG!
HOME! HOME! HE'S COMIN' HOME!
BLAST!
WUMP!
YER OUT!
!
WHAT WERE YOU SAYING?
Peirce

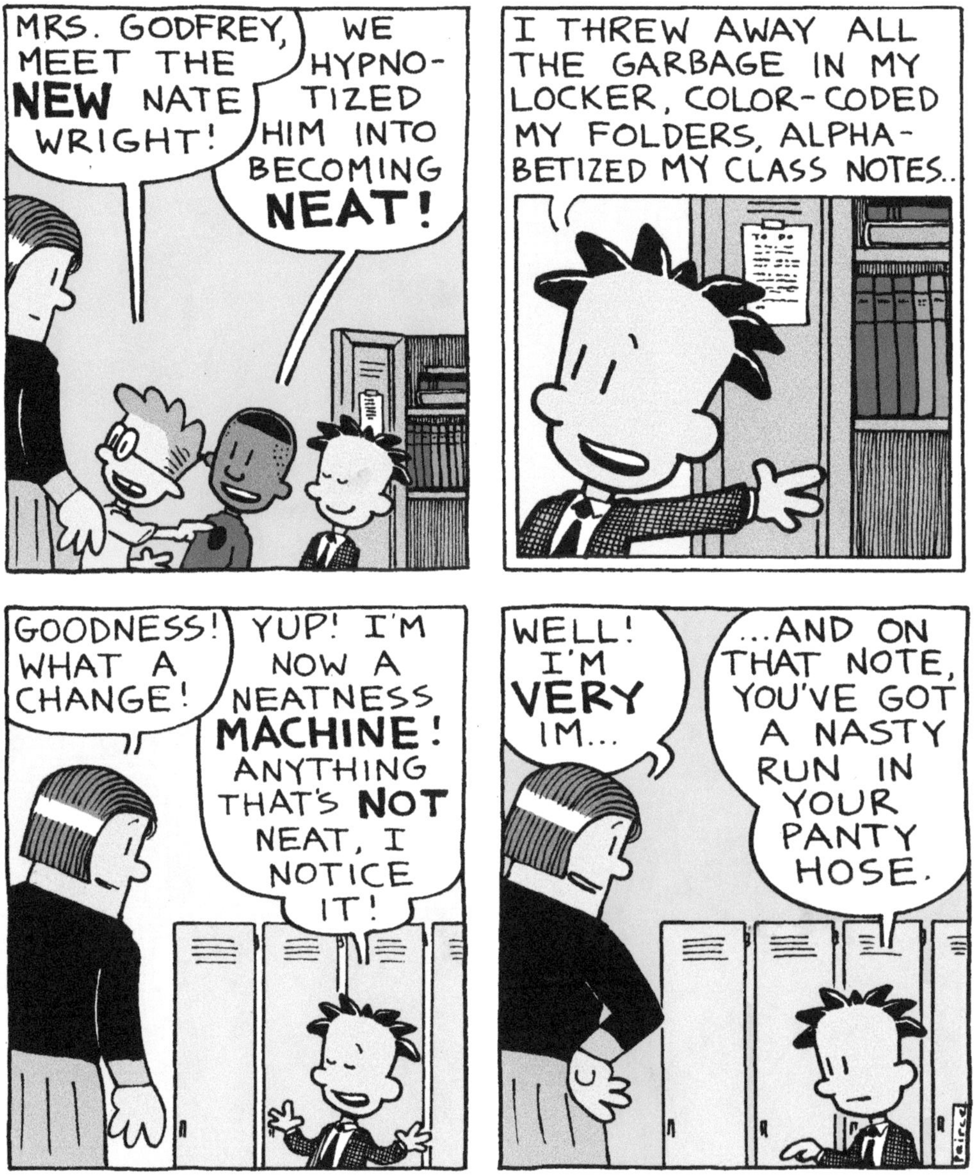
MRS. GODFREY, MEET THE **NEW** NATE WRIGHT!
WE HYPNO-TIZED HIM INTO BECOMING **NEAT!**
I THREW AWAY ALL THE GARBAGE IN MY LOCKER, COLOR-CODED MY FOLDERS, ALPHA-BETIZED MY CLASS NOTES..
TO DO
GOODNESS! WHAT A CHANGE!
YUP! I'M NOW A NEATNESS **MACHINE!** ANYTHING THAT'S **NOT** NEAT, I NOTICE IT!
WELL! I'M **VERY** IM...
...AND ON THAT NOTE, YOU'VE GOT A NASTY RUN IN YOUR PANTY HOSE.
Peirce

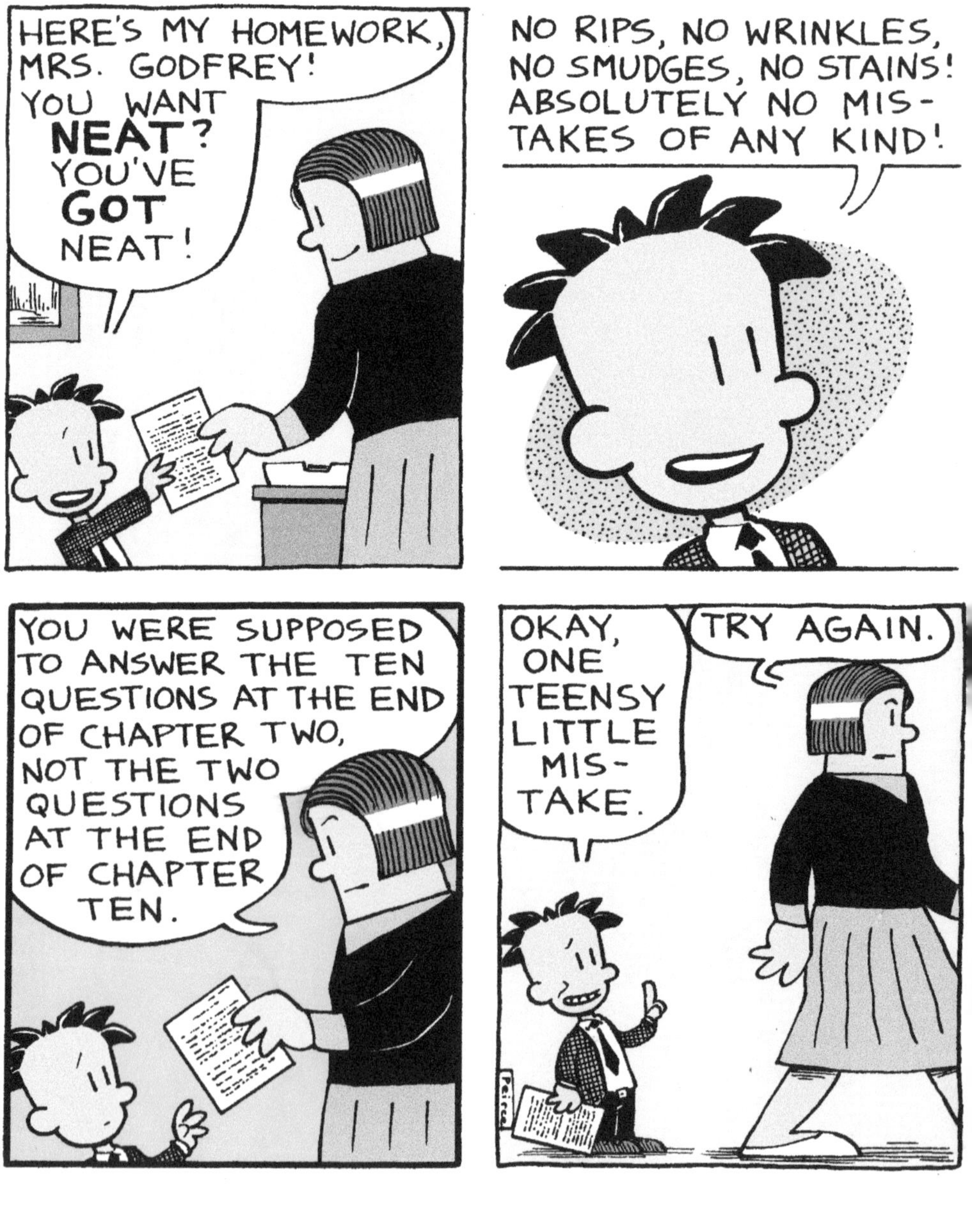
HERE'S MY HOMEWORK, MRS. GODFREY! YOU WANT **NEAT**? YOU'VE **GOT** NEAT!
NO RIPS, NO WRINKLES, NO SMUDGES, NO STAINS! ABSOLUTELY NO MIS-TAKES OF ANY KIND!
YOU WERE SUPPOSED TO ANSWER THE TEN QUESTIONS AT THE END OF CHAPTER TWO, NOT THE TWO QUESTIONS AT THE END OF CHAPTER TEN.
OKAY, ONE TEENSY LITTLE MIS-TAKE.
TRY AGAIN.
Peirce

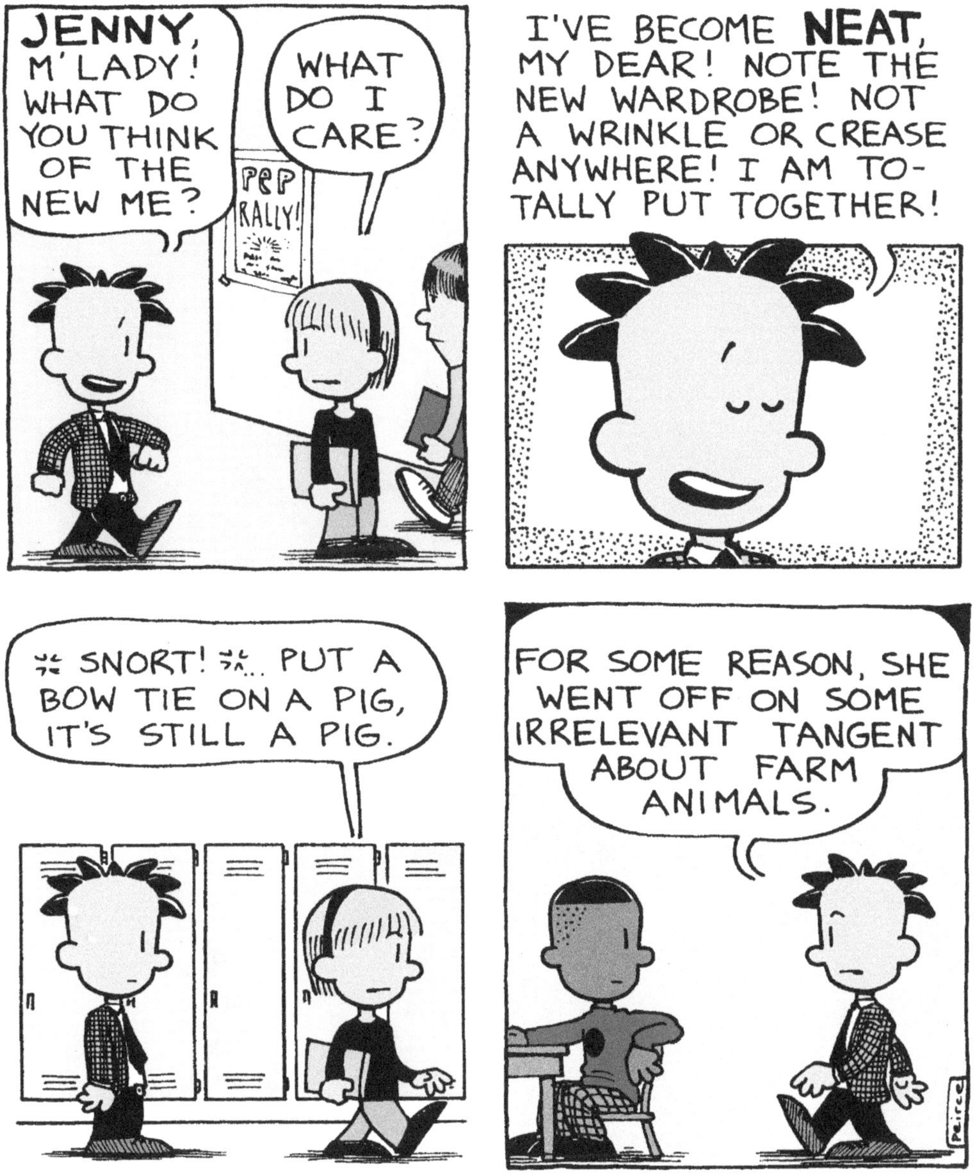
JENNY, M'LADY! WHAT DO YOU THINK OF THE NEW ME?
WHAT DO I CARE?
PEP RALLY!
I'VE BECOME NEAT, MY DEAR! NOTE THE NEW WARDROBE! NOT A WRINKLE OR CREASE ANYWHERE! I AM TOTALLY PUT TOGETHER!
SNORT! ... PUT A BOW TIE ON A PIG, IT'S STILL A PIG.
FOR SOME REASON, SHE WENT OFF ON SOME IRRELEVANT TANGENT ABOUT FARM ANIMALS.
Peirce

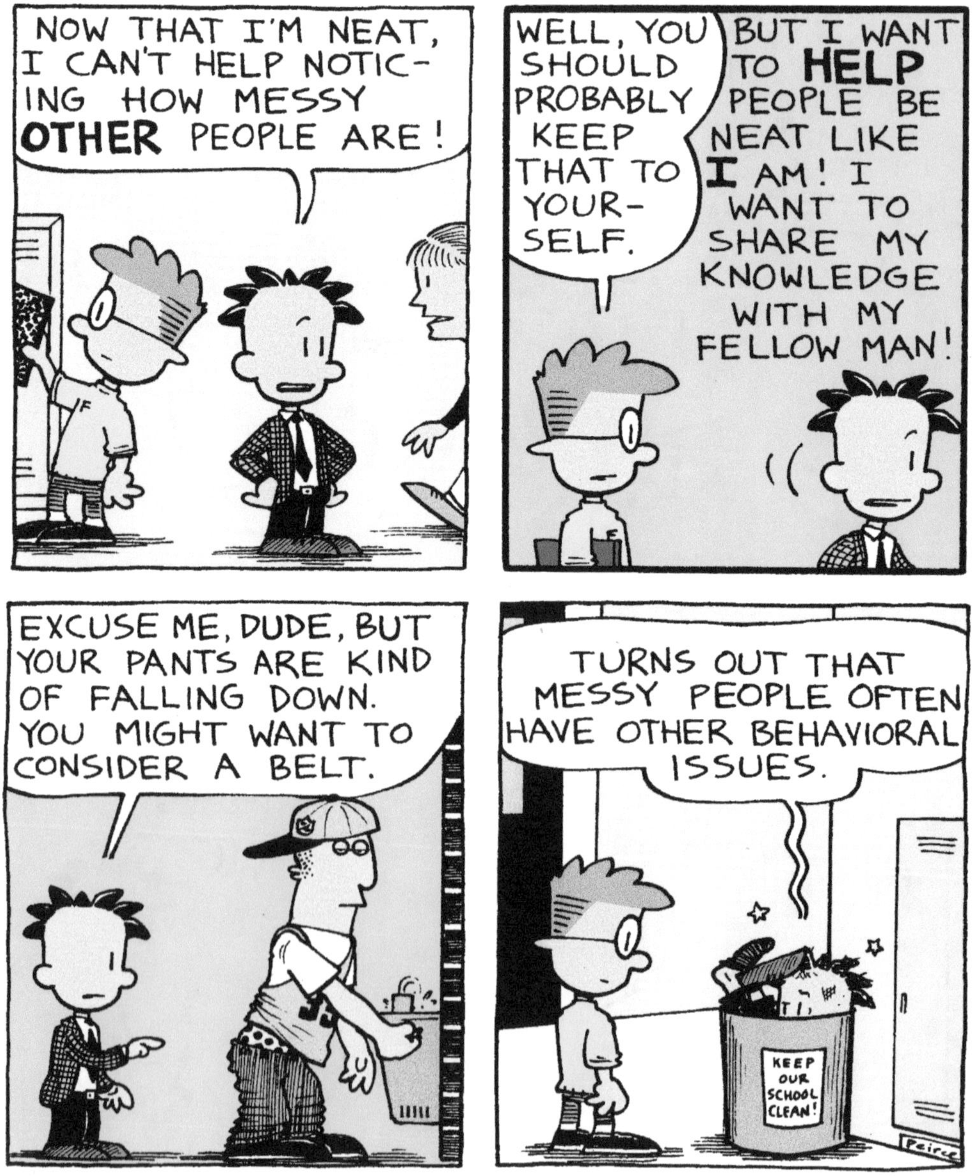
NOW THAT I'M NEAT, I CAN'T HELP NOTICING HOW MESSY **OTHER** PEOPLE ARE!
WELL, YOU SHOULD PROBABLY KEEP THAT TO YOURSELF.
BUT I WANT TO **HELP** PEOPLE BE NEAT LIKE **I** AM! I WANT TO SHARE MY KNOWLEDGE WITH MY FELLOW MAN!
EXCUSE ME, DUDE, BUT YOUR PANTS ARE KIND OF FALLING DOWN. YOU MIGHT WANT TO CONSIDER A BELT.
TURNS OUT THAT MESSY PEOPLE OFTEN HAVE OTHER BEHAVIORAL ISSUES.
KEEP OUR SCHOOL CLEAN!
Peirce

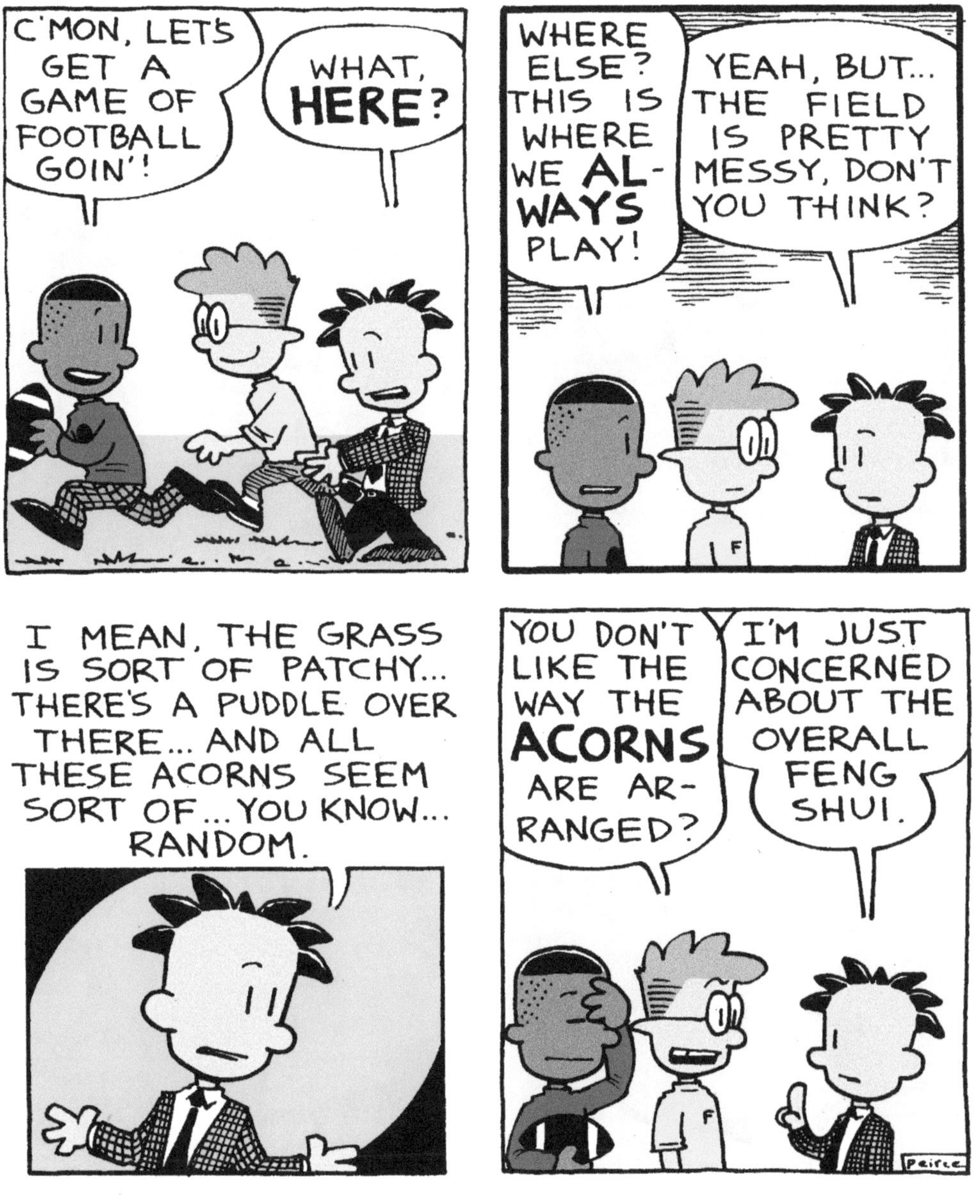

C'MON, LET'S GET A GAME OF FOOTBALL GOIN'!
WHAT, **HERE**?
WHERE ELSE? THIS IS WHERE WE **AL-WAYS** PLAY!
YEAH, BUT... THE FIELD IS PRETTY MESSY, DON'T YOU THINK?
I MEAN, THE GRASS IS SORT OF PATCHY... THERE'S A PUDDLE OVER THERE... AND ALL THESE ACORNS SEEM SORT OF... YOU KNOW... RANDOM.
YOU DON'T LIKE THE WAY THE **ACORNS** ARE AR-RANGED?
I'M JUST CONCERNED ABOUT THE OVERALL FENG SHUI.
Peirce

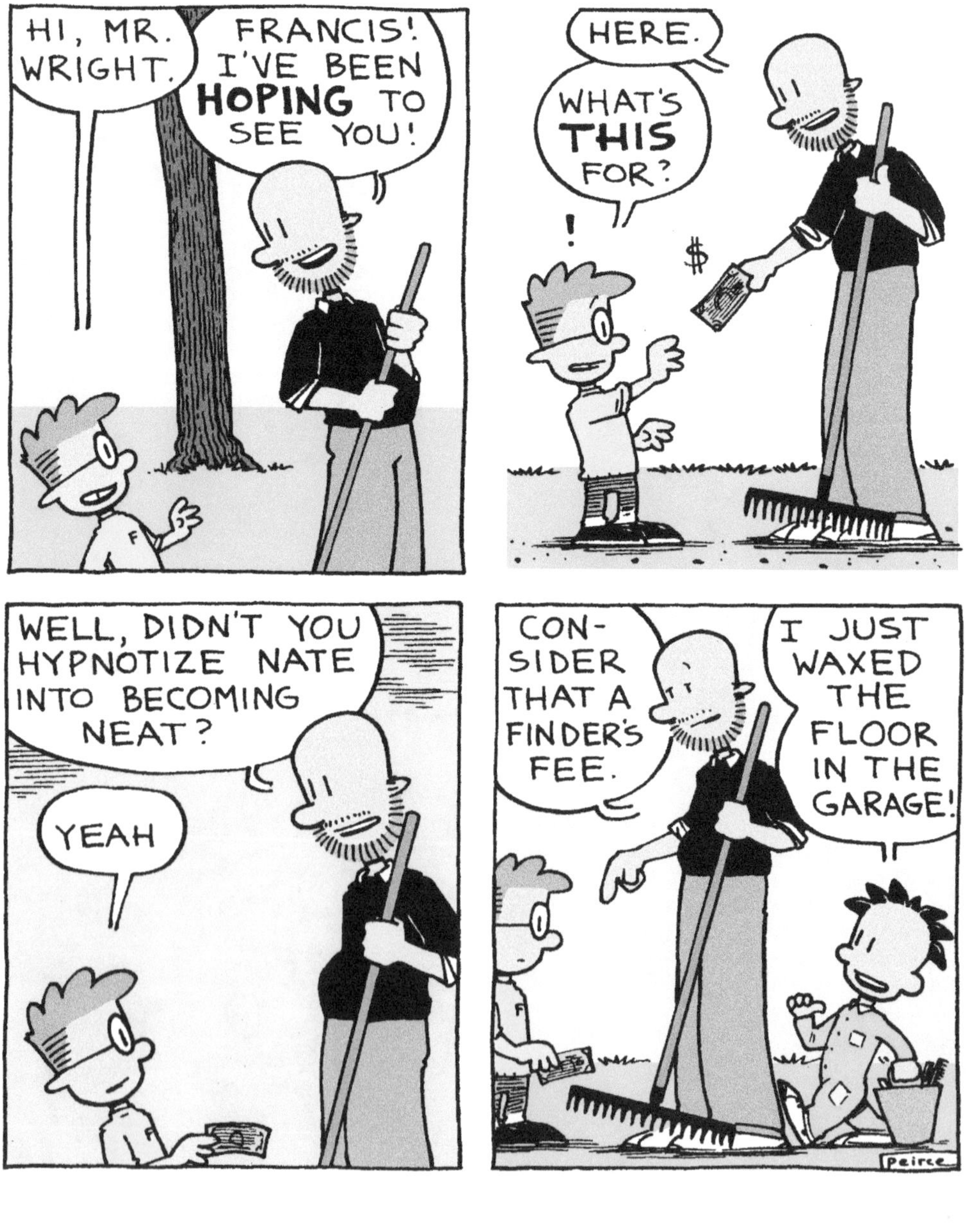
HI, MR. WRIGHT.
FRANCIS! I'VE BEEN **HOPING** TO SEE YOU!
HERE.
WHAT'S **THIS** FOR?
!
$
WELL, DIDN'T YOU HYPNOTIZE NATE INTO BECOMING NEAT?
YEAH
CONSIDER THAT A FINDER'S FEE.
I JUST WAXED THE FLOOR IN THE GARAGE!
Peirce

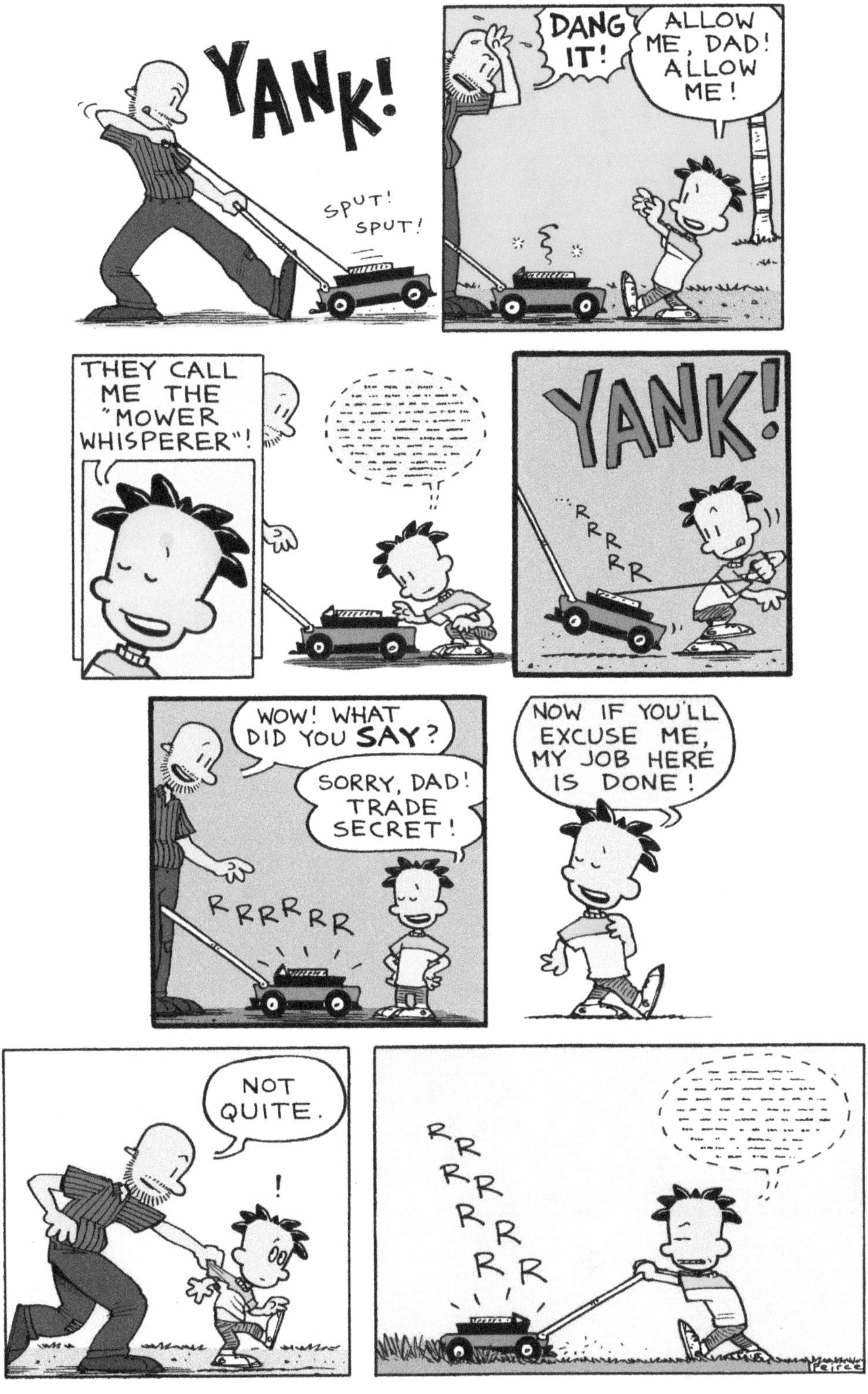

YANK!
SPUT!
SPUT!
DANG IT!
ALLOW ME, DAD! ALLOW ME!
THEY CALL ME THE "MOWER WHISPERER"!
YANK!
RRRRR
WOW! WHAT DID YOU **SAY**?
SORRY, DAD! TRADE SECRET!
RRRRRR
NOW IF YOU'LL EXCUSE ME, MY JOB HERE IS DONE!
NOT QUITE.
!
RRRRRRRR
Peirce

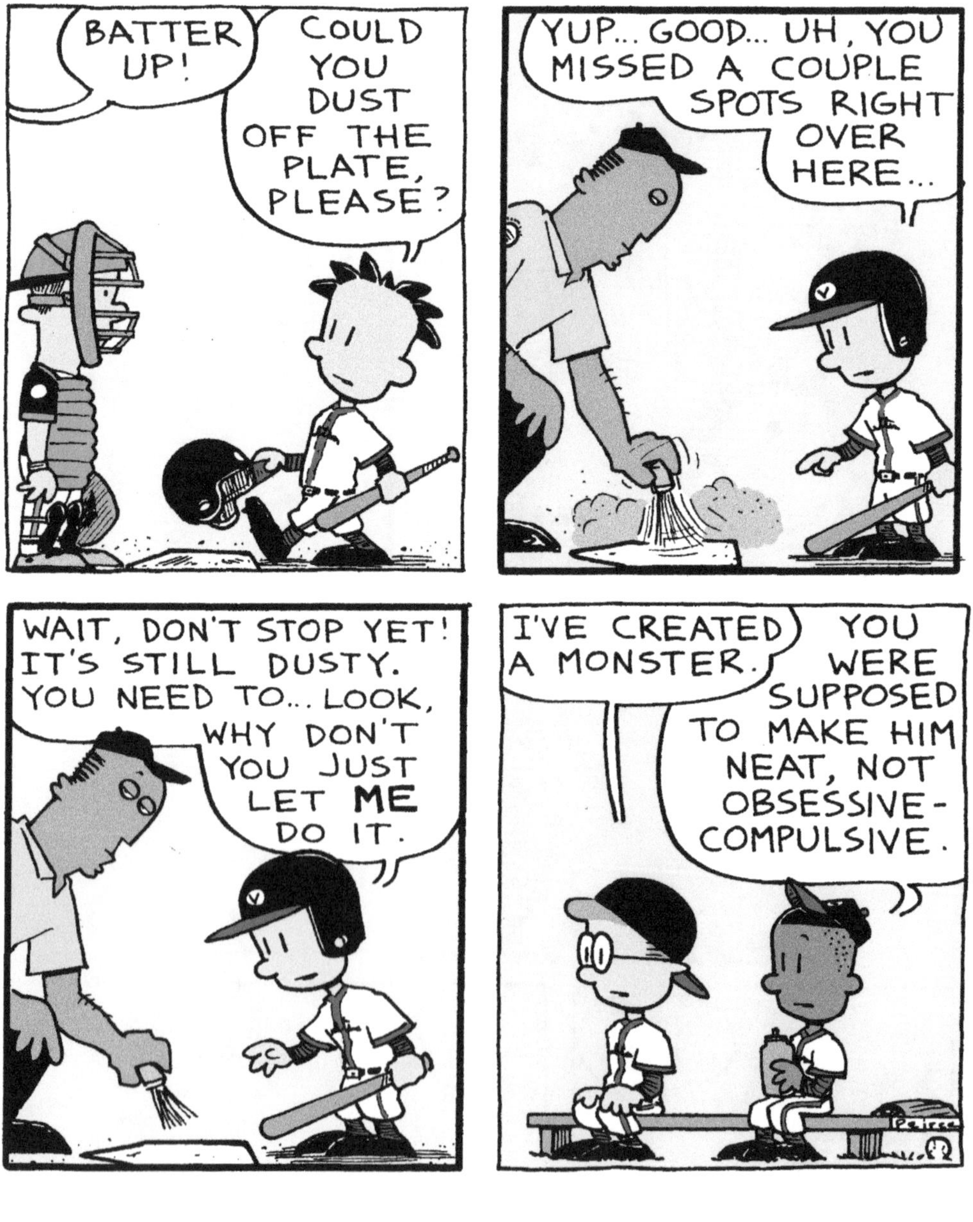
BATTER UP!
COULD YOU DUST OFF THE PLATE, PLEASE?
YUP... GOOD... UH, YOU MISSED A COUPLE SPOTS RIGHT OVER HERE...
WAIT, DON'T STOP YET! IT'S STILL DUSTY. YOU NEED TO... LOOK, WHY DON'T YOU JUST LET **ME** DO IT.
I'VE CREATED A MONSTER.
YOU WERE SUPPOSED TO MAKE HIM NEAT, NOT OBSESSIVE-COMPULSIVE.
Peirce

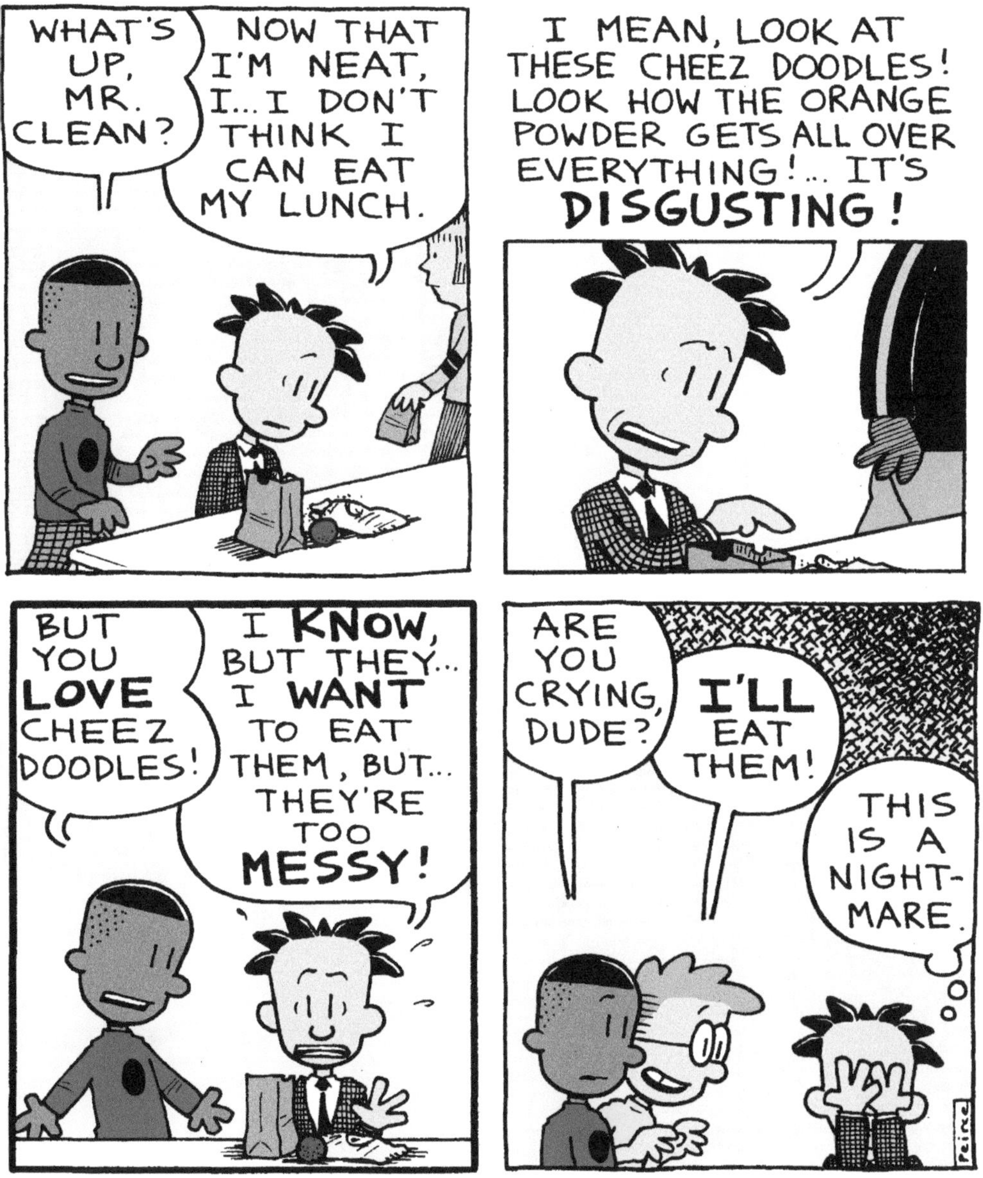
WHAT'S UP, MR. CLEAN?
NOW THAT I'M NEAT, I... I DON'T THINK I CAN EAT MY LUNCH.
I MEAN, LOOK AT THESE CHEEZ DOODLES! LOOK HOW THE ORANGE POWDER GETS ALL OVER EVERYTHING!... IT'S **DISGUSTING!**
BUT YOU **LOVE** CHEEZ DOODLES!
I **KNOW**, BUT THEY... I **WANT** TO EAT THEM, BUT... THEY'RE TOO **MESSY!**
ARE YOU CRYING, DUDE?
I'LL EAT THEM!
THIS IS A NIGHT-MARE.
PEIRCE

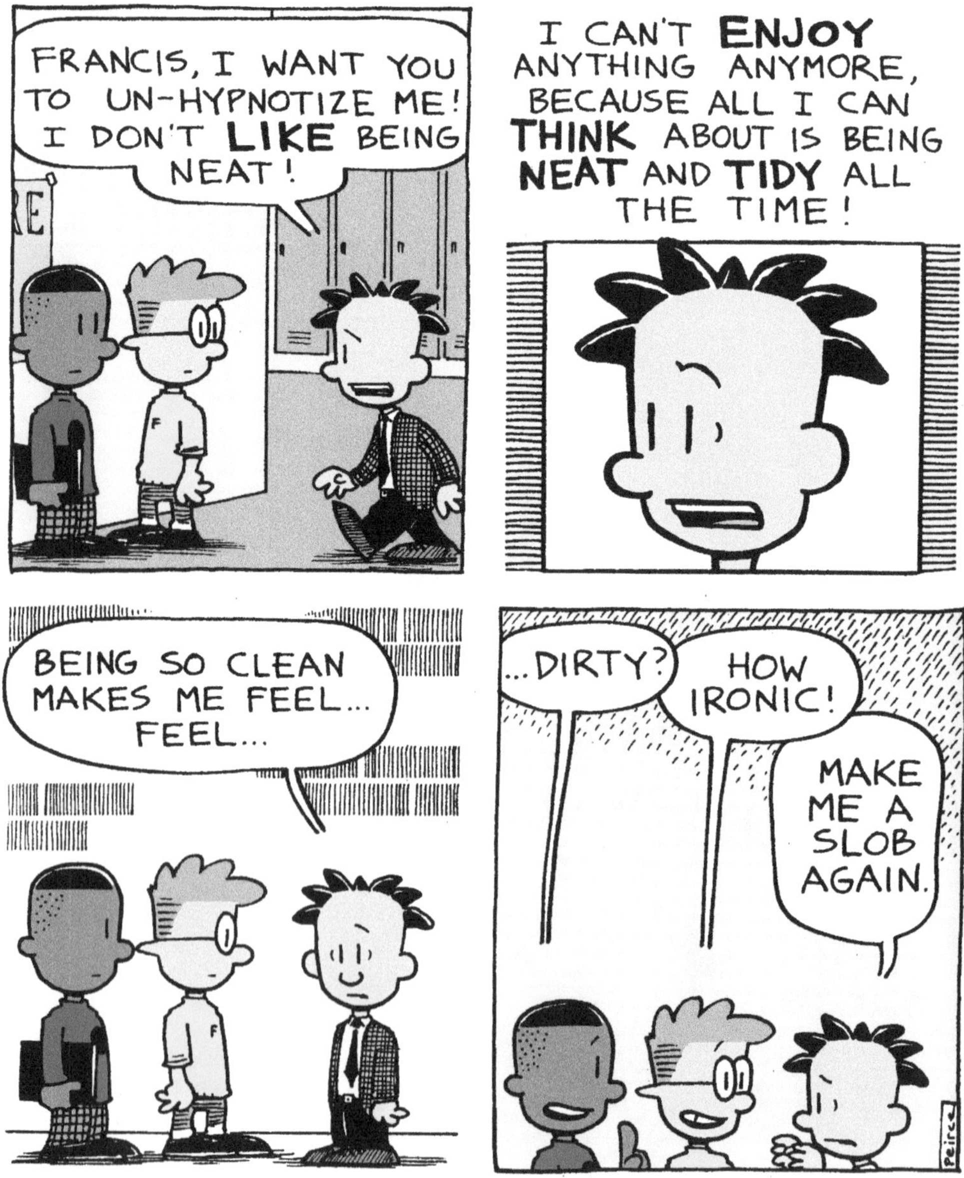
FRANCIS, I WANT YOU TO UN-HYPNOTIZE ME! I DON'T **LIKE** BEING NEAT!
I CAN'T **ENJOY** ANYTHING ANYMORE, BECAUSE ALL I CAN **THINK** ABOUT IS BEING **NEAT** AND **TIDY** ALL THE TIME!
BEING SO CLEAN MAKES ME FEEL... FEEL...
...DIRTY?
HOW IRONIC!
MAKE ME A SLOB AGAIN.
Peirce

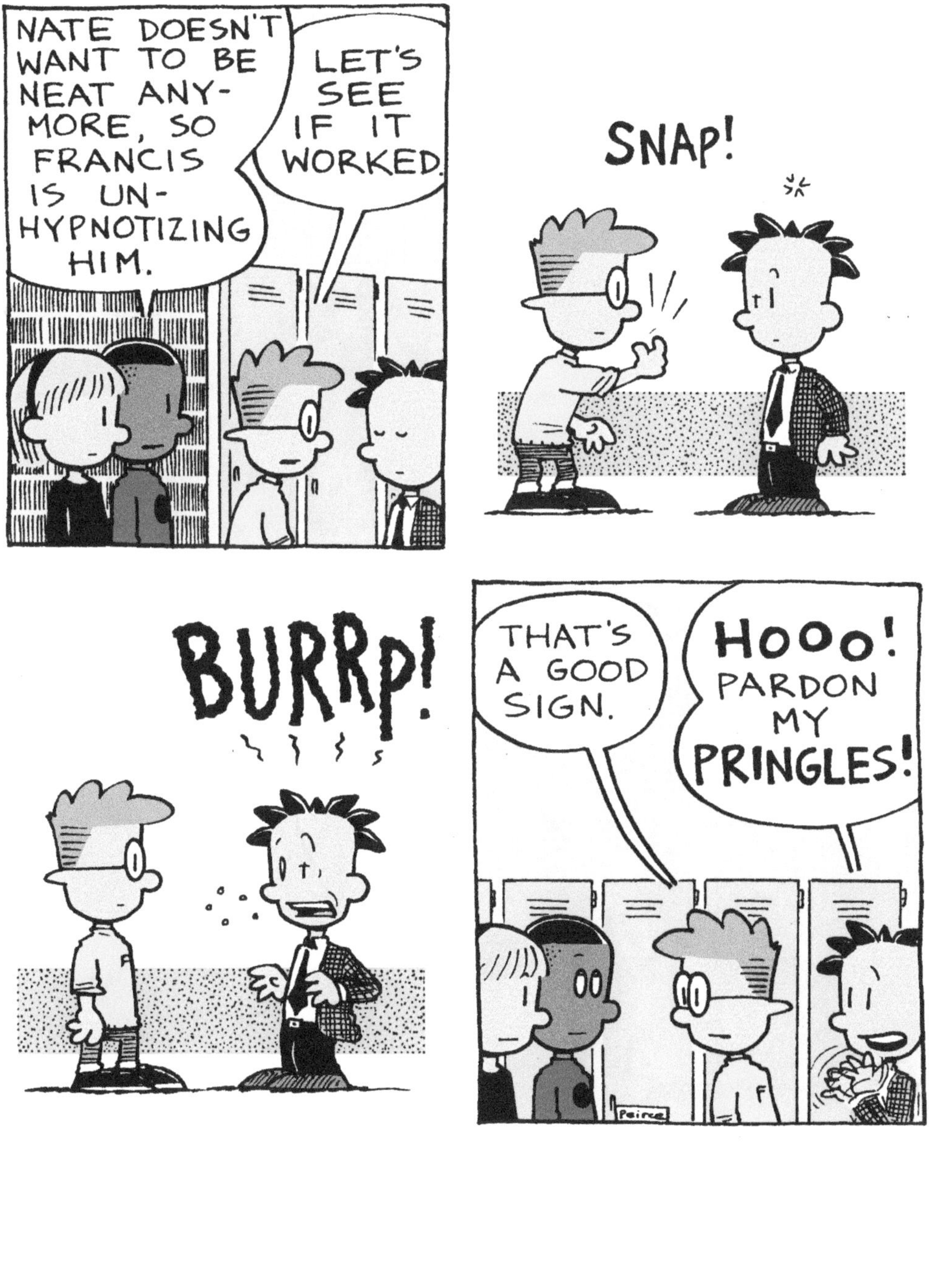
NATE DOESN'T WANT TO BE NEAT ANY-MORE, SO FRANCIS IS UN-HYPNOTIZING HIM.
LET'S SEE IF IT WORKED.
SNAP!
BURRP!
THAT'S A GOOD SIGN.
HOOo! PARDON MY PRINGLES!
Peirce

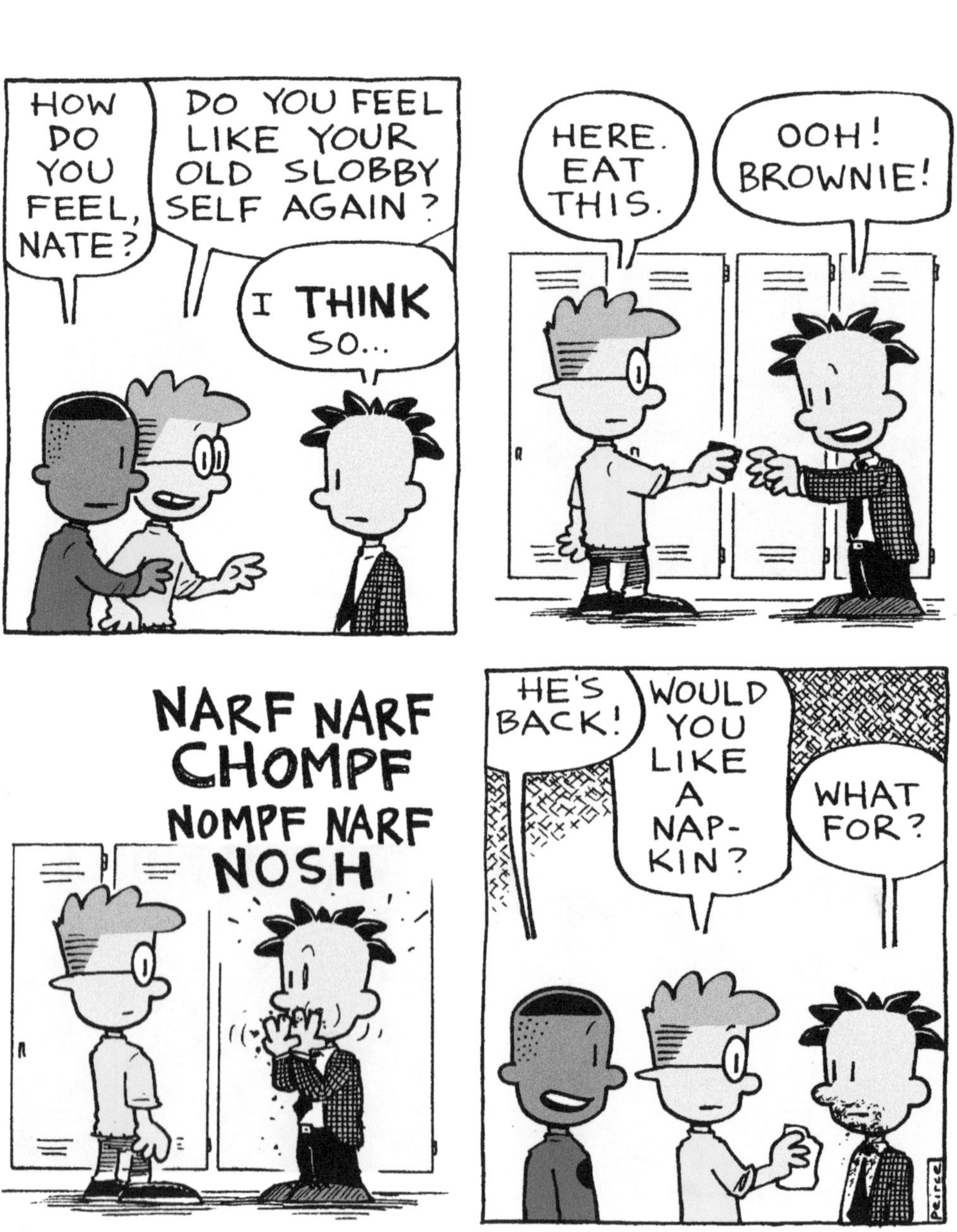
HOW DO YOU FEEL, NATE?
DO YOU FEEL LIKE YOUR OLD SLOBBY SELF AGAIN?
I THINK SO...
HERE. EAT THIS.
OOH! BROWNIE!
NARF NARF CHOMPF NOMPF NARF NOSH
HE'S BACK!
WOULD YOU LIKE A NAP-KIN?
WHAT FOR?
PEIRCE

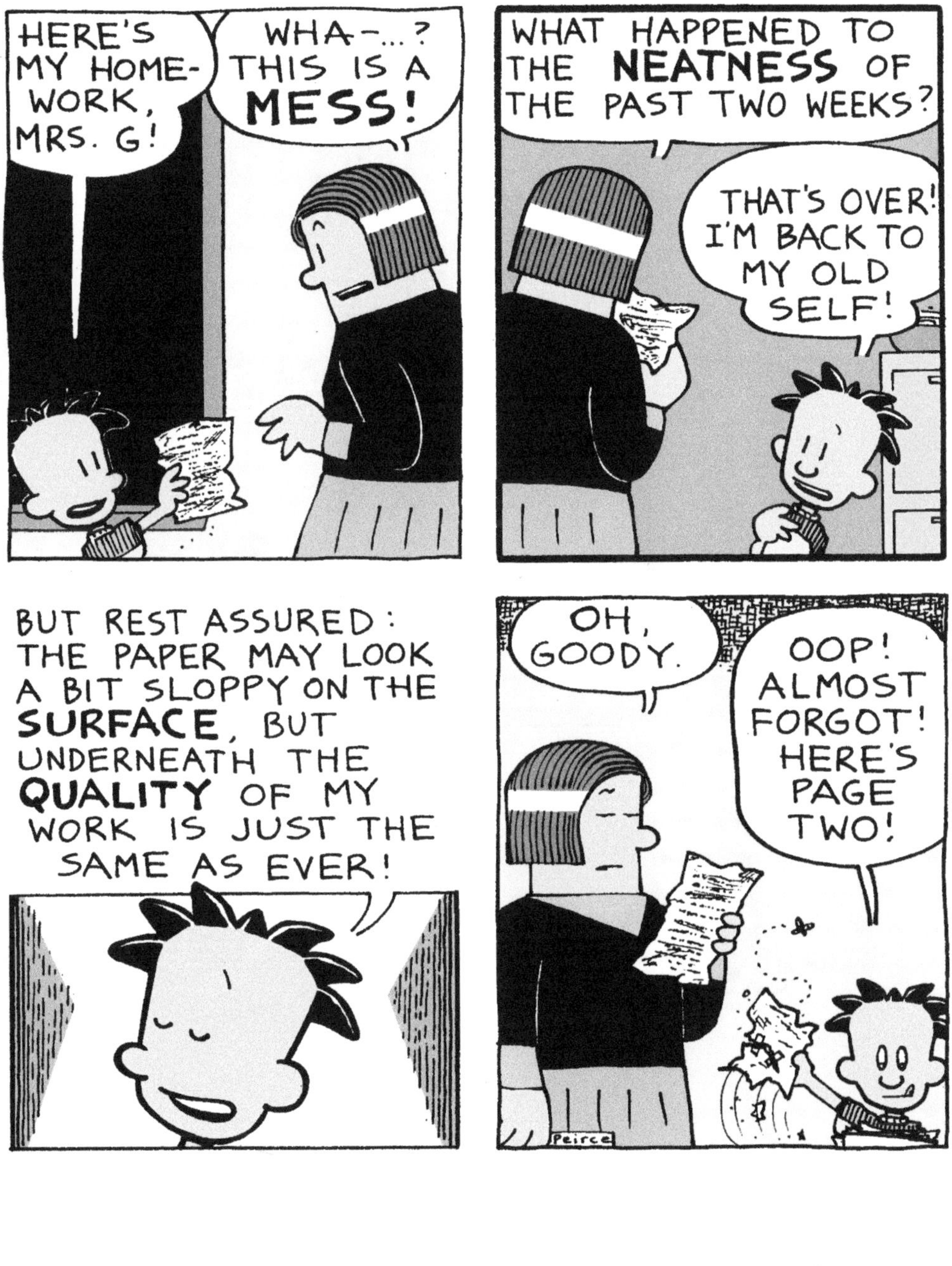
HERE'S MY HOME-WORK, MRS. G!
WHA-...? THIS IS A MESS!
WHAT HAPPENED TO THE NEATNESS OF THE PAST TWO WEEKS?
THAT'S OVER! I'M BACK TO MY OLD SELF!
BUT REST ASSURED: THE PAPER MAY LOOK A BIT SLOPPY ON THE SURFACE, BUT UNDERNEATH THE QUALITY OF MY WORK IS JUST THE SAME AS EVER!
OH, GOODY.
OOP! ALMOST FORGOT! HERE'S PAGE TWO!
Peirce

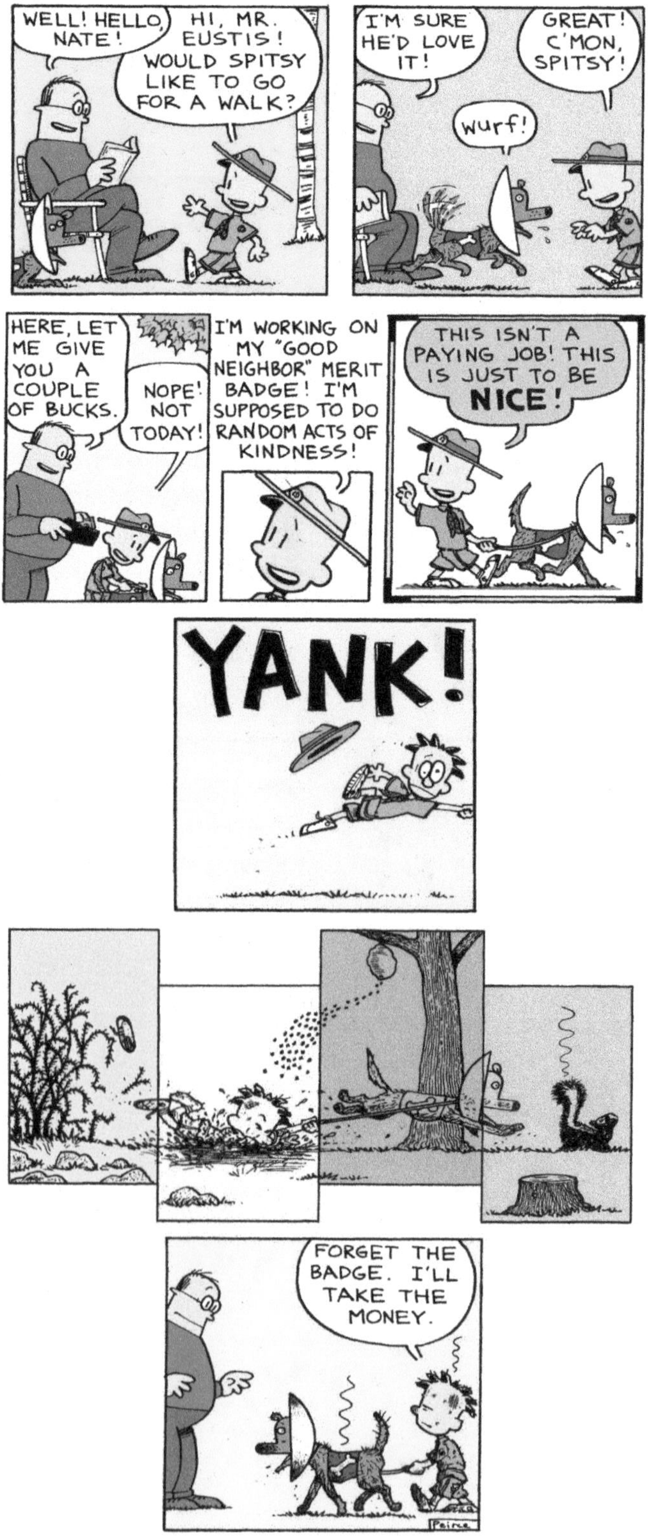
WELL! HELLO, NATE!
HI, MR. EUSTIS! WOULD SPITSY LIKE TO GO FOR A WALK?
I'M SURE HE'D LOVE IT!
GREAT! C'MON, SPITSY!
wurf!
HERE, LET ME GIVE YOU A COUPLE OF BUCKS.
NOPE! NOT TODAY!
I'M WORKING ON MY "GOOD NEIGHBOR" MERIT BADGE! I'M SUPPOSED TO DO RANDOM ACTS OF KINDNESS!
THIS ISN'T A PAYING JOB! THIS IS JUST TO BE NICE!
YANK!
FORGET THE BADGE. I'LL TAKE THE MONEY.
Peirce

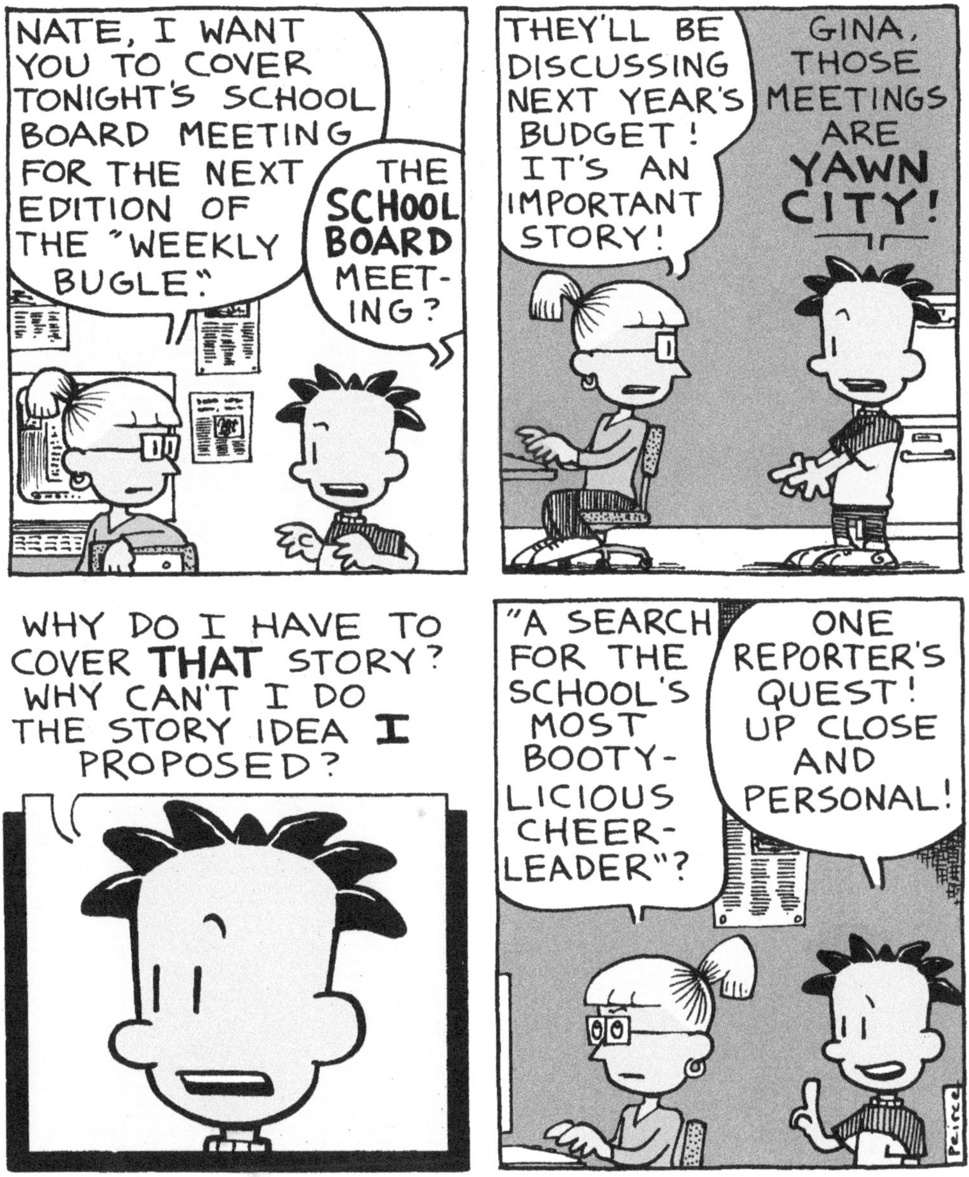
NATE, I WANT YOU TO COVER TONIGHT'S SCHOOL BOARD MEETING FOR THE NEXT EDITION OF THE "WEEKLY BUGLE."
THE **SCHOOL BOARD** MEETING?
THEY'LL BE DISCUSSING NEXT YEAR'S BUDGET! IT'S AN IMPORTANT STORY!
GINA, THOSE MEETINGS ARE **YAWN CITY!**
WHY DO I HAVE TO COVER **THAT** STORY? WHY CAN'T I DO THE STORY IDEA **I** PROPOSED?
"A SEARCH FOR THE SCHOOL'S MOST BOOTY-LICIOUS CHEER-LEADER"?
ONE REPORTER'S QUEST! UP CLOSE AND PERSONAL!
Peirce

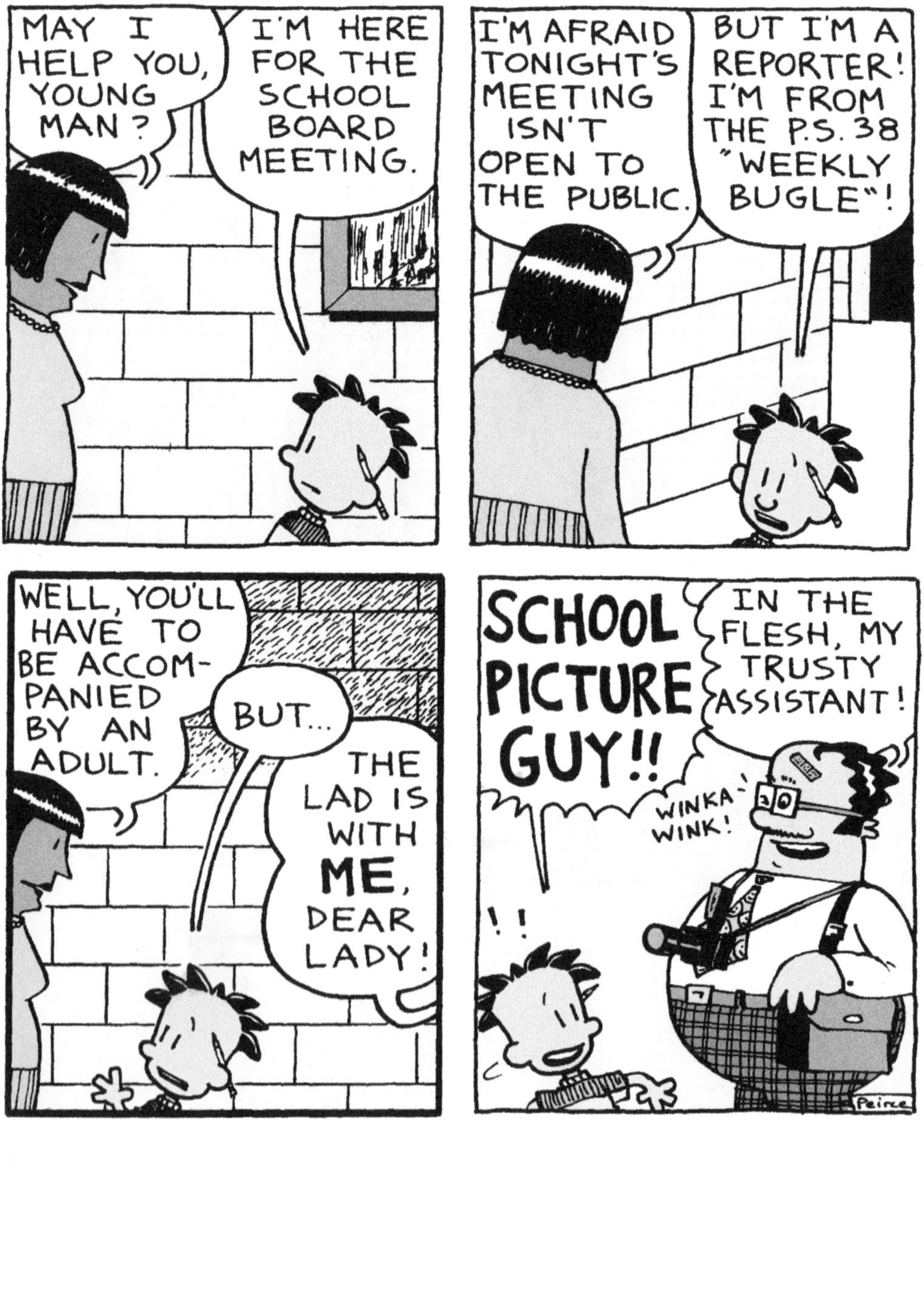
MAY I HELP YOU, YOUNG MAN?
I'M HERE FOR THE SCHOOL BOARD MEETING.
I'M AFRAID TONIGHT'S MEETING ISN'T OPEN TO THE PUBLIC.
BUT I'M A REPORTER! I'M FROM THE P.S. 38 "WEEKLY BUGLE"!
WELL, YOU'LL HAVE TO BE ACCOMPANIED BY AN ADULT.
BUT...
THE LAD IS WITH ME, DEAR LADY!
SCHOOL PICTURE GUY!!
IN THE FLESH, MY TRUSTY ASSISTANT!
WINKA WINK!
!!
Peirce

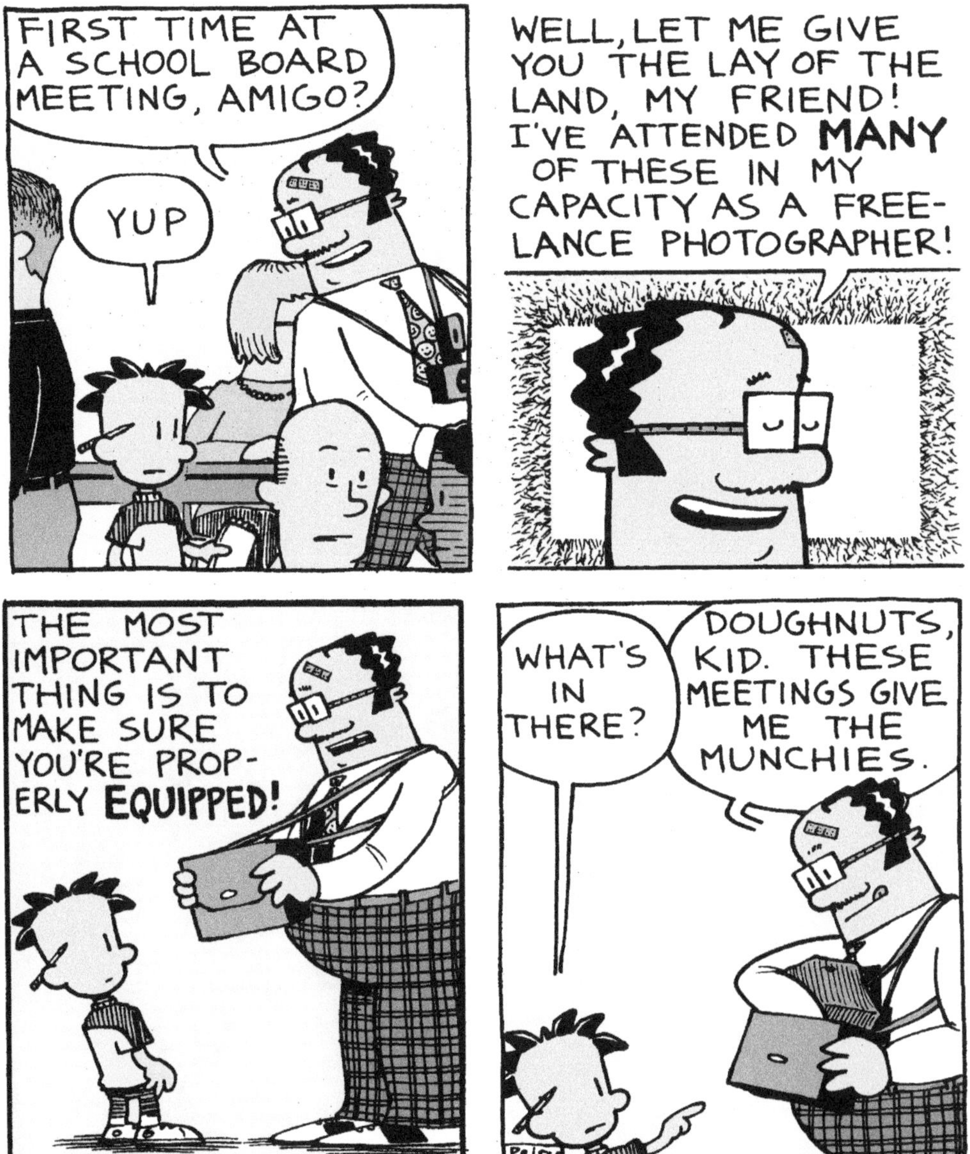
FIRST TIME AT A SCHOOL BOARD MEETING, AMIGO?
YUP
WELL, LET ME GIVE YOU THE LAY OF THE LAND, MY FRIEND! I'VE ATTENDED **MANY** OF THESE IN MY CAPACITY AS A FREE-LANCE PHOTOGRAPHER!
THE MOST IMPORTANT THING IS TO MAKE SURE YOU'RE PROPERLY **EQUIPPED!**
WHAT'S IN THERE?
DOUGHNUTS, KID. THESE MEETINGS GIVE ME THE MUNCHIES.

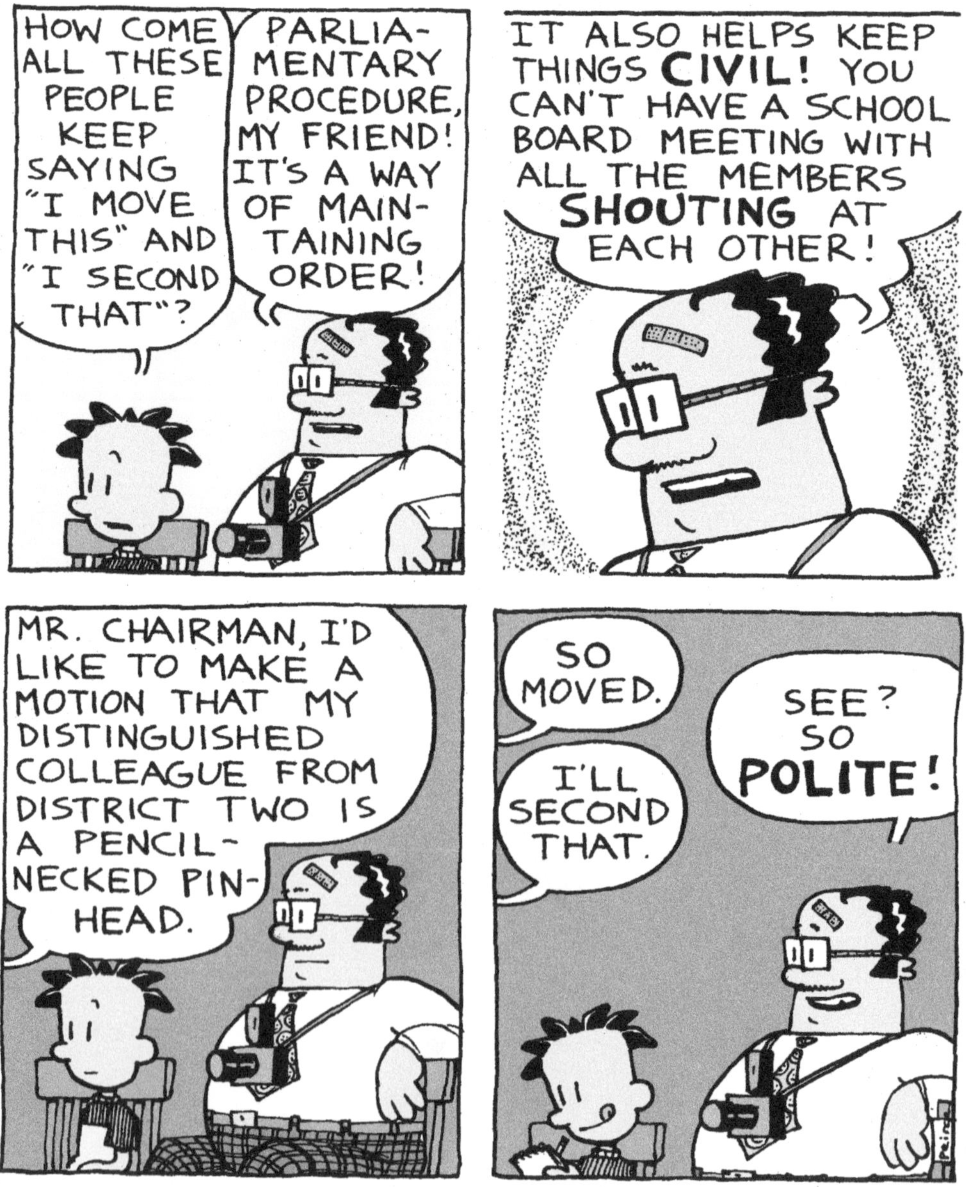
HOW COME ALL THESE PEOPLE KEEP SAYING "I MOVE THIS" AND "I SECOND THAT"?
PARLIAMENTARY PROCEDURE, MY FRIEND! IT'S A WAY OF MAINTAINING ORDER!
IT ALSO HELPS KEEP THINGS CIVIL! YOU CAN'T HAVE A SCHOOL BOARD MEETING WITH ALL THE MEMBERS SHOUTING AT EACH OTHER!
MR. CHAIRMAN, I'D LIKE TO MAKE A MOTION THAT MY DISTINGUISHED COLLEAGUE FROM DISTRICT TWO IS A PENCIL-NECKED PIN-HEAD.
SO MOVED.
I'LL SECOND THAT.
SEE? SO POLITE!

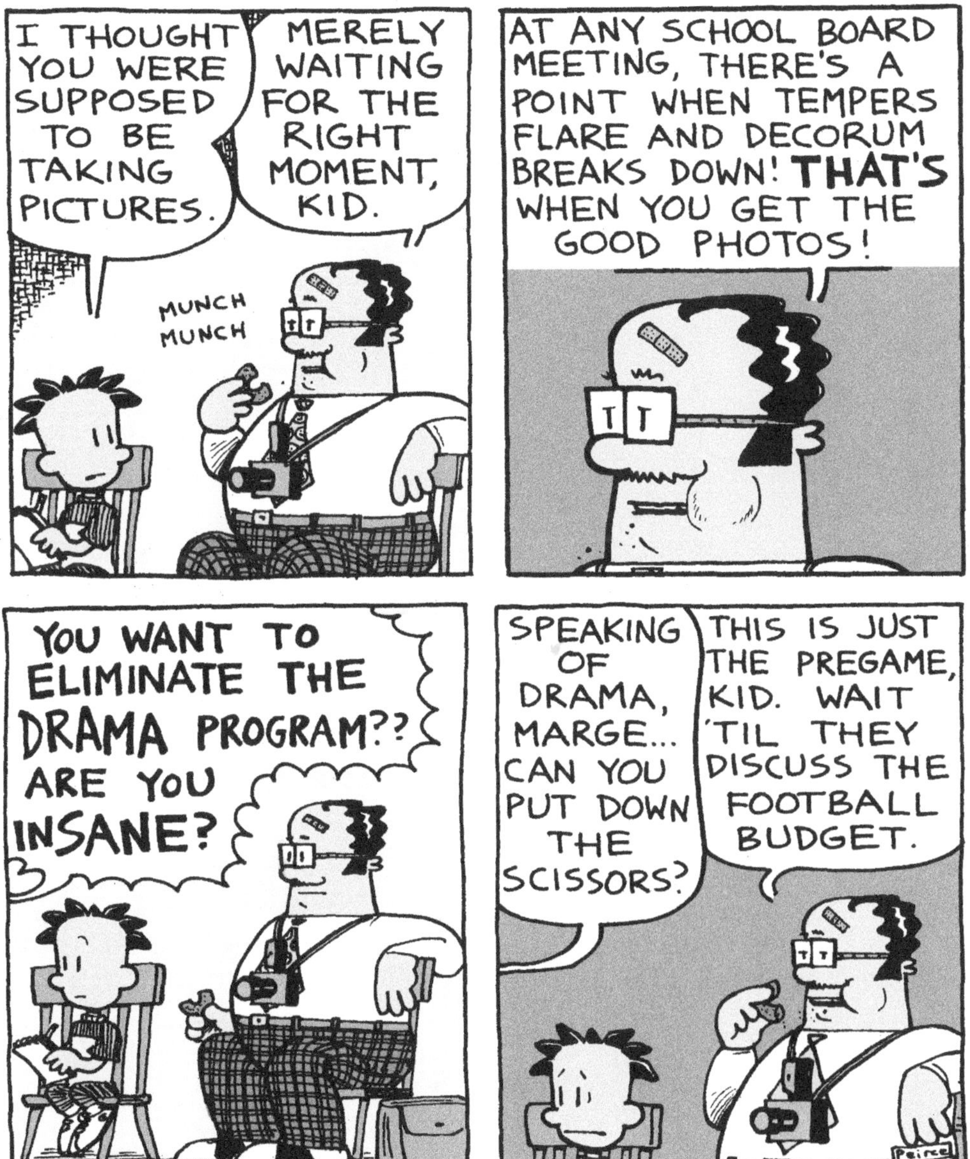
I THOUGHT YOU WERE SUPPOSED TO BE TAKING PICTURES.
MERELY WAITING FOR THE RIGHT MOMENT, KID.
MUNCH MUNCH
AT ANY SCHOOL BOARD MEETING, THERE'S A POINT WHEN TEMPERS FLARE AND DECORUM BREAKS DOWN! THAT'S WHEN YOU GET THE GOOD PHOTOS!
YOU WANT TO ELIMINATE THE DRAMA PROGRAM?? ARE YOU INSANE?
SPEAKING OF DRAMA, MARGE... CAN YOU PUT DOWN THE SCISSORS?
THIS IS JUST THE PREGAME, KID. WAIT 'TIL THEY DISCUSS THE FOOTBALL BUDGET.
Peirce

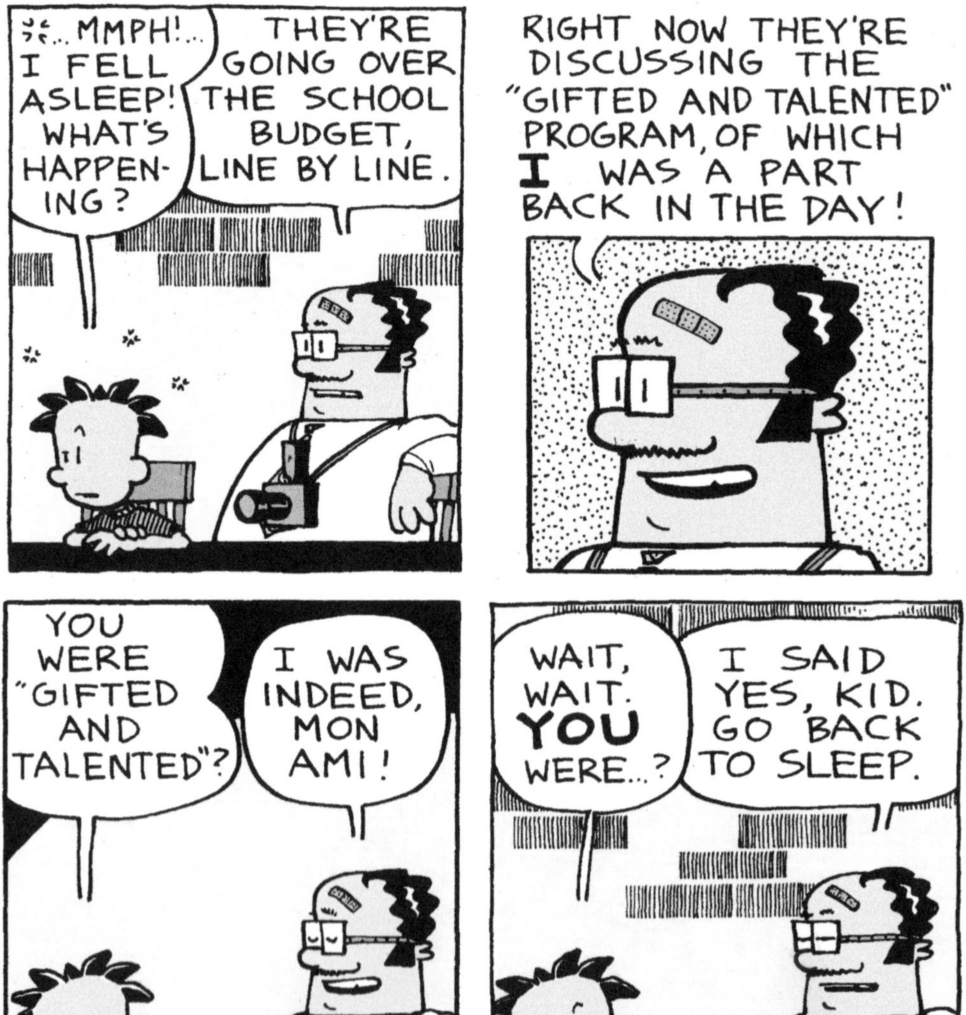
...MMPH!... I FELL ASLEEP! WHAT'S HAPPENING?
THEY'RE GOING OVER THE SCHOOL BUDGET, LINE BY LINE.
RIGHT NOW THEY'RE DISCUSSING THE "GIFTED AND TALENTED" PROGRAM, OF WHICH I WAS A PART BACK IN THE DAY!
YOU WERE "GIFTED AND TALENTED"?
I WAS INDEED, MON AMI!
WAIT, WAIT. YOU WERE...?
I SAID YES, KID. GO BACK TO SLEEP.
Peirce

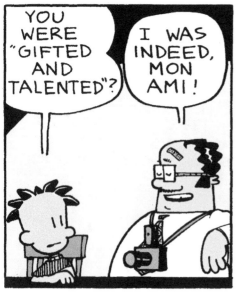

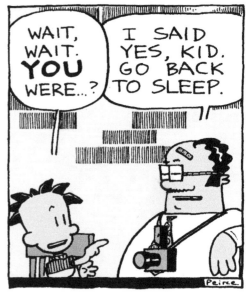

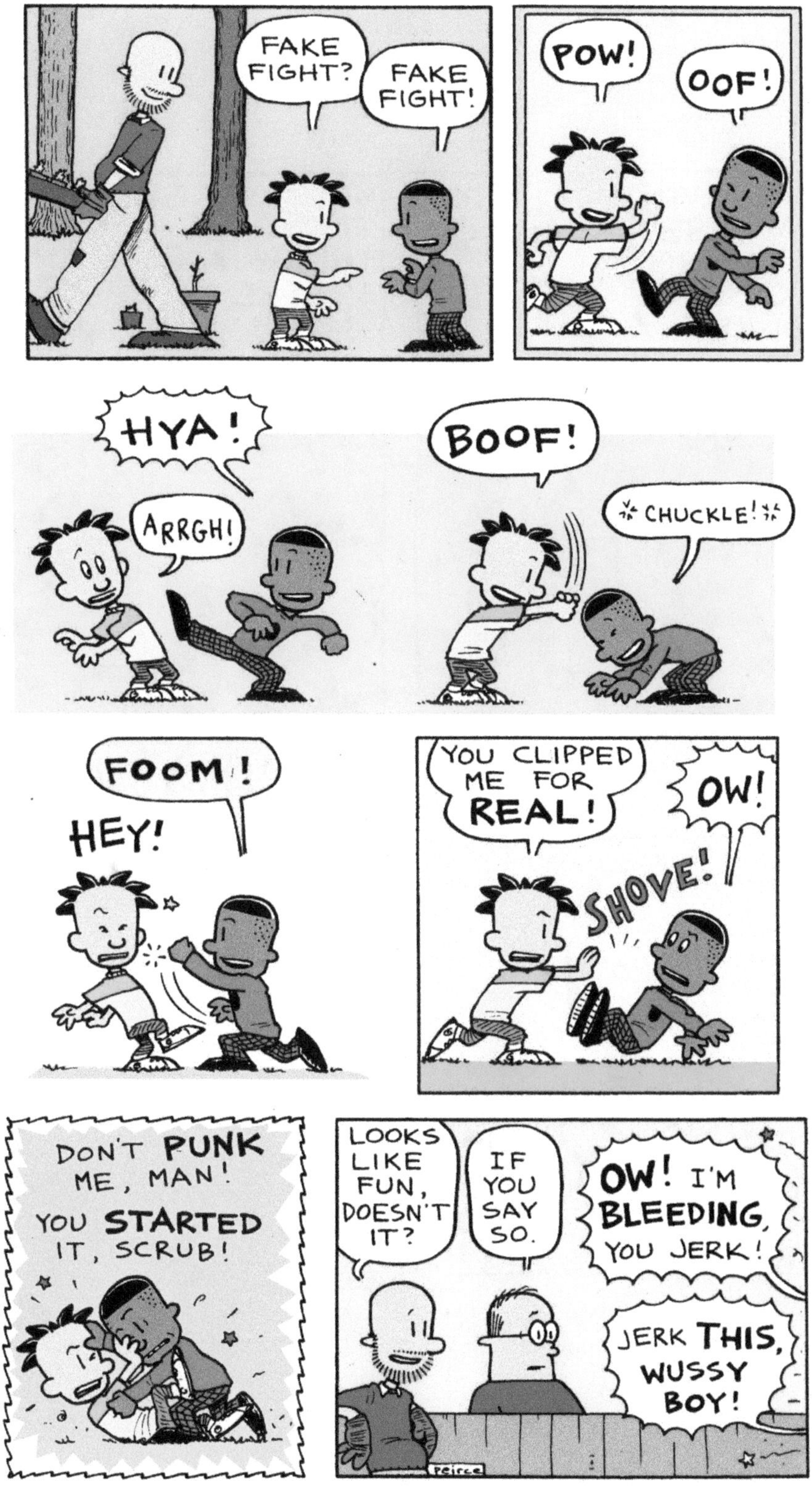
FAKE FIGHT?
FAKE FIGHT!
POW!
OOF!
HYA!
ARRGH!
BOOF!
CHUCKLE!
FOOM!
HEY!
YOU CLIPPED ME FOR REAL!
OW!
SHOVE!
DON'T PUNK ME, MAN!
YOU STARTED IT, SCRUB!
LOOKS LIKE FUN, DOESN'T IT?
IF YOU SAY SO.
OW! I'M BLEEDING, YOU JERK!
JERK THIS, WUSSY BOY!
PEIRCE

MR. GALVIN, WHAT ARE WE DOING IN CLASS TODAY?
PHOTO-SYNTHESIS.
LEMENTS
WELL... CARE TO MAKE THINGS A LITTLE MORE... INTER-ESTING?
MORE INTER...? WHAT?
ARE YOU SUGGESTING SOME SORT OF **WAGER**?
UH... I WAS SUGGESTING MAYBE A FILMSTRIP.
YEAH, PHOTO-SYNTHESIS IS REALLY BORING.
LEMENTS
Peirce

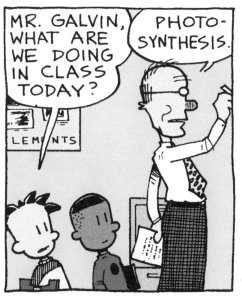

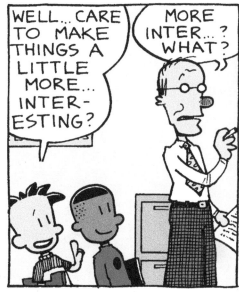

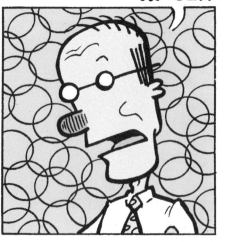

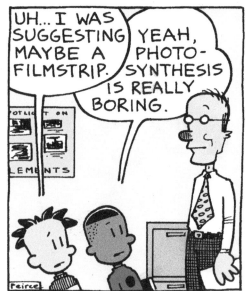

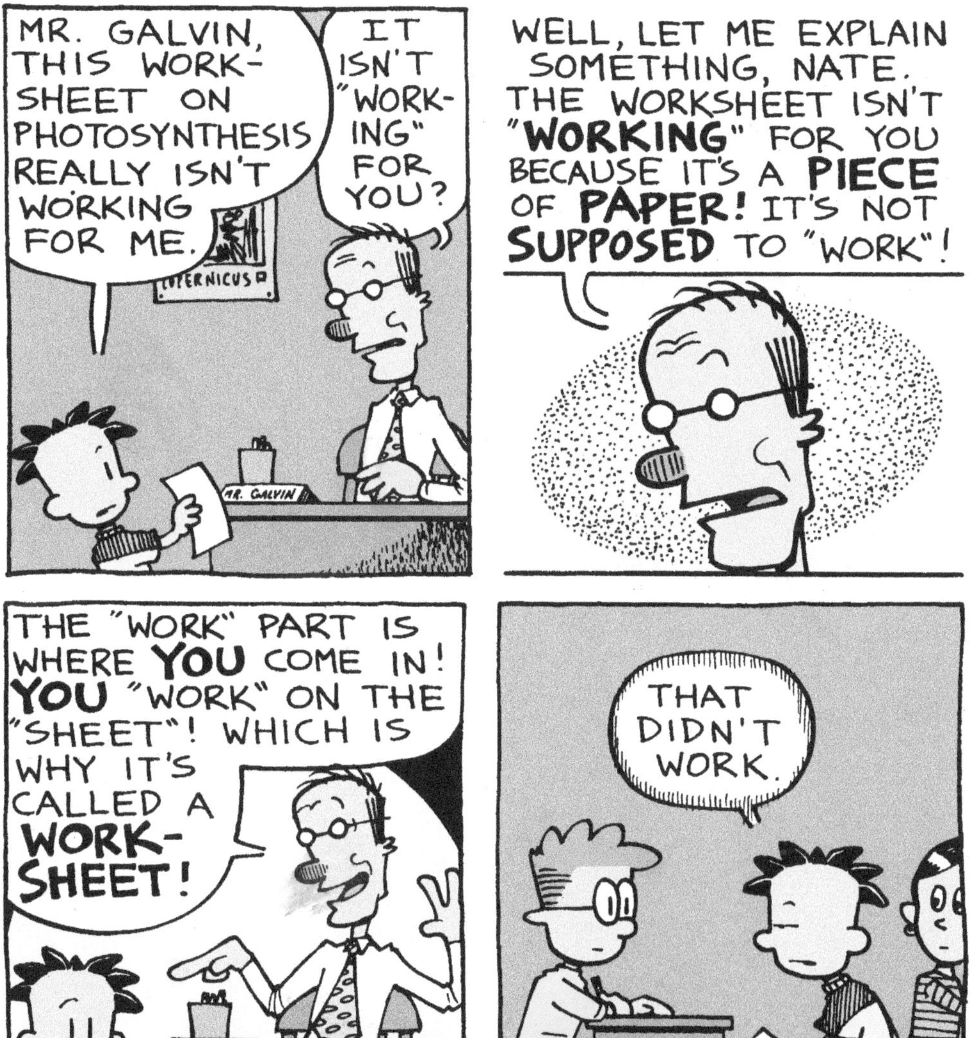
MR. GALVIN, THIS WORK-SHEET ON PHOTOSYNTHESIS REALLY ISN'T WORKING FOR ME.
IT ISN'T "WORKING" FOR YOU?
COPERNICUS
MR. GALVIN
WELL, LET ME EXPLAIN SOMETHING, NATE. THE WORKSHEET ISN'T "WORKING" FOR YOU BECAUSE IT'S A PIECE OF PAPER! IT'S NOT SUPPOSED TO "WORK"!
THE "WORK" PART IS WHERE YOU COME IN! YOU "WORK" ON THE "SHEET"! WHICH IS WHY IT'S CALLED A WORK-SHEET!
MR. GALVIN
THAT DIDN'T WORK.
Peirce

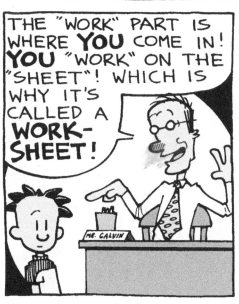

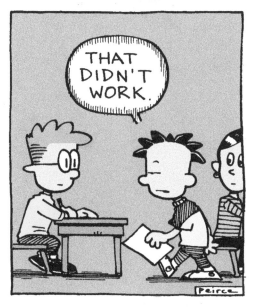

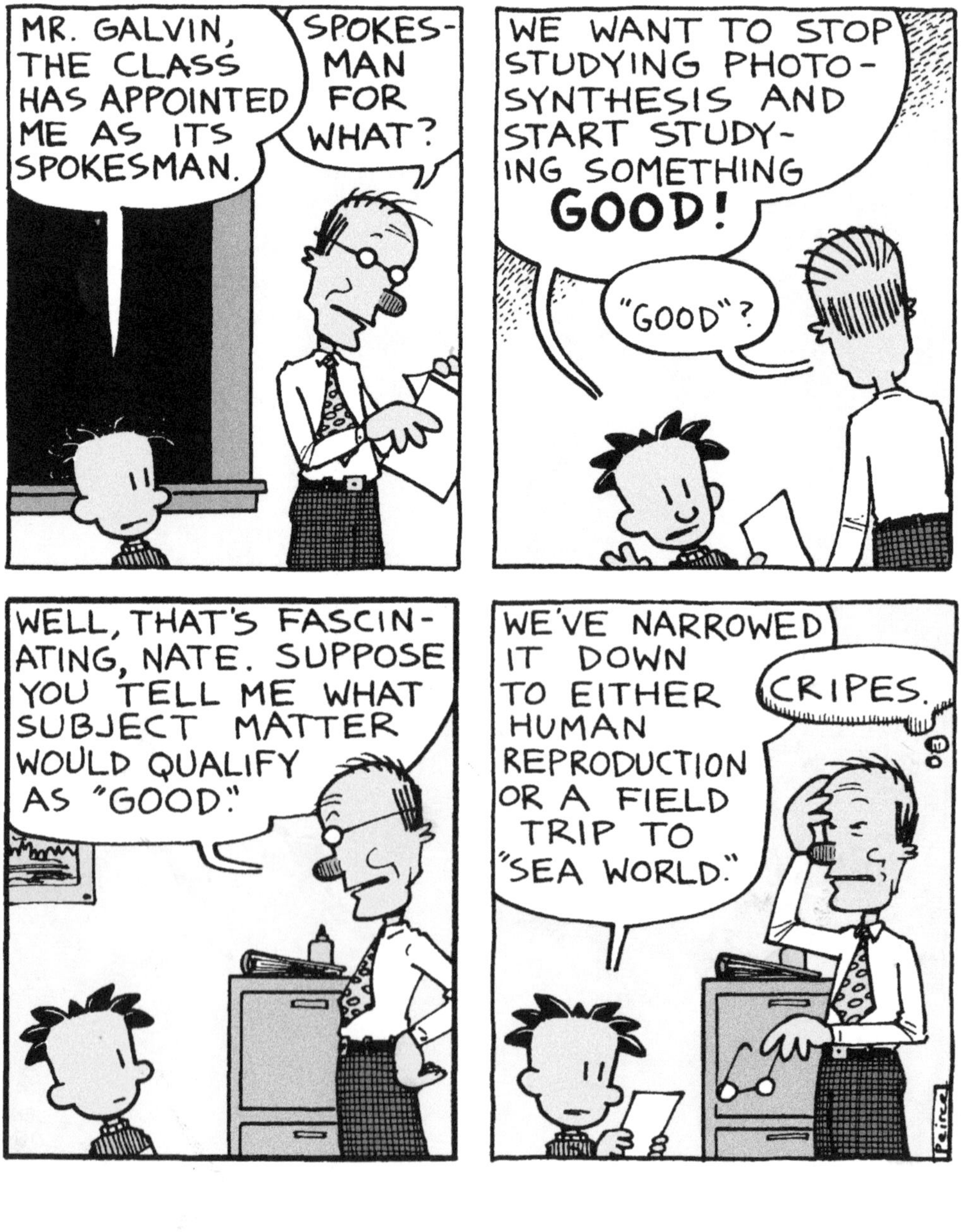
MR. GALVIN, THE CLASS HAS APPOINTED ME AS ITS SPOKESMAN.
SPOKES-MAN FOR WHAT?
WE WANT TO STOP STUDYING PHOTO-SYNTHESIS AND START STUDYING SOMETHING GOOD!
"GOOD"?
WELL, THAT'S FASCINATING, NATE. SUPPOSE YOU TELL ME WHAT SUBJECT MATTER WOULD QUALIFY AS "GOOD."
WE'VE NARROWED IT DOWN TO EITHER HUMAN REPRODUCTION OR A FIELD TRIP TO "SEA WORLD."
CRIPES.
Peirce

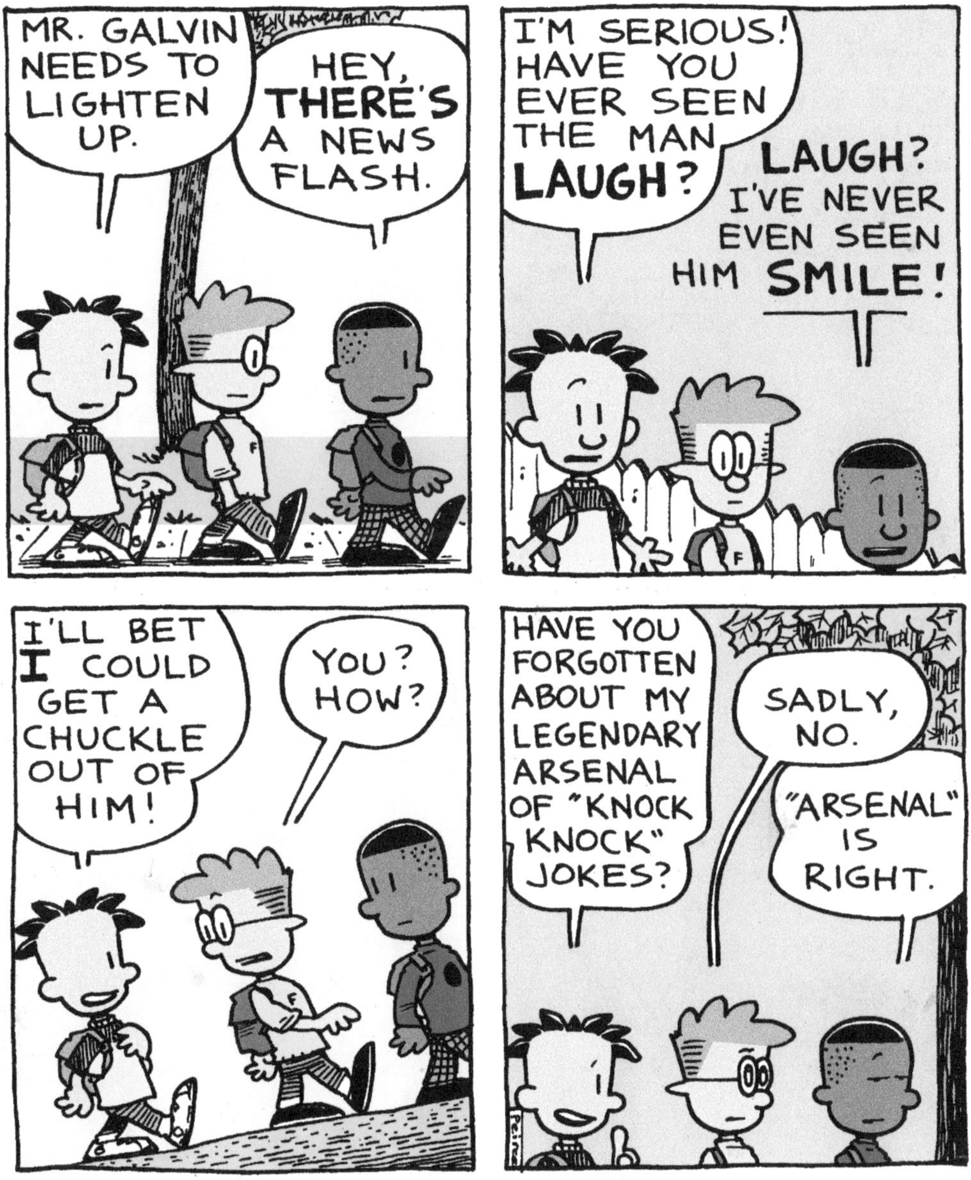

MR. GALVIN NEEDS TO LIGHTEN UP.
HEY, THERE'S A NEWS FLASH.
I'M SERIOUS! HAVE YOU EVER SEEN THE MAN LAUGH?
LAUGH? I'VE NEVER EVEN SEEN HIM SMILE!
I'LL BET I COULD GET A CHUCKLE OUT OF HIM!
YOU? HOW?
HAVE YOU FORGOTTEN ABOUT MY LEGENDARY ARSENAL OF "KNOCK KNOCK" JOKES?
SADLY, NO.
"ARSENAL" IS RIGHT.

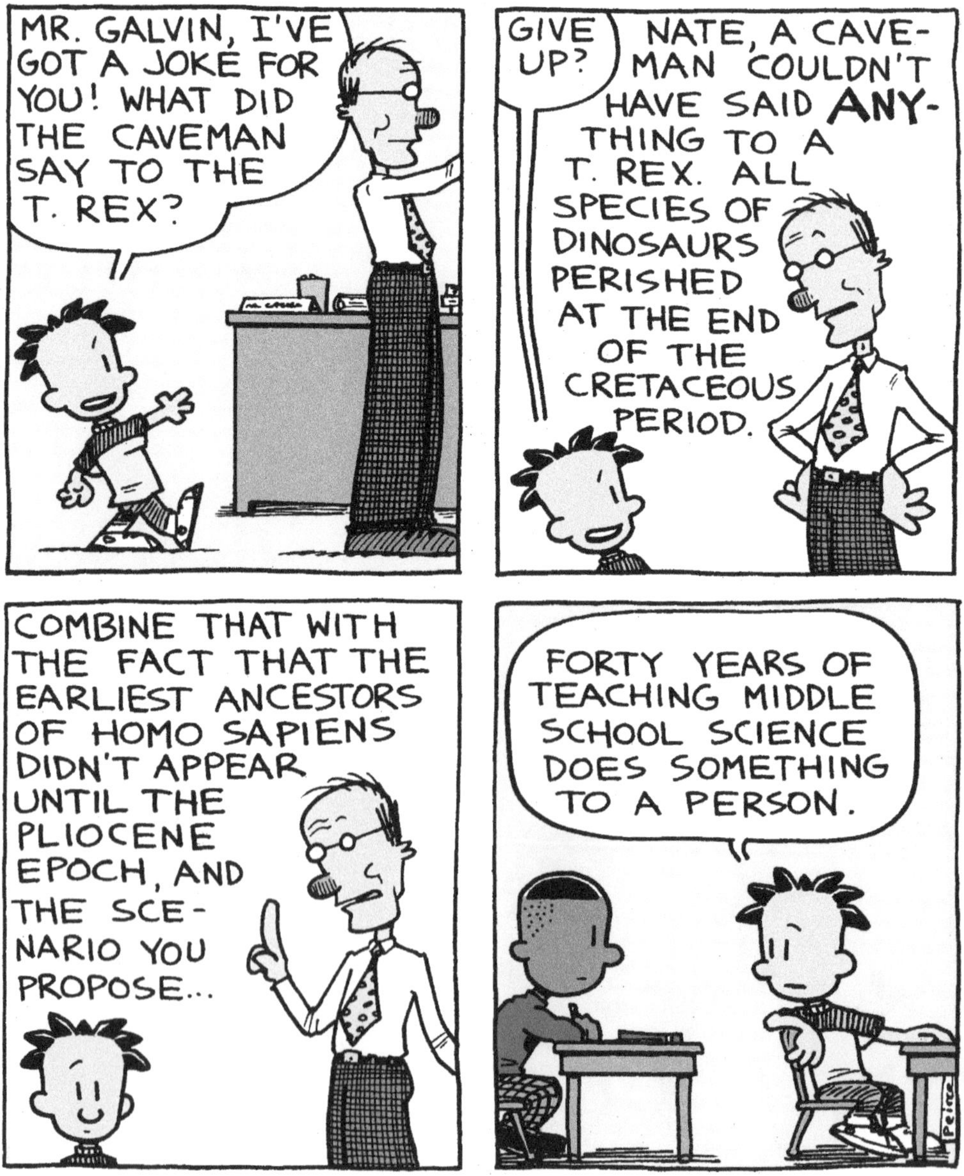
MR. GALVIN, I'VE GOT A JOKE FOR YOU! WHAT DID THE CAVEMAN SAY TO THE T. REX?
GIVE UP?
NATE, A CAVEMAN COULDN'T HAVE SAID ANYTHING TO A T. REX. ALL SPECIES OF DINOSAURS PERISHED AT THE END OF THE CRETACEOUS PERIOD.
COMBINE THAT WITH THE FACT THAT THE EARLIEST ANCESTORS OF HOMO SAPIENS DIDN'T APPEAR UNTIL THE PLIOCENE EPOCH, AND THE SCENARIO YOU PROPOSE...
FORTY YEARS OF TEACHING MIDDLE SCHOOL SCIENCE DOES SOMETHING TO A PERSON.

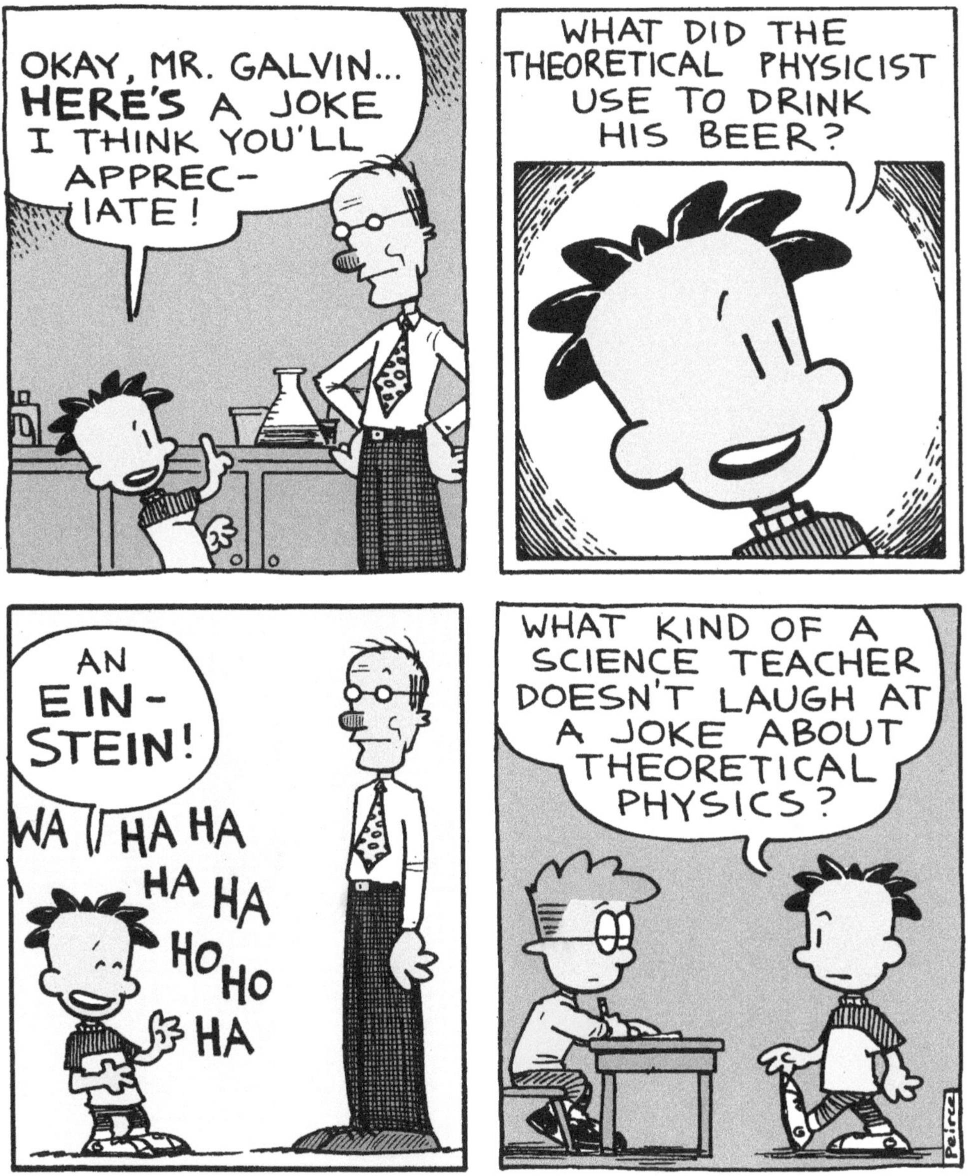
OKAY, MR. GALVIN... **HERE'S** A JOKE I THINK YOU'LL APPREC-IATE!
WHAT DID THE THEORETICAL PHYSICIST USE TO DRINK HIS BEER?
AN EIN-STEIN!
WA HA HA HA HA HA HO HO HA
WHAT KIND OF A SCIENCE TEACHER DOESN'T LAUGH AT A JOKE ABOUT THEORETICAL PHYSICS?
Peirce

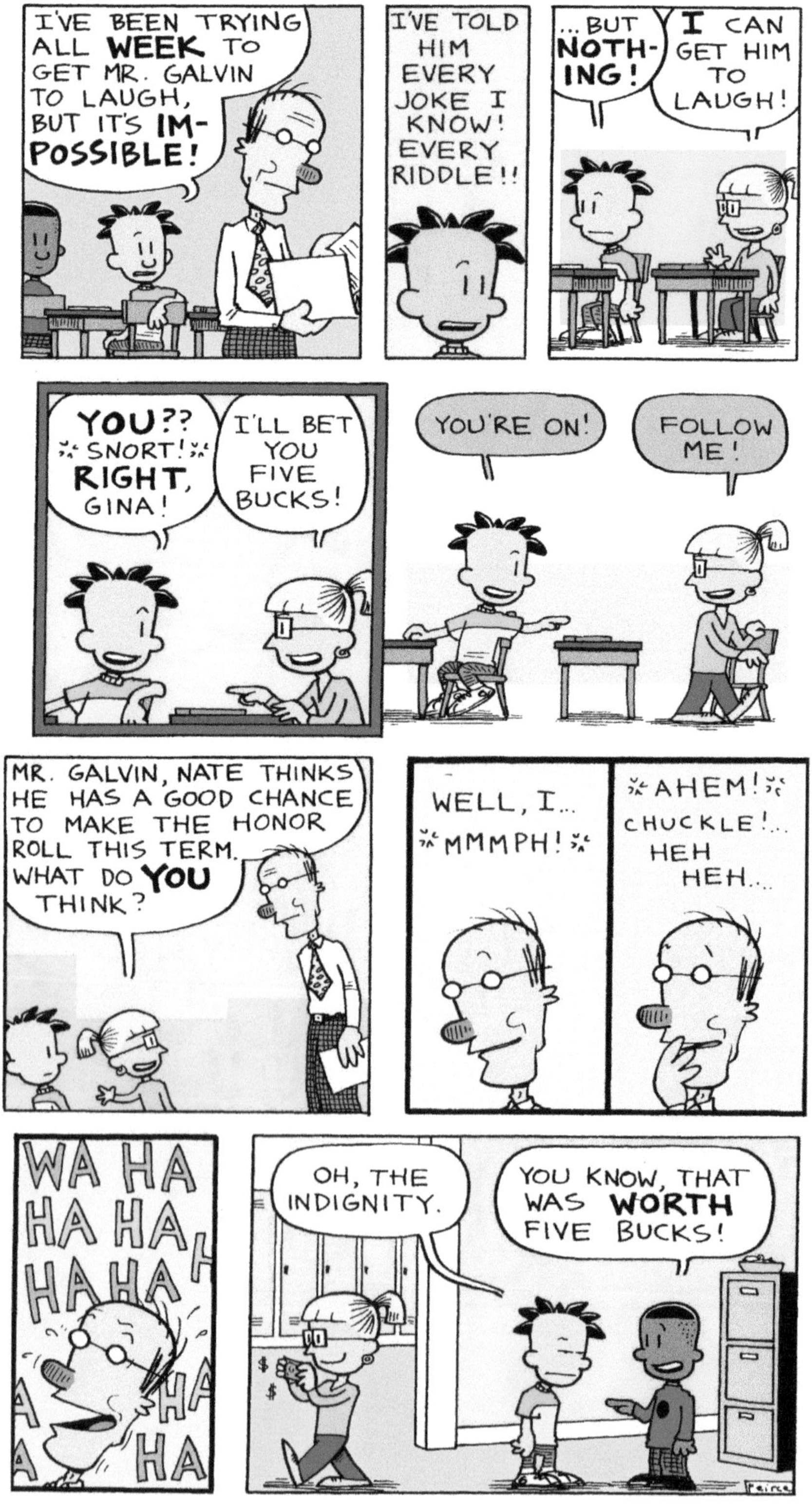
I'VE BEEN TRYING ALL WEEK TO GET MR. GALVIN TO LAUGH, BUT IT'S IM-POSSIBLE!
I'VE TOLD HIM EVERY JOKE I KNOW! EVERY RIDDLE!!
...BUT NOTH-ING!
I CAN GET HIM TO LAUGH!
YOU?? SNORT! RIGHT, GINA!
I'LL BET YOU FIVE BUCKS!
YOU'RE ON!
FOLLOW ME!
MR. GALVIN, NATE THINKS HE HAS A GOOD CHANCE TO MAKE THE HONOR ROLL THIS TERM. WHAT DO YOU THINK?
WELL, I... MMMPH!
AHEM! CHUCKLE!... HEH HEH...
WA HA HA HA HA HA HA HA HA HA
OH, THE INDIGNITY.
YOU KNOW, THAT WAS WORTH FIVE BUCKS!
Peirce

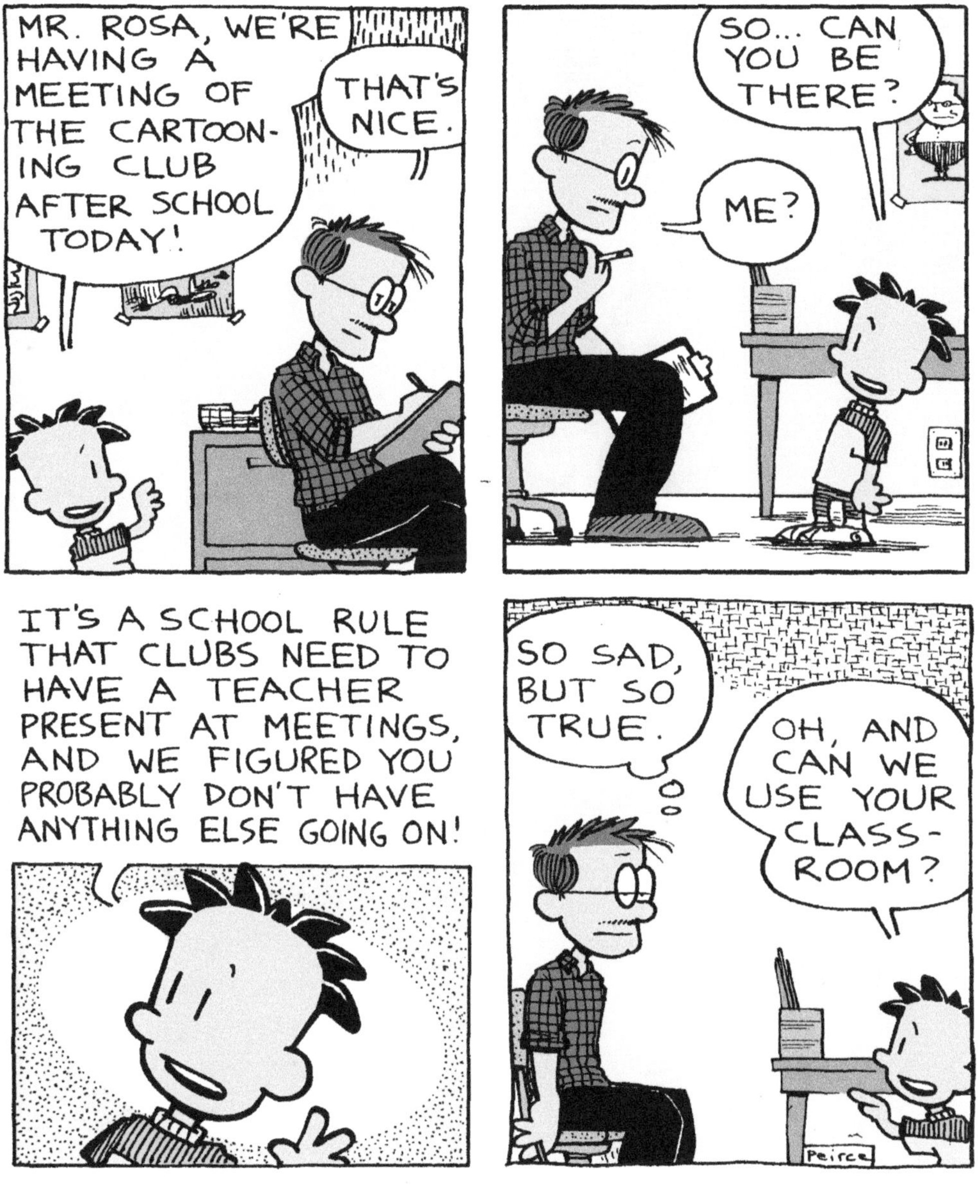
MR. ROSA, WE'RE HAVING A MEETING OF THE CARTOONING CLUB AFTER SCHOOL TODAY!
THAT'S NICE.
SO... CAN YOU BE THERE?
ME?
IT'S A SCHOOL RULE THAT CLUBS NEED TO HAVE A TEACHER PRESENT AT MEETINGS, AND WE FIGURED YOU PROBABLY DON'T HAVE ANYTHING ELSE GOING ON!
SO SAD, BUT SO TRUE.
OH, AND CAN WE USE YOUR CLASSROOM?
Peirce

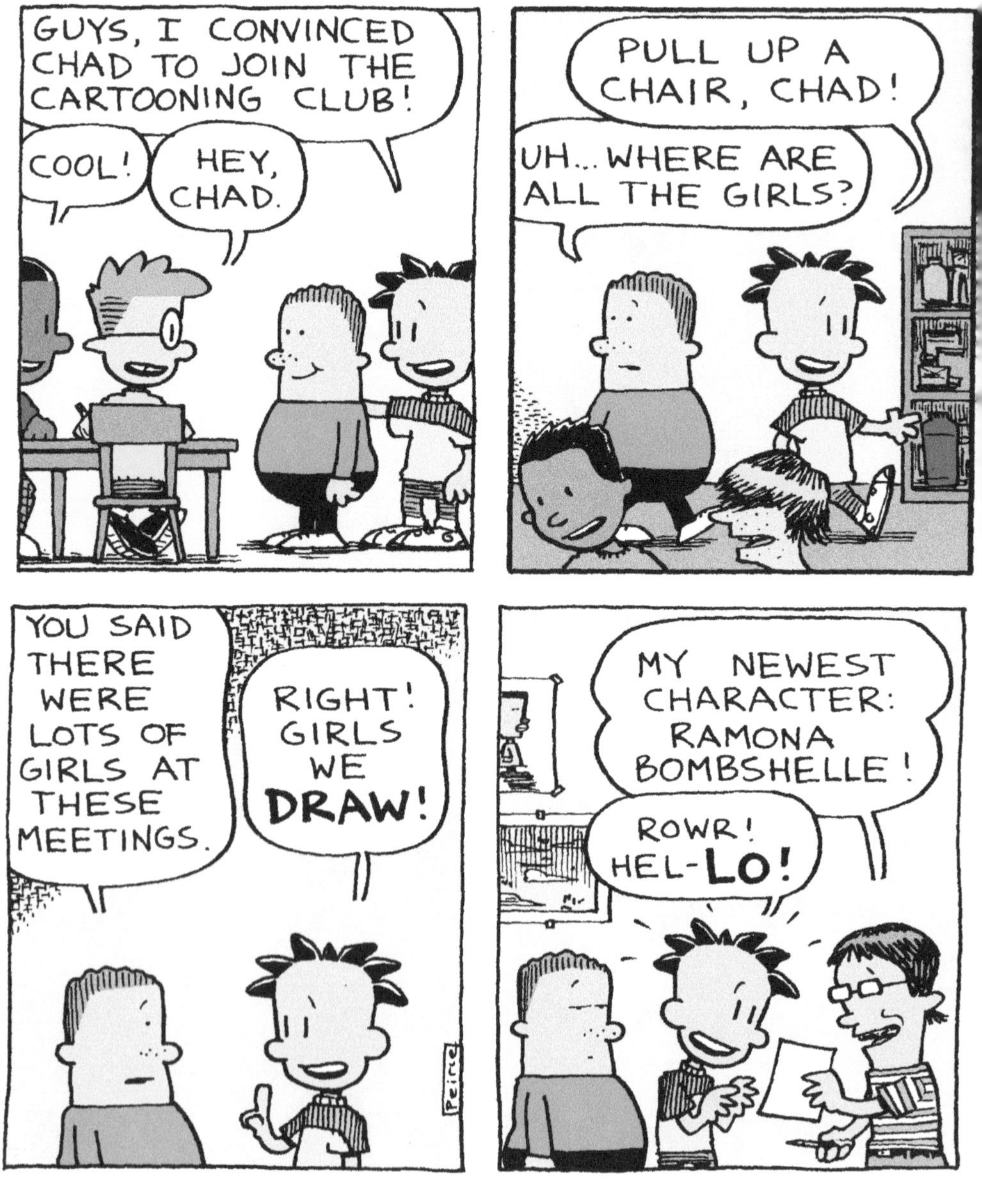
GUYS, I CONVINCED CHAD TO JOIN THE CARTOONING CLUB!
COOL!
HEY, CHAD.
PULL UP A CHAIR, CHAD!
UH... WHERE ARE ALL THE GIRLS?
YOU SAID THERE WERE LOTS OF GIRLS AT THESE MEETINGS.
RIGHT! GIRLS WE **DRAW**!
Peirce
MY NEWEST CHARACTER: RAMONA BOMBSHELLE!
ROWR! HEL-**LO**!

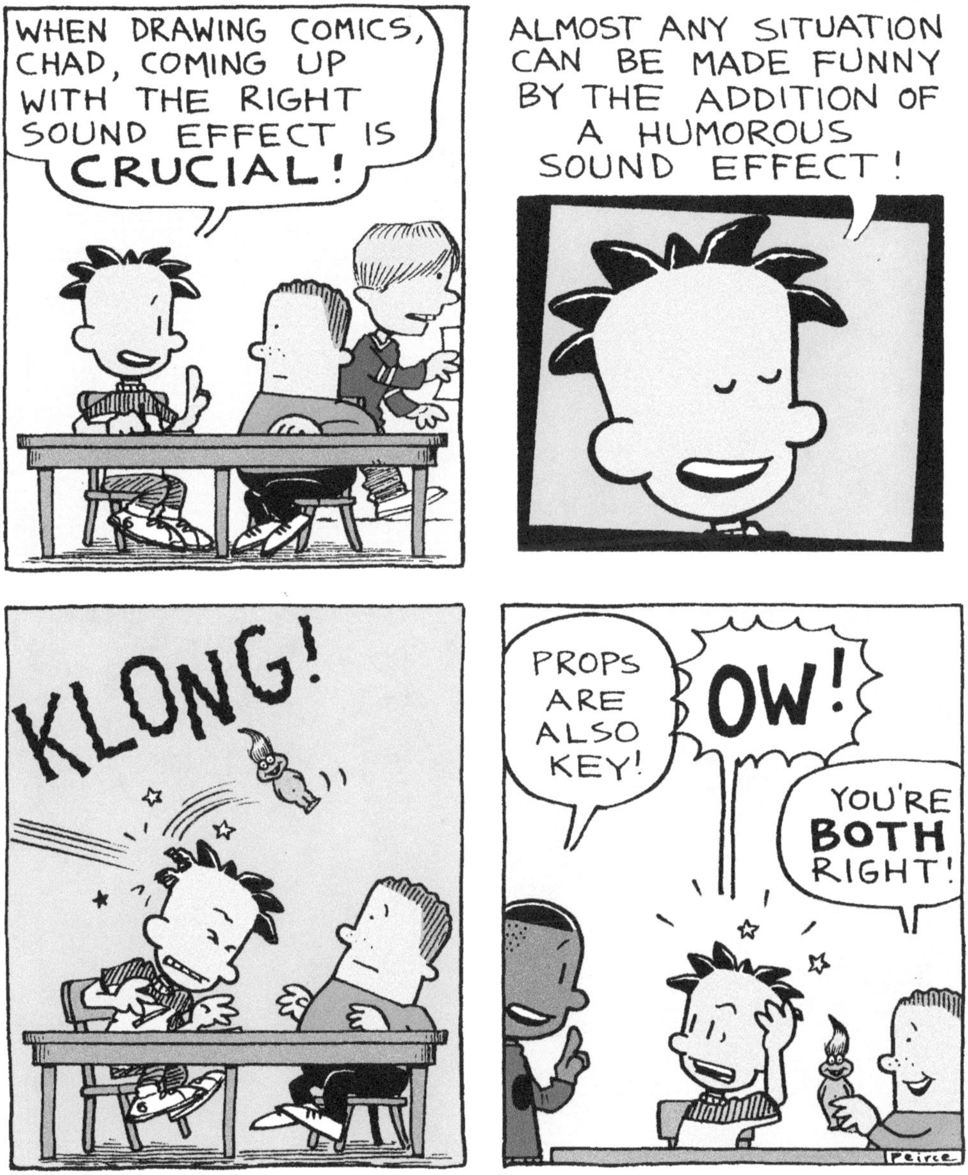
WHEN DRAWING COMICS, CHAD, COMING UP WITH THE RIGHT SOUND EFFECT IS CRUCIAL!
ALMOST ANY SITUATION CAN BE MADE FUNNY BY THE ADDITION OF A HUMOROUS SOUND EFFECT!
KLONG!
PROPS ARE ALSO KEY!
OW!
YOU'RE BOTH RIGHT!
Peirce

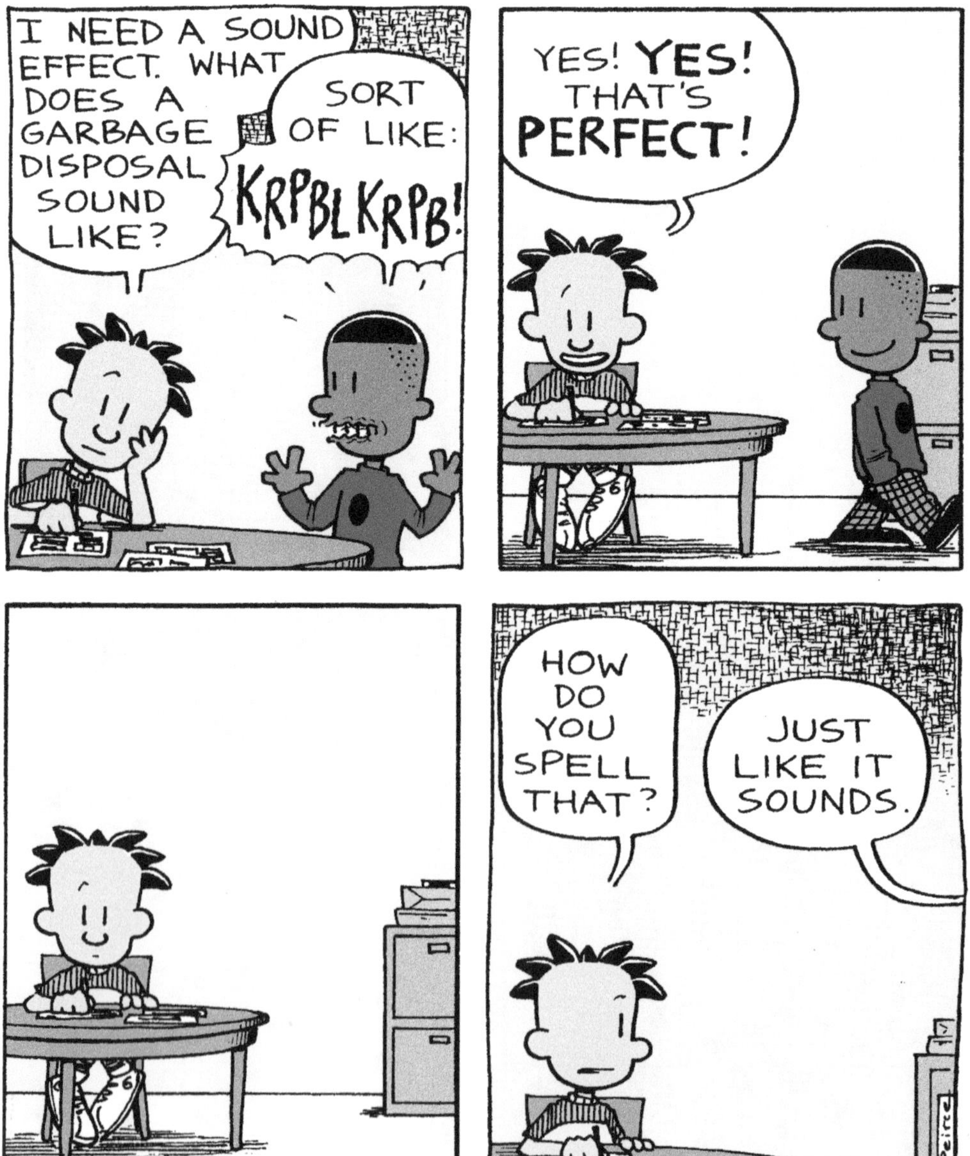
I NEED A SOUND EFFECT. WHAT DOES A GARBAGE DISPOSAL SOUND LIKE?
SORT OF LIKE:
KRPBLKRPB!
YES! YES! THAT'S PERFECT!
HOW DO YOU SPELL THAT?
JUST LIKE IT SOUNDS.
Peirce

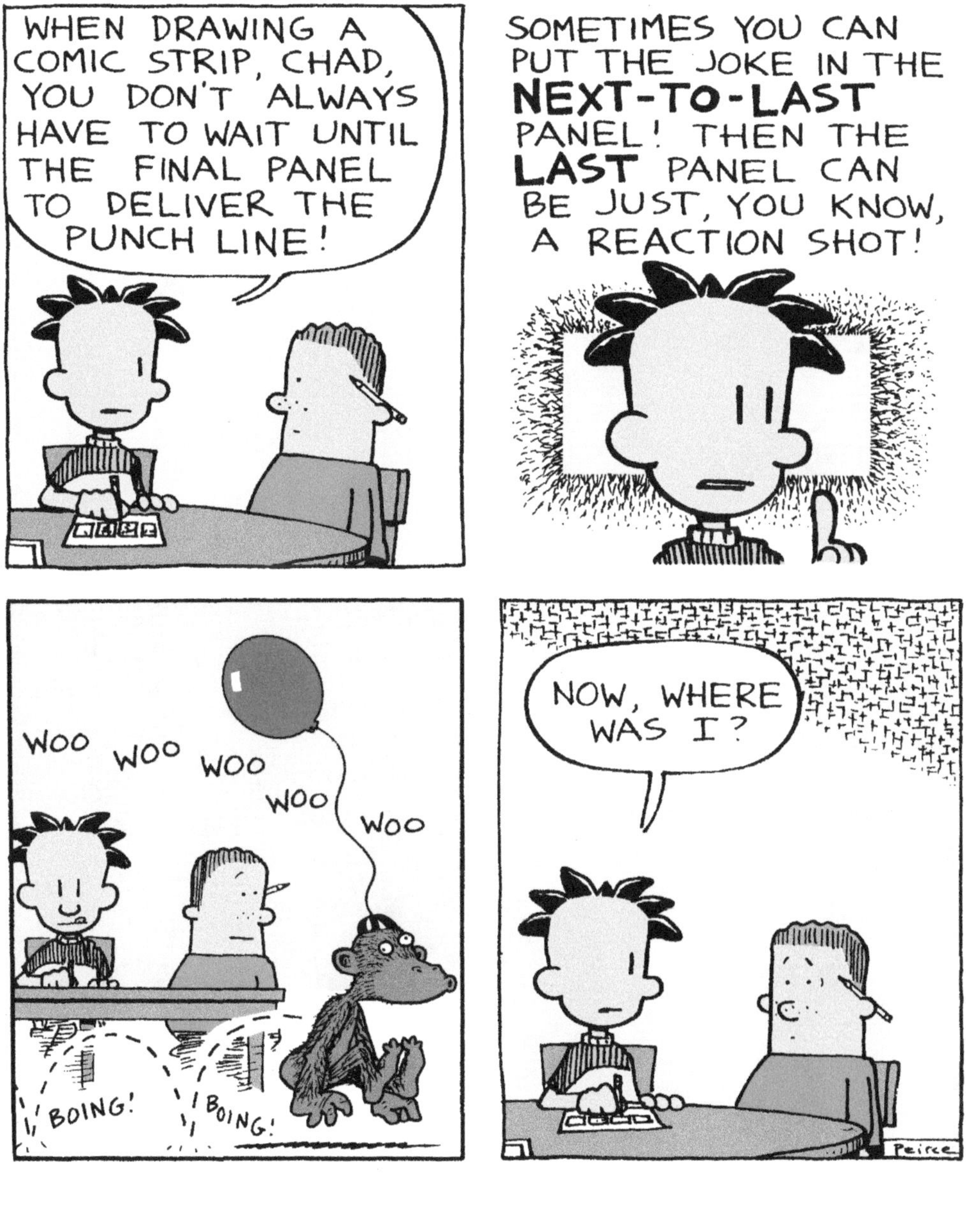
WHEN DRAWING A COMIC STRIP, CHAD, YOU DON'T ALWAYS HAVE TO WAIT UNTIL THE FINAL PANEL TO DELIVER THE PUNCH LINE!
SOMETIMES YOU CAN PUT THE JOKE IN THE **NEXT-TO-LAST** PANEL! THEN THE **LAST** PANEL CAN BE JUST, YOU KNOW, A REACTION SHOT!
WOO WOO WOO WOO WOO
BOING!
BOING!
NOW, WHERE WAS I?
Peirce

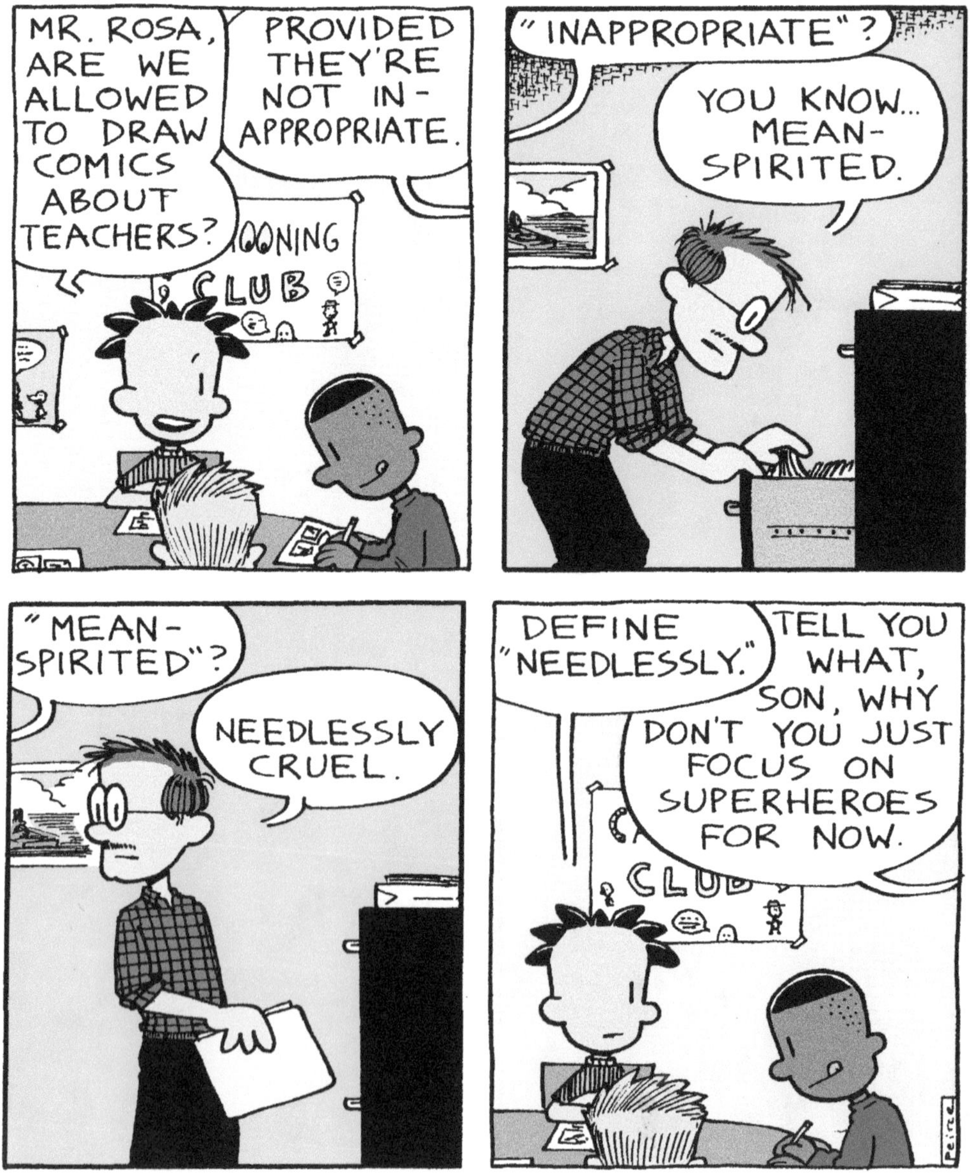
MR. ROSA, ARE WE ALLOWED TO DRAW COMICS ABOUT TEACHERS?
PROVIDED THEY'RE NOT IN-APPROPRIATE.
"INAPPROPRIATE"?
YOU KNOW... MEAN-SPIRITED.
"MEAN-SPIRITED"?
NEEDLESSLY CRUEL.
DEFINE "NEEDLESSLY."
TELL YOU WHAT, SON, WHY DON'T YOU JUST FOCUS ON SUPERHEROES FOR NOW.
PEIRCE

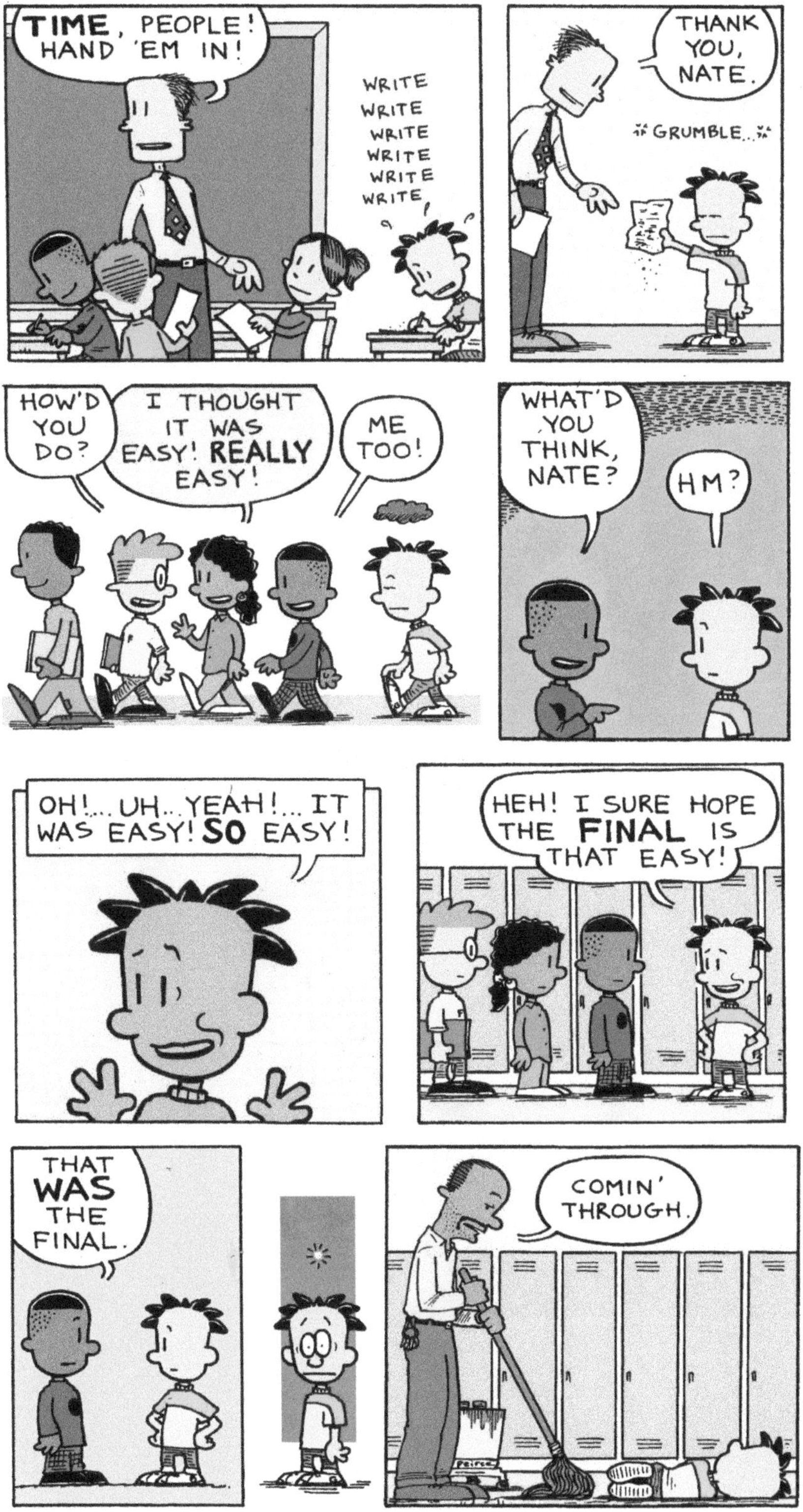
TIME, PEOPLE! HAND 'EM IN!
WRITE WRITE WRITE WRITE WRITE WRITE
THANK YOU, NATE.
GRUMBLE...
HOW'D YOU DO?
I THOUGHT IT WAS EASY! REALLY EASY!
ME TOO!
WHAT'D YOU THINK, NATE?
HM?
OH!... UH... YEAH!... IT WAS EASY! SO EASY!
HEH! I SURE HOPE THE FINAL IS THAT EASY!
THAT WAS THE FINAL.
COMIN' THROUGH.

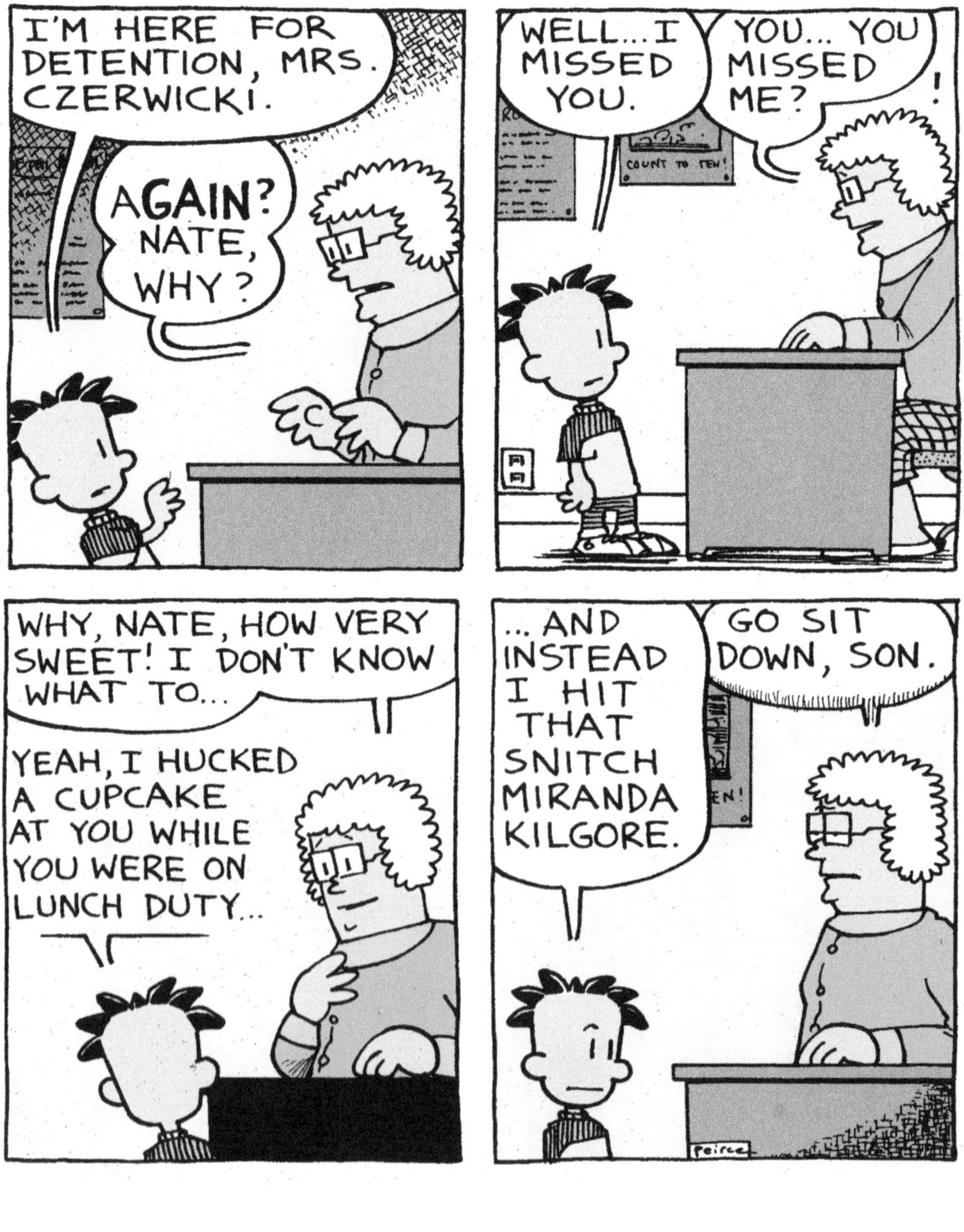
I'M HERE FOR DETENTION, MRS. CZERWICKI.
AGAIN? NATE, WHY?
WELL... I MISSED YOU.
YOU... YOU MISSED ME?
!
COUNT TO TEN!
WHY, NATE, HOW VERY SWEET! I DON'T KNOW WHAT TO...
YEAH, I HUCKED A CUPCAKE AT YOU WHILE YOU WERE ON LUNCH DUTY...
... AND INSTEAD I HIT THAT SNITCH MIRANDA KILGORE.
GO SIT DOWN, SON.
peirce

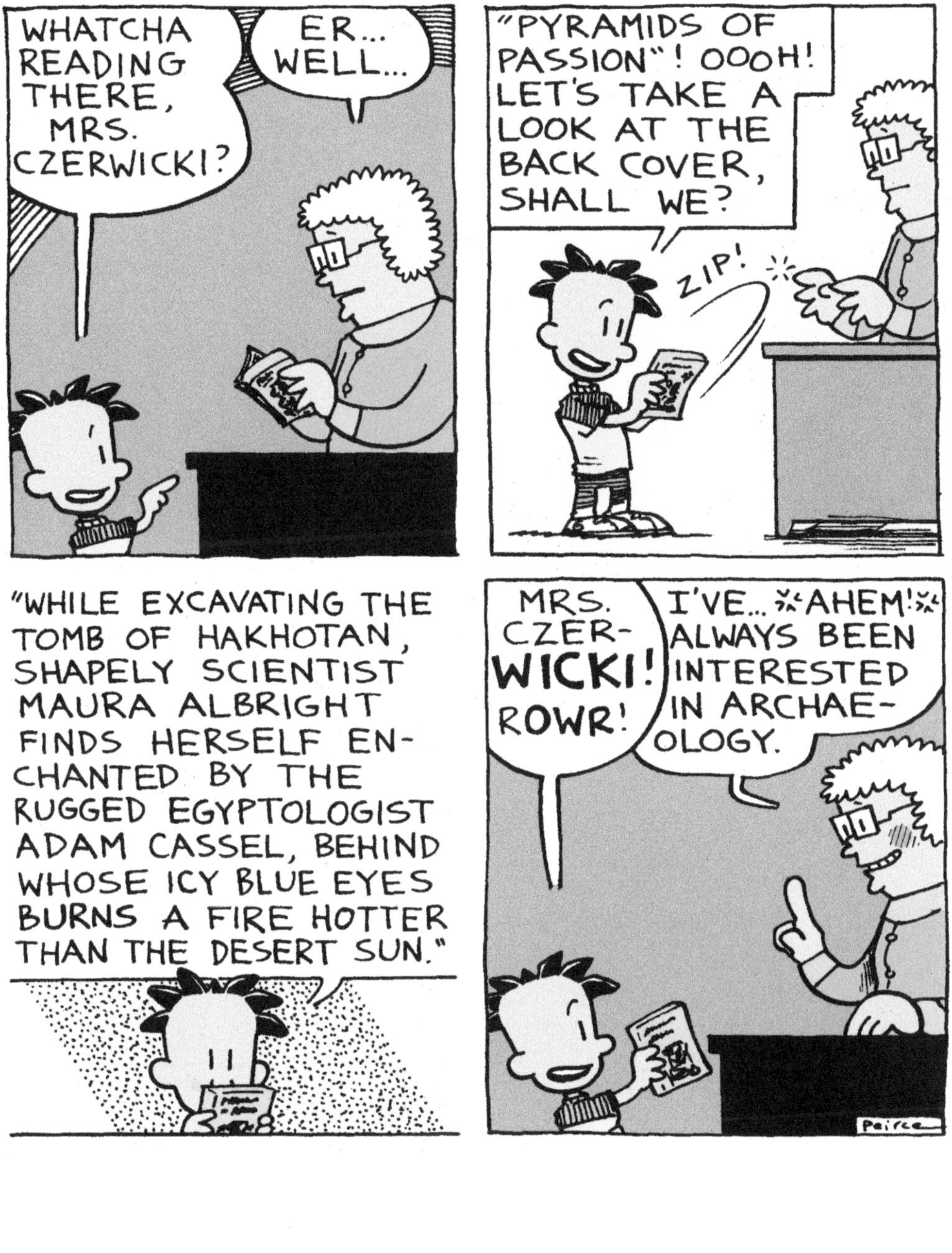

WHATCHA READING THERE, MRS. CZERWICKI?
ER... WELL...
"PYRAMIDS OF PASSION"! OOOH! LET'S TAKE A LOOK AT THE BACK COVER, SHALL WE?
ZIP!
"WHILE EXCAVATING THE TOMB OF HAKHOTAN, SHAPELY SCIENTIST MAURA ALBRIGHT FINDS HERSELF EN-CHANTED BY THE RUGGED EGYPTOLOGIST ADAM CASSEL, BEHIND WHOSE ICY BLUE EYES BURNS A FIRE HOTTER THAN THE DESERT SUN."
MRS. CZER-**WICKI**! ROWR!
I'VE... AHEM! ALWAYS BEEN INTERESTED IN ARCHAE-OLOGY.
Peirce

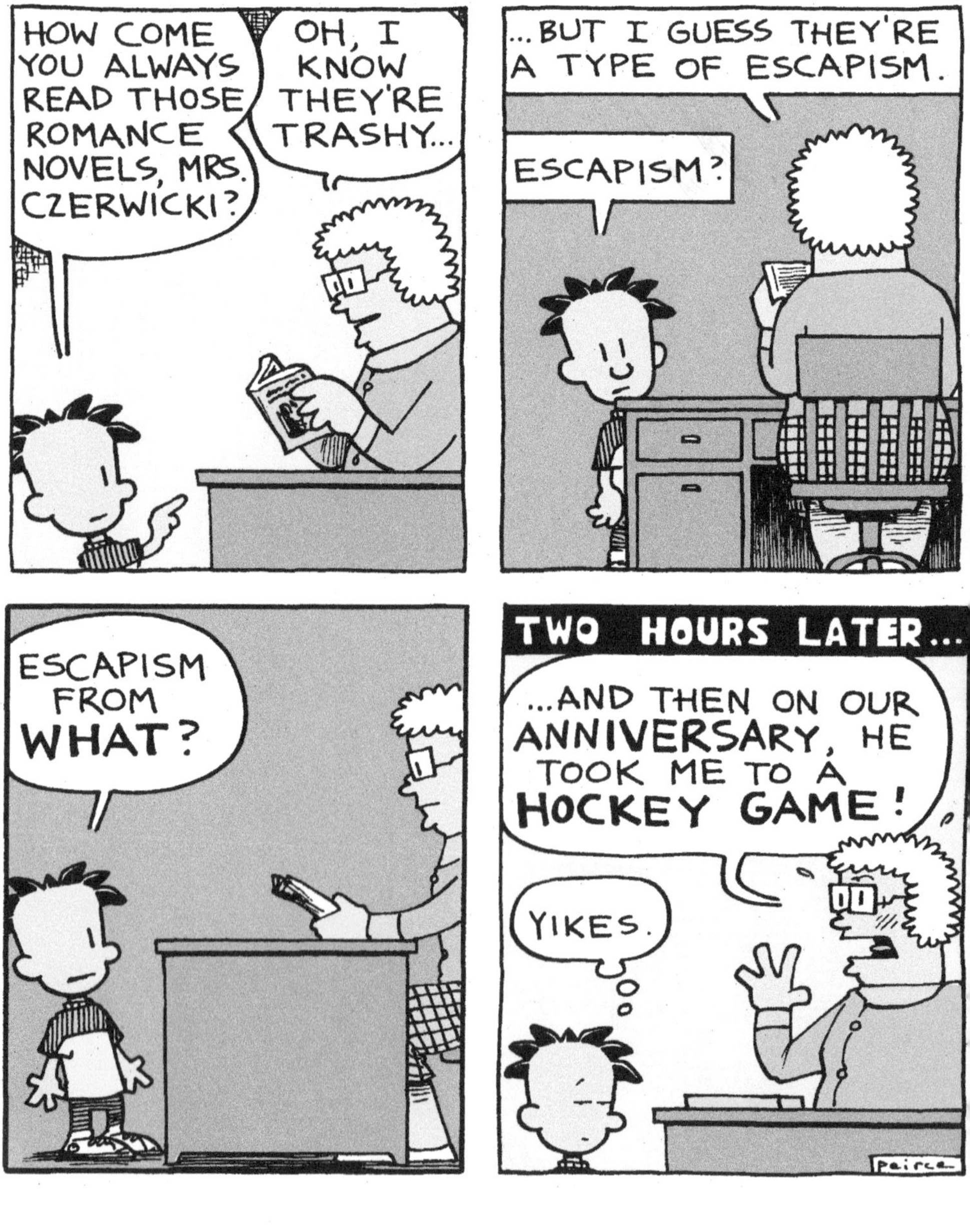
HOW COME YOU ALWAYS READ THOSE ROMANCE NOVELS, MRS. CZERWICKI?
OH, I KNOW THEY'RE TRASHY...
...BUT I GUESS THEY'RE A TYPE OF ESCAPISM.
ESCAPISM?
ESCAPISM FROM WHAT?
TWO HOURS LATER...
...AND THEN ON OUR ANNIVERSARY, HE TOOK ME TO A HOCKEY GAME!
YIKES.
peirce

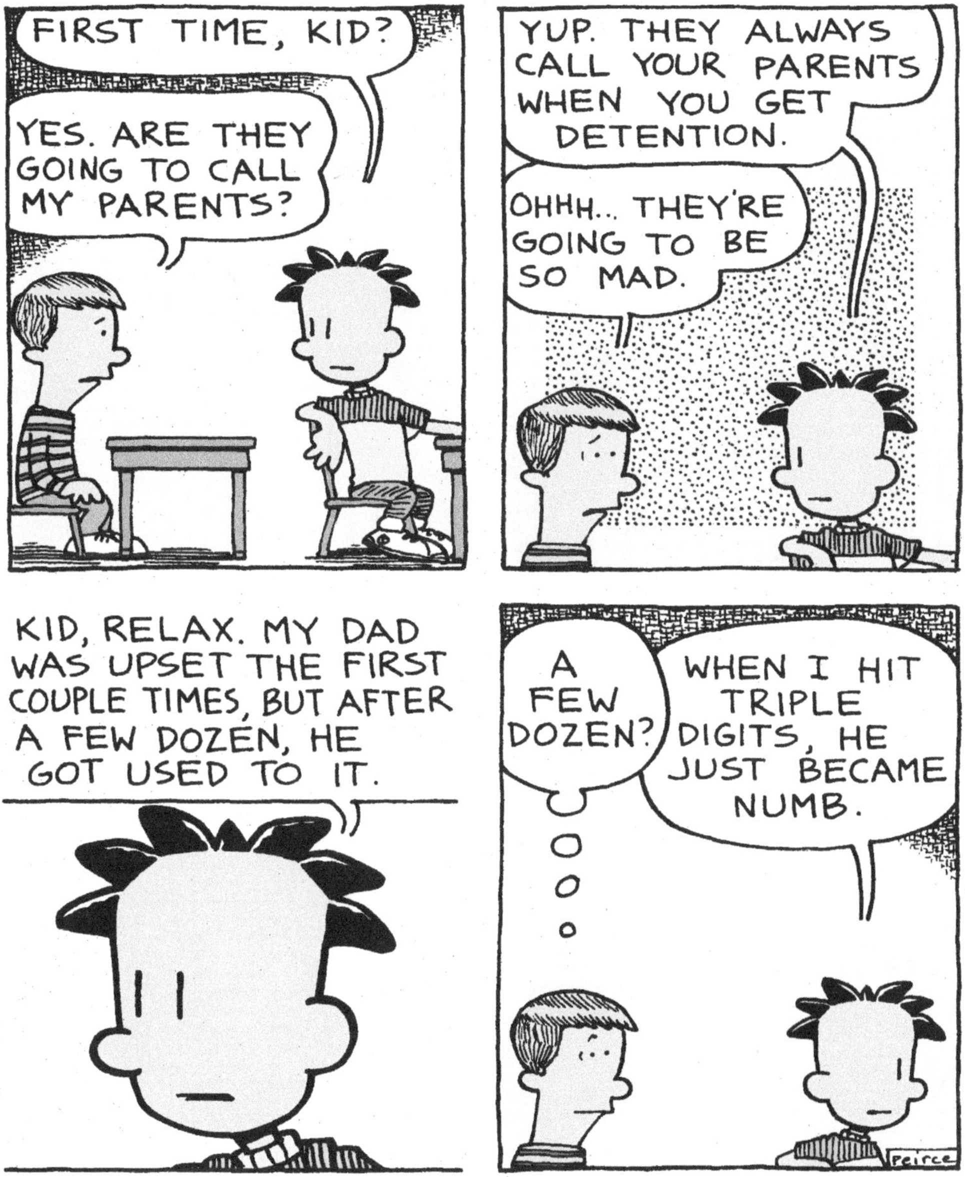
FIRST TIME, KID?
YES. ARE THEY GOING TO CALL MY PARENTS?
YUP. THEY ALWAYS CALL YOUR PARENTS WHEN YOU GET DETENTION.
OHHH... THEY'RE GOING TO BE SO MAD.
KID, RELAX. MY DAD WAS UPSET THE FIRST COUPLE TIMES, BUT AFTER A FEW DOZEN, HE GOT USED TO IT.
A FEW DOZEN?
WHEN I HIT TRIPLE DIGITS, HE JUST BECAME NUMB.
PEIRCE

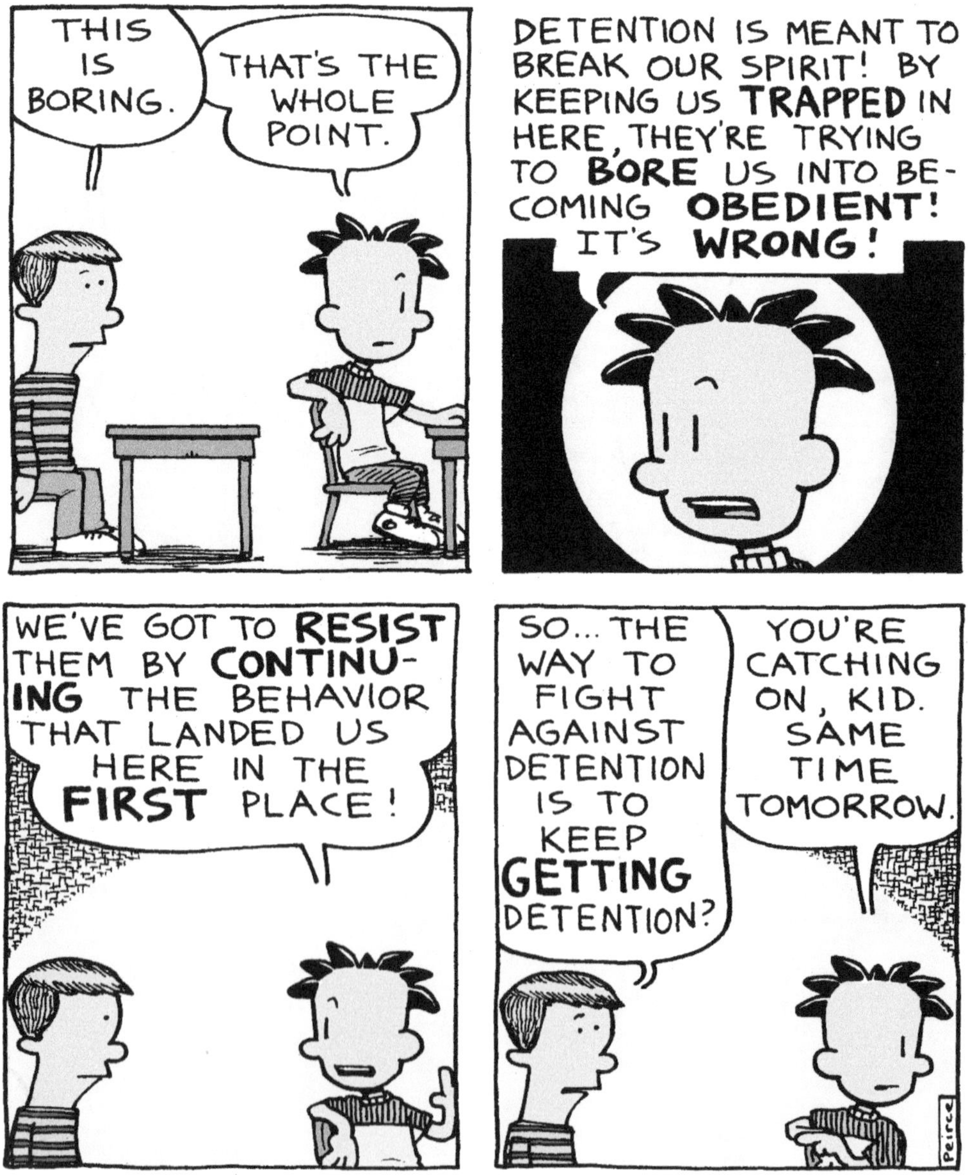
THIS IS BORING.
THAT'S THE WHOLE POINT.
DETENTION IS MEANT TO BREAK OUR SPIRIT! BY KEEPING US TRAPPED IN HERE, THEY'RE TRYING TO BORE US INTO BECOMING OBEDIENT! IT'S WRONG!
WE'VE GOT TO RESIST THEM BY CONTINUING THE BEHAVIOR THAT LANDED US HERE IN THE FIRST PLACE!
SO... THE WAY TO FIGHT AGAINST DETENTION IS TO KEEP GETTING DETENTION?
YOU'RE CATCHING ON, KID. SAME TIME TOMORROW.
Peirce

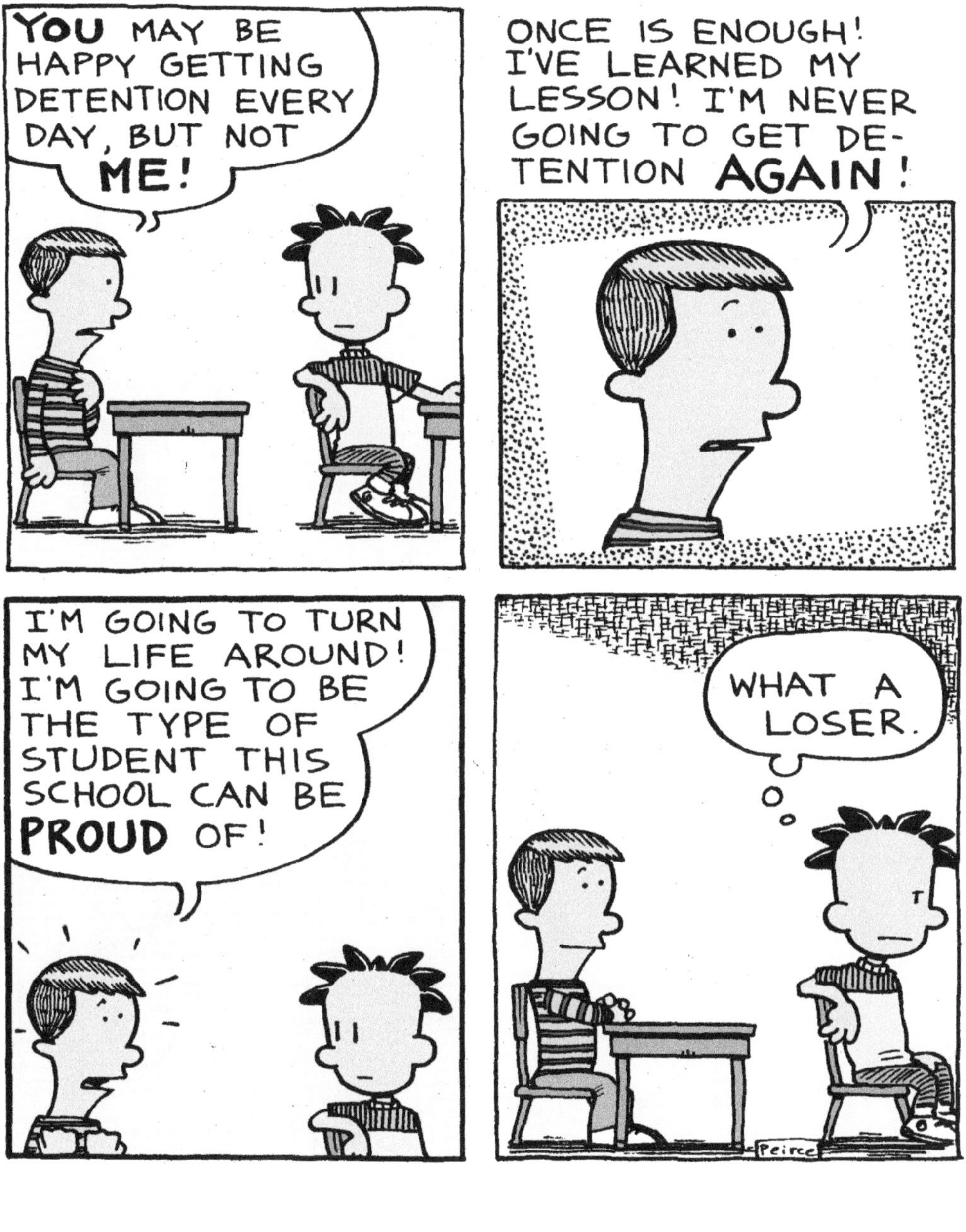
YOU MAY BE HAPPY GETTING DETENTION EVERY DAY, BUT NOT ME!
ONCE IS ENOUGH! I'VE LEARNED MY LESSON! I'M NEVER GOING TO GET DETENTION AGAIN!
I'M GOING TO TURN MY LIFE AROUND! I'M GOING TO BE THE TYPE OF STUDENT THIS SCHOOL CAN BE PROUD OF!
WHAT A LOSER.
Peirce

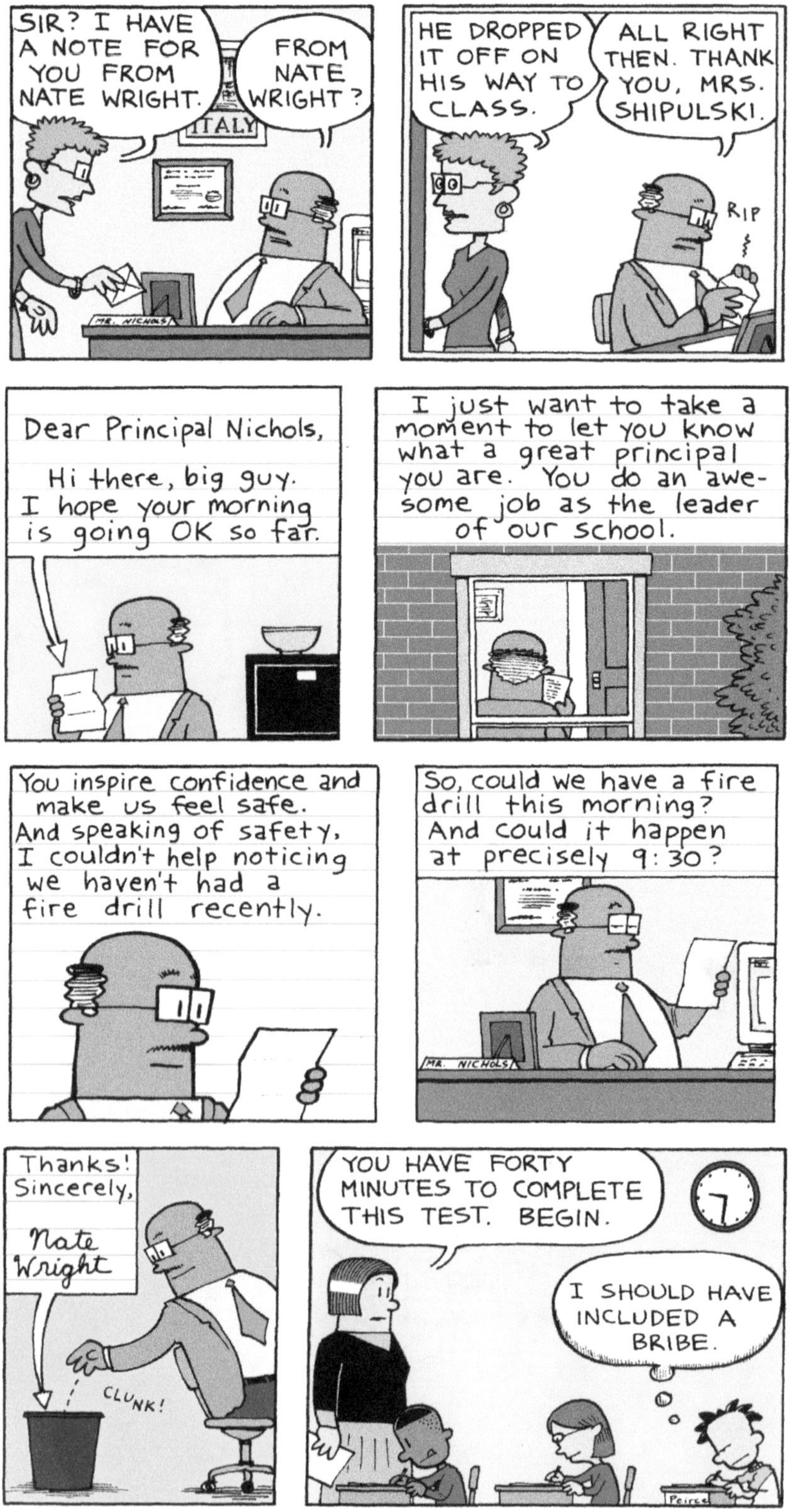

SIR? I HAVE A NOTE FOR YOU FROM NATE WRIGHT.
FROM NATE WRIGHT?
ITALY
MR. NICHOLS
HE DROPPED IT OFF ON HIS WAY TO CLASS.
ALL RIGHT THEN. THANK YOU, MRS. SHIPULSKI.
RIP
Dear Principal Nichols,
Hi there, big guy. I hope your morning is going OK so far.
I just want to take a moment to let you know what a great principal you are. You do an awesome job as the leader of our school.
You inspire confidence and make us feel safe. And speaking of safety, I couldn't help noticing we haven't had a fire drill recently.
So, could we have a fire drill this morning? And could it happen at precisely 9:30?
MR. NICHOLS
Thanks! Sincerely,
Nate Wright
CLUNK!
YOU HAVE FORTY MINUTES TO COMPLETE THIS TEST. BEGIN.
I SHOULD HAVE INCLUDED A BRIBE.
Peirce

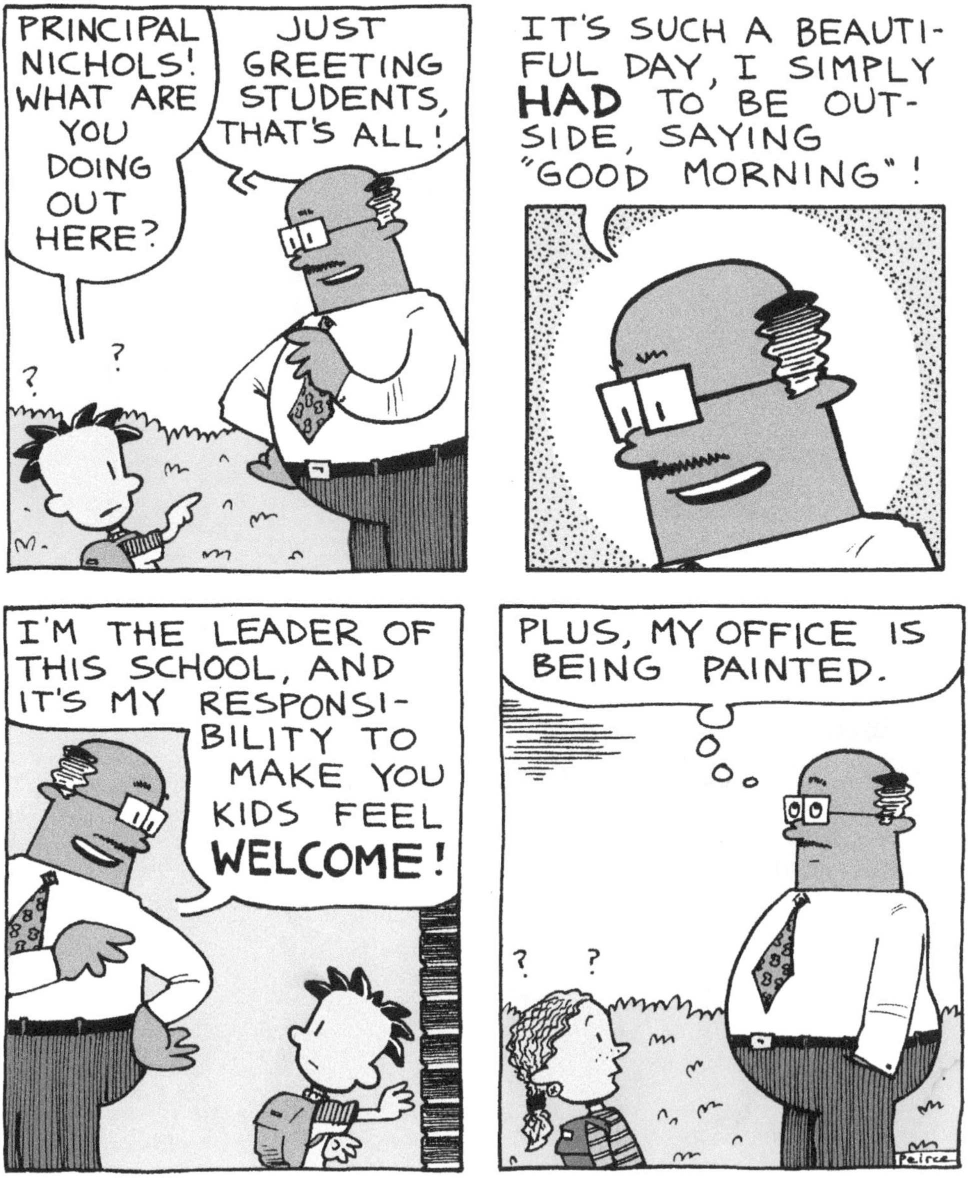
PRINCIPAL NICHOLS! WHAT ARE YOU DOING OUT HERE?
JUST GREETING STUDENTS, THAT'S ALL!
? ?
IT'S SUCH A BEAUTIFUL DAY, I SIMPLY HAD TO BE OUTSIDE, SAYING "GOOD MORNING"!
I'M THE LEADER OF THIS SCHOOL, AND IT'S MY RESPONSIBILITY TO MAKE YOU KIDS FEEL WELCOME!
PLUS, MY OFFICE IS BEING PAINTED.
? ?
Peirce

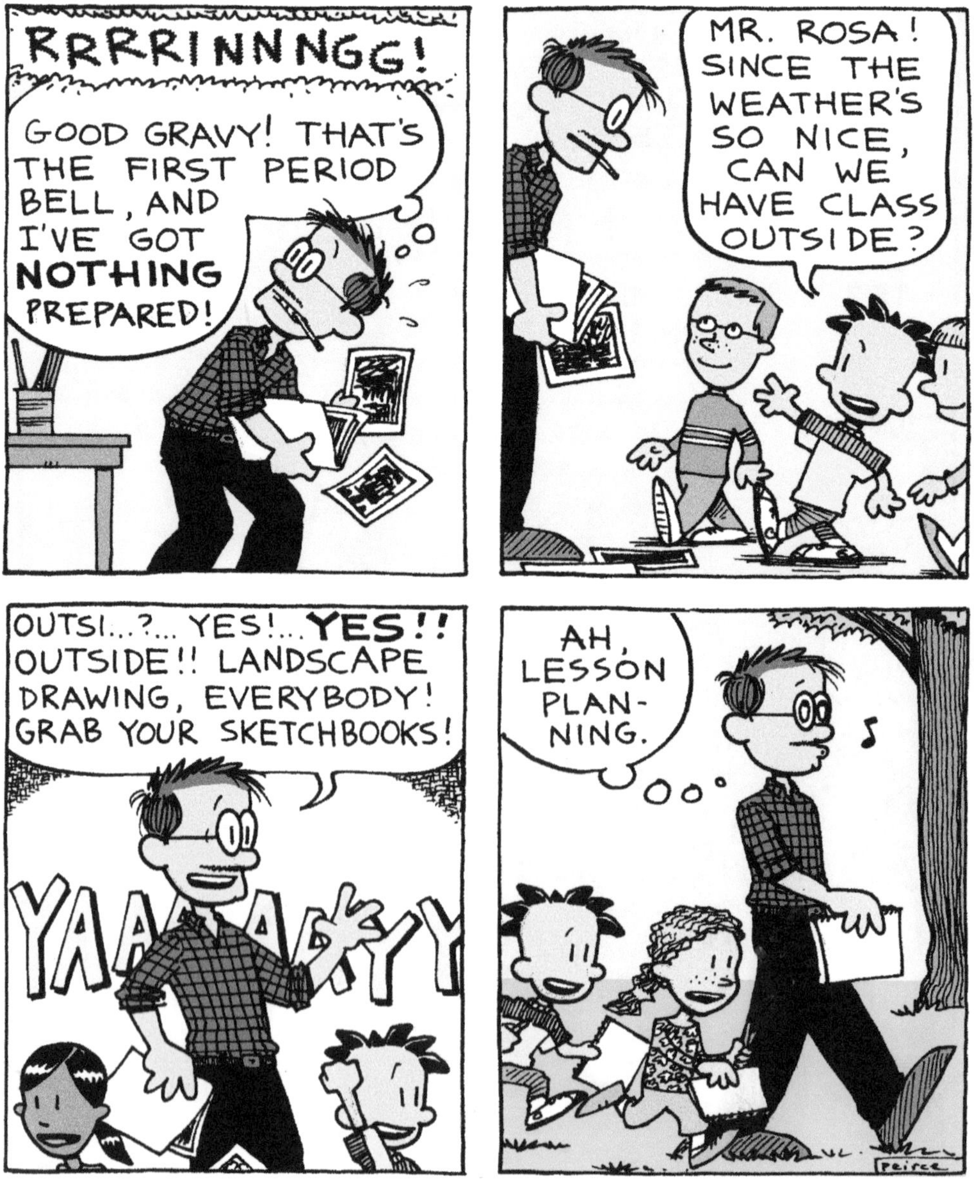
RRRRINNNGG!
GOOD GRAVY! THAT'S THE FIRST PERIOD BELL, AND I'VE GOT **NOTHING** PREPARED!
MR. ROSA! SINCE THE WEATHER'S SO NICE, CAN WE HAVE CLASS OUTSIDE?
OUTSI...?... YES!... **YES!!** OUTSIDE!! LANDSCAPE DRAWING, EVERYBODY! GRAB YOUR SKETCHBOOKS!
YAAAAYYY
AH, LESSON PLAN-NING.
PEIRCE

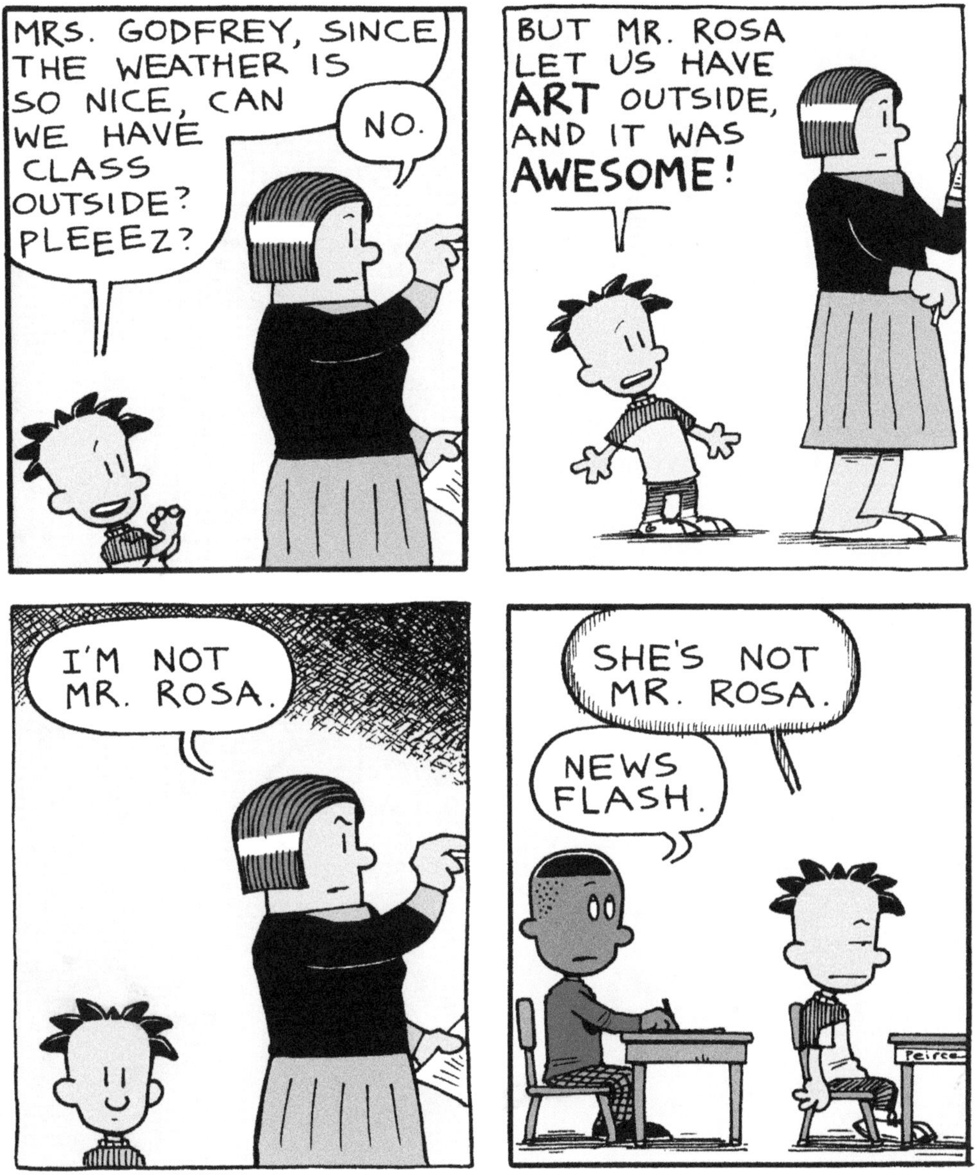
MRS. GODFREY, SINCE THE WEATHER IS SO NICE, CAN WE HAVE CLASS OUTSIDE? PLEEEZ?
NO.
BUT MR. ROSA LET US HAVE **ART** OUTSIDE, AND IT WAS **AWESOME**!
I'M NOT MR. ROSA.
SHE'S NOT MR. ROSA.
NEWS FLASH.
Peirce

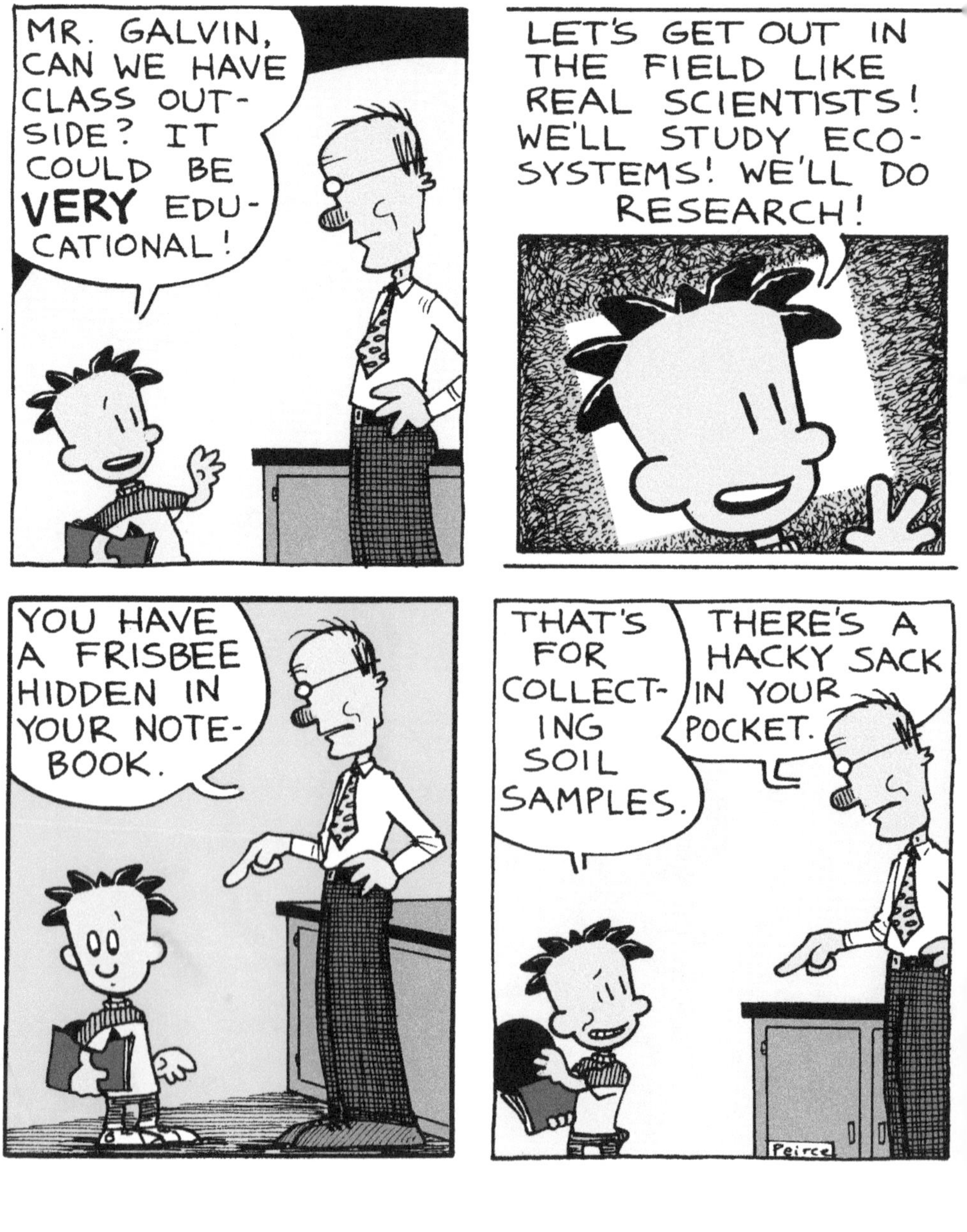
MR. GALVIN, CAN WE HAVE CLASS OUT-SIDE? IT COULD BE **VERY** EDU-CATIONAL!
LET'S GET OUT IN THE FIELD LIKE REAL SCIENTISTS! WE'LL STUDY ECO-SYSTEMS! WE'LL DO RESEARCH!
YOU HAVE A FRISBEE HIDDEN IN YOUR NOTE-BOOK.
THERE'S A HACKY SACK IN YOUR POCKET.
THAT'S FOR COLLECT-ING SOIL SAMPLES.
Peirce

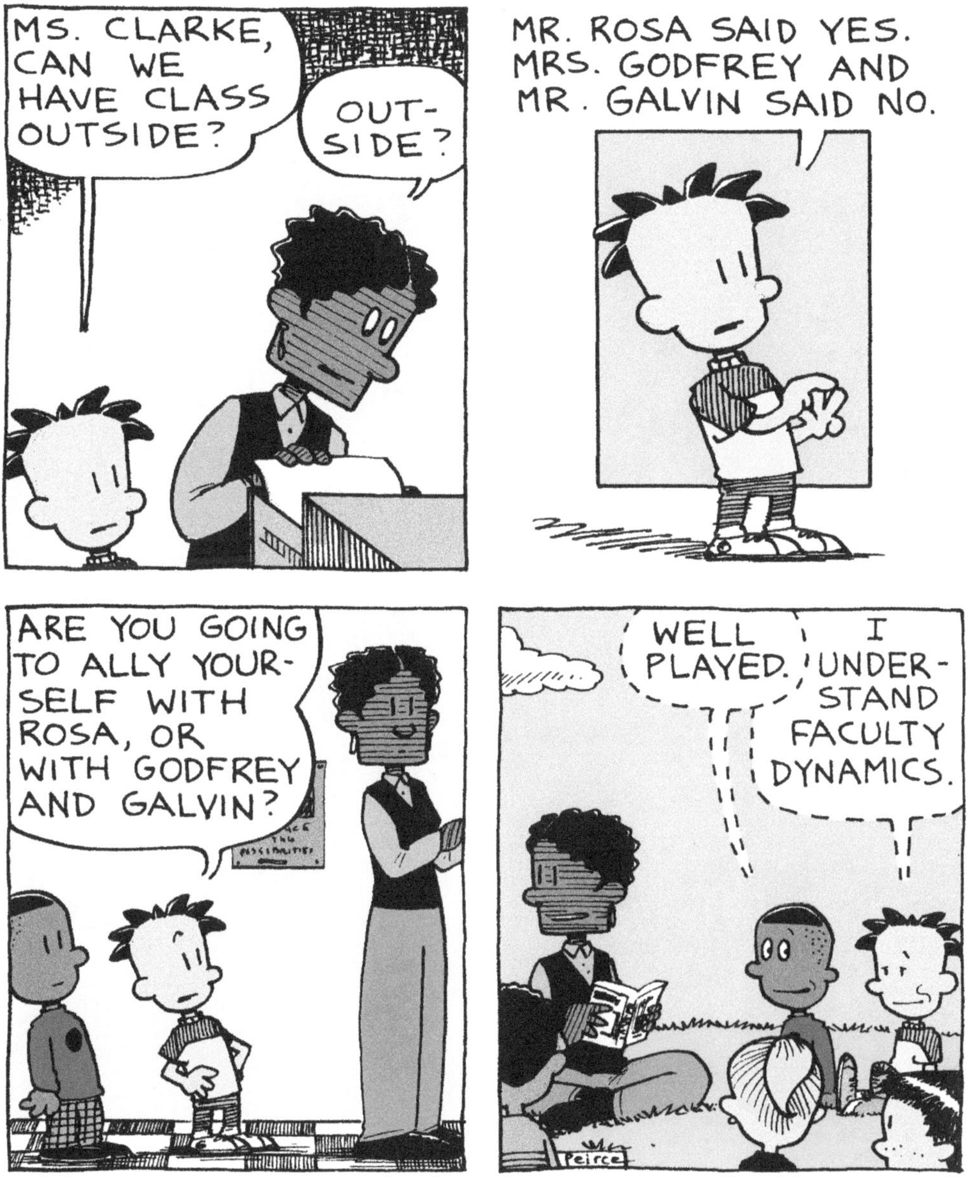
MS. CLARKE, CAN WE HAVE CLASS OUTSIDE?
OUT-SIDE?
MR. ROSA SAID YES. MRS. GODFREY AND MR. GALVIN SAID NO.
ARE YOU GOING TO ALLY YOURSELF WITH ROSA, OR WITH GODFREY AND GALVIN?
WELL PLAYED.
I UNDERSTAND FACULTY DYNAMICS.
Peirce

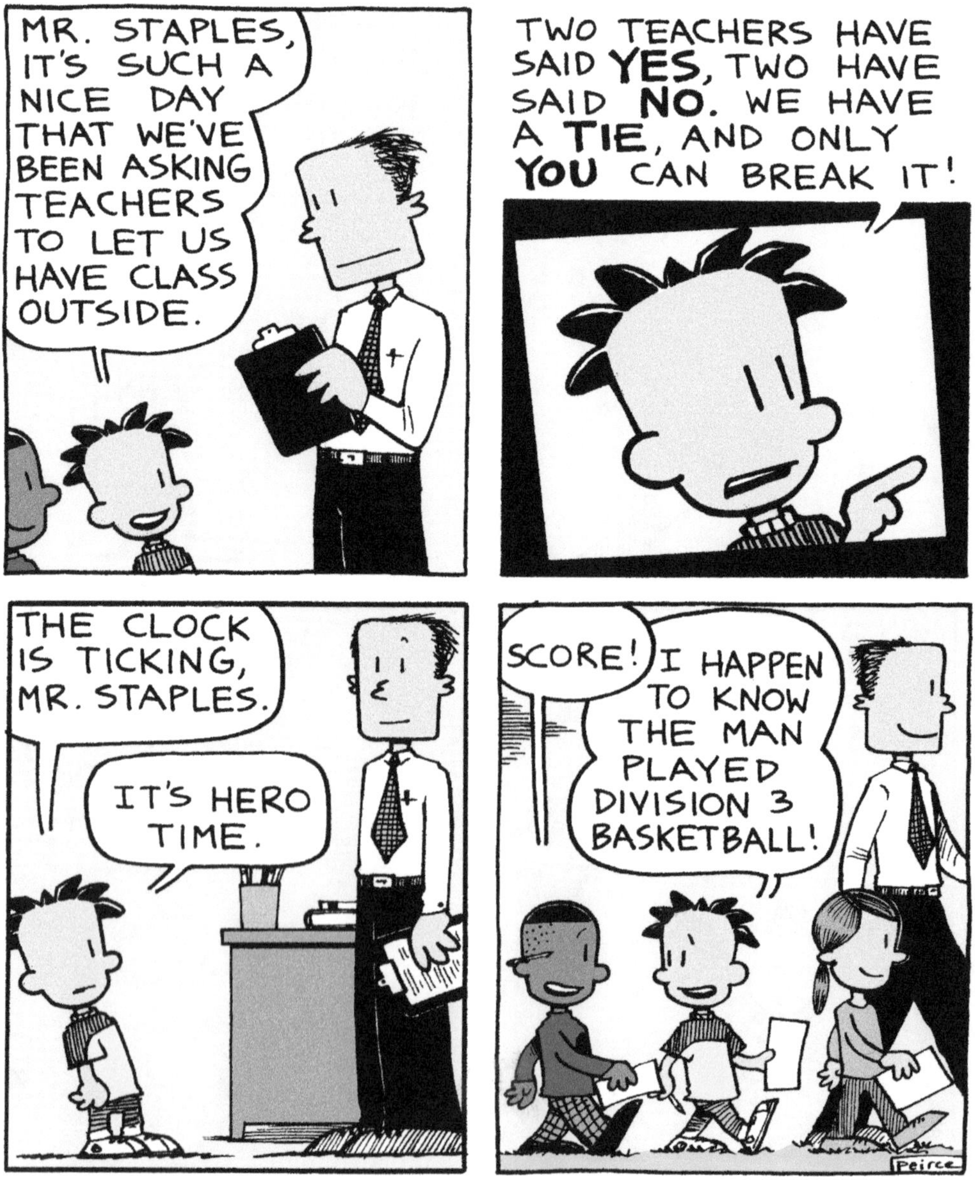
MR. STAPLES, IT'S SUCH A NICE DAY THAT WE'VE BEEN ASKING TEACHERS TO LET US HAVE CLASS OUTSIDE.
TWO TEACHERS HAVE SAID **YES**, TWO HAVE SAID **NO**. WE HAVE A **TIE**, AND ONLY **YOU** CAN BREAK IT!
THE CLOCK IS TICKING, MR. STAPLES.
IT'S HERO TIME.
SCORE!
I HAPPEN TO KNOW THE MAN PLAYED DIVISION 3 BASKETBALL!
Peirce

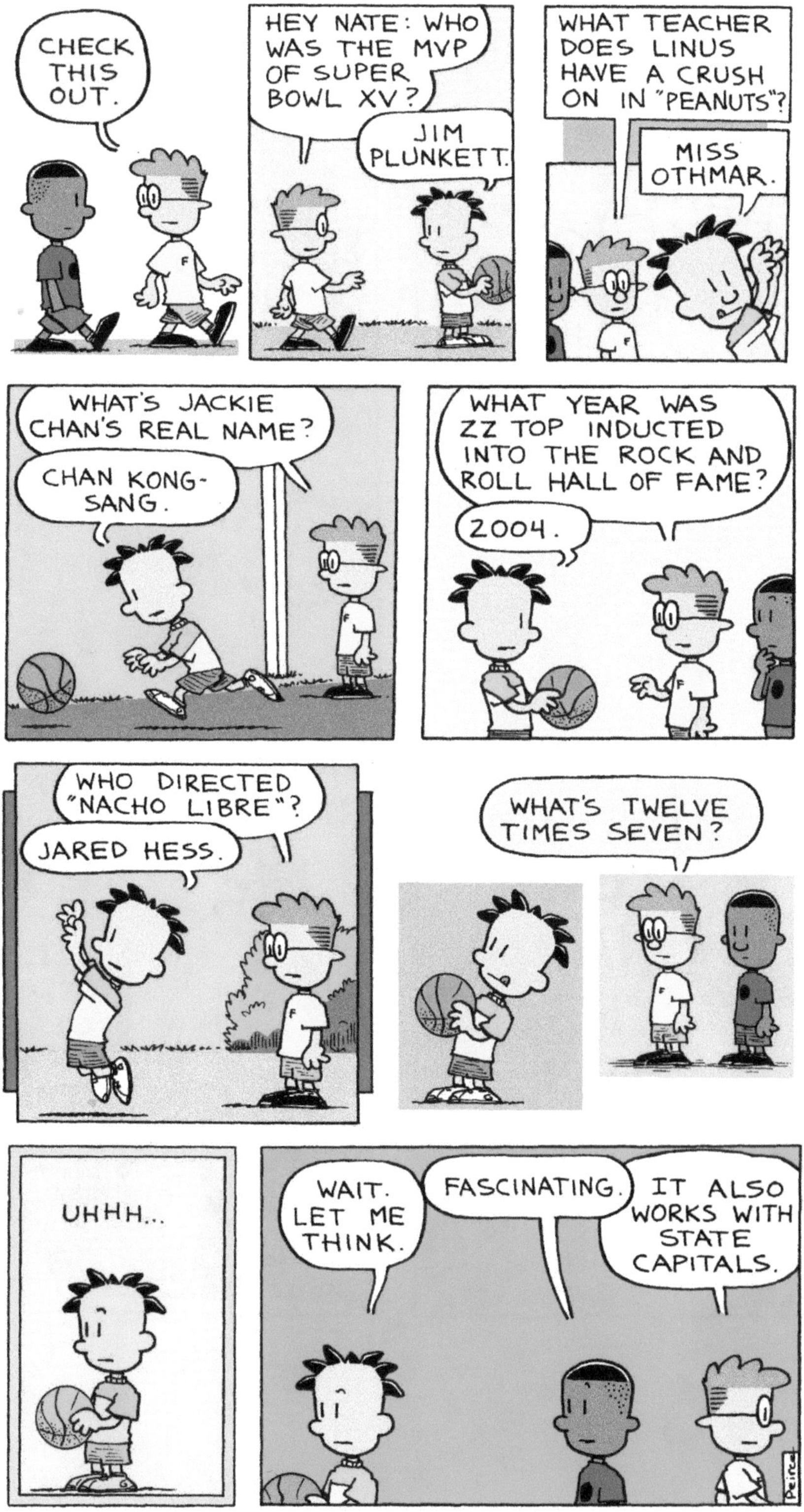

CHECK THIS OUT.
HEY NATE: WHO WAS THE MVP OF SUPER BOWL XV?
JIM PLUNKETT.
WHAT TEACHER DOES LINUS HAVE A CRUSH ON IN "PEANUTS"?
MISS OTHMAR.
WHAT'S JACKIE CHAN'S REAL NAME?
CHAN KONG-SANG.
WHAT YEAR WAS ZZ TOP INDUCTED INTO THE ROCK AND ROLL HALL OF FAME?
2004.
WHO DIRECTED "NACHO LIBRE"?
JARED HESS.
WHAT'S TWELVE TIMES SEVEN?
UHHH...
WAIT. LET ME THINK.
FASCINATING.
IT ALSO WORKS WITH STATE CAPITALS.
Peirce

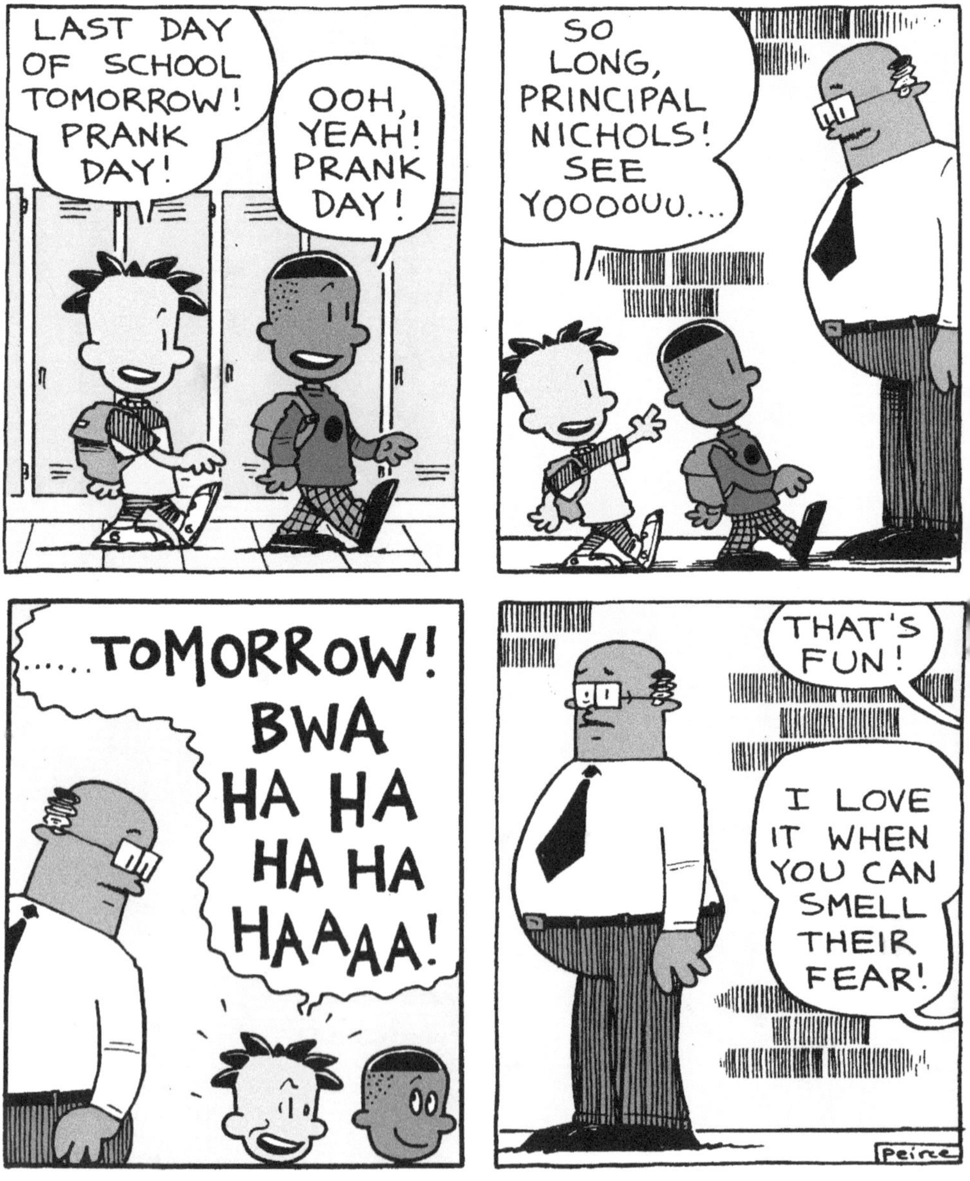
LAST DAY OF SCHOOL TOMORROW! PRANK DAY!
OOH, YEAH! PRANK DAY!
SO LONG, PRINCIPAL NICHOLS! SEE YOOOOUU....
......TOMORROW! BWA HA HA HA HA HAAAAA!
THAT'S FUN!
I LOVE IT WHEN YOU CAN SMELL THEIR FEAR!
Peirce

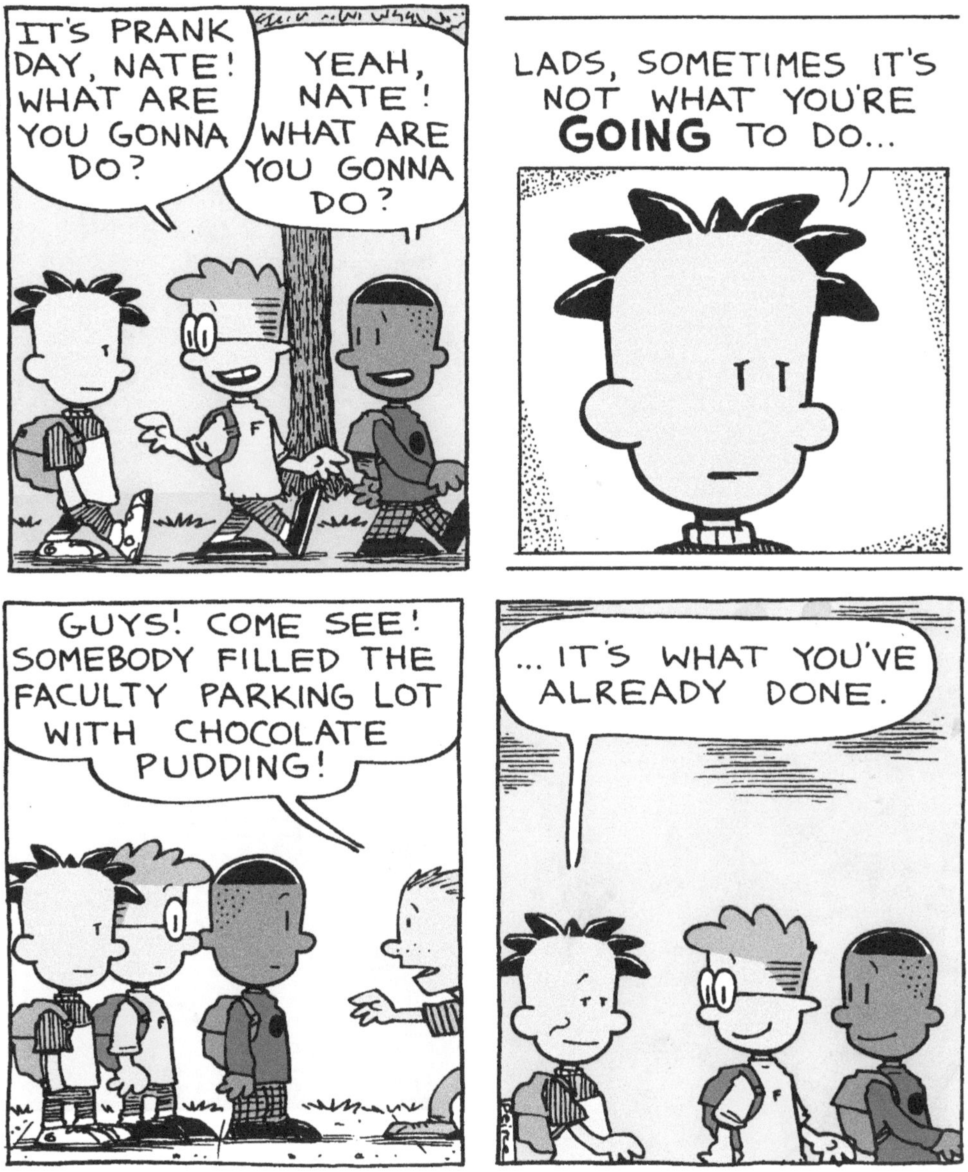
IT'S PRANK DAY, NATE! WHAT ARE YOU GONNA DO?
YEAH, NATE! WHAT ARE YOU GONNA DO?
LADS, SOMETIMES IT'S NOT WHAT YOU'RE **GOING** TO DO...
GUYS! COME SEE! SOMEBODY FILLED THE FACULTY PARKING LOT WITH CHOCOLATE PUDDING!
... IT'S WHAT YOU'VE ALREADY DONE.

ALL RIGHT, PEOPLE, SETTLE DOWN! THERE WILL BE NO "PRANK DAY" SHENANIGANS IN THIS ROOM!
WE STILL HAVE ONE FINAL CLASS TO GET THROUGH, AND...
DELIVERY.
WHAT?
THE "THIGHMASTER" YOU ORDERED, MA'AM.
HA HA HA HA
CRIPES.
HI, KIDS.
HA HA
HA HA
Peirce

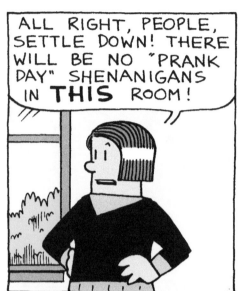

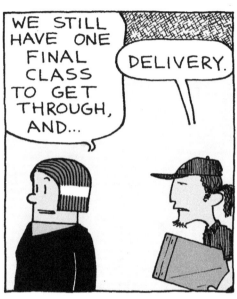

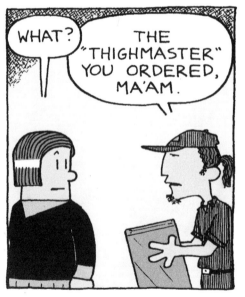

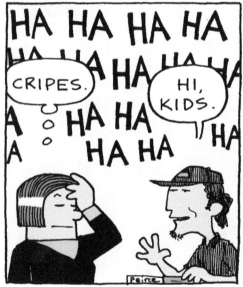

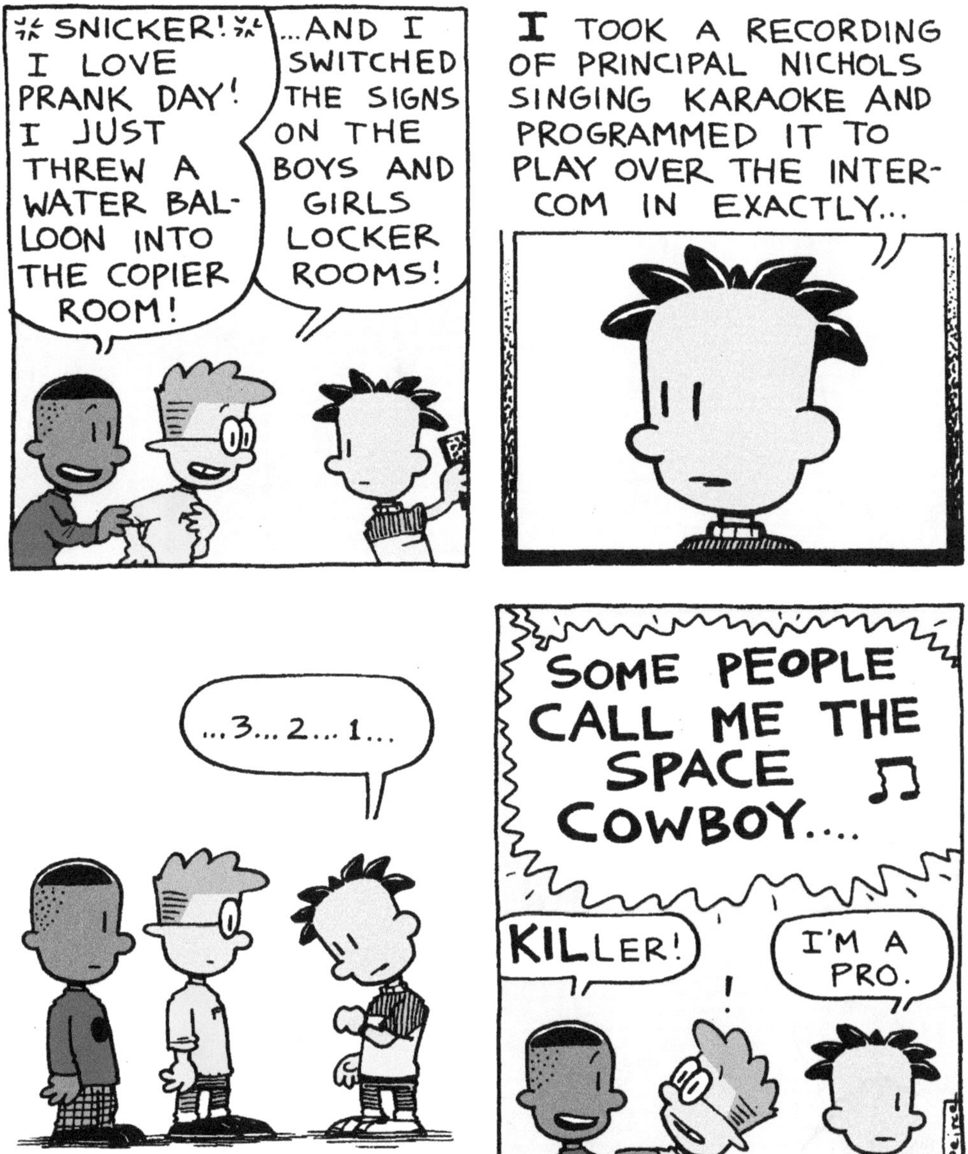
SNICKER! I LOVE PRANK DAY! I JUST THREW A WATER BALLOON INTO THE COPIER ROOM!
...AND I SWITCHED THE SIGNS ON THE BOYS AND GIRLS LOCKER ROOMS!
I TOOK A RECORDING OF PRINCIPAL NICHOLS SINGING KARAOKE AND PROGRAMMED IT TO PLAY OVER THE INTERCOM IN EXACTLY...
...3... 2... 1...
SOME PEOPLE CALL ME THE SPACE COWBOY....
KILLER!
!
I'M A PRO.
Peirce

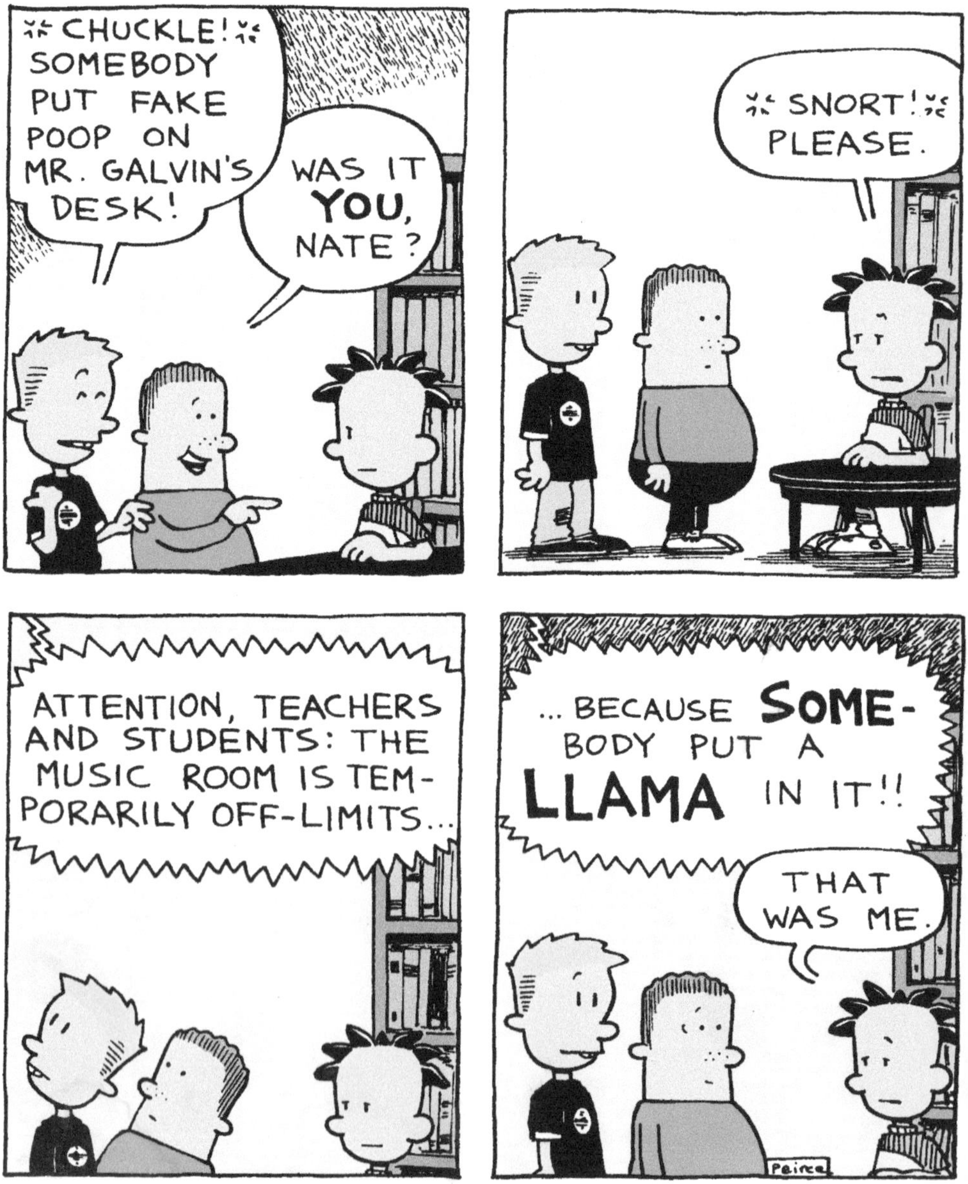

CHUCKLE!
SOMEBODY PUT FAKE POOP ON MR. GALVIN'S DESK!
WAS IT **YOU**, NATE?
SNORT! PLEASE.
ATTENTION, TEACHERS AND STUDENTS: THE MUSIC ROOM IS TEMPORARILY OFF-LIMITS...
...BECAUSE **SOMEBODY** PUT A **LLAMA** IN IT!!
THAT WAS ME.
Peirce

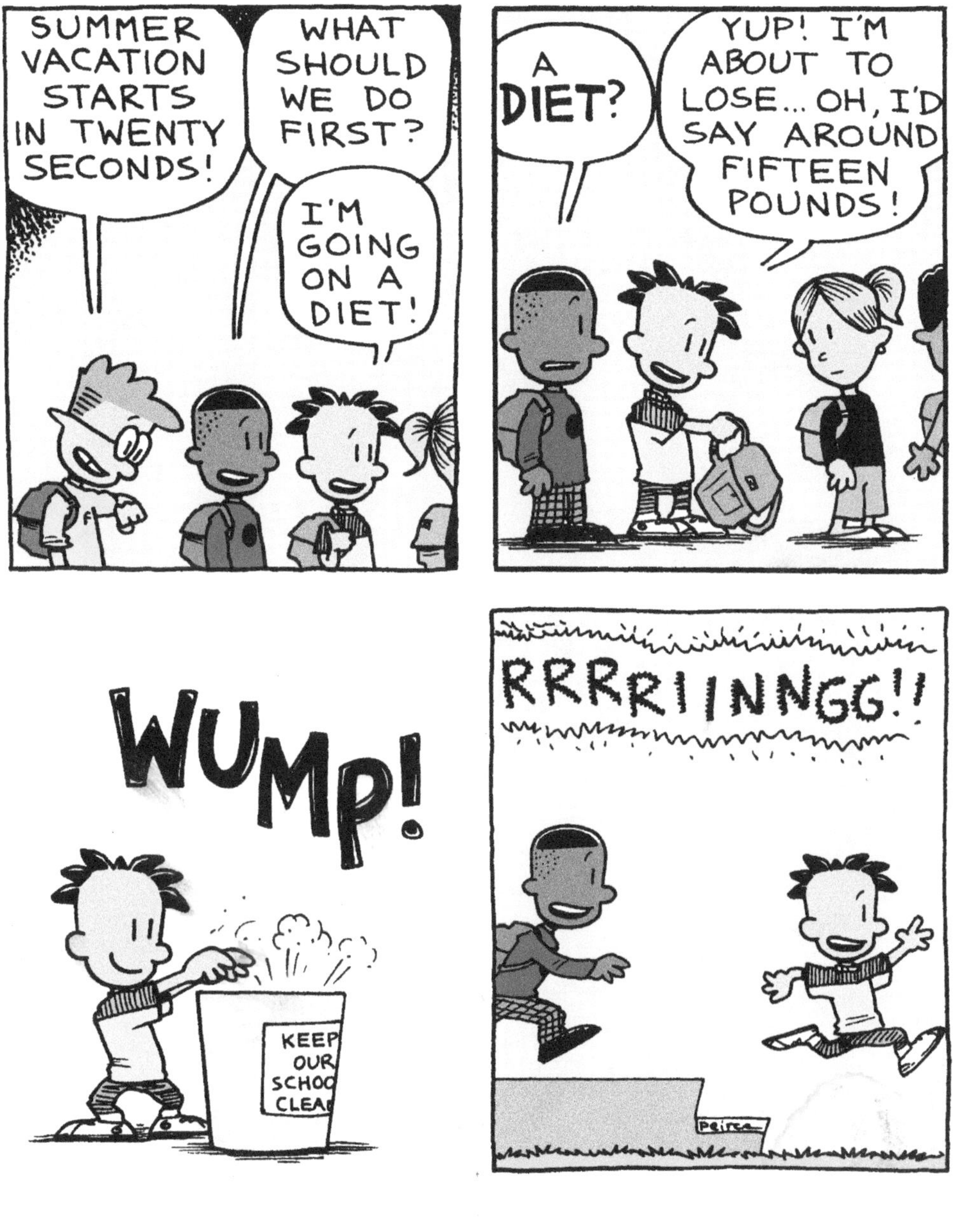
SUMMER VACATION STARTS IN TWENTY SECONDS!
WHAT SHOULD WE DO FIRST?
I'M GOING ON A DIET!
A DIET?
YUP! I'M ABOUT TO LOSE... OH, I'D SAY AROUND FIFTEEN POUNDS!
WUMP!
KEEP OUR SCHOO CLEA
RRRRIINNGG!!
Peirce

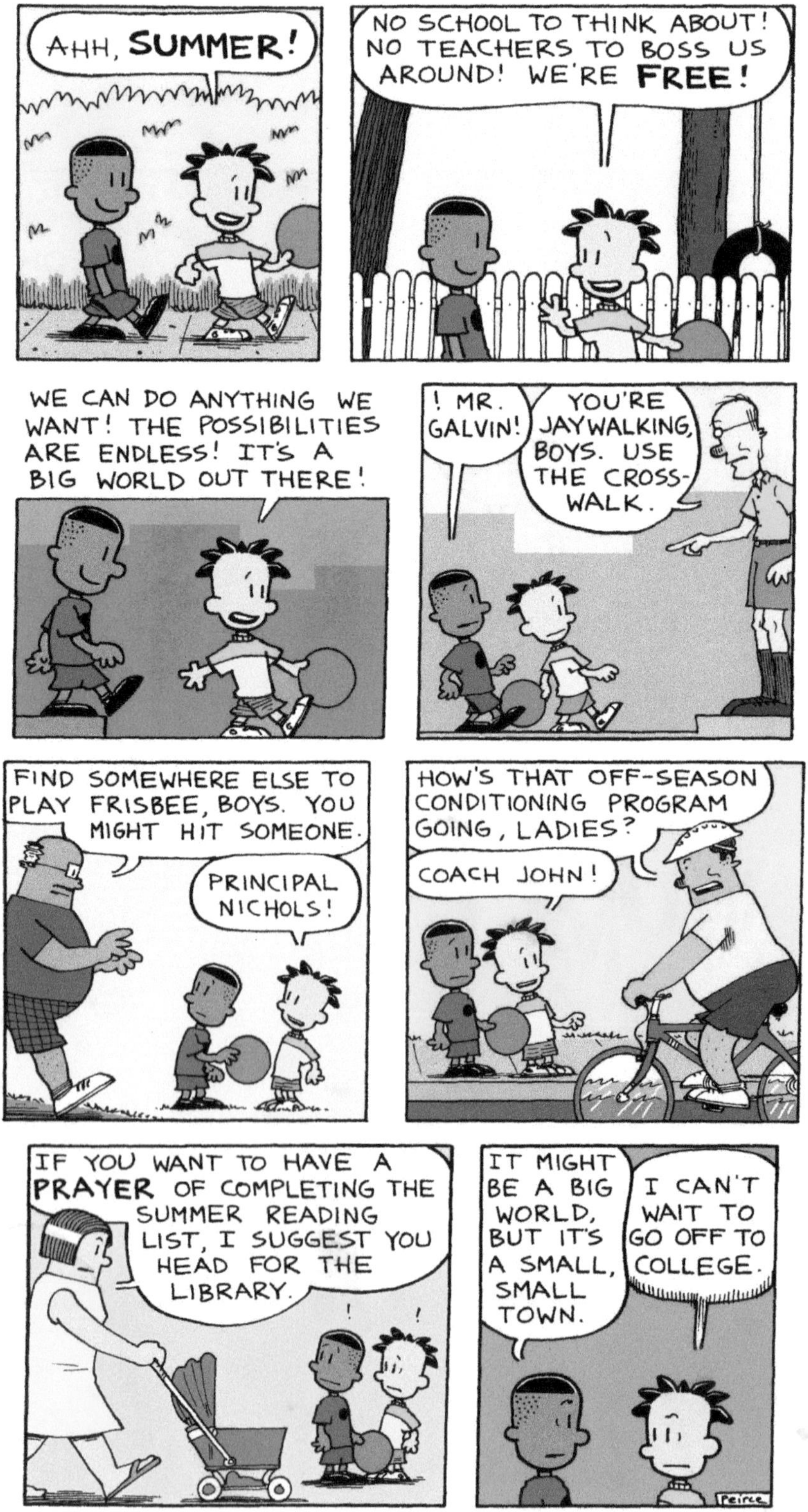
AHH, SUMMER!
NO SCHOOL TO THINK ABOUT! NO TEACHERS TO BOSS US AROUND! WE'RE FREE!
WE CAN DO ANYTHING WE WANT! THE POSSIBILITIES ARE ENDLESS! IT'S A BIG WORLD OUT THERE!
! MR. GALVIN!
YOU'RE JAYWALKING, BOYS. USE THE CROSS-WALK.
FIND SOMEWHERE ELSE TO PLAY FRISBEE, BOYS. YOU MIGHT HIT SOMEONE.
PRINCIPAL NICHOLS!
HOW'S THAT OFF-SEASON CONDITIONING PROGRAM GOING, LADIES?
COACH JOHN!
IF YOU WANT TO HAVE A PRAYER OF COMPLETING THE SUMMER READING LIST, I SUGGEST YOU HEAD FOR THE LIBRARY.
!
!
IT MIGHT BE A BIG WORLD, BUT IT'S A SMALL, SMALL TOWN.
I CAN'T WAIT TO GO OFF TO COLLEGE.
Peirce

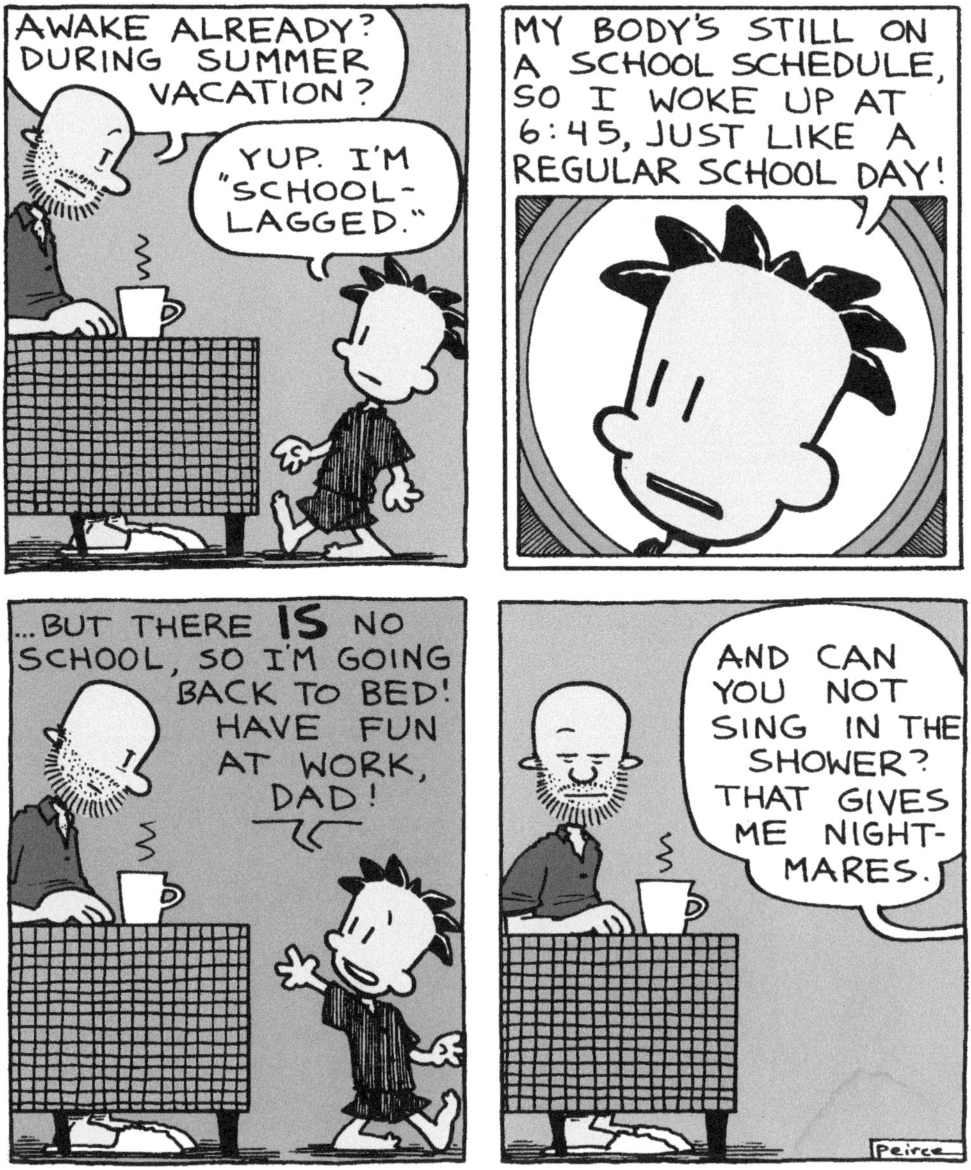
AWAKE ALREADY? DURING SUMMER VACATION?
YUP. I'M "SCHOOL-LAGGED."
MY BODY'S STILL ON A SCHOOL SCHEDULE, SO I WOKE UP AT 6:45, JUST LIKE A REGULAR SCHOOL DAY!
...BUT THERE IS NO SCHOOL, SO I'M GOING BACK TO BED! HAVE FUN AT WORK, DAD!
AND CAN YOU NOT SING IN THE SHOWER? THAT GIVES ME NIGHT-MARES.
Peirce

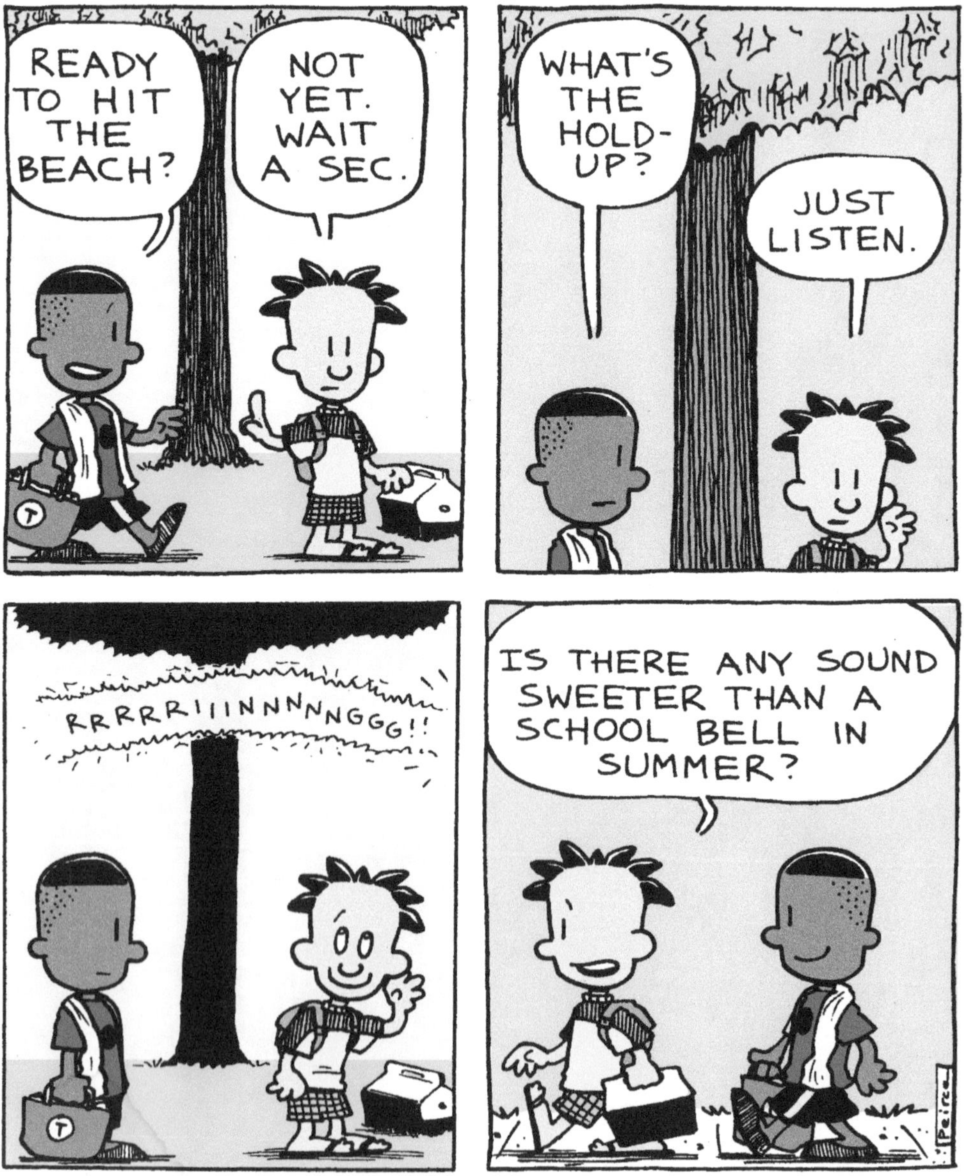
READY TO HIT THE BEACH?
NOT YET. WAIT A SEC.
WHAT'S THE HOLD-UP?
JUST LISTEN.
RRRRRIIIINNNNNNGGGG!!
IS THERE ANY SOUND SWEETER THAN A SCHOOL BELL IN SUMMER?
Peirce

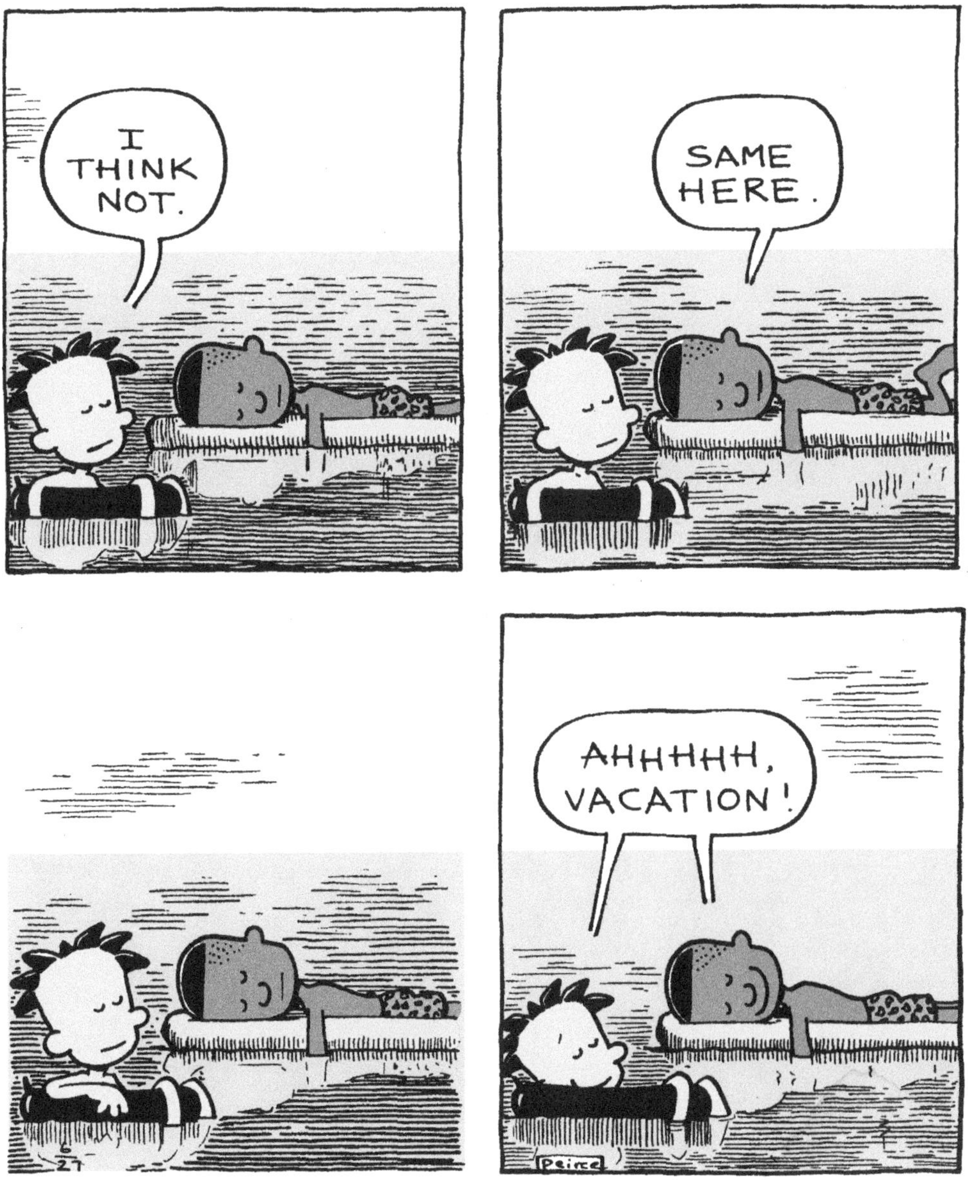
I THINK NOT.
SAME HERE.
AHHHHH, VACATION!

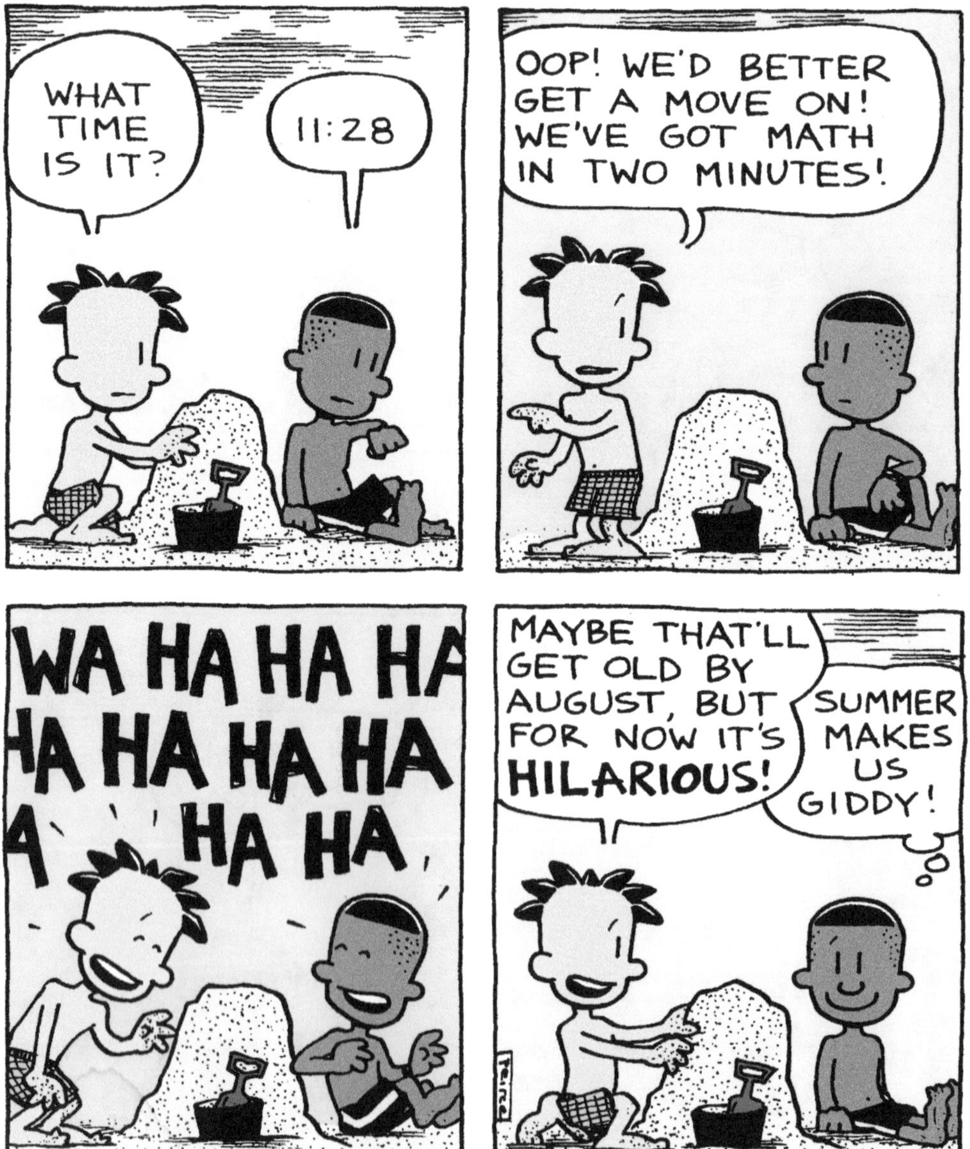
WHAT TIME IS IT?
11:28
OOP! WE'D BETTER GET A MOVE ON! WE'VE GOT MATH IN TWO MINUTES!
WA HA HA HA HA HA HA HA HA A HA HA
MAYBE THAT'LL GET OLD BY AUGUST, BUT FOR NOW IT'S **HILARIOUS!**
SUMMER MAKES US GIDDY!

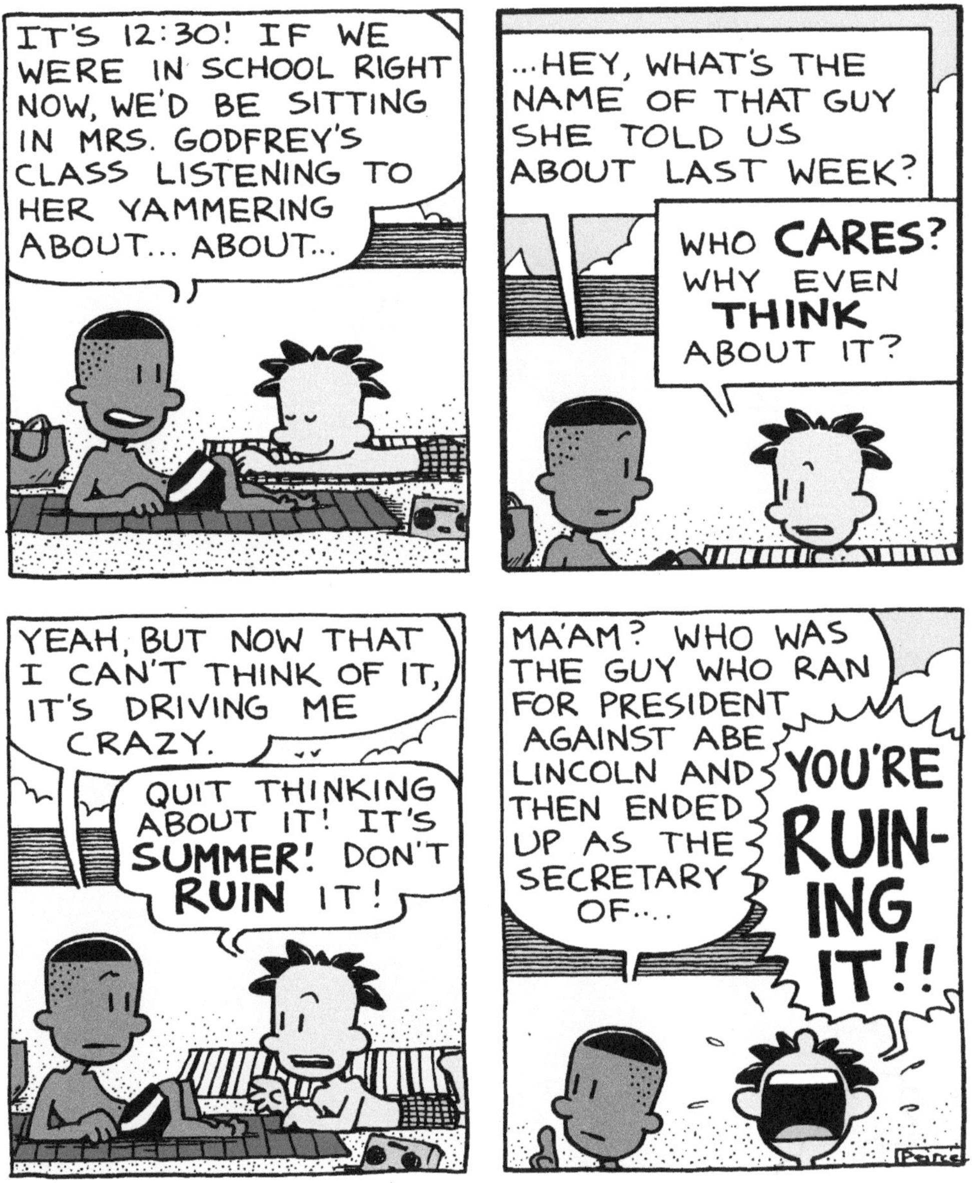
IT'S 12:30! IF WE WERE IN SCHOOL RIGHT NOW, WE'D BE SITTING IN MRS. GODFREY'S CLASS LISTENING TO HER YAMMERING ABOUT... ABOUT...
...HEY, WHAT'S THE NAME OF THAT GUY SHE TOLD US ABOUT LAST WEEK?
WHO CARES? WHY EVEN THINK ABOUT IT?
YEAH, BUT NOW THAT I CAN'T THINK OF IT, IT'S DRIVING ME CRAZY.
QUIT THINKING ABOUT IT! IT'S SUMMER! DON'T RUIN IT!
MA'AM? WHO WAS THE GUY WHO RAN FOR PRESIDENT AGAINST ABE LINCOLN AND THEN ENDED UP AS THE SECRETARY OF...
YOU'RE RUIN-ING IT!!

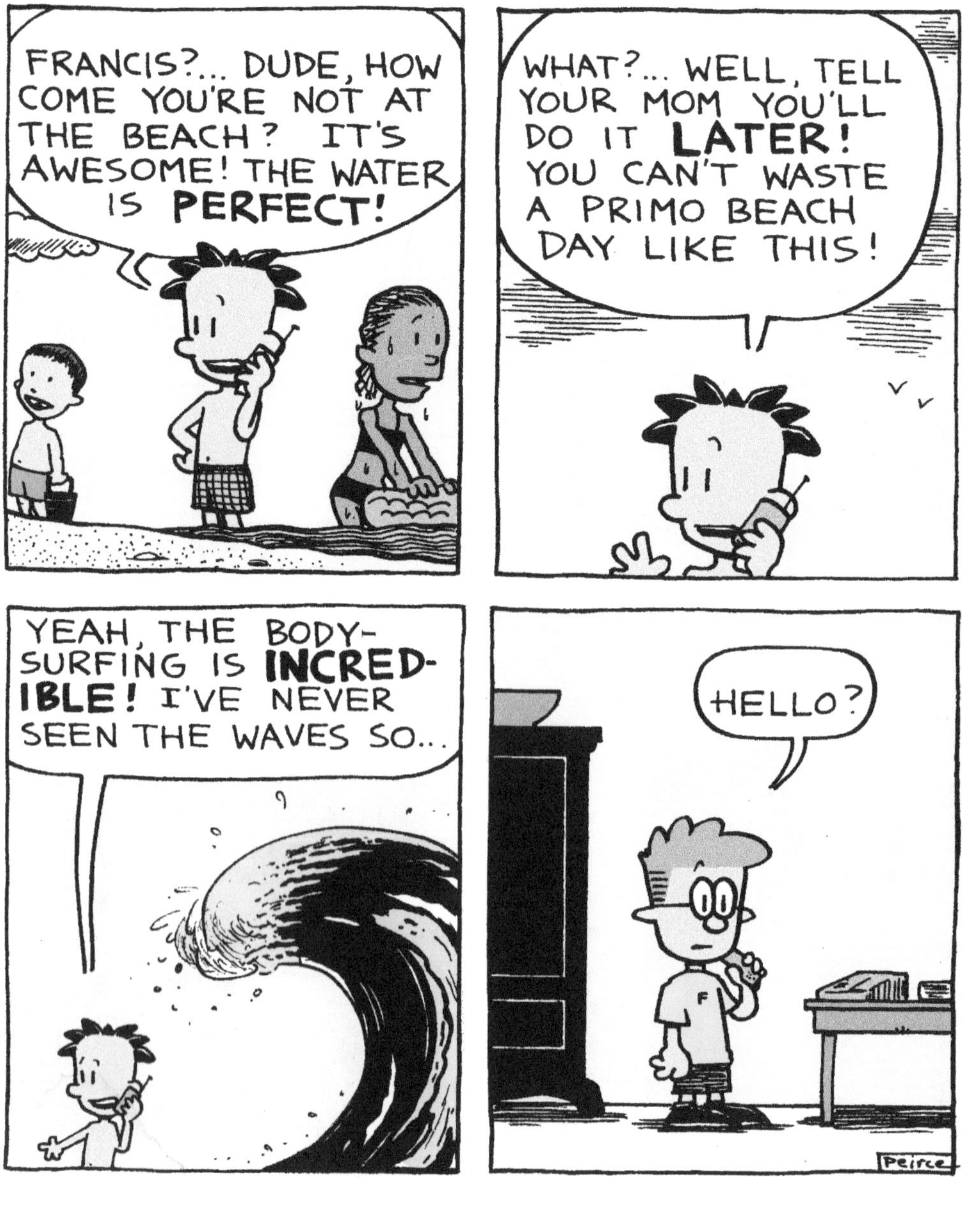
FRANCIS?... DUDE, HOW COME YOU'RE NOT AT THE BEACH? IT'S AWESOME! THE WATER IS PERFECT!
WHAT?... WELL, TELL YOUR MOM YOU'LL DO IT LATER! YOU CAN'T WASTE A PRIMO BEACH DAY LIKE THIS!
YEAH, THE BODY-SURFING IS INCRED-IBLE! I'VE NEVER SEEN THE WAVES SO...
HELLO?
Peirce

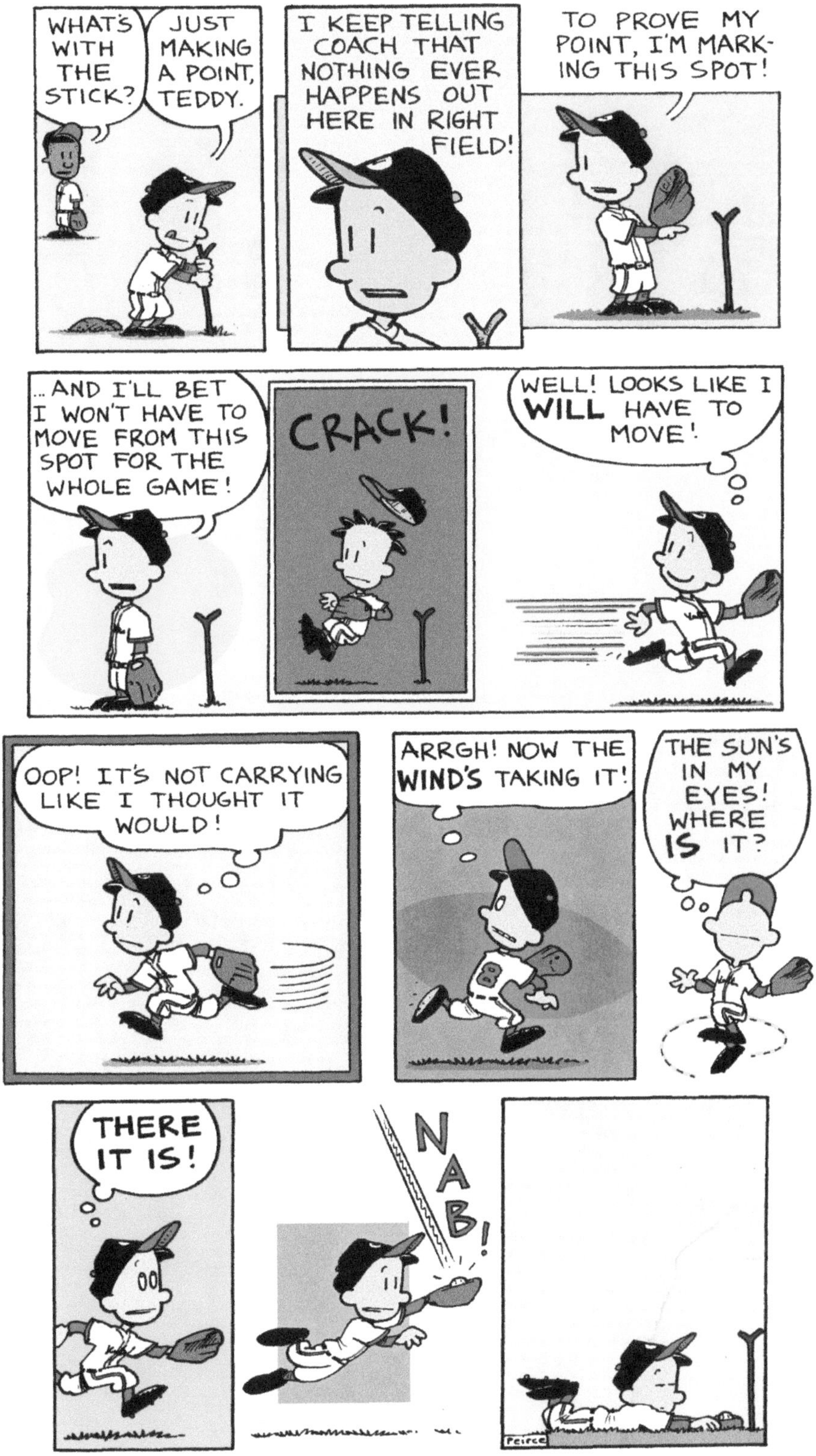
WHAT'S WITH THE STICK?
JUST MAKING A POINT, TEDDY.
I KEEP TELLING COACH THAT NOTHING EVER HAPPENS OUT HERE IN RIGHT FIELD!
TO PROVE MY POINT, I'M MARKING THIS SPOT!
... AND I'LL BET I WON'T HAVE TO MOVE FROM THIS SPOT FOR THE WHOLE GAME!
CRACK!
WELL! LOOKS LIKE I WILL HAVE TO MOVE!
OOP! IT'S NOT CARRYING LIKE I THOUGHT IT WOULD!
ARRGH! NOW THE WIND'S TAKING IT!
THE SUN'S IN MY EYES! WHERE IS IT?
THERE IT IS!
NAB!
PEIRCE

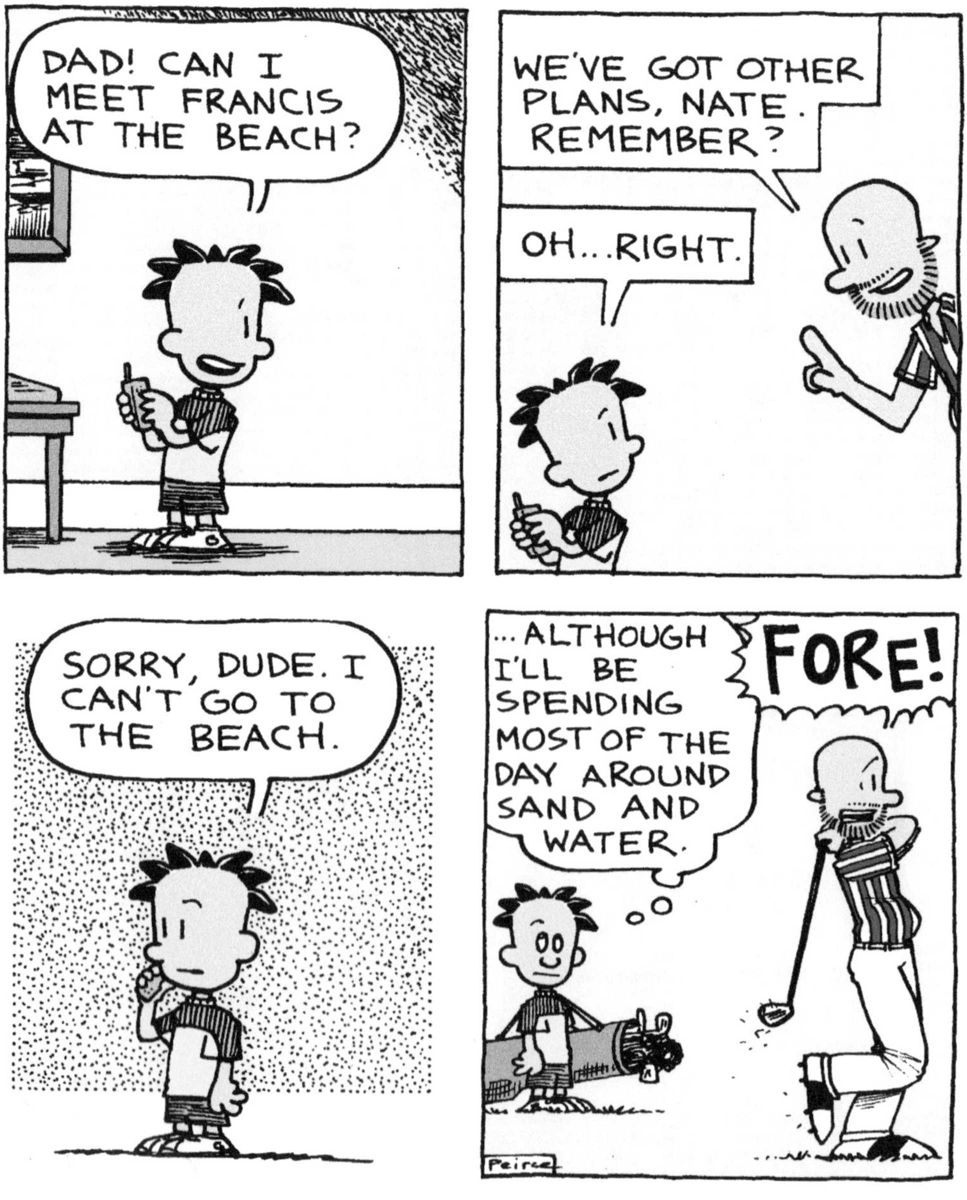
DAD! CAN I MEET FRANCIS AT THE BEACH?
WE'VE GOT OTHER PLANS, NATE. REMEMBER?
OH...RIGHT.
SORRY, DUDE. I CAN'T GO TO THE BEACH.
...ALTHOUGH I'LL BE SPENDING MOST OF THE DAY AROUND SAND AND WATER.
FORE!
Peirce

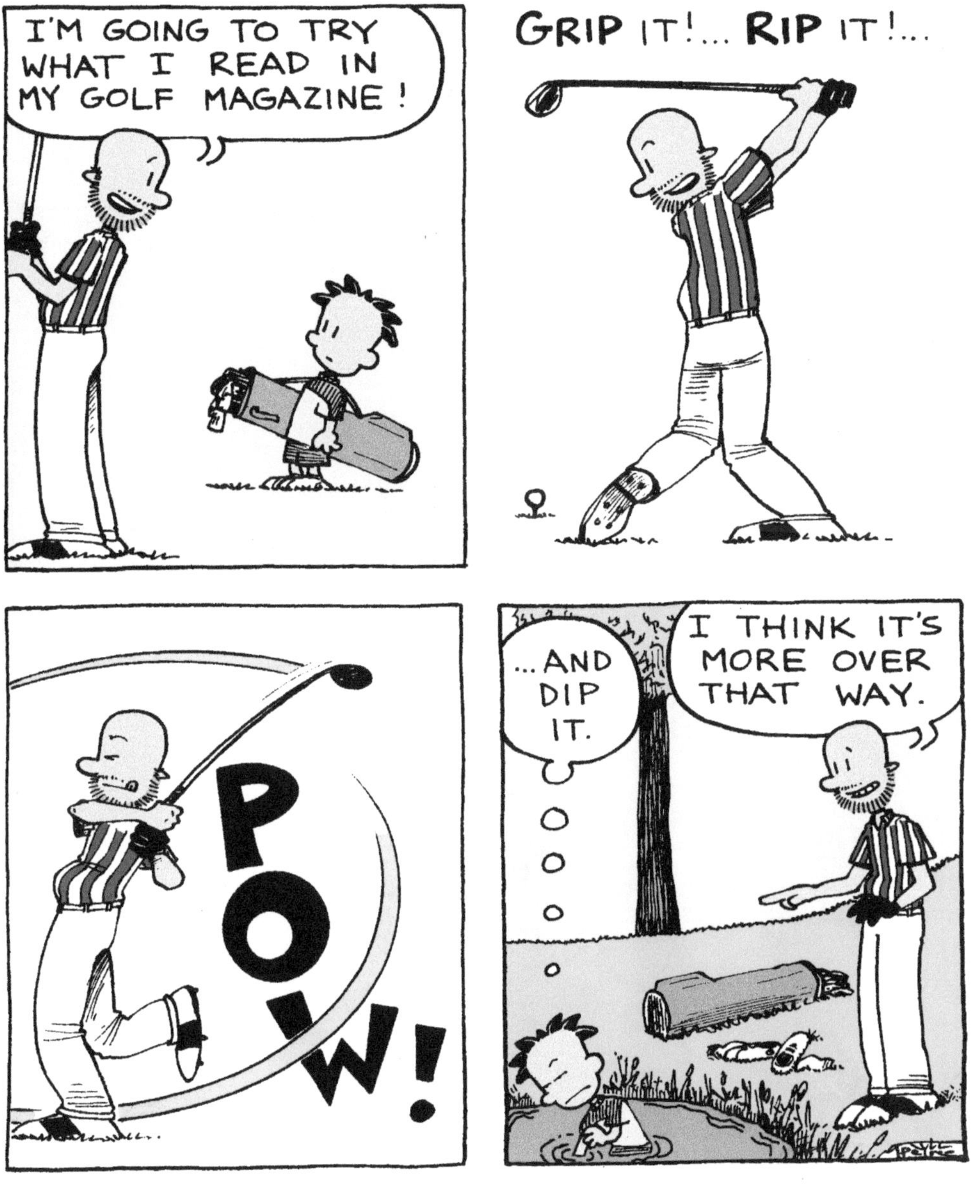
I'M GOING TO TRY WHAT I READ IN MY GOLF MAGAZINE!
GRIP IT!... RIP IT!...
POW!
...AND DIP IT.
I THINK IT'S MORE OVER THAT WAY.

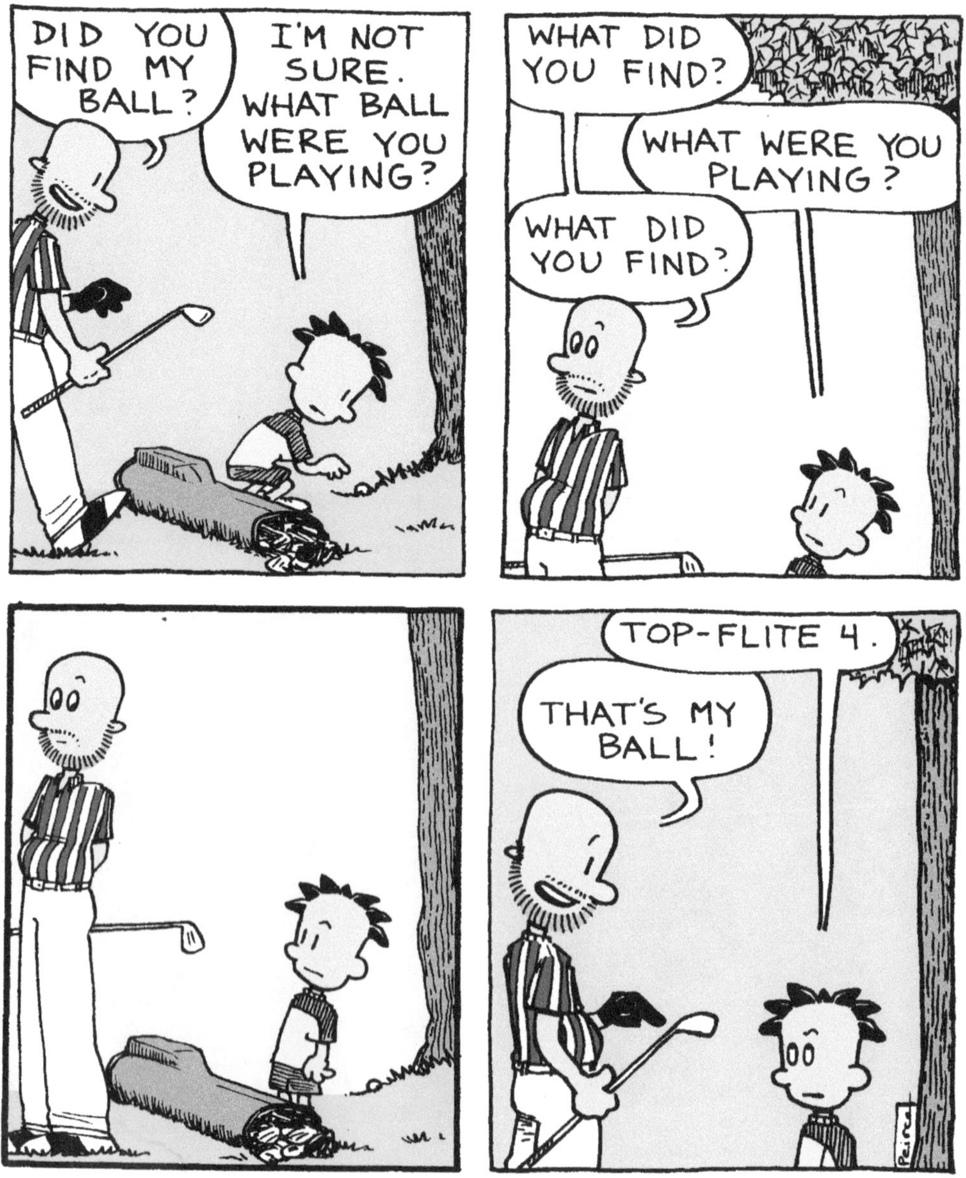
DID YOU FIND MY BALL?
I'M NOT SURE. WHAT BALL WERE YOU PLAYING?
WHAT DID YOU FIND?
WHAT WERE YOU PLAYING?
WHAT DID YOU FIND?
TOP-FLITE 4.
THAT'S MY BALL!

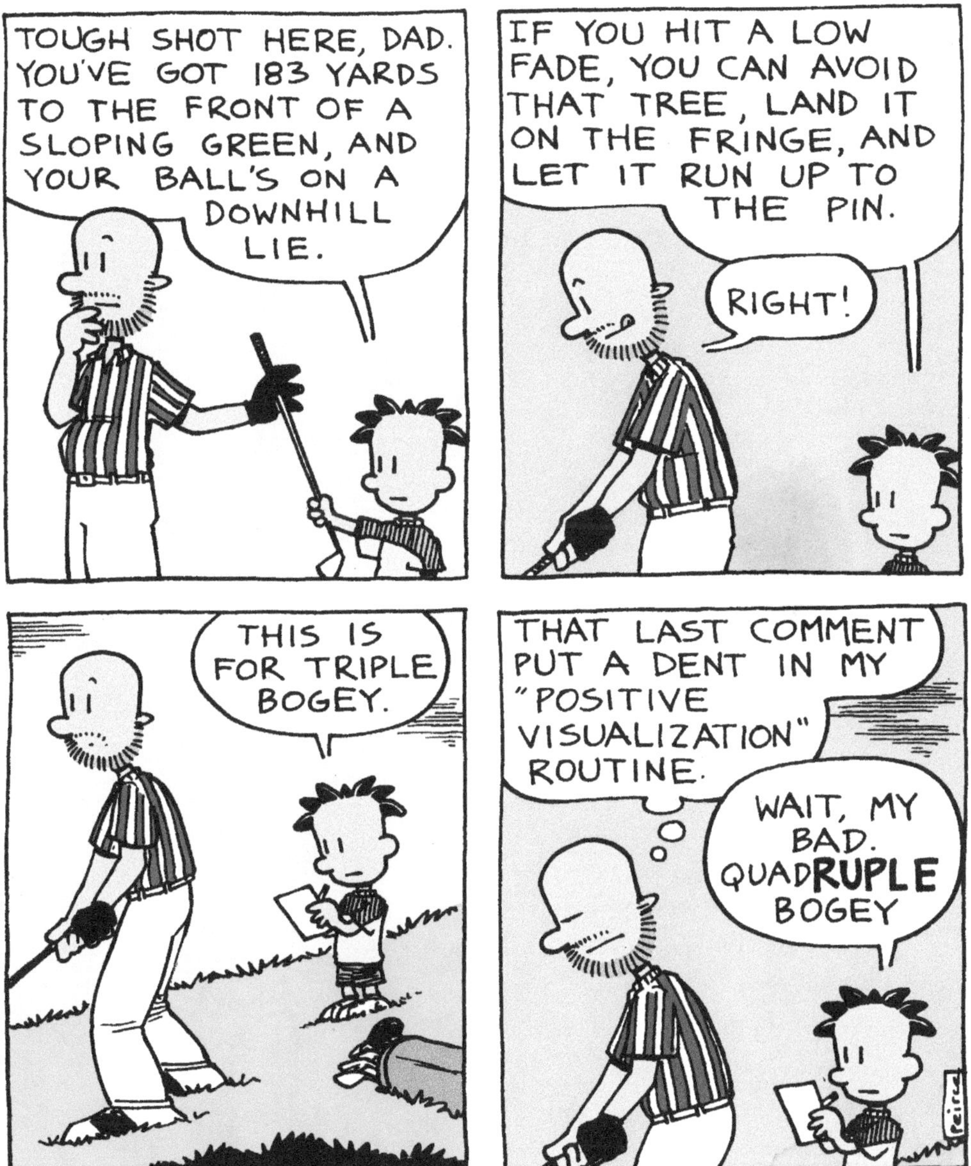
TOUGH SHOT HERE, DAD. YOU'VE GOT 183 YARDS TO THE FRONT OF A SLOPING GREEN, AND YOUR BALL'S ON A DOWNHILL LIE.
IF YOU HIT A LOW FADE, YOU CAN AVOID THAT TREE, LAND IT ON THE FRINGE, AND LET IT RUN UP TO THE PIN.
RIGHT!
THIS IS FOR TRIPLE BOGEY.
THAT LAST COMMENT PUT A DENT IN MY "POSITIVE VISUALIZATION" ROUTINE.
WAIT, MY BAD. QUADRUPLE BOGEY
PEIRCE

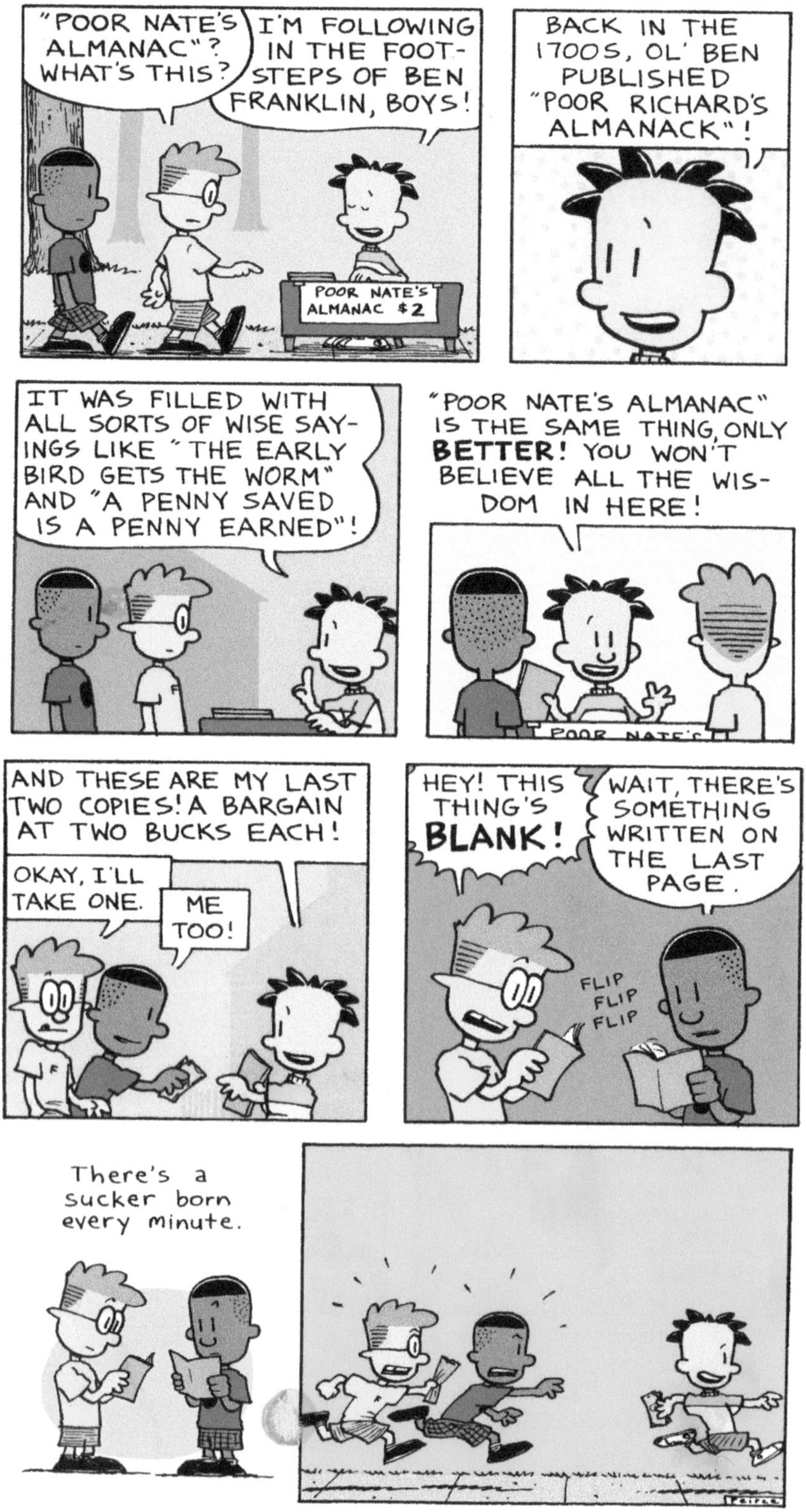
"POOR NATE'S ALMANAC"? WHAT'S THIS?
I'M FOLLOWING IN THE FOOTSTEPS OF BEN FRANKLIN, BOYS!
POOR NATE'S ALMANAC $2
BACK IN THE 1700S, OL' BEN PUBLISHED "POOR RICHARD'S ALMANACK"!
IT WAS FILLED WITH ALL SORTS OF WISE SAYINGS LIKE "THE EARLY BIRD GETS THE WORM" AND "A PENNY SAVED IS A PENNY EARNED"!
"POOR NATE'S ALMANAC" IS THE SAME THING, ONLY BETTER! YOU WON'T BELIEVE ALL THE WISDOM IN HERE!
AND THESE ARE MY LAST TWO COPIES! A BARGAIN AT TWO BUCKS EACH!
OKAY, I'LL TAKE ONE.
ME TOO!
HEY! THIS THING'S BLANK!
WAIT, THERE'S SOMETHING WRITTEN ON THE LAST PAGE.
FLIP FLIP FLIP
There's a sucker born every minute.

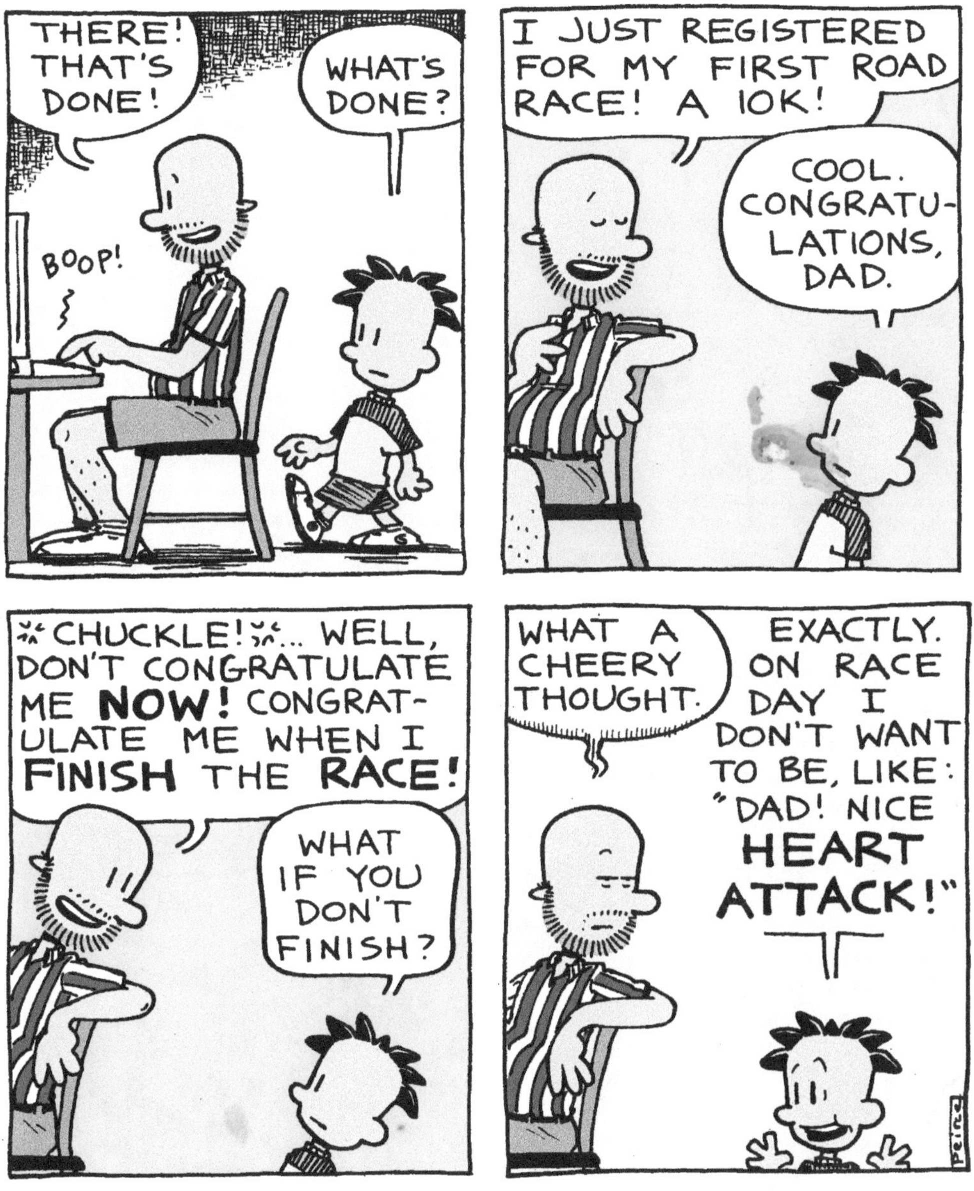
THERE! THAT'S DONE!
WHAT'S DONE?
BOOP!
I JUST REGISTERED FOR MY FIRST ROAD RACE! A 10K!
COOL. CONGRATU-LATIONS, DAD.
CHUCKLE!... WELL, DON'T CONGRATULATE ME NOW! CONGRAT-ULATE ME WHEN I FINISH THE RACE!
WHAT IF YOU DON'T FINISH?
WHAT A CHEERY THOUGHT.
EXACTLY. ON RACE DAY I DON'T WANT TO BE, LIKE: "DAD! NICE HEART ATTACK!"
PEIRCE

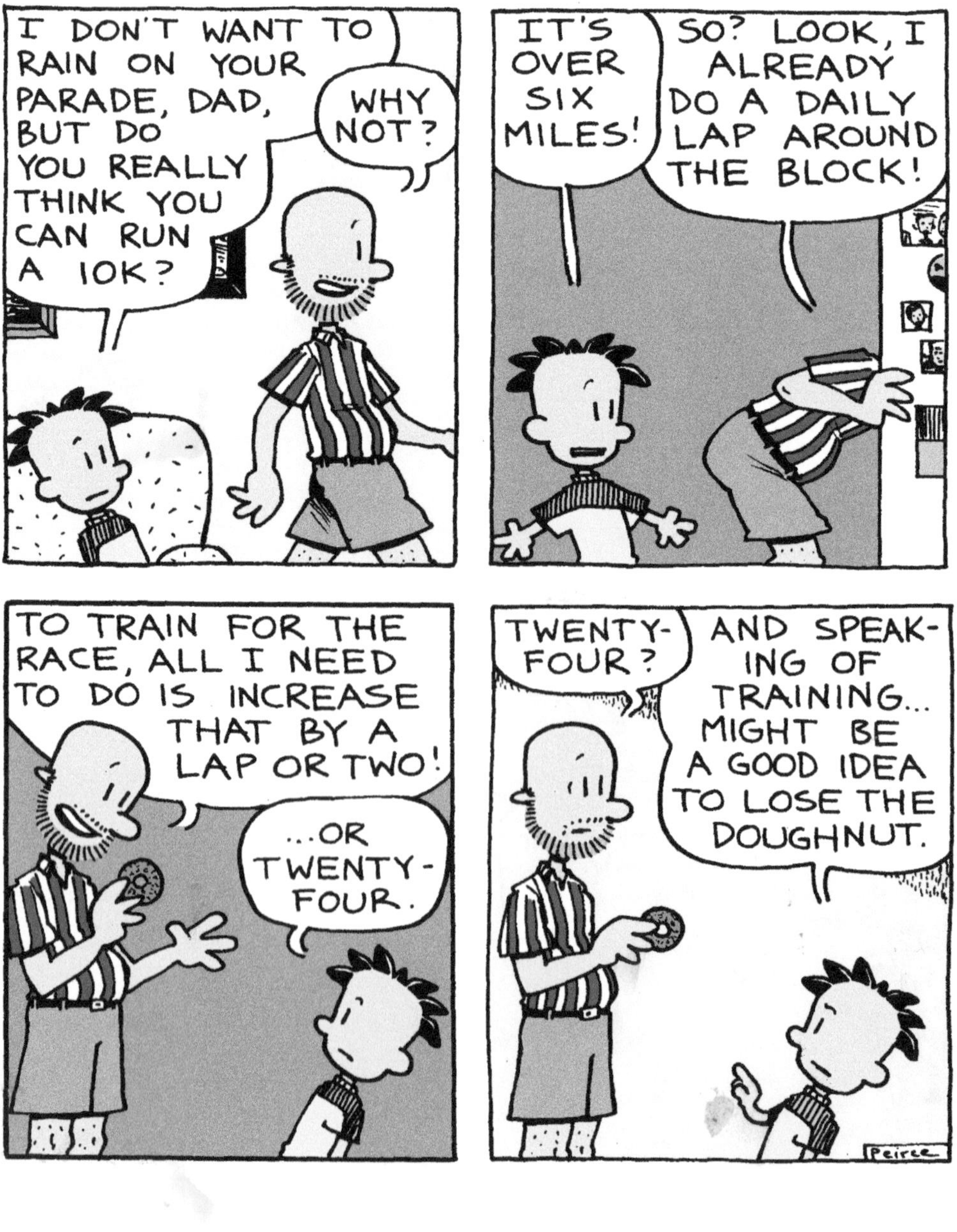
I DON'T WANT TO RAIN ON YOUR PARADE, DAD, BUT DO YOU REALLY THINK YOU CAN RUN A 10K?
WHY NOT?
IT'S OVER SIX MILES!
SO? LOOK, I ALREADY DO A DAILY LAP AROUND THE BLOCK!
TO TRAIN FOR THE RACE, ALL I NEED TO DO IS INCREASE THAT BY A LAP OR TWO!
...OR TWENTY-FOUR.
TWENTY-FOUR?
AND SPEAKING OF TRAINING... MIGHT BE A GOOD IDEA TO LOSE THE DOUGHNUT.
Peirce

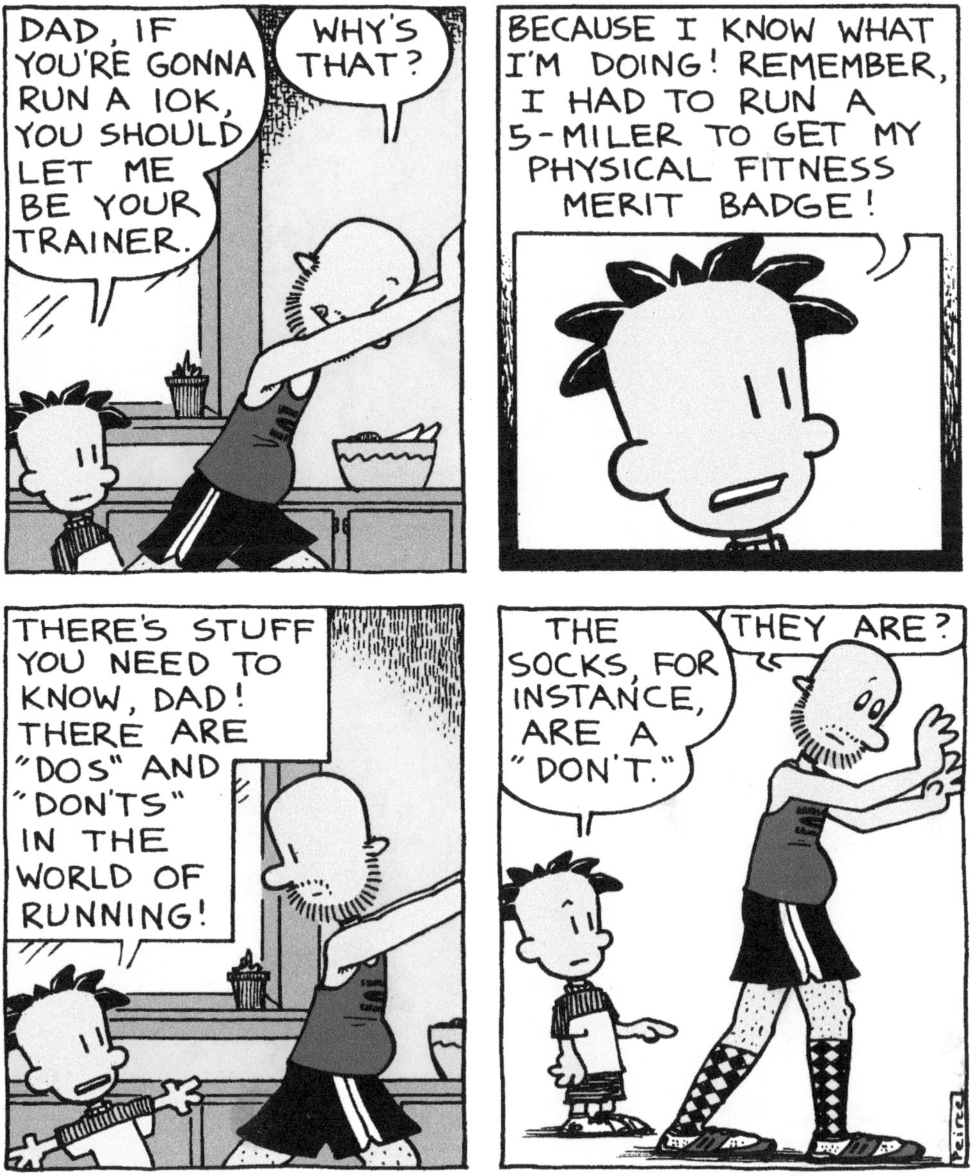
DAD, IF YOU'RE GONNA RUN A 10K, YOU SHOULD LET ME BE YOUR TRAINER.
WHY'S THAT?
BECAUSE I KNOW WHAT I'M DOING! REMEMBER, I HAD TO RUN A 5-MILER TO GET MY PHYSICAL FITNESS MERIT BADGE!
THERE'S STUFF YOU NEED TO KNOW, DAD! THERE ARE "DOS" AND "DON'TS" IN THE WORLD OF RUNNING!
THE SOCKS, FOR INSTANCE, ARE A "DON'T."
THEY ARE?
Peirce

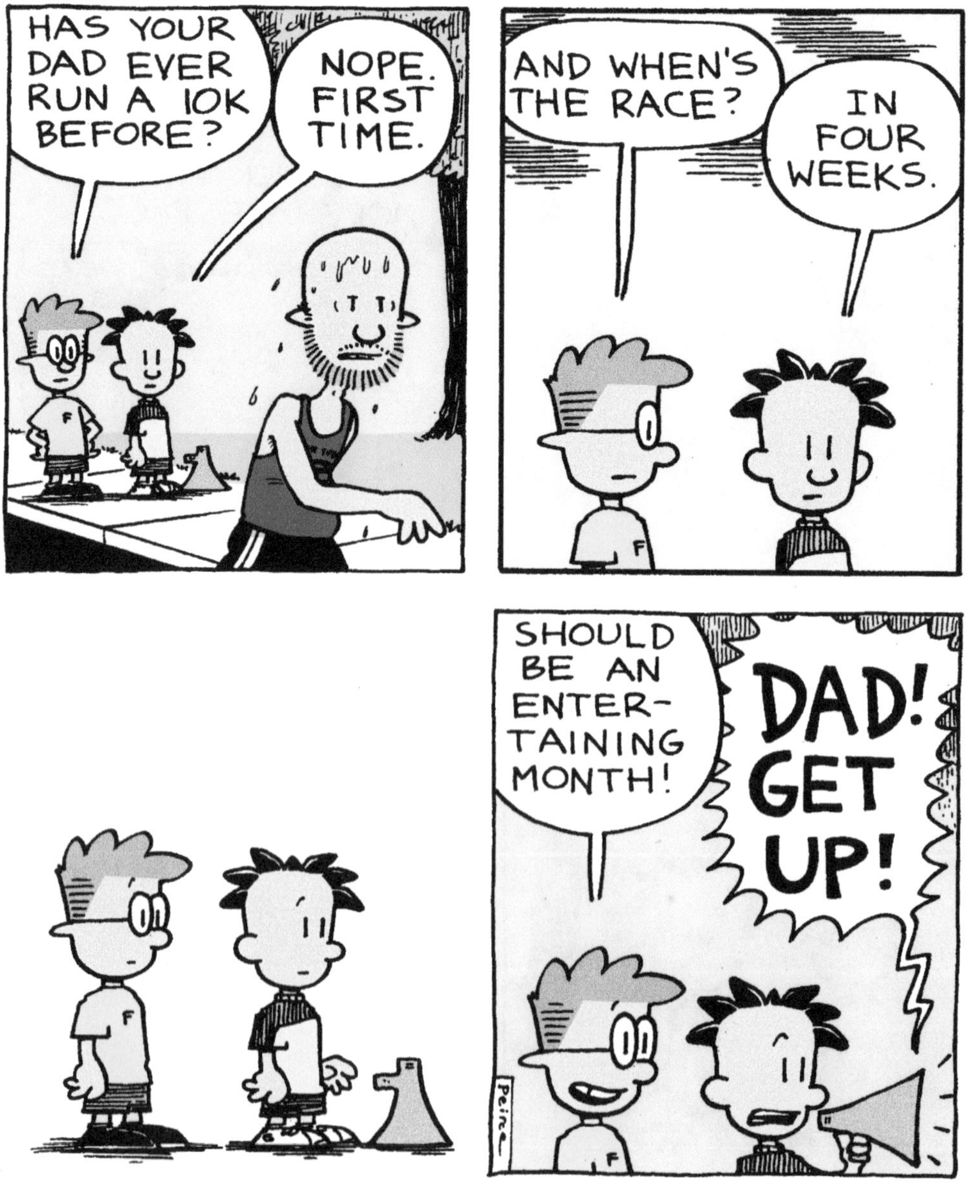
HAS YOUR DAD EVER RUN A 10K BEFORE?
NOPE. FIRST TIME.
AND WHEN'S THE RACE?
IN FOUR WEEKS.
SHOULD BE AN ENTER-TAINING MONTH!
DAD! GET UP!
Peirce

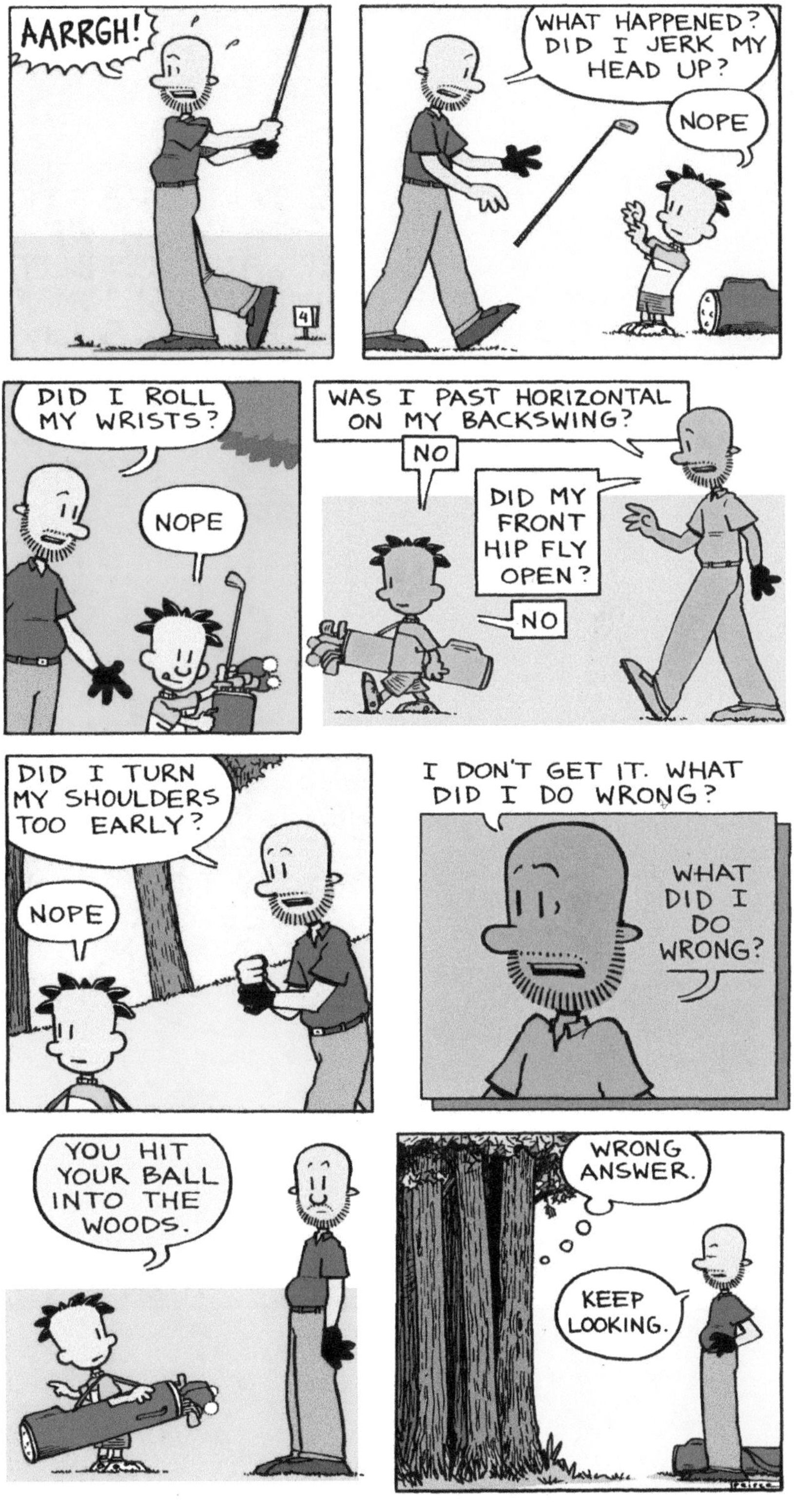
AARRGH!
WHAT HAPPENED? DID I JERK MY HEAD UP?
NOPE
DID I ROLL MY WRISTS?
NOPE
WAS I PAST HORIZONTAL ON MY BACKSWING?
NO
DID MY FRONT HIP FLY OPEN?
NO
DID I TURN MY SHOULDERS TOO EARLY?
NOPE
I DON'T GET IT. WHAT DID I DO WRONG?
WHAT DID I DO WRONG?
YOU HIT YOUR BALL INTO THE WOODS.
WRONG ANSWER.
KEEP LOOKING.

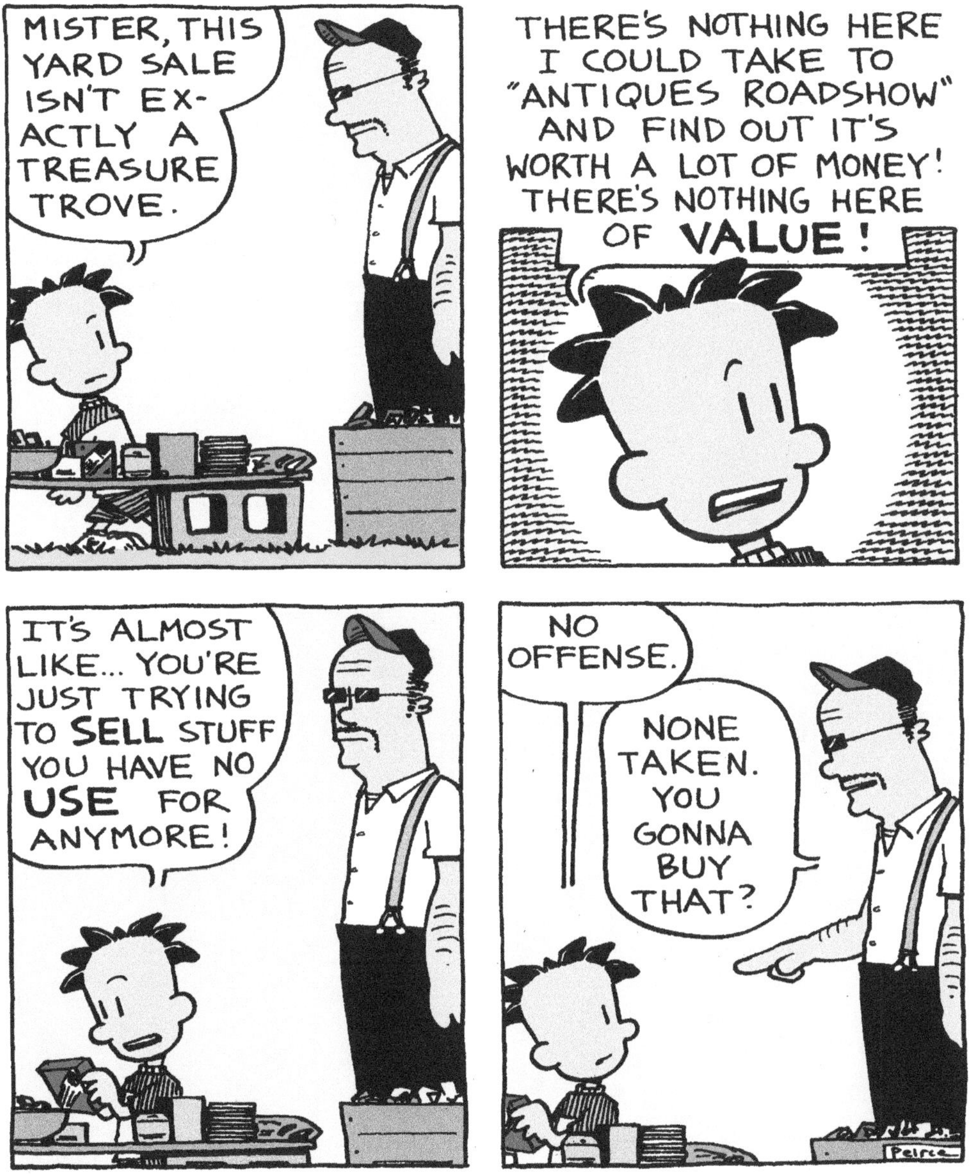
MISTER, THIS YARD SALE ISN'T EXACTLY A TREASURE TROVE.
THERE'S NOTHING HERE I COULD TAKE TO "ANTIQUES ROADSHOW" AND FIND OUT IT'S WORTH A LOT OF MONEY! THERE'S NOTHING HERE OF VALUE!
IT'S ALMOST LIKE... YOU'RE JUST TRYING TO SELL STUFF YOU HAVE NO USE FOR ANYMORE!
NO OFFENSE.
NONE TAKEN. YOU GONNA BUY THAT?
Peirce

CHESTER SEEMED SLUGGISH WARMING UP. HIS FASTBALL WAS SLOWER THAN USUAL.

I'LL FIX THAT.

CHESTER PITCHES BEST WHEN HE PITCHES **ANGRY!** SO ALL WE HAVE TO DO IS MAKE HIM **MAD!**

HOW DO WE...

YO, CHESTER! FRANCIS JUST CALLED YOU "SLOW"!

WHAT?!

THERE YOU GO! PROBLEM SOLVED!

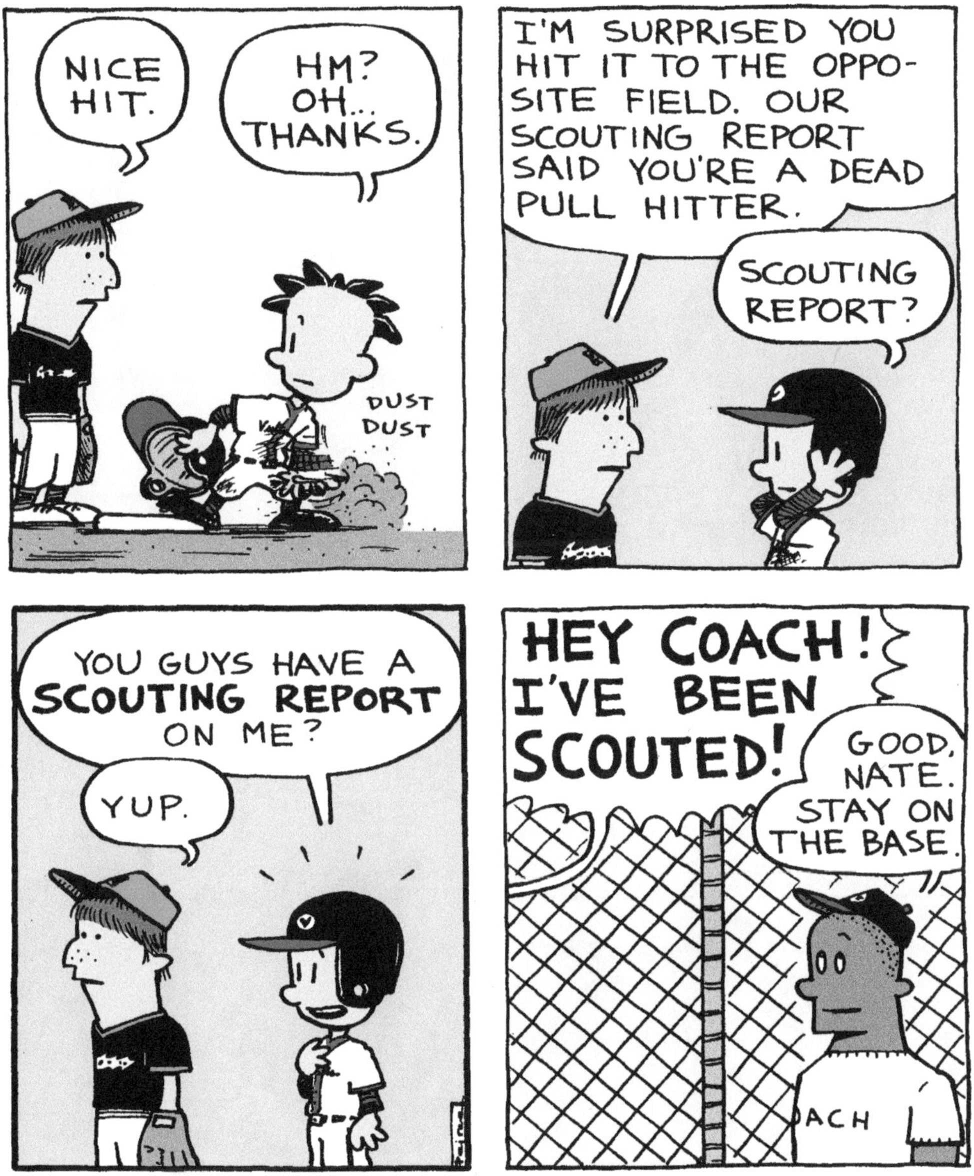
NICE HIT.
HM? OH... THANKS.
DUST DUST
I'M SURPRISED YOU HIT IT TO THE OPPOSITE FIELD. OUR SCOUTING REPORT SAID YOU'RE A DEAD PULL HITTER.
SCOUTING REPORT?
YOU GUYS HAVE A SCOUTING REPORT ON ME?
YUP.
HEY COACH! I'VE BEEN SCOUTED!
GOOD, NATE. STAY ON THE BASE.
ACH

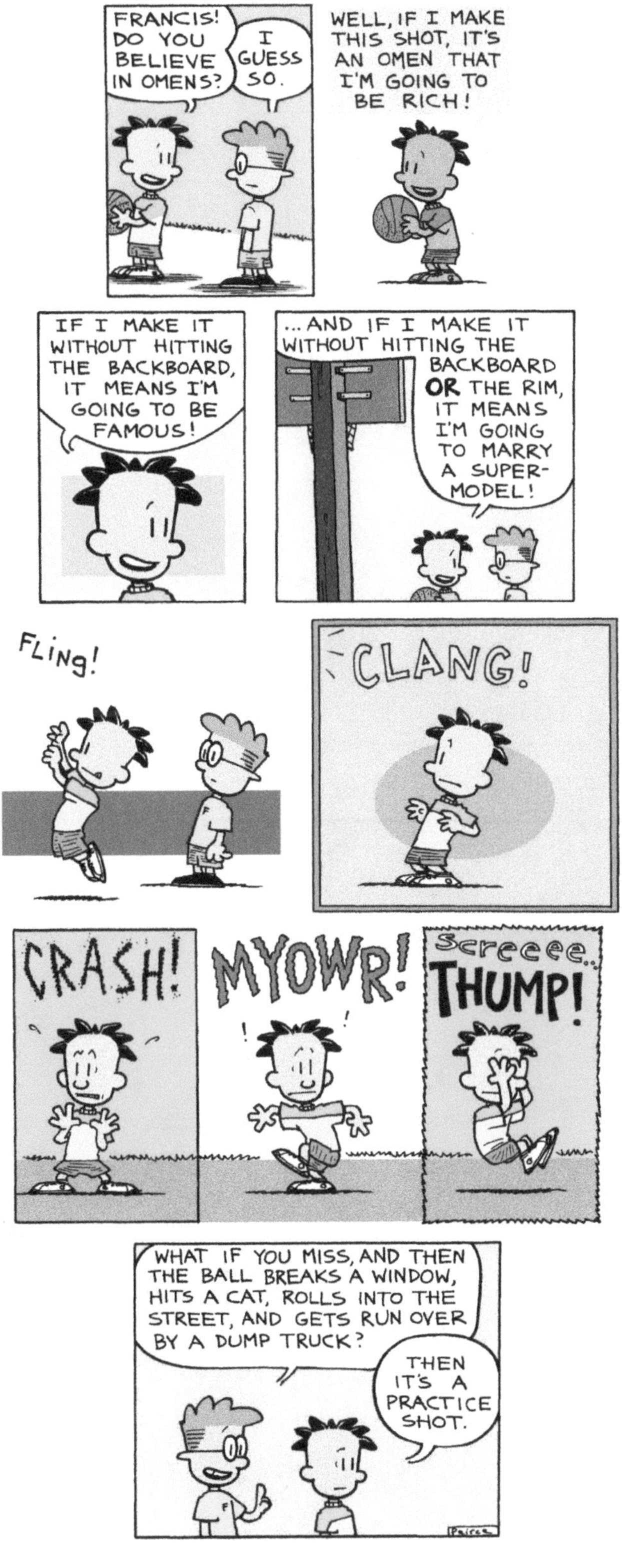
FRANCIS! DO YOU BELIEVE IN OMENS?
I GUESS SO.
WELL, IF I MAKE THIS SHOT, IT'S AN OMEN THAT I'M GOING TO BE RICH!
IF I MAKE IT WITHOUT HITTING THE BACKBOARD, IT MEANS I'M GOING TO BE FAMOUS!
...AND IF I MAKE IT WITHOUT HITTING THE BACKBOARD OR THE RIM, IT MEANS I'M GOING TO MARRY A SUPER-MODEL!
FLING!
CLANG!
CRASH!
MYOWR!
Screeee..
THUMP!
WHAT IF YOU MISS, AND THEN THE BALL BREAKS A WINDOW, HITS A CAT, ROLLS INTO THE STREET, AND GETS RUN OVER BY A DUMP TRUCK?
THEN IT'S A PRACTICE SHOT.

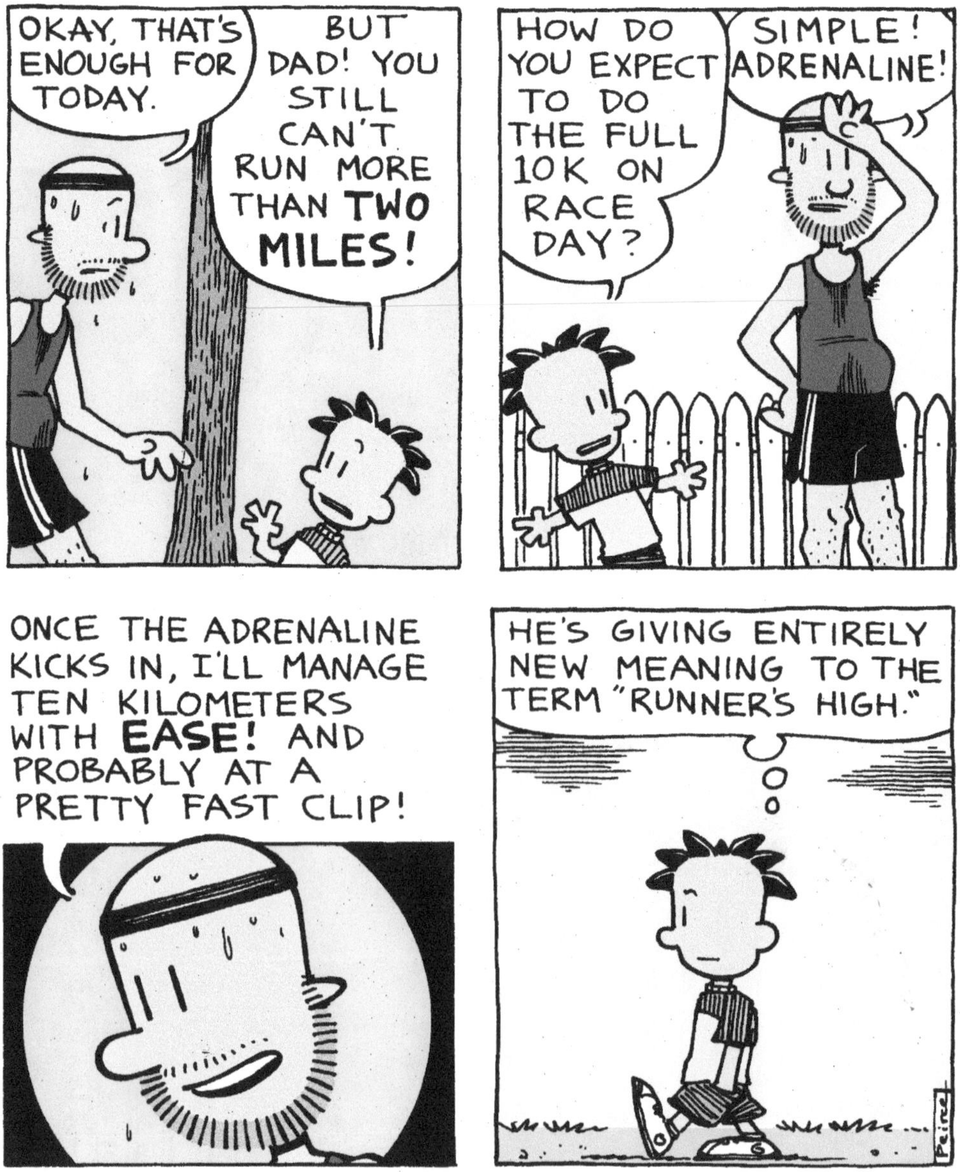
OKAY, THAT'S ENOUGH FOR TODAY.
BUT DAD! YOU STILL CAN'T RUN MORE THAN **TWO MILES!**
HOW DO YOU EXPECT TO DO THE FULL 10K ON RACE DAY?
SIMPLE! ADRENALINE!
ONCE THE ADRENALINE KICKS IN, I'LL MANAGE TEN KILOMETERS WITH **EASE!** AND PROBABLY AT A PRETTY FAST CLIP!
HE'S GIVING ENTIRELY NEW MEANING TO THE TERM "RUNNER'S HIGH."
Peirce

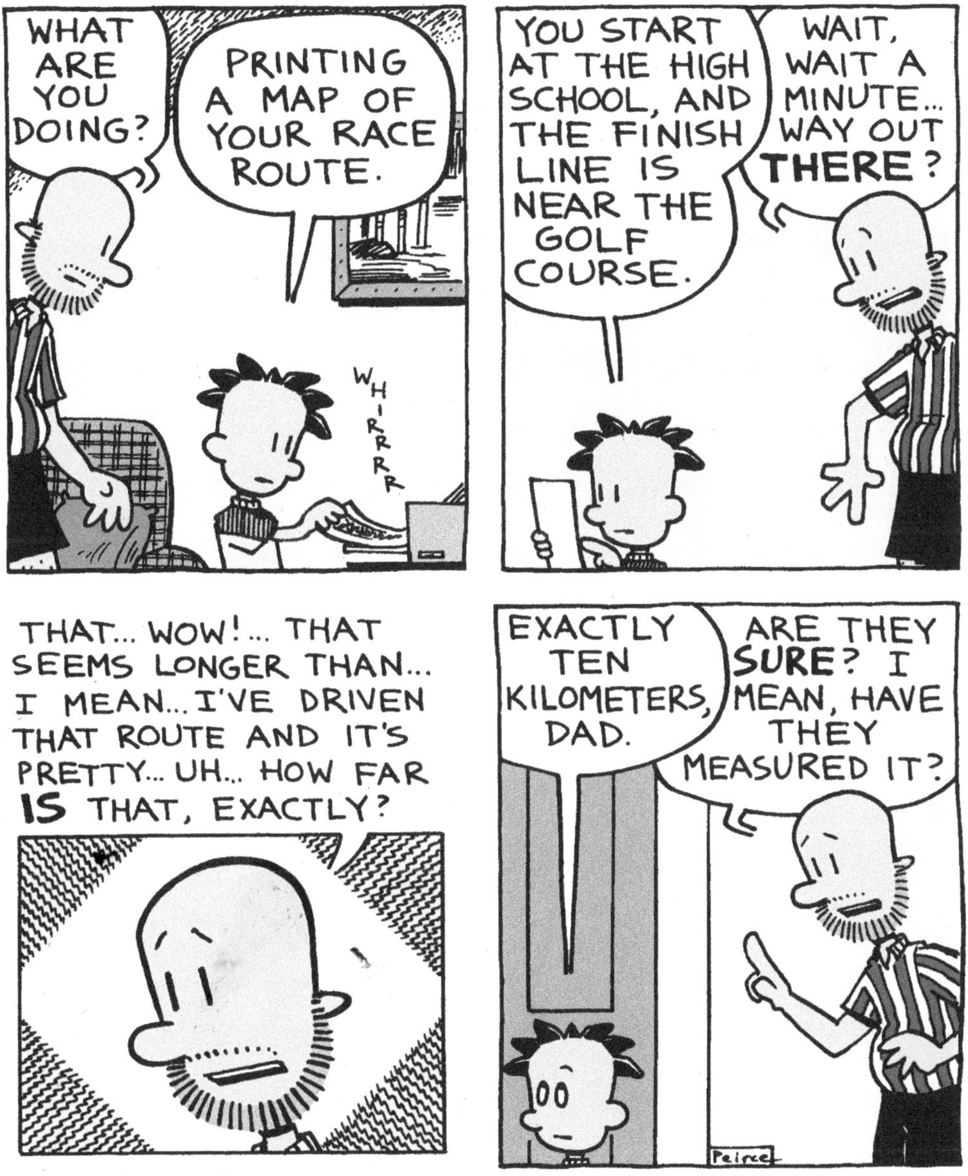
WHAT ARE YOU DOING?
PRINTING A MAP OF YOUR RACE ROUTE.
WHIRRRR
YOU START AT THE HIGH SCHOOL, AND THE FINISH LINE IS NEAR THE GOLF COURSE.
WAIT, WAIT A MINUTE... WAY OUT **THERE**?
THAT... WOW!... THAT SEEMS LONGER THAN... I MEAN... I'VE DRIVEN THAT ROUTE AND IT'S PRETTY... UH... HOW FAR **IS** THAT, EXACTLY?
EXACTLY TEN KILOMETERS, DAD.
ARE THEY **SURE**? I MEAN, HAVE THEY MEASURED IT?
Peirce

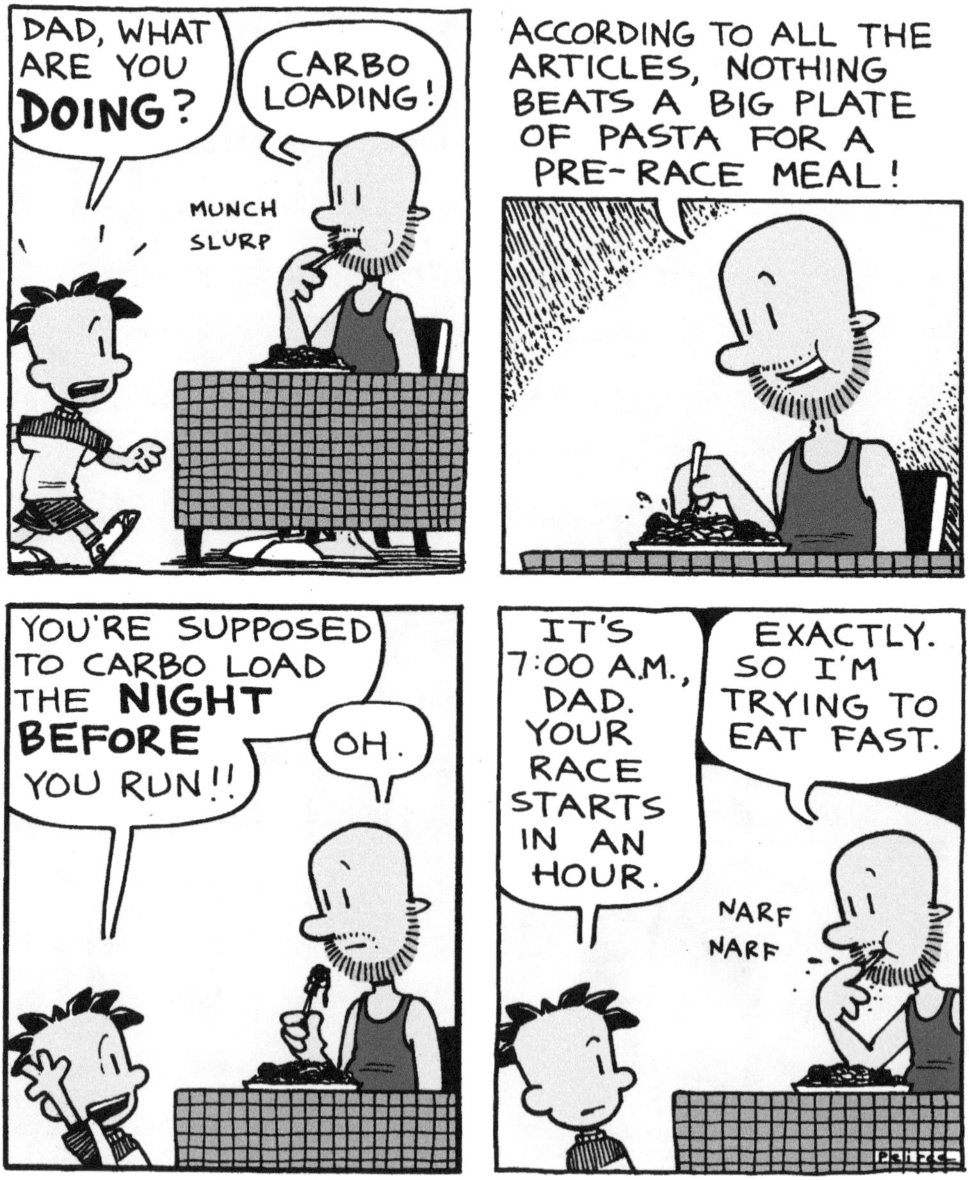
DAD, WHAT ARE YOU DOING?
CARBO LOADING!
MUNCH
SLURP
ACCORDING TO ALL THE ARTICLES, NOTHING BEATS A BIG PLATE OF PASTA FOR A PRE-RACE MEAL!
YOU'RE SUPPOSED TO CARBO LOAD THE NIGHT BEFORE YOU RUN!!
OH.
IT'S 7:00 A.M., DAD. YOUR RACE STARTS IN AN HOUR.
EXACTLY. SO I'M TRYING TO EAT FAST.
NARF
NARF

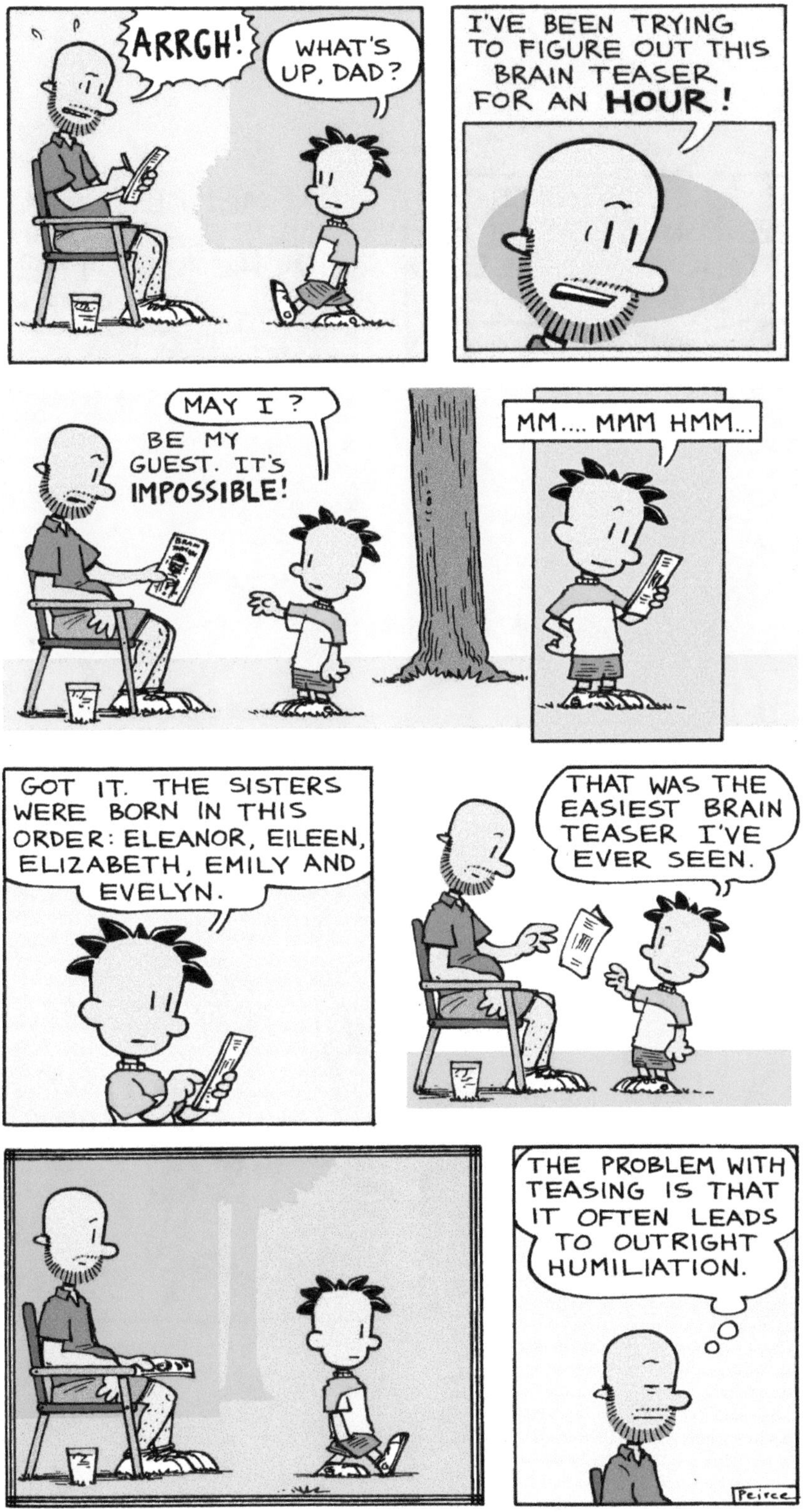
ARRGH!
WHAT'S UP, DAD?
I'VE BEEN TRYING TO FIGURE OUT THIS BRAIN TEASER FOR AN HOUR!
MAY I?
BE MY GUEST. IT'S IMPOSSIBLE!
MM.... MMM HMM...
GOT IT. THE SISTERS WERE BORN IN THIS ORDER: ELEANOR, EILEEN, ELIZABETH, EMILY AND EVELYN.
THAT WAS THE EASIEST BRAIN TEASER I'VE EVER SEEN.
THE PROBLEM WITH TEASING IS THAT IT OFTEN LEADS TO OUTRIGHT HUMILIATION.
Peirce

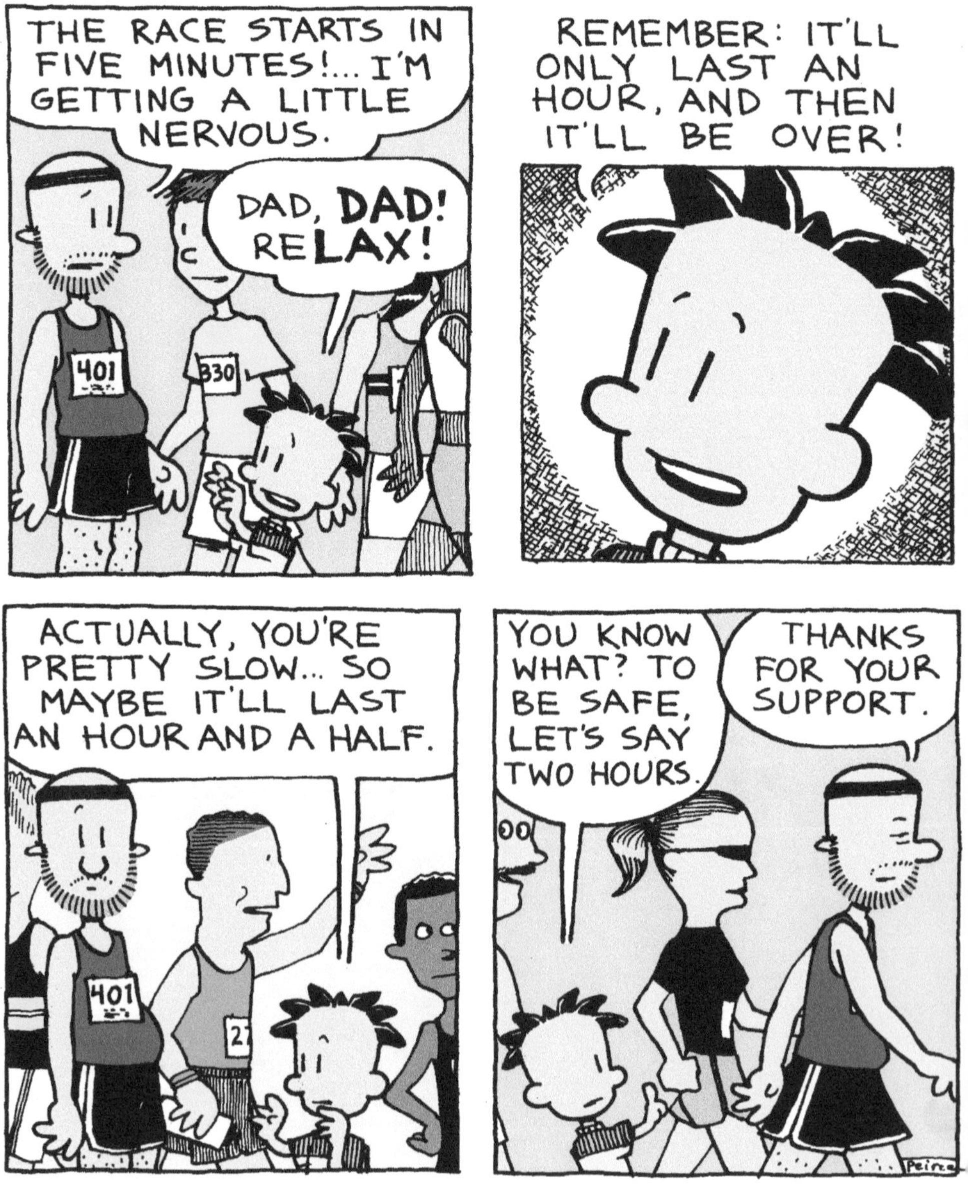
THE RACE STARTS IN FIVE MINUTES!... I'M GETTING A LITTLE NERVOUS.
DAD, DAD! RELAX!
401
330
REMEMBER: IT'LL ONLY LAST AN HOUR, AND THEN IT'LL BE OVER!
ACTUALLY, YOU'RE PRETTY SLOW... SO MAYBE IT'LL LAST AN HOUR AND A HALF.
401
YOU KNOW WHAT? TO BE SAFE, LET'S SAY TWO HOURS.
THANKS FOR YOUR SUPPORT.
Peirce

WHERE **IS** IT? I REMEMBER BURYING MY TIME CAP-SULE **RIGHT HERE**!

MAYBE YOUR MEM-ORY IS WRONG.

MY MEMORY IS **PER-FECT!** I REMEMBER DIGGING FOR HOURS IN THE BLAZING SUN, AND IT WAS ALL DUSTY, AND I FOUND THIS LITTLE THING WITH INITIALS ON IT, AND...

DUDE, THAT WAS "HOLES." WE WATCHED IT AT MY HOUSE LAST WEEK.

WELL, THAT WOULD EX-PLAIN THE PRESENCE OF JON VOIGHT.

HE'S EASILY CONFUSED.

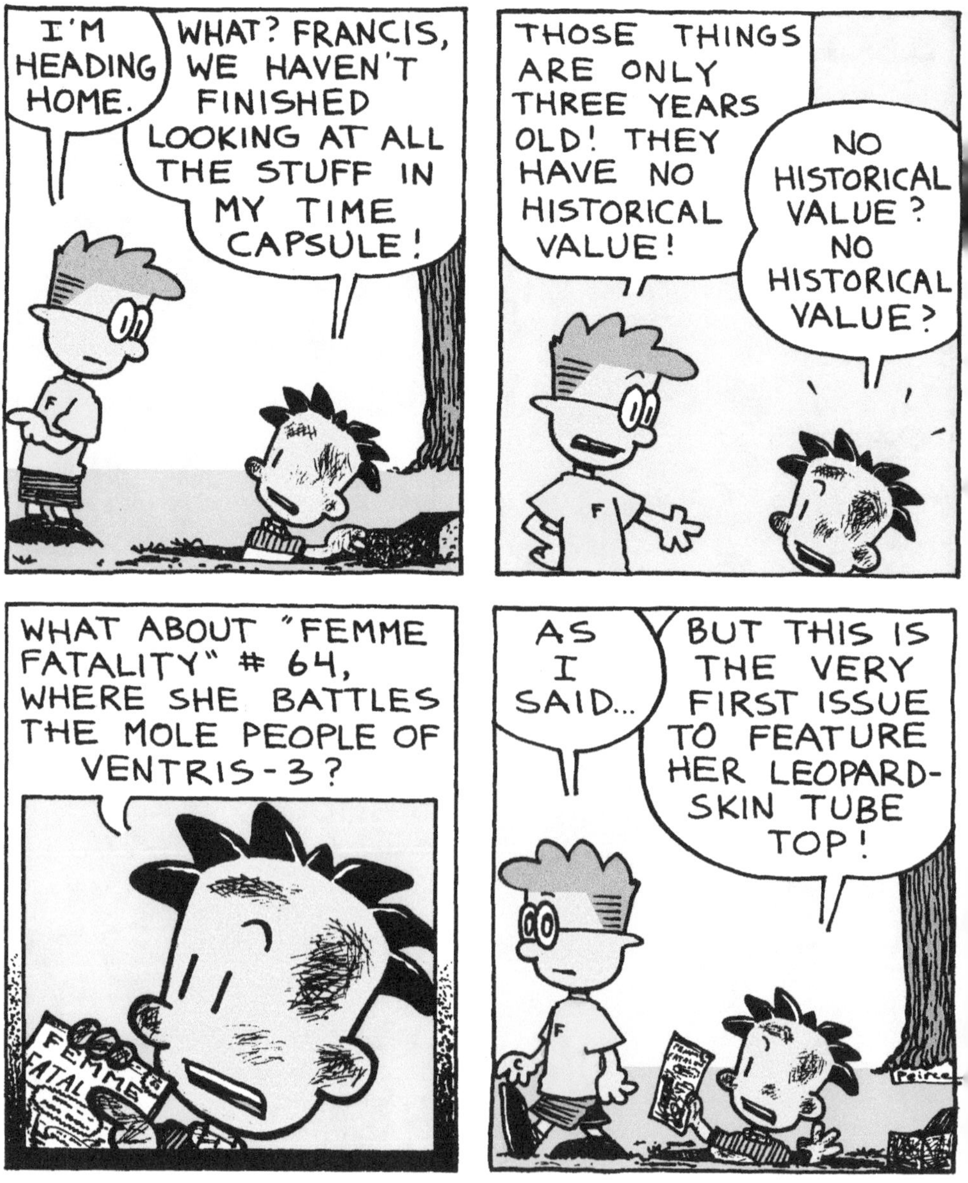
I'M HEADING HOME.
WHAT? FRANCIS, WE HAVEN'T FINISHED LOOKING AT ALL THE STUFF IN MY TIME CAPSULE!
THOSE THINGS ARE ONLY THREE YEARS OLD! THEY HAVE NO HISTORICAL VALUE!
NO HISTORICAL VALUE? NO HISTORICAL VALUE?
WHAT ABOUT "FEMME FATALITY" # 64, WHERE SHE BATTLES THE MOLE PEOPLE OF VENTRIS-3?
FEMME FATAL
AS I SAID...
BUT THIS IS THE VERY FIRST ISSUE TO FEATURE HER LEOPARD-SKIN TUBE TOP!
Peirce

CALEB, MY YOUNG FRIEND! WANT TO BUY A CARICATURE?

WHAT ARE CARICATURES?

CARICATURES $1

YOU KNOW, CARTOONY PORTRAITS OF PEOPLE!

OOH! I'M PRETTY GOOD AT THAT MY-SELF!

HERE'S ONE OF MY SISTER RENATA...

....LUKE SKYWALKER WITH OBI-WAN KENOBI...

...AND HERE! JACK SPARROW FROM "PIRATES OF THE CARIBBEAN"!

WELL...UH... ※ KOFF! ※... THESE ARE OKAY, CALEB, BUT...

WOW, NATE! DID YOU DO THOSE?

THEY'RE GOOD!

! ! !

HOW MUCH FOR THE PIRATE?

CARICATURES $1

UHHH...

CARICATURES $1

CARICATURES $2.00

Peirce

153

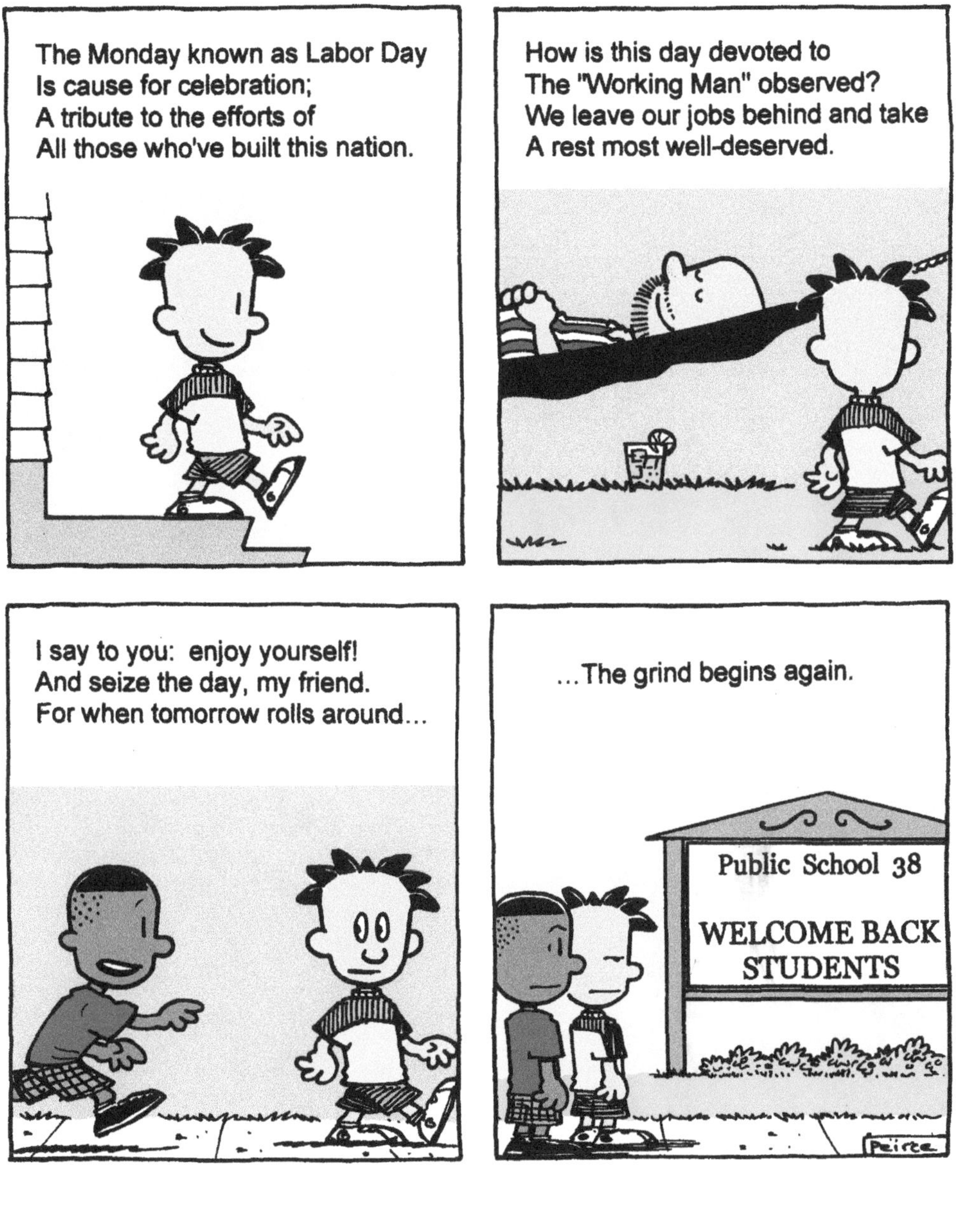
The Monday known as Labor Day
Is cause for celebration;
A tribute to the efforts of
All those who've built this nation.
How is this day devoted to
The "Working Man" observed?
We leave our jobs behind and take
A rest most well-deserved.
I say to you: enjoy yourself!
And seize the day, my friend.
For when tomorrow rolls around...
...The grind begins again.
Public School 38
WELCOME BACK
STUDENTS
Peirce

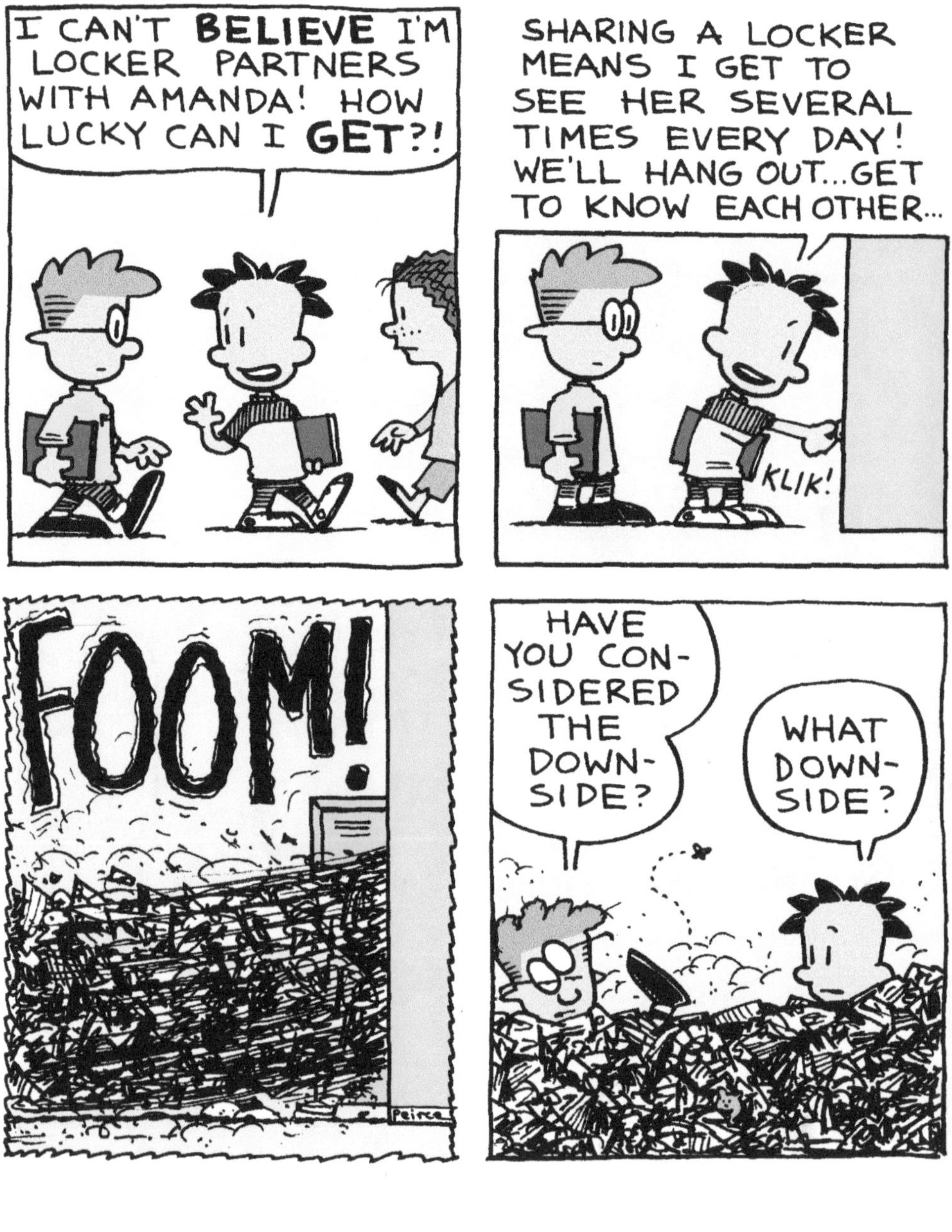
I CAN'T BELIEVE I'M LOCKER PARTNERS WITH AMANDA! HOW LUCKY CAN I GET?!
SHARING A LOCKER MEANS I GET TO SEE HER SEVERAL TIMES EVERY DAY! WE'LL HANG OUT...GET TO KNOW EACH OTHER...
KLIK!
FOOM!
Peirce
HAVE YOU CONSIDERED THE DOWNSIDE?
WHAT DOWNSIDE?

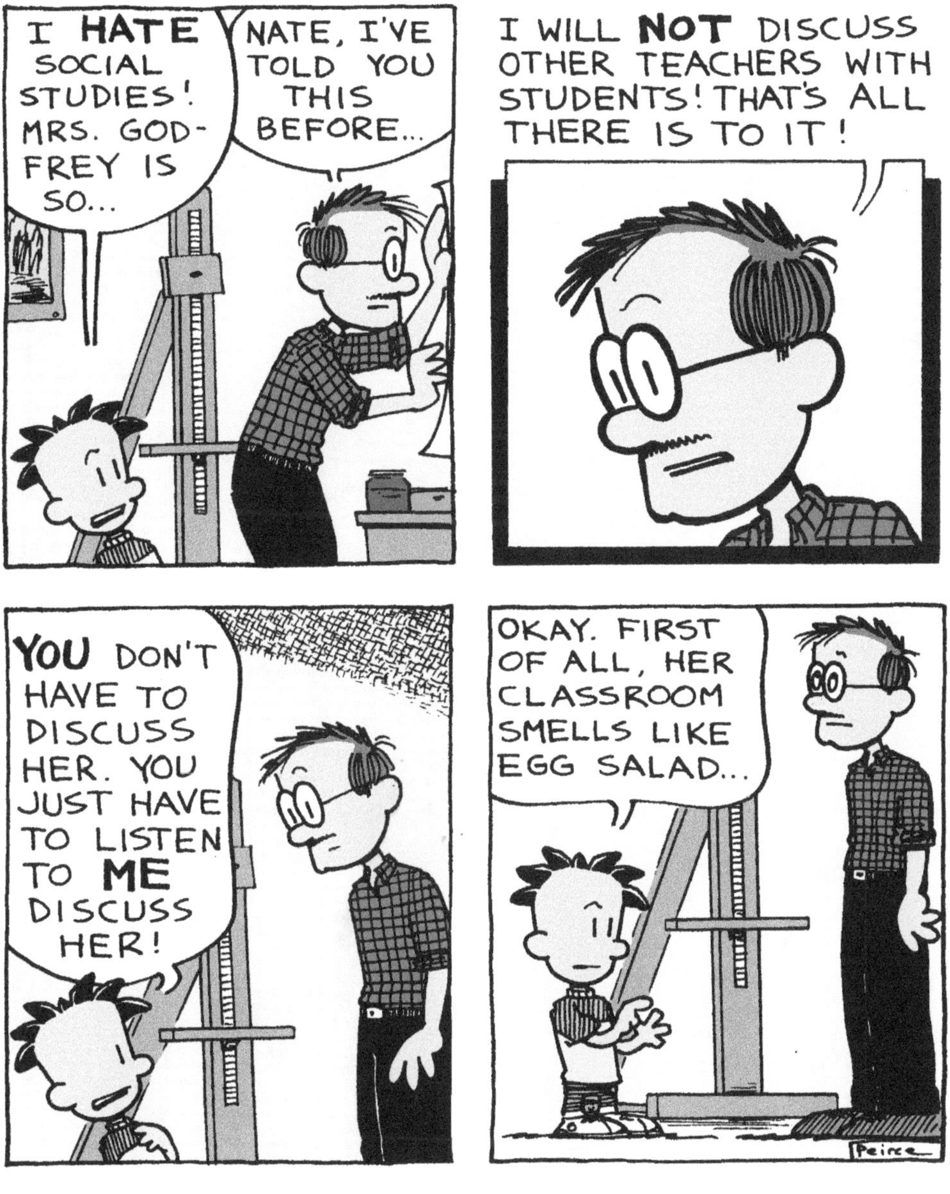
I **HATE** SOCIAL STUDIES! MRS. GODFREY IS SO...
NATE, I'VE TOLD YOU THIS BEFORE...
I WILL **NOT** DISCUSS OTHER TEACHERS WITH STUDENTS! THAT'S ALL THERE IS TO IT!
YOU DON'T HAVE TO DISCUSS HER. YOU JUST HAVE TO LISTEN TO **ME** DISCUSS HER!
OKAY. FIRST OF ALL, HER CLASSROOM SMELLS LIKE EGG SALAD...
Peirce

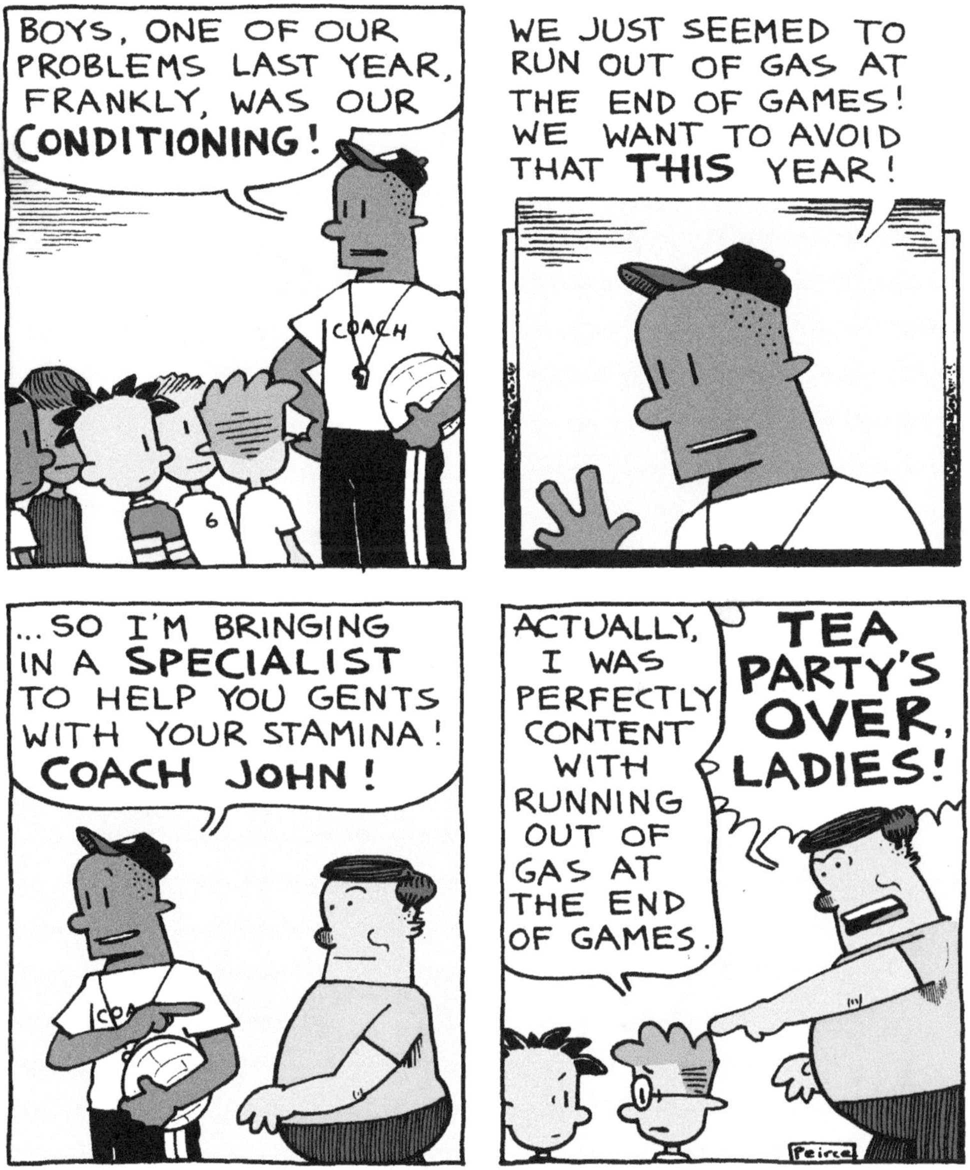
BOYS, ONE OF OUR PROBLEMS LAST YEAR, FRANKLY, WAS OUR CONDITIONING!
COACH
6
WE JUST SEEMED TO RUN OUT OF GAS AT THE END OF GAMES! WE WANT TO AVOID THAT THIS YEAR!
...SO I'M BRINGING IN A SPECIALIST TO HELP YOU GENTS WITH YOUR STAMINA! COACH JOHN!
ACTUALLY, I WAS PERFECTLY CONTENT WITH RUNNING OUT OF GAS AT THE END OF GAMES.
TEA PARTY'S OVER, LADIES!
Peirce

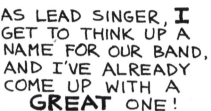

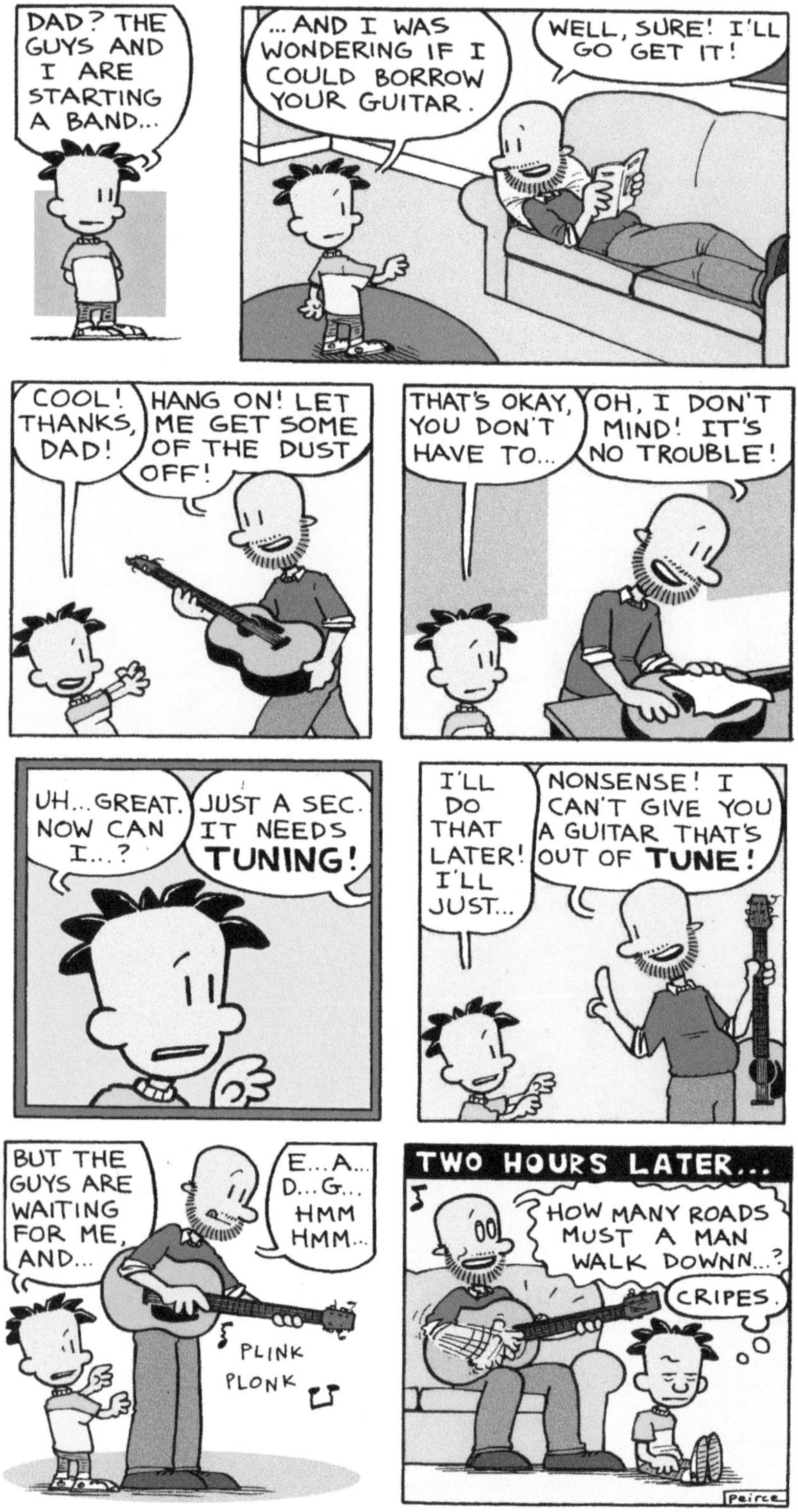
DAD? THE GUYS AND I ARE STARTING A BAND...
...AND I WAS WONDERING IF I COULD BORROW YOUR GUITAR.
WELL, SURE! I'LL GO GET IT!
COOL! THANKS, DAD!
HANG ON! LET ME GET SOME OF THE DUST OFF!
THAT'S OKAY, YOU DON'T HAVE TO...
OH, I DON'T MIND! IT'S NO TROUBLE!
UH...GREAT. NOW CAN I...?
JUST A SEC. IT NEEDS **TUNING!**
I'LL DO THAT LATER! I'LL JUST...
NONSENSE! I CAN'T GIVE YOU A GUITAR THAT'S OUT OF **TUNE!**
BUT THE GUYS ARE WAITING FOR ME, AND...
E...A... D...G... HMM HMM...
PLINK
PLONK
TWO HOURS LATER...
HOW MANY ROADS MUST A MAN WALK DOWNN...?
CRIPES.
Peirce

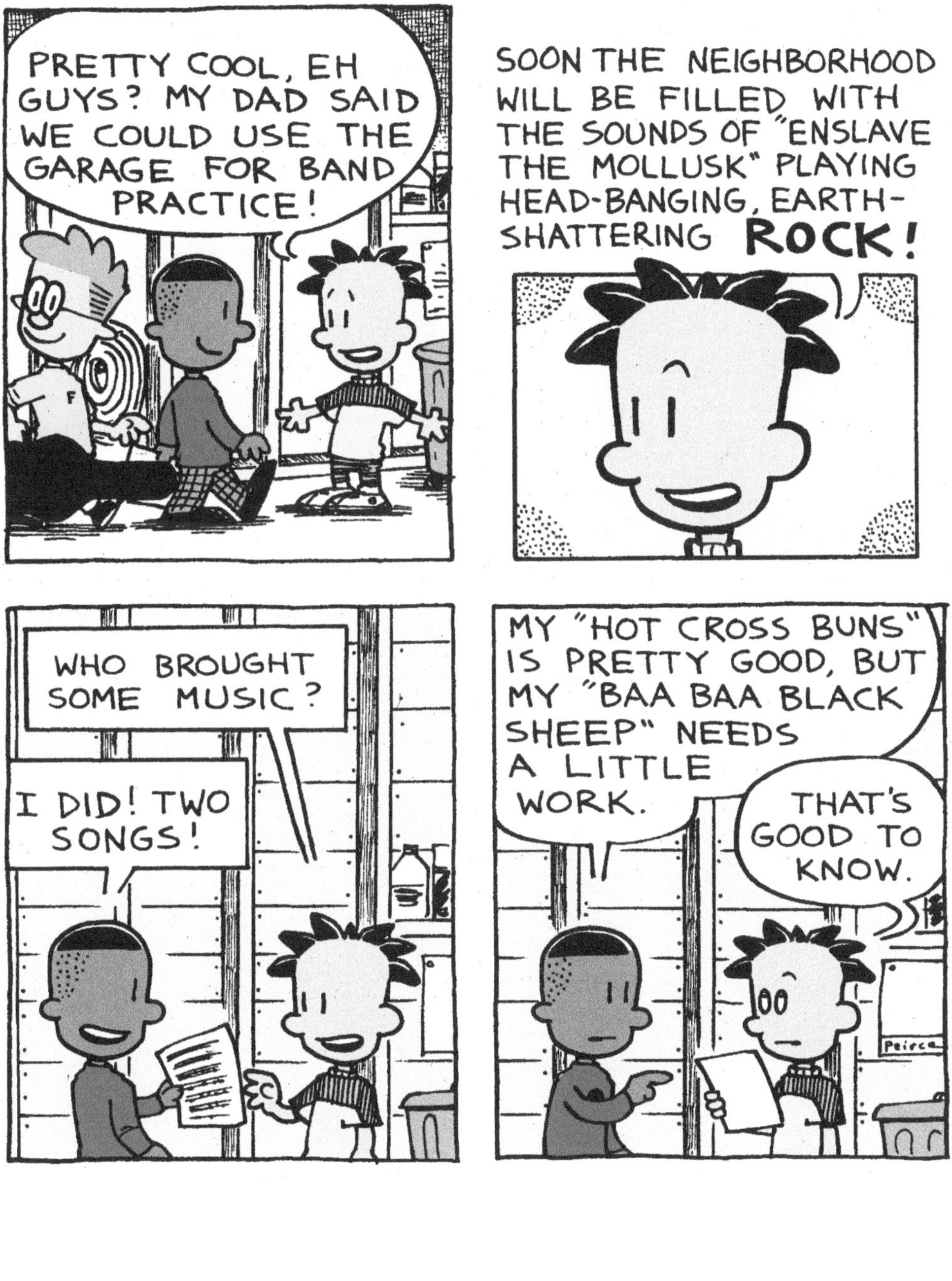
PRETTY COOL, EH GUYS? MY DAD SAID WE COULD USE THE GARAGE FOR BAND PRACTICE!
SOON THE NEIGHBORHOOD WILL BE FILLED WITH THE SOUNDS OF "ENSLAVE THE MOLLUSK" PLAYING HEAD-BANGING, EARTH-SHATTERING ROCK!
F
WHO BROUGHT SOME MUSIC?
I DID! TWO SONGS!
MY "HOT CROSS BUNS" IS PRETTY GOOD, BUT MY "BAA BAA BLACK SHEEP" NEEDS A LITTLE WORK.
THAT'S GOOD TO KNOW.
Peirce

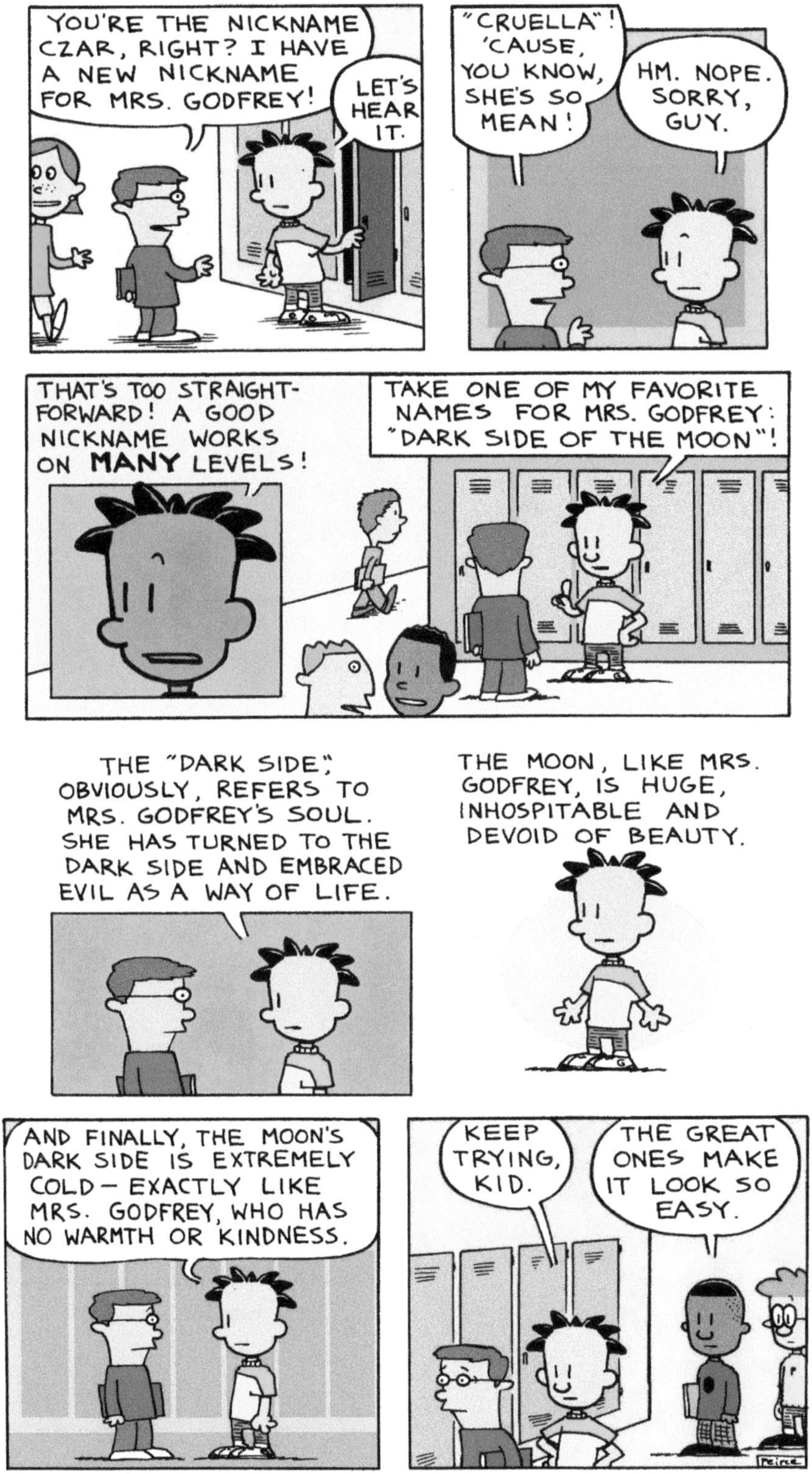
YOU'RE THE NICKNAME CZAR, RIGHT? I HAVE A NEW NICKNAME FOR MRS. GODFREY!
LET'S HEAR IT.
"CRUELLA"! 'CAUSE, YOU KNOW, SHE'S SO MEAN!
HM. NOPE. SORRY, GUY.
THAT'S TOO STRAIGHT-FORWARD! A GOOD NICKNAME WORKS ON MANY LEVELS!
TAKE ONE OF MY FAVORITE NAMES FOR MRS. GODFREY: "DARK SIDE OF THE MOON"!
THE "DARK SIDE," OBVIOUSLY, REFERS TO MRS. GODFREY'S SOUL. SHE HAS TURNED TO THE DARK SIDE AND EMBRACED EVIL AS A WAY OF LIFE.
THE MOON, LIKE MRS. GODFREY, IS HUGE, INHOSPITABLE AND DEVOID OF BEAUTY.
AND FINALLY, THE MOON'S DARK SIDE IS EXTREMELY COLD — EXACTLY LIKE MRS. GODFREY, WHO HAS NO WARMTH OR KINDNESS.
KEEP TRYING, KID.
THE GREAT ONES MAKE IT LOOK SO EASY.
Peirce

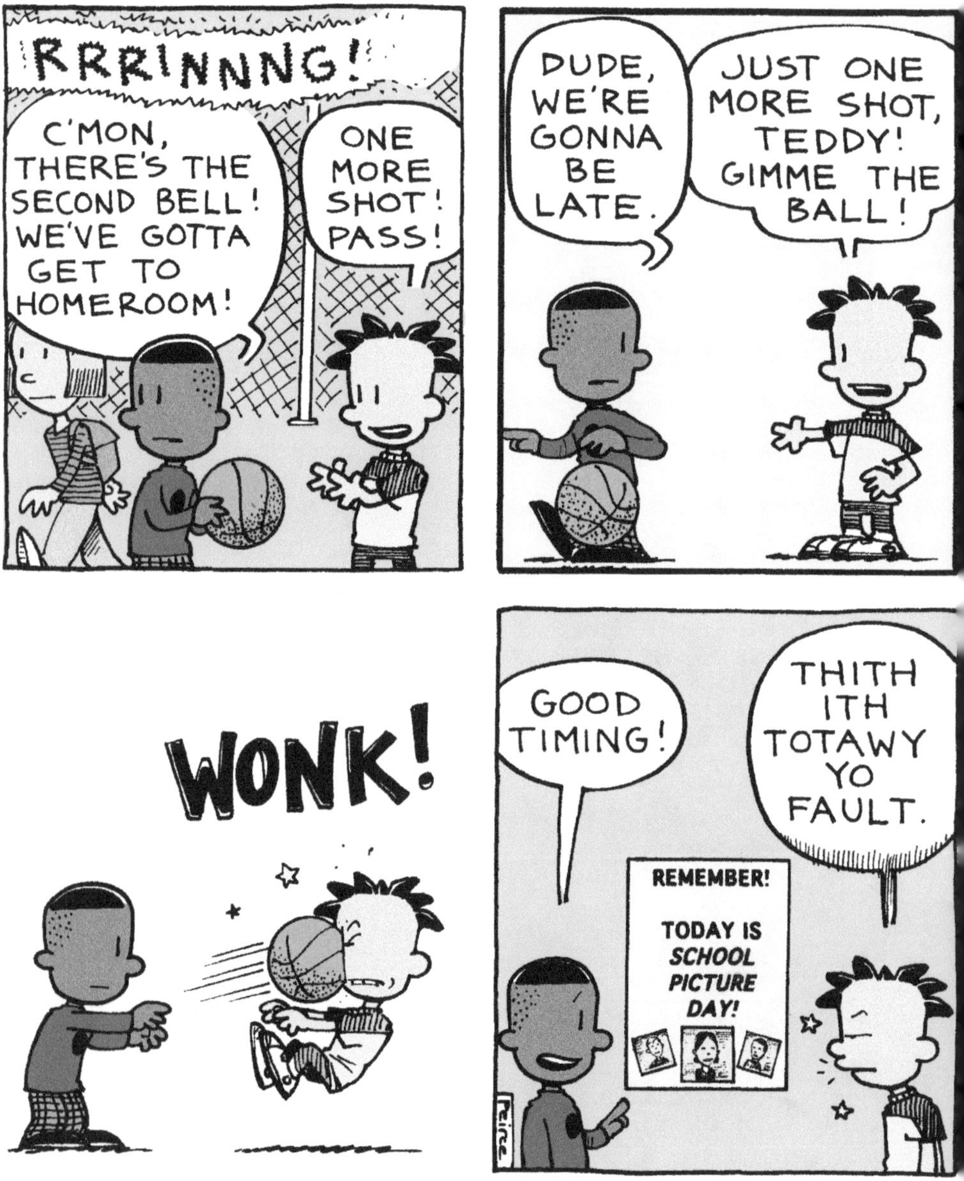
RRRINNNG!
C'MON, THERE'S THE SECOND BELL! WE'VE GOTTA GET TO HOMEROOM!
ONE MORE SHOT! PASS!
DUDE, WE'RE GONNA BE LATE.
JUST ONE MORE SHOT, TEDDY! GIMME THE BALL!
WONK!
GOOD TIMING!
THITH ITH TOTAWY YO FAULT.
REMEMBER!
TODAY IS SCHOOL PICTURE DAY!
Peirce

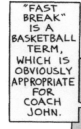

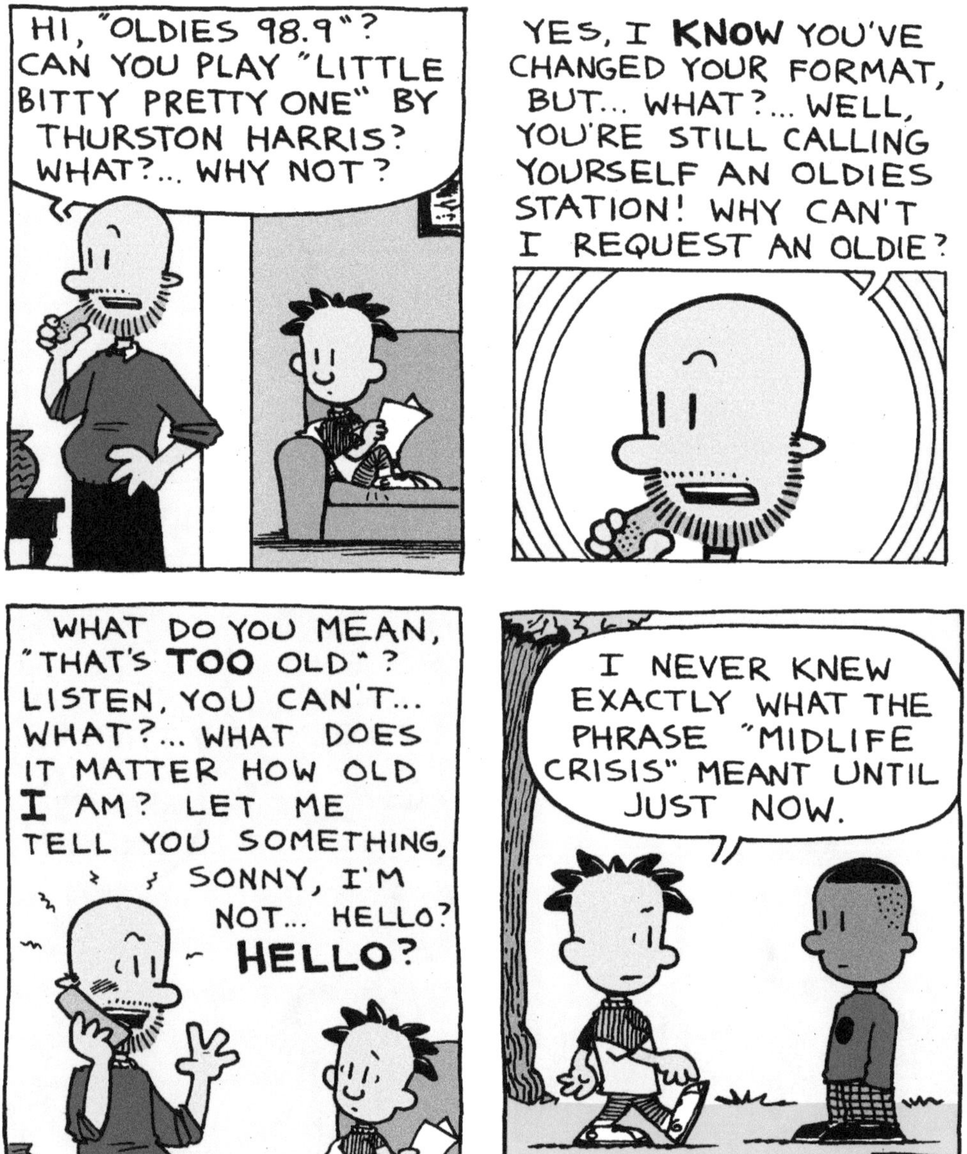
HI, "OLDIES 98.9"? CAN YOU PLAY "LITTLE BITTY PRETTY ONE" BY THURSTON HARRIS? WHAT?... WHY NOT?
YES, I **KNOW** YOU'VE CHANGED YOUR FORMAT, BUT... WHAT?... WELL, YOU'RE STILL CALLING YOURSELF AN OLDIES STATION! WHY CAN'T I REQUEST AN OLDIE?
WHAT DO YOU MEAN, "THAT'S **TOO** OLD"? LISTEN, YOU CAN'T... WHAT?... WHAT DOES IT MATTER HOW OLD **I** AM? LET ME TELL YOU SOMETHING, SONNY, I'M NOT... HELLO? **HELLO**?
I NEVER KNEW EXACTLY WHAT THE PHRASE "MIDLIFE CRISIS" MEANT UNTIL JUST NOW.
PEIRCE

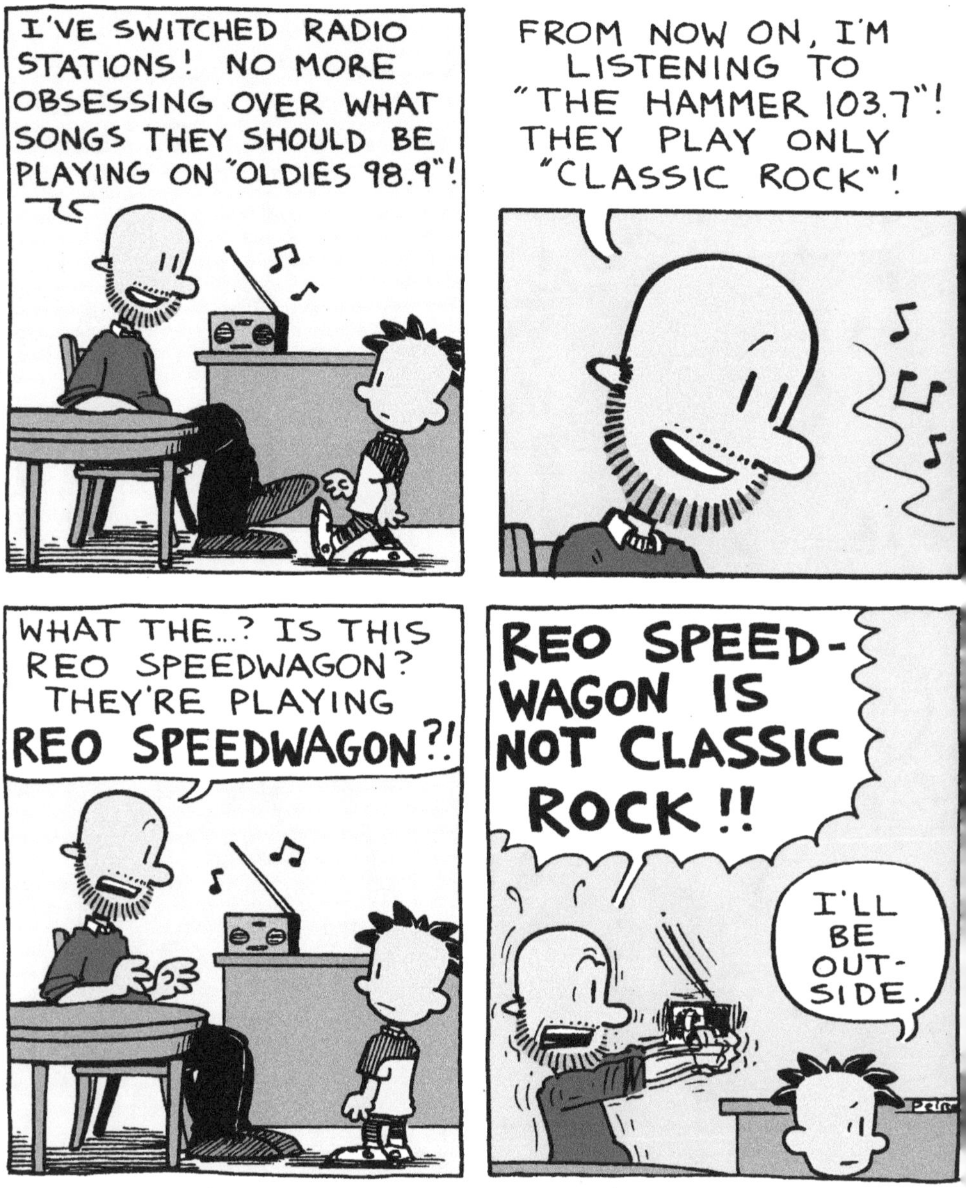
I'VE SWITCHED RADIO STATIONS! NO MORE OBSESSING OVER WHAT SONGS THEY SHOULD BE PLAYING ON "OLDIES 98.9"!
FROM NOW ON, I'M LISTENING TO "THE HAMMER 103.7"! THEY PLAY ONLY "CLASSIC ROCK"!
WHAT THE...? IS THIS REO SPEEDWAGON? THEY'RE PLAYING REO SPEEDWAGON?!
REO SPEED-WAGON IS NOT CLASSIC ROCK!!
I'LL BE OUT-SIDE.

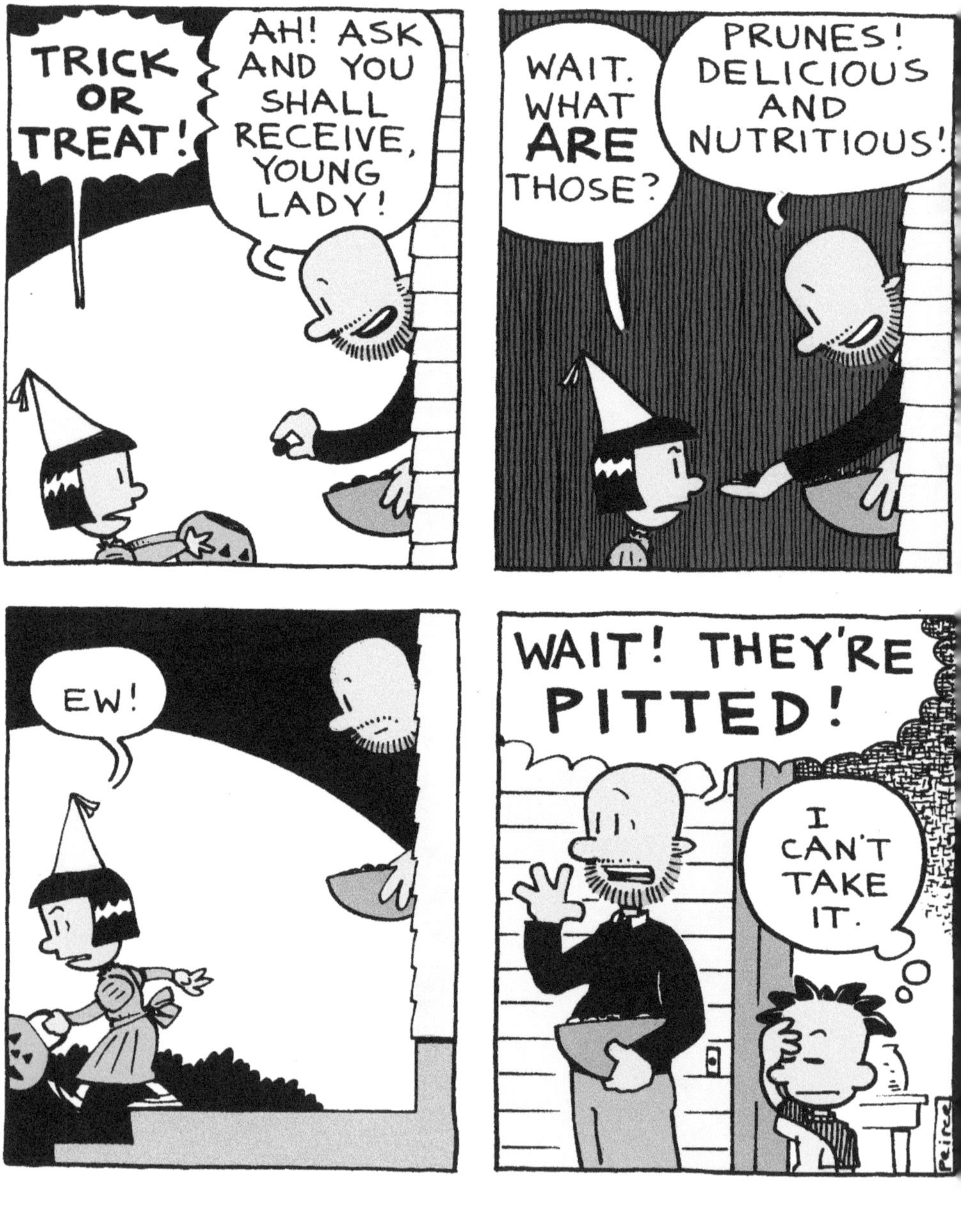
TRICK OR TREAT!
AH! ASK AND YOU SHALL RECEIVE, YOUNG LADY!
WAIT. WHAT ARE THOSE?
PRUNES! DELICIOUS AND NUTRITIOUS!
EW!
WAIT! THEY'RE PITTED!
I CAN'T TAKE IT.
PEIRCE

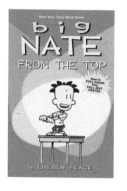 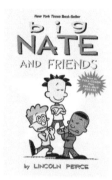  
  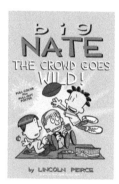 
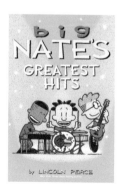 

CPSIA information can be obtained
at www.ICGtesting.com
Printed in the USA
LVHW070128100222
710754LV00007B/224

9 781449 473945